Praise for
What Time is Love?

'A startlingly great debut. Holly's beautiful prose smoulders, crackles and roars, but it's the storytelling that really astonishes'
Daisy Buchanan

'*What Time is Love?* is not only a beautifully told love story but also a fascinating account of the changing social mores of the 20th century. I found it delightful, insightful and immersive'
Kate Eberlen

'A unique and wonderfully crafted debut, *What Time Is Love?* has it all – nostalgia and romance, captivating characters and stunning prose... an unforgettable story with writing that sparkles: a gem of a read'
Holly Miller

'A stunning, skilful, deftly drawn, cockle-warmer of a novel that somehow sweeps you through half a century while feeling like a leisurely afternoon. Prose so good I couldn't stop underlining'
Lauren Bravo

'A wonderful, original and powerful debut by the very talented Holly Williams. She is wild and brilliant'
Elaine Feeney

'Exquisitely conceived and with the most beautiful sense of place, *What Time is Love?* is such an original and thoughtful take on the age-old question of whether it's possible to have met the right person at the plain wrong time'
Abbie Greaves

'A brilliant, witty, defiantly unsentimental examination of privilege and class and sex and selfhood. And most of all, it's a gorgeous love story'
Marianne Levy

Holly Williams was born and grew up in Mid Wales, and now lives in Sheffield. After six years as a staff writer at the *Independent*, she became a freelance journalist – reviewing books and theatre, and writing and editing for the arts pages for many publications including the *Observer*, the *New York Times*, *Time Out*, the *Times Literary Supplement*, and the *Financial Times*. In 2020, she received funding from Arts Council England to complete *What Time is Love?*, her first published novel.

what
time
is
love?

HOLLY WILLIAMS

ORION

First published in Great Britain in 2022 by Orion Fiction
an imprint of The Orion Publishing Group Ltd
Carmelite House, 50 Victoria Embankment
London EC4Y 0DZ

An Hachette UK Company

3 5 7 9 10 8 6 4

A CIP catalogue record for this book is
available from the British Library.

ISBN (Hardback) 978 1 3987 0629 3
ISBN (eBook) 978 1 3987 0632 3

Typeset at The Spartan Press Ltd,
Lymington, Hants

Printed and bound in Great Britain by Clays Ltd,
Elcograf S.p.A.

www.orionbooks.co.uk

For my parents, Lynda and Martin.

21 January, 1927

The clock reads 6.42 a.m., and in a small bedroom at the top of a terraced cottage in Abergavenny, Angharad Lewis clenches her jaw for a final push. She gives birth to a baby girl she will shortly call Violet, a tiny bundle whose dark blue eyes gaze at her mother in total silence as she's whisked away, swaddled and bound by the midwife. At the same moment – 6.42 – on the other side of the country, in a towel-covered room in the east wing of Farley Hall near Knaresborough, Amelia Brinkforth machineguns out one last line of expletives as her baby boy tears and rips his way into the world. Red and ready to unfurl his long limbs, Albert Peregrine Brinkforth opens his mouth, and howls.

Chapter 1

April 1947

It started with the letter. A letter Letty had read over and over in the two months since it arrived on the doorstep, written on her friend's Rose's signature mauve-coloured notepaper.

Bertie and I are taking a walking holiday in the Brecon Beacons in April – isn't that your part of the world? Would you like to meet us? I'm simply dying to see you again!

Since the moment she'd opened it, Letty had felt a fine fizz of excitement running through her – at the thought of seeing Rose again, and at finally getting to meet her younger brother, Bertie.

Now the day was here, and Letty sipped nervously at the lemonade she'd bought, bubbles hissing at the back of her throat. She'd arrived at The Lamb half an hour early, not trusting the buses between Abergavenny and Brecon. Shifting in a threadbare armchair, in the snug at the back of the pub where women were allowed, she rearranged the folds of her favourite skirt and tugged at a few of her dark curls. Daft, Letty scorned herself, to feel this fluttery. But she hadn't seen Rose since the end of the war, the end of their time working together as telegraphists in London – and she had never met Bertie.

She had always been fascinated by the idea of him, however, ever since discovering that they shared a birthday. Rose had been in charge of the whole squadron of telegraphists in the central post office during the war, and on each new girl's first day liked to note down their birthday so she could treat them when the time came.

'Twenty-first January? Do you know, that's the same day as my little brother, Bertie!' Rose had exclaimed. 'And are you eighteen too?'

Letty had nodded.

'Well I never!' Rose had looked closely at her, clearly tickled by the coincidence, and Letty felt pleased at having some connection with her. There was something about the tall, bright woman that attracted Letty, despite it being obvious that they came from very different worlds. Letty had never heard such plummy tones outside of the wireless.

She had asked Rose as many questions about Bertie as she could without prying. In her head, Letty had painted a picture of him: an elegant, urbane young man in a dinner jacket, spouting Homer. She was certain that reading Classics at Oxford was the most highbrow activity anyone had ever undertaken, and that he must be horribly impressive.

She realised she'd nearly finished her lemonade and wondered whether she had time to get another drink before Rose – and the mythical Bertie – arrived. She couldn't believe they were actually coming here, to one of her local pubs.

If it hadn't been for the war, she and Rose would surely never have met. Letty thought it was unlikely she would even have left south Wales, and society ladies like Rose didn't tend to crop up in places like Abergavenny post office. Nonetheless, their time together was brief: it was 1945, and the end of the war was almost glimmering into view, when Letty started working in London.

The huge building on the corner of St Martin's Le Grand was full of other young women who never expected to have a job in London, or even really to do such work at all. They chattered and fluttered like a tree full of sparrows, distracted from the heart-ticking, fear-spiking sirens and rubble by a steady stream of soldiers, dance bands at Hammersmith Palais, and the glamour of the West End.

Letty arrived as full of nerves as any of them; she'd never been to the capital before. But after a few weeks, she fell in love with London. Swinging on to the back of a bus, its *ding* and motored rush. The tall buildings that blocked out the sky and the wide parks full of people. The long walks she wasn't meant to take through damaged, anonymous streets. She was alone and away from home for the first time in her life, and the independence was thrilling. But there was also a growing pleasure in getting to know all kinds of other people: Letty shared her tea each night with fourteen girls in her boarding house, and they bonded quickly, deeply. It was as if all the invisible walls between people had been blown apart too.

Rose was their unflappable leader at the central post office – her cheery certainty about the importance of their work to the war effort helped lift the lonely, the overwhelmed, and the nervous. Rose had taken Letty under her wing in her early, wide-eyed weeks, even marching her into a hotel for tea and cake one afternoon ('I have all this silly money – let me treat you!'). But Letty was surprised to find how easy it was to talk to Rose – to properly talk to her – despite their differences.

'It's a funny thing about this war,' Rose said once, over a cup of tea in Letty's mould-spotted boarding house, 'but having to work has given us a sense of purpose, I think.'

Letty raised her eyes to look at Rose square on. '"Us"? Do you mean women, or folk like you?'

Rose fiddled with one of her pale brown puffs of hair, and Letty felt bad for alluding to the difference in their backgrounds. She usually tried not to think too much about the fact that Rose's father was an actual lord, that her friend was titled and landed.

'Women. Girls,' said Rose. 'If it weren't for the war, our only work would be finding a husband, and all that.'

'Well, I was working at the post office in Abergavenny already. Lots of us do have to work...' Letty spoke gently.

Letty had got her job at fifteen, when she left school; she'd already studied a year longer than her father wanted. Mrs Ketterick had said sternly to him that Violet 'had a very fine mind', and insisted she be put up for one of the vanishingly few council scholarships so she could continue to secondary school. But then they found out that Carrie Jones who worked at the dinky post office on the high street in Abergavenny was having a fourth baby, and being offered Carrie's job was too good an opportunity for Letty to refuse, scholarship or no.

'But wasn't that job just a stop gap?' pressed Rose. 'Something to fill the time while you were wooed?'

'I suppose. Didn't feel like that for me, though. Although I daresay that's all my dad thinks it is.'

'I just think a lot of these girls – us girls – well, we've never expected to do much, never been asked really,' Rose continued. 'Oh, I know raising children and running a household will become our work – and very important work it is too. But all this is different, isn't it?'

Letty cocked her head, indicating that Rose should go on.

'Our war work is the *un*expected, the needs-must. And it lets you have your head a bit. It's about time – I think women need that.'

Letty and Rose enjoyed an intimacy accelerated by circumstances, but it was only a few months before the end came. The flag-waving, impulse-kissing end; Letty watched the relief dredging everyone's faces and felt, instead, a cold trickle of disappointment. It was a bad thought, she knew, one she couldn't even tell Rose. The image of the wide fields around her home in winter – the bare, purple-brown earth hardened into ridges and stretching endlessly away – kept appearing to her.

Back in Abergavenny, it was as if Letty's time in London was sealed off and floating away, an almost unreal memory. Then one day, a mauve envelope arrived in the post. All the girls had sworn to keep in contact – but only Rose actually did, proving an avid, highly entertaining pen pal. And then she started sending books.

'What's all these packages for you then, Letty?' her father asked, his large moustache prickling, as it did when he felt threatened. Letty didn't respond, just took the latest from his hands, unwrapping a heavy, leather-bound copy of *Wuthering Heights*, sent from the 'absolutely enormous library' at Farley Hall, Rose's majestic-sounding home.

Letty's father wasn't a big reader, although his prowess at the crossword was legendary across several valleys. Evan was a chapel man, a choir man, a railway man, and a Labour man. But while he approved of his sons – both younger than Letty, both furious at missing the war – picking up George Orwell, he showed a scratchy irritation at seeing Letty pass a Sunday reading in the old armchair by the fire, its stuffing bursting out around her curled-up feet.

She didn't care. The letters, and the books, were her portal to another world – not quite frantic, purposeful London, but certainly not sleepy south Wales either. They made up for how her life had shrunk back.

Letty slept in her narrow bed, separated from her brothers by a heavy old woven curtain, worked five days a week
and Saturday mornings, and drank halves in The Fountain on
Saturday nights. But sometimes her old friends' shrill gaiety in
the pub made things worse. Really, it was all just near-hysterical
relief at not being dead, she thought, watching their eyes shine
and their mouths stretch, not saying anything really, as if being
alive was worthwhile if you did nothing at all with it.

Letty picked up her lemonade again, and was draining the
very last of it, when a man lurched towards her across the
straw-strewn floor of The Lamb.

'Letty?'

And there he was.

Even though she had been waiting for him, Letty was slightly
taken aback by the very tall, thin man. His blonde-brown hair
was dishevelled with sweat, and several strands drooped into a
pair of soft, wide brown eyes.

'Bertie?'

Where is Rose? Letty thought, a panic rising, still gripping
the empty glass.

Why didn't I wait for Rose? Bertie thought, deeply regretting
his decision to arrive, alone, ahead of her.

He'd not given too much consideration to meeting this friend
of his sister's. Now he found himself confronted by the darkest,
deepest, bluest eyes he thought he had ever seen.

Bertie had yomped ahead of Rose for the final stretch of their
twelve-mile ramble through the damp, ever-deepening green of
the Brecon Beacons, a competitive habit from childhood that
neither sibling was yet quite ready to give up. At twenty-two,
Rose was two years older than Bertie and, with sturdy legs that
had shot up during adolescence, it used to be a fair match. But
these days he outstripped her regularly, and so he had ended up

8

at the low-beamed inn where they had rather shabby rooms for the weekend by himself, out of breath, and with aching feet.

'Hullo. Hullo! Very good to meet you, Letty. I've heard— I mean Rose— she's ...'

Bertie gave the impression of having many more limbs than is quite normal, and seemed unsure what to do with them. He started to put out his long hand to shake Letty's, before appearing to think better of it, running it through his hair instead, fine strands of which stayed springing up into the air. Eventually, he gestured decisively towards Letty's empty glass.

'Would you like a drink? Another – I mean— what can I ...'

'A half of mild, please,' Letty said, quickly.

Bertie nodded very enthusiastically, looking everywhere except her eyes, then after gesturing with his whole long body towards the bar repeatedly, finally manoeuvred both limbs and wallet towards it to procure a pint of bitter and a half of mild.

Letty stared at him – tried not to stare at him – and realised she'd been imagining the past, some tailed vision of aristocracy from the pictures, not a normal twenty-year-old, with unkempt hair and muddy trousers.

Bertie returned with their drinks, and sat down abruptly on a brown armchair next to her, spilling his pint slightly. They both stared into the little fire, hissing in a gnarly iron grate. It could only have been a few seconds, but the silence seemed to tighten all through Letty's body. Her crossed ankles clenched together.

'Would you mind if I took off my boots?' Bertie said.

His feet were throbbing. But dealing with his damp laces would also give Bertie a convenient excuse to look at the floor. It seemed preferable to looking into the face, into the eyes, of this Letty.

Letty shook her head and tried to compose her expression. Men she knew would never take off their boots in the pub

– but then they would be arriving after work, standing up and downing pints like they were a final task of the day, not the reward. Bertie, however, set to taking off hiking boots as if he were about to put his feet up, like a man of leisure.

Letty sipped the mild while watching him tussle with his laces. Although she had always expected that Bertie would seem as alien as Rose had when they first met, the sensation was heightened by his ... *maleness.* The wonder of this strange new species of man, with his tweed jacket and clipped consonants and gentle, fumbling eagerness.

'How was your walk?'

'Ah!' Bertie managed to remove the first boot, relief swiftly tainted by the realisation that his socks smelled like wet dog. 'Yes, very good. Excellent country round here.' He tried to wrap and tuck the leg under the armchair, surreptitiously.

'Pen y Fan, is it?'

'That's right. Spectacular, quite ... spectacular. And such a relief to get out and about, after the winter we've had!'

Both boots deposited by the fire, Bertie drained half his pint, cast his eyes about the walls then the ceiling as if powerfully interested in the polished horse brasses hanging there, then back to the bar, before giving up and sneaking a look at Letty. She also seemed to be avoiding his gaze, glancing away as if there might be something very interesting happening on the other side of the pub. She had small dimples in her pale cheeks; her eyebrows – thin and neat – were lightly drawn up. An unusually narrow nose, with a bobbly end, also seemed tilted upwards, in amusement, surely.

Or because of the smell? Oh lord, thought Bertie, he smelled like a deceased sheep.

'Letty! Darling girl!'

Thank Christ, both Letty and Bertie thought as Rose's buoyant tones bounced across the pub.

Not quite as tall as her brother, Rose still walked in strides at least twice the length of Letty's, as Letty had discovered when trying to keep up with her in London. After the dawdling pavements of Abergavenny, Letty had felt tossed and blown by the city's crowds, but they always seemed to part before Rose like water from the bow of a ship. She crossed the pub in about two of these strides, and wrapped her sturdy arms around Letty's narrow shoulders, nearly lifting her out of the chair.

'How are you, how are you? Glad to see he found you – Bertie! You've taken off your boots? Honestly. And where's my drink then, eh?'

'It's wonderful to see you,' said Letty. 'How long's it been now then?'

'Well, at least two years. Oh, and I've missed you, darling darling girl.' Rose flung an arm around her friend again as she perched on the end of the armchair. She tapped the end of Letty's nose, who wrinkled it, and stuck out her tongue. She felt, for a second, like she was back at school – not that she'd ever had a friend as clever or confident as Rose at school. Perhaps that was just something bred into people like her, Letty thought, impressed as always at how easily Rose moved through the world.

Bertie was so beside himself, he pointed at the bar, mouthed a potential order for Rose wordlessly – which Letty knew would be a single G&T, the only thing her friend ever drank – and had followed his finger before he even remembered he was not wearing anything on his feet.

Word will get around, Letty thought suddenly, watching the bootless Bertie lope and nod and smile and pull out a too-large note. Twm behind the bar, all forearm and forehead, leaned solid and still as Bertie bent and fumbled; the Davies boys watched with heavy eyes.

Well, let them! Letty felt her face flush with pleasure at the thought of being associated with him – but even more so with Rose. Let word get about! There was a wriggling in her belly at the simple and absolute joy of being reunited with her friend, her friend that she loved, her friend that she had thought she might never see again.

Bertie delivered the G&T and settled back into the armchair with the remainder of his own drink as the fire crackled and threatened to scorch his boots, and found he could barely get a word into the girls' conversation. His sister asked Letty a stream of overlapping questions about the local area, and her favourite walks, and her job, and the books they'd both been reading.

Letty found the only way she could manage to say poised and intelligent things about *Mrs Dalloway* was if she didn't look in the direction of Bertie's long legs (and socked feet) at all.

But, eventually, she forced herself to turn to face him properly.

'What about you, Bertie? You must be reading lots of interesting things at Oxford, is it?'

'I wish I was reading all the things that you two are getting stuck into. Much more interesting than most of my tutes!' he said with a charming, lopsided smile. 'Greats – that is, I mean, Classics – is very hard and incredibly dull. You'd honestly never think a war had just happened, it's so irrelevant, so ...'

'Stuck in the past?' Letty asked, with a twitch of eyebrow.

His eyes flicked to hers, and then they finally, properly met. There was a split-second charge, like a static shock. The ends of Letty's fingers prickled; tiny stars burst in Bertie's peripheral vision.

Letty looked away hastily, unsure what had just happened.

Then she was surprised to find herself feeling emboldened by the spark.

'Surely classics is full of war, isn't it? Nothing but war, I'd've thought – Trojans and that. That's all of an-*ti*-quity' – Bertie swooned inwardly at the way her Welsh accent picked through the word – 'but that's all that the present is too, isn't it: men, lots of men, killing each other.'

'I think, Letty, that you should study in my place and leave me to work in the post office.'

The merest hint of a scowl. *Oh no,* thought Bertie, *she thinks I'm patronising her. Oh God.*

'I doubt I'd be up to it actually, I've no organisational skills whatsoever, and I'm dreadful at arithmetic. Although I would enjoy using the stamp ...' He mimed franking parcels, absent-mindedly.

'Become a librarian, then. You've plenty of experience with dusty old books under your belt, haven't you?'

Letty saw the edges of Rose's wide mouth twitching as if there were small strings pulling at it. Then Letty blushed, and Bertie couldn't help but wonder, *Did she also feel it ...?* Surely he wasn't imagining—

And at that thought, Bertie also blushed. And he noticed his sister's mouth break, irresistibly, into the most enormous grin.

Later, after Letty had left the pub – Bertie's eyes glued to her short, neat frame as she hurried out the door to the last bus – he sank immediately and gloomily into a third pint. How unlikely it was that their paths should ever have crossed! How unlikely, too, that they ever would again.

Then Rose handed him a gift.

'It was such a treat to see Letty again today. Do you know, I really have missed having a friend like her. I was wondering if I oughtn't to invite her up for the garden party—'

'Yes, absolutely, what an excellent thought! Yes, you must.'

'Oh, do you think so?' asked Rose, innocently. 'I wasn't sure it'd really be her—'

'Well you know her better than I,' interrupted Bertie, trying to cover up his enthusiasm. He took a gulp of bitter and tried to look thoughtful. 'But I can't see why not. She likes cake, I presume? And gardens? We've seen where she lives, be nice for her to see where you live too...'

He paused, noticing a shadow of worry pass over Rose's face, and realised that, of course, they hadn't seen her home. And whatever it was like, it surely wasn't going to be very similar to Farley Hall at all.

But Bertie shook off this flicker of doubt; none of that stuff mattered, not really. What mattered was that he wanted to see her again.

'Anyway, Rosie — doesn't she have the most absurdly large number of your books to return?'

Chapter 2

July 1947

'Bertie!' Rose's voice came from the next room. 'She's here!'

Bertie, who had been pacing around Farley Hall all day, anxiously awaiting Letty's arrival, found himself bolting upstairs to his bedroom.

'Bertie!' Rose bellowed up the stairs, exasperated. 'Can you answer the door? I've got my hands full and I don't want to send a *maid*!'

He did not reply. He absolutely could not answer the door. His pulse appeared to have gone haywire.

'*Bertie!*'

Instead, he hid at the side of the thick curtain in his bedroom and looked down at the driveway. There she was, getting out of the car they'd sent to meet her train at Knaresborough station, arriving some hours before the party was due to start.

Letty looked up, and Bertie shrank away from the window.

As she craned up at it, the handsome, grey-yellow stone of Farley Hall seemed to loom over Letty out of the rain. So many windows! Behind each of those must be a room. And behind one of them, must be Bertie...

Letty dropped her gaze to the floor, quickly.

The driver scurried up the steps to deliver her brown, scuffed suitcase to the imposing front door. Silly, to arrive for just one night with such a large case, but it was the only one the Lewis family owned.

Letty felt momentarily paralysed. A few droplets of rain fell off the brim of her hat, and down her collar. She shivered, then lifted her pointed chin, and walked up the steps. Just as she was about to press the bell, the door flew open.

'Letty!' Rose, one arm full of cut flowers, kissed her hastily on the cheek, and then almost dragged her inside. 'Welcome, welcome, welcome. How was the journey? I hope it wasn't *too* long and terrible? It's all a bit chaotic here because of the weather' – Rose gestured vaguely behind her – 'but I am *quite* sure it's about to brighten up, don't you think? Anyway, I'll show you to your room, and then we can do the grand tour later – such as it is!'

Farley Hall certainly seemed grand to Letty as Rose whisked her across the glossy hallway floor, up a curved staircase and along a panelled corridor with six doors in it, depositing Letty at one. Her own private bedroom. As soon as a servant (*a servant!*) brought up a tray of tea and began to run Letty a bath, Rose made her excuses and left to hurry back to getting the hall and garden prepared.

Letty tried to relax in a little armchair, telling herself to savour the experience of being waited on. But she wasn't sure how long it was acceptable to take, getting ready for a party, and besides, she was too nervous to eat much. A good job really, given how thinly the sandwiches were cut. The weak-looking tea tasted strangely floral.

When would she see him?

The question continued to whirl round Letty's mind as she sank into the cavernous, cast iron bathtub. She tried to enjoy the luxury of having it all to herself for as long as she liked, rather than a quick splash in a tin bath while her brothers shouted at her to hurry up before the water went cold. But her limbs refused to unwind themselves. What if the party was starting already? What if Rose – *if Bertie* – was wondering where she'd got to? Perhaps they'd guess how shy she felt, thought she was hiding up here, thought she was a pathetic little ...

Letty dressed as quickly as she could, in her favourite frock: cornflower blue, with tiny yellow flower sprigs. The day before, she'd sewn on a lace collar to cover a worn seam. It wasn't fancy, but it fitted perfectly. She carefully fluffed out a few of her curls that had gone flat under her hat on the train, dabbed just a little rouge to her cheeks.

Her tread felt almost portentous, coming down the echoey staircase. She hovered, for a moment, in the hallway, before hearing Rose's voice in the next room.

'Oh! You're ready!'

Letty's heart sank. Rose was still dressed in an old brown worsted skirt, and busy choreographing an elaborate dance of party planning. Uniformed women span around her, holding crates of bottles, linen cloths, and trays of silverware. Rose held up a finger to indicate she'd be with Letty in one minute, and then turned back to a bewilderingly in-depth discussion about cake forks.

Feeling awkward and unhelpful, Letty slipped away, thinking to go back in her room. But then, out of some thrown-open doors, she spied the garden, suddenly drenched in a bright, peachy light.

Letty felt herself drawn outside. The rain had left tiny jewels across the lawn's jade surface, glinting in the sun that had obligingly come out to dry it before guests arrived. The light slanted through the late afternoon, picking out the curves of the day-lilies, the velvety peeling back of rose petals. Letty thought she could smell their scent in trails, floating past her on the wet, warm air.

The rain-water crept up the toes of her low-heeled, best navy shoes. Letty breathed in the possibility of the evening to come.

'Hullo.'

A start, a twist, and Letty had the exact sensation of being in a lift: a rush but a drop, the ground vanishing beneath you even though you remain still on the spot.

For there was Bertie, in a blue blazer and cream trousers and an open shirt. Something about the small triangle of exposed flesh made Letty forget what to do with her hands. She did a funny sort of bob, cringed inwardly, then put them behind her back.

'Hello, thanks very much for inviting me – well for Rose inviting— I mean, it's very pretty here.'

'How was your journey?' Bertie said. A small, cartwheeling furry animal appeared to have taken up residence at the base of his oesophagus. It had taken Rose running upstairs, banging on his door and hissing at him to 'get outside and entertain her, she's all by herself' to finally make Bertie leave his room.

'Oh, yes, fine.' It had been very long and cramped in third, actually. She'd brought *Tender is the Night*, but somehow most of the journey had passed in looking out the window and thinking about how she'd have clever conversations with Bertie about it rather than actually reading it.

'Ah, good. Long way.'

'Yes, rather.' *Rather? That's not something you say*, she thought.

'And … is the room? To your comfort—'

'Oh yes, it's got a terrific bath!'

Bertie went red, which made Letty colour too.

He had very little experience with women, but after the

easy, teasing conversation with Letty in the pub, he'd thought about her all summer term, as he cycled along the canal, ate in the long hall, and certainly as he put his head down on his badly sprung single bed. Once Rose had confirmed she was coming to the party, his days were spent largely imagining their continued verbiage.

In his head, he had been considerably wittier than this.

'Well, the weather looks to be perking up,' he managed, woefully.

'Yes. That's ... nice. For the party. Although I suppose for the flowers too.'

'I suppose so.'

'They must get battered by that rain!'

'Yes.' Bertie paused. *Stumped by my idiocy, presumably*, thought Letty.

'Well, it'll be better for the guests anyway,' he managed.

'Yes, I do hate a wet party.'

'I suppose, ah, people will be here before too long,' said Bertie, who seemed very interested in the sodden grass at their feet.

'It'll be busy, I daresay?'

'Should be, if I know Rose. Well, I won't keep you – I know what girls are like – don't let me stop you, you know, getting togged up ...' He gestured with his whole body back to Farley Hall, its thick stone lit a creamy yellow against the now blue sky.

Her mouth opened, but she didn't know what to say. He thought she hadn't yet changed for the party, didn't realise that this *was* her best dress.

Letty nodded, unable to speak, and instead stepped rapidly off the lawn and back to the house, head down.

She is ready, Bertie realised. He had just assumed it was too early for anyone female to be done – but now she must think … she must think …

Bertie groaned softly to himself.

In her room, Letty pretended to read again, until the party had definitely begun, the noise of shrieking voices unignorable. Thankfully, as she stepped gingerly back outside, Rose – now dressed in a cerise frock with a neat waist – spotted her, dashed across the grass a little clumsily and linked arms.

She steered Letty towards a table of impossibly glamorous food (lobster! Smoked salmon! Rationing was apparently an irrelevancy when you had tastes this fine), and presented her with several flutes of actual Champagne in quick succession, before introducing her in the most effusive tones to all of her glamourous, grown-up friends. The last of the sun warmed the back of Letty's neck, and her cheeks began to hurt from all the smiling and nodding. It was a burning sensation she'd not known in two years.

She kept an awareness of where Bertie was at all times, in order never to look in his direction.

Her dress might be plain compared to all the other party frocks that seemed to float around her, but Letty soon found she no longer cared. Because there was dancing. And men. Not enough, but still: men, again, at last. A light, quick mover, Letty had no problem drawing them to her. As she twirled across the lawn, the crepe folds of her dress flared out and back, gently caressing her; she wished she had bare legs, so she could feel it better.

It was all so different to the brown evenings passed at dances in Aber, the same old faces and the general shabbiness of things after the war. Letty felt like she'd been dropped into one of the novels Rose lent her.

'Are you having a nice time, my darling?' asked Rose, flinging an arm around her between numbers and gently tugging her left earlobe.

'Of course – it's wonderful. I just had the most delightful talk with – um – Freddie? – about Fitzgerald. He's reading *Tender* too!' Letty wanted to reassure Rose that she could fit in in this world. That Rose didn't need to be worried about her (or embarrassed by her, a small voice wanted to pledge).

'Super. I'm so pleased,' replied Rose, before swizzling away to discuss India very loudly with a tired-looking young man recently back from negotiations. And Letty thought briefly, disloyally, that perhaps it was Rose that needed to not try so hard with the men that she blasted with the full force of personality.

Letty caught sight of Bertie, shoulders drooping as he leaned against a large carved stone flowerpot, and wondered if he was watching her. She said yes immediately to the next offer of a dance from a stranger, and let herself be lifted, drifting in the night air that spun round her shoulders, her face hot, her waist held tight. Dance after dance. The evening rainbowed around her, sherbet dresses swirling through the half-lit flower beds, the bright Chinese lanterns above them glowing like gaudy little moons.

Then she began to notice it: the same giddy, gritted deter-mination to enjoy oneself here that she saw at home. Too loud; too hard. The way that some of the men's eyes had nothing behind them, the orange hiss of the trumpet, the burning in her cheeks ... *A bit of air*, she thought, before remembering she was already outside.

And then, quite certainly, she needed to sit down.

Letty had tottered down almost to the end of the garden

when she saw the oak tree, with a low iron bench curving round it.

She sat, pressing her hands to the iron bars and then to her cheeks to cool them, and sighed. She wasn't sure if she was excited or exhausted. But the sturdiness of the oak was reassuring, and Letty breathed deeply, inhaling a country smell that was familiar and yet not, earth and young green leaves and something else. Yorkshire. It was the furthest north she'd ever been.

Bertie, around the other side of the tree in his preferred hiding place, felt the vibration through the metal bars more than he really heard her sit down.

It couldn't be, thought Bertie. Could it? He weighed up the risk: lose his solitude, or lose the possibility ...

He lit a cigarette.

Letty registered the click-hiss-crackle before she remembered to be startled. Someone behind the tree. She looked down; yes, the bench curved the whole way around its massive trunk.

A cigarette. That could be just the thing. She hated the cigarette smoke that clogged The Fountain, but here the way the men lit them for you, so debonair yet strangely tender ... Yes, a cigarette.

Letty gripped the bars, and used them to swish herself around the bench to see who was there.

And there she was.

'Oh!'

'Letty. I ... I was just having a quiet smoke, I didn't hear— Are you ...?'

'Yes, fine. Just wanted a moment ...'

He half stood, face contorting into at least six different expressions. 'I should ... I can leave you ... I mean—'

'Oh don't be daft.' Letty grabbed his arm and pulled him

back down on the bench, a little unsteadily, their sides half-colliding, at which Bertie couldn't prevent a laugh escaping.

And then she was giggling too, and the awkwardness he'd carried round like tortoise shell on his back all night lifted away.

'Oh, Bertie, I've had a few glasses of Champagne.'

'I know,' he said, looking mock-mournfully down at his hand, which held an empty flute. 'So have I. What a terrible state of affairs.'

'Do give me a cigarette, and talk to me about books.'

And so he lit a cigarette, looking really at the curve of her white neck, and shared his cleverest thoughts about Wordsworth. Only they seemed to come out as rather woolly and sentimental aphorisms about the simplicity of the life of the shepherd, and suchlike.

'If this belief from heaven be sent, if such be Nature's holy plan, have I not reason to lament what man has made of man?" he quoted in desperation, declaring it out and up to the stars, which winked in apparent approval.

Letty wanted to clutch her heart. A man was actually reciting poetry to her! At a garden party! *Under the stars!*

Instead, she rolled her eyes as she smoked, which Bertie thought made her seem quite excellently worldly.

'The countryside isn't like that though, is it. Not the proper countryside, it isn't – it's not all God in a primrose and tweeting birds. It's dark and dirty and *hard.*'

'Ah, but isn't there something transcendent in that too – in the honesty of it, man and nature, beasts and soil? Machines, and-and planes, and speed, and weapons... they all take us further from that essential dialogue between human nature and the earth.'

'We've never not had weapons though, Bertie, have we, even

if it was just bits of metal or–or swords, or whatsit, you know … *sticks.*'

She picked up a fallen oak branch and adopted a fencing stance. His earnestness might be enchanting and she might want to lie under the tree and listen to him read her the complete works of Wordsworth, but she also must prick it, somehow couldn't allow these grandiose statements about Mankind and Nature to stand, to impress her so very easily.

Bertie had never been mocked by a woman like this before – an occasional cynical laugh from a haughty creature who thought him pathetic: certainly. Regularly. But never one waving a branch at him.

He slowly reached down, picked a stick of his own, and then rose to his feet in a flash, startling her.

'*En garde!*'

Letty yelped, and they fenced, badly.

'For nature!'

'For progress!' She parried rapidly, forcing him onto a back foot, which impressed him as much as the fact that she was determined to spar intellectually.

'For … for the sublime!'

'For the future! I want a new, thrilling future! With excitement, and purpose, and, and … action!'

'Oh, I bet you do …'

She gasped lightly at his husky insinuation that came from who knew where and then it appeared his stick had fallen to the floor and his arm was around her and he had pulled her tighter into him than any of the men on the dancefloor, and her mind was suddenly quite clear: *Remember this.*

The moment before their lips touched stretched forever, in anticipation. Like the moment between the lights dimming, and the curtain rising.

And then they were kissing. And it felt miraculous, to Bertie, who knew he would always remember this kiss, under this oak tree.

Her arm still dangled at her side, holding the branch, one young green leaf trembling.

Chapter 3

October 1947

'But it's ridiculous,' Letty hissed at him, her feet planted at the edge of the lawn of Worcester College like a particularly stubborn sheep.

'I know, but the rules are the rules and they're honestly real sticklers.' Bertie grimaced, his long narrow face seeming to drag towards his chest.

'No. Walking. On. The. Grass. No. Women. Allowed. Inside.' She delivered the words like they were a personal, devastating insult. 'But you live here. You study here.'

'Well, yes, I think that's the thing, distraction ...' said Bertie weakly, trailing off.

Since the garden party, they'd stayed in touch, writing carefully crafted letters about poetry and politics, alongside gently nosing questions about each other's lives that belied an almost feverish interest on both sides. Bertie had burned with pleasure when Letty said yes to his suggestion that he might visit her in Abergavenny; now, it was his turn to host her in his world. He had been proud at the thought of introducing Letty to Oxford: showing her the cloisters and mullioned windows, the concentrated hush of academia. Even if he hadn't wildly taken to his studies, the aesthetics of his situation pleased Bertie – the crumble-edged splendour of the quad, and the tangled staircase that tripped over its own steepness as it led to his cosy bedroom and study, the old red armchair with its shiny, worn-smooth leather.

It had never occurred to him that she'd expect to see that bit too, yet here she was, furious at being prevented. It wasn't that Letty had any particular designs on his bedroom – this was only their fourth meeting; she was staying in a room above a tea shop – it was just that she wanted to know every single thing about Bertie. She wanted to be able to imagine him by the fire that he wrote of. To smell his books. To get inside these great walls!

Not to be stuck outside in the autumn grey, the chill seeming to come from those forbidding stones themselves.

Bertie had daydreamed incessantly about Letty in the six weeks since he had visited her in Wales. But at her arrival in Oxford, he felt tilted by her presence, the reality of her; she was lightly different to his worn and worked-over memories. Not quite as pale. Her stride shorter, trotting almost. There was a seriousness in her gaze that made the strangeness of her being in Oxford – actually present in his everyday life – feel simultaneously perfectly correct and charged with unpredictable electricity.

'Come on – I'll show you the dining hall at least,' he said, kissing her hand, hoping to soften her.

'All right then.' Letty tossed her curls, which she'd had set specially for the trip, in a display of disgruntlement.

Inside the huge room – grandeur in every panel, privilege in every breath – she felt suddenly very small. But she wouldn't show it. She could feel Bertie looking at her, wanting her to be impressed, but she wouldn't give in.

Why did something inside her resist showing him her admiration, she wondered. He'd had no such reservations when visiting

Aber. If Bertie was bemused by the small town, he'd managed to smile through it all.

She'd been bursting to see him, at the train station a full twenty minutes before the train, tapping up and down the platform on newly re-heeled shoes. When he'd stepped off, in his smart suit and a hat threatened by gusts of Welsh wind, a sudden shyness overtook her. She walked and talked very fast towards The Fountain, where he had a room, gesturing stagily at her local landmarks ('that's the cottage where my dad grew up', 'that's where I had my first job, behind the counter on a Saturday').

When he came outside after dropping his small smart case in the dark, boiled-vegetable-smelling room, he had handed her a paper-wrapped parcel, a little self-consciously. Letty unwrapped it with the indecorous haste of a child.

'*Sons and Lovers*? I've never read any DH Lawrence – oh, Bertie, thank you, it's beautiful!'

And then she stood on tiptoes and kissed him dead on the mouth, astonishing Bertie, who thought that it was highly improbable he would ever be allowed to touch her again.

'All right, boyo! On you go!' yelled someone from across the street, but Letty just laughed at the old man, whose trousers were actually torn and ragged.

'Don't mind him, rude old thing,' she whispered to Bertie with a smile that seemed to curl all the way into his ear.

Letty had tried to keep him away from her family – her parents knew that he was visiting, and her brothers teased her mercilessly about her 'fancy man' when anyone else was around, but in the privacy of the home, they all said absolutely nothing. She was unsure if it was because he was the first man she had announced she was courting, or if it was because he was from away. But come Saturday night it wasn't possible to keep Bertie to herself, and in the crush and press of bodies in the pub, she was astonished to find him warmly accepted.

It was thanks to his experience in the war that he could manage it, Bertie reflected. He had signed up the day after his eighteenth birthday. The end was obviously nearing, but to miss out entirely seemed cowardly. Yet, once he'd done his officer training and got out to Italy, Bologna was nearly in the army's grasp. He was part of something, but just barely.

What the war did teach him was how to talk to men who were nothing like him. He learnt the camaraderie of sharing the last cigarette, making small talk about cricket, the collective shot of testosterone that fear – and in their case, victory – could bring. But he learnt, too, how to neutralise masculine bluster in all its many variations, rather than become a target for it.

Bertie's schooling had been entirely geared towards fashioning him, and boys like him, into leaders. He was sent, at seven, to board at an imposing building made of such thick stone it was freezing even in the summer term. Many hours' train ride away from Farley Hall, his parents rarely visited; Bertie was to learn to stand on his own two feet, to learn how to wield power and authority on behalf of the British Empire, no less. That hadn't remotely worked – but what his schooling had given him was an inner confidence that allowed Bertie to be always and only himself. Bumbling, non-threatening, bookish, and yet under-pinning these qualities with such self-assurance and generous good cheer that even the toughest, coarsest of soldiers realised there was no sense in trying to pull him down or give him a kicking for his privilege. There was simply no need.

At The Fountain, this ebullient openness once more stood in him in good stead. Bertie had proved horrendously bad at darts, trodden on a dog, and failed to follow scores of jokes that were just too fast, too Welsh for him. But he laughed long and loud when he did get them, and more importantly laughed at himself, and bought several rounds. Letty's brothers, their friends, and assorted old boys all afterwards said 'funny sort' and 'bit different, that one', but also declared him 'a good lad'. Letty felt like she'd been lightly gold-plated.

But in Oxford, it was as if some cheap metal below was showing. She'd known it would be grand; she was excited for grand. But she hadn't expected to feel so shut out. Even at his college, Bertie didn't introduce her to anyone. Oxford was somehow closed off, all walls.

'What did you think of the book?'

Bertie's voice was soft, and Letty felt a pang in her chest as she walked.

'*Sons and Lovers*?' She'd read it, twice, in advance of seeing him again. Its glossy, oxblood leather cover seemed to almost glow on her bedside table, and she'd snatched it back furiously when her brother Geraint picked it up, leafing through its treasured pages with fat, grubby fingers.

'Yes, I liked it very much.' Letty felt herself stall, sounding stiff when really she had so much she had planned to say, about the strange intensity of the way Lawrence wrote about relationships, all that was going on in a person beneath the surface. But what if, compared to other girls Bertie talked to in Oxford, she seemed naive? Dim?

Bertie's heart sank. He'd thought Lawrence might speak to her, more than the Wodehouse and Waugh that Rose had lately been sending; had thought that Letty might like to read about communities like hers in great literature, too. But perhaps she considered that patronising of him...?

'Oh, well. Good.' There was so much more for them to discuss, Bertie just knew it, but before he could find the words they were at the river.

'I, uh, I thought we might take a punt?' Bertie said, trying to sound spontaneous.

'Oh, yes?' Letty heard how cool she sounded, but secretly she'd hoped they might. It was one of the only things she knew about the university towns, really – spires and punts. 'That's what you do with all the university girls, is it?'

She felt it wounding him. He opened his mouth, halfway towards a joke. Closed it.

Bertie walked sheepishly up to a man in a tatty cap and muttered something; nodding, he went to a low shed and dragged out a punt, with a huge wicker hamper on it, bedecked with red velvet cushions and thick tartan blankets. Letty frowned.

'Your carriage awaits...' Bertie spoke with offhand irony, as if the whole enterprise was a joke, but kept his eyes cast down as he held out his hand to help her onto the low wooden vessel, then busied himself paying the boatman and pushing them off the side of the bank. And so he missed the look of growing wonder in Letty's eyes.

The water flowed smooth round the punt, and the current began to tug as Bertie steered them deftly into the middle of the river. Letty shuffled into the cushions. She hoped everyone in Oxford could see her: on a punt, with this man, who had arranged it all specially. And actually for her.

Once they had some slight speed, and were out the way of the rowers who passed, grunting, in loose vests and tiny shorts, Bertie sat down opposite her, and busied himself in the basket.

'Are you cold? There's blankets... I thought in case you got cold sitting. And, ah, I brought a picnic. Are you hungry?'

'Always.'

'Excellent. Well it isn't much but some sandwiches' – a paper-wrapped packet, tied up with string, yet posed on a china plate emerged – 'and cheese and apples' – a little platter, ready cut up – 'and some cake' – fruit cake! And iced buns! – 'and some wine? If you'd like?' Crystal glasses caught the autumn light, which helpfully cracked through the thick cloud and cut through the fine yellowing leaves of the weeping willow they'd drifted towards. Letty starred dumbstruck at the feast. The only sweet thing she'd had for weeks was jam.

Bertie rummaged more. Paused, shot a look to the sky, and then pulled out a tiny glass vase with a single rose in it, the palest pink. He passed it to her, with a shrug.

A vibration in the air. Was she going to … *laugh*? He would need to capsize the punt and drown immediately.

Letty couldn't move, fearing that the whole thing was about to be revealed as an elaborate fiction, or a joke at her expense. Then she took the flower and set it down with grave tenderness next to her, at the edge of the gingham tablecloth he'd spread out between them.

'This is … magical,' was all she managed.

Her eyes stung with it.

And so Bertie could exhale again, and busied himself further with gently steering them under the willow, a cool and pale bower, the orange light and lilac shadow dappling his eager face, turned hopefully now towards her, and she knew with certainty he'd never done this for anyone before.

And she looked at him so intently it almost seemed like she was in pain.

Then it was Letty who nearly capsized them, lunging towards him and taking hold of Bertie's narrow trunk as tight as if she might break him.

'Hey now!' he laughed, gulping a mouthful of wine, somehow leafy, its taste all mingled with the fresh wet green of the river and the tree.

She held on and on, until he tried to feed her a bit of cheese and apple. She took it gently in her mouth and carried nibbling on to the tips of his fingers. She pressed her teeth gently, then firmly down onto their pads. Ran her tongue over them.

When he let out a low groan, she released him. Turned to nuzzle into his neck. Its warmth, and slight stubble; its buttery smell.

'Thank you,' Letty said, fully muffled into him.

'What's that?' Bertie tried to pull her out, to hear her, but she burrowed further.

When she did let him pull her away, she could barely flick her eyes at him. 'I can't believe you did all this, for me.'

She had no more words, just tried to radiate her feelings into him.

Bertie took Letty's pointed face, easily cupped by his long, nobbled fingers, and kissed her.

The fluttering in the chest she'd always felt at his touch dived down into her belly, which seemed to turn to a fiery liquid. Something quickening and churning and insistent. When his mouth moved to her neck, a gasp slipped out, unintended. He smiled, as his heart hit his sternum like a hammer, and his whole body knew.

Chapter 4

January 1948

'Well, *really*, Bertie.' His mother, Amelia, half sighed, half drawled out her disgust, her disappointment, as she held a wine glass aloft. The slick flick of her other wrist alerted Martha that it should be refilled.

Given the circumstances, even Harold didn't object. Bertie's father remained silent. His gaze rested on – or, rather, bore into – the vase of artfully arranged hot-house dahlias at the centre of the dining table, almost reflected in its high sheen. They looked, Bertie thought, like a contained explosion, paused mid-burst.

His father's own contained reaction to the announcement frightened him. So far Harold had not spoken a word.

'She's a sweet thing, I grant you that. But this is the rest of your life, darling.' Amelia's words already had that glaze on them, the smeared polish drink gave her.

'I love her,' said Bertie, as simply as he could, and glanced at Rose, who looked anguished, sat very straight and tall on their high-backed dining chairs.

'Mummy, Violet is one of my dearest friends, she's a very clever, good, hardworking sort of person,' Rose tried, but as she spoke Bertie heard how the words sounded all wrong, not at all what their mother hoped for in a daughter-in-law.

During Letty's weekend visits, both Bertie and Rose pounced

on her company hungrily, the girls' friendship as sturdy a tripod leg of the relationship as the romance. But Amelia, while glass-ily polite, practically ignored Letty's now frequent presence at Farley Hall. Even when Letty had recently visited for her and Bertie's birthday dinner, Amelia had barely acknowledged that there were two celebrations happening.

But then Amelia didn't lavish much attention on her own children either. Tall, with rich chestnut hair still not showing a single grey, she could glide into a room and gather up everyone in it on the wave of her slim arms, the swooping charm of her voice – if she so chose. When it came to Bertie and Rose, she rarely bothered.

Even in school holidays as children Amelia had barely spent time with them, and would often be in foul, black moods that Bertie and Rose had found bewildering. She had looked at them as if they were in the way, preventing her from get-ting things done. What things, Bertie still couldn't imagine: his mother did nothing. Had never done anything. 'Imagine a life that pointless,' Rose had once burst out, frustrated at the waste, the spite.

As they got older, the fresheners began starting earlier; in the afternoon, with lunch. The crack of the ice. Then there might be an hour of intruding, heavy affection – her breath sweet as she insisted on doing Rose's hair, badly, or reading over Bertie's shoulder, a sudden cloying abundance. Bertie had tried to turn into stone, still and unreactive, to stave off the moment when she'd turn. Because then there would come a fine slicing up of their personalities, achievements, looks. A needle inserted into the flesh tenderised, despite his efforts to resist, by her earlier affection.

Any fiancé would be wrong for their eternally disappointed mother. But Bertie also recognised that she had no power, beyond the power to hurt. And so he looked, really, at his father.

'Bertie, study, please.'

'Father, I really think if you have something to say—' interrupted Rose, hotly.

'You seem to be under the impression that this is a family matter, Rose, when it is precisely nothing to do with you.'

Rose went beetroot and glared. Amelia rolled her eyes extravagantly.

Harold rose. The same height as his wife, although thirteen years older, with a chest that now domed out in front of him, he had a compact, meaty solidity. What little dark hair remained on his head met a still full but scrupulously neat beard.

His study. A sanctum, the hallowed place where Harold passed most of his hours, reading papers for the Lords and accounts for the estate. The dark wood panels seemed to press inwards in agonising silence as they sat down in two rigid armchairs by the fire.

Bertie was only ever called there for a telling-off. At sixteen, he'd spent a whole long week in a corner of the room, copying out Bible verses by hand while Harold worked (or read *The Times* cover to cover). Bertie and two of his equally clever, self-satisfied schoolfriends had got worked up about the war and decided Nietzsche was right and God must be dead, and mounted a protest against enforced church-going at school, accompanied by an essay on 'the tyranny of organised religion' in the school newspaper. Harold had been told to come to collect his son.

Harold attended church every week without fail, and informed Bertie that he considered his soul a poor price to pay in exchange for teenage rebellion. Amelia, who hadn't been to church since her brother had been gunned down in the First World War, had let out a small barking laugh.

The thick smell of beeswax and pipe smoke and leather,

the lack of air, or light – all was unchanged, claustrophobically familiar. This, Bertie had always assumed, was what the world of men would be like. Power in the back room, the heavy weight of the whisky glass. He wished for a wind to rush through the room, to blow it all away.

'The world seems different to you, I suppose.'

Bertie started, unnerved by his father's unanticipated accuracy.

'Nothing is ever the same after a war. But we still go forwards, Bertie. And you do know what's expected of you. Your duty.'

Harold adjusted the pile of books on a side table so that their spines aligned exactly, and sat back in his chair, the leather creaking as if in quiet support. The carriage clock on the mantelpiece struck the hour, with painful slowness. In the silence that followed, Bertie was sure he could feel dust motes settle softly around them.

Bertie got to his feet suddenly, and listed towards the mantelpiece. He stared at the clock face, its impassive gold expression, then turned.

'Father, things *are* different. But not because of the war. Just because of *her* – I simply don't want to be with anyone else.'

Harold's eyes blazed, and Bertie realised his father had hoped this was going to be simpler. He hadn't understood that there would be this new battle, hadn't reckoned with Bertie's new core of determination, that could win against his paternal authority.

'Sorry, Pa, but I'm afraid that's all there is to it. I'm going to ask her to marry me.'

Bertie watched the second hand turn, with its set, aggressive tick.

'And you'll live where?' asked Harold in a low rumble, eventually. 'Cramped in a cottage, with the rest of her family?'

'Perhaps,' Bertie answered with provoking lightness. He hadn't given too much thought to practicalities, in truth.

'You'd be willing to dispense with your past as well as your future then? What on earth have we been fighting for but this, our heritage?' Harold gestured, as if every stately home in England were under the wave of his hand.

'The hills. The countryside. And freedom!' Bertie was surprised at how the words rushed out, surprised at how earnest they sounded. 'And the people – the people of this whole green and pleasant land, Father, which isn't just ... isn't *just* people like us.'

'So you spend a few months in the army and come back a *man of the people.*'

Yes, Bertie wanted to say. That was exactly what the army had given him: a window into the lives of all different kinds of men. An understanding that what they had in common was greater than what divided them – and that what divided them, really, was this entrenched inequality that only benefited people like Harold. *Like him.*

'Our country is made up of fine people, Father,' Bertie replied, holding his power – displaying it – in his breezy refusal to be rattled. Or to be cowed. 'And the finest of them is Let— is Violet. She makes me very happy.'

'*Happy.*' Scorn dripped into the pause. 'So you'll be just as happy in the mucky Welsh hills, with nothing as your inheritance. Just as happy to never see your mother and me again.'

And then the room tilted on its axis, and the clock seemed even louder in the silence as Bertie recognised what was really behind the threat: his father's own fear and dread, at the thought of being alone forever and solely responsible for his wife, at the rooms being even emptier and yet even more suffocatingly airless than they already were, at passing the hall on to no one.

Hold fast, thought Bertie. Actually, he has more to lose.

He slowly moved towards his father's chair, crouched down on his heels, and took his father's hand. Harold bristled, but did not pull away.

'Father. Of course I don't want that. I feel a profound sense of duty to you, to Mother, to Farley Hall. Let me serve. But I must have Violet by my side.'

He kept his tone warm, but certain, trying to speak his father's language, searching for and finally finding his gaze.

'I am going to do this anyway, Father. Please let's go forward into this new world together.'

Bertie stood, re-establishing the usual distance. His blood was pounding round his body, despite the easy demeanour. But that was the trick: never let on. Stay cheery. Stay solid.

'The war taught you nothing, I see.'

And now the shock was that his father could so little see the change in his son. Still thought him an unformed schoolboy, not a man.

'When I went into the army, I already loved my country,' continued Harold. 'But I came out ready to do anything – *any-thing* – to preserve it. We had to win, and we did win, because of enormous sacrifice and suf—'

Suffering. Suffering was the word he couldn't say, Bertie realised.

Harold had been shot in his lower back at Amiens. Nine months in a hospital outside Harrogate. Amelia married him soon – presumably too soon – afterwards.

Harold cleared his throat. 'There was a lot of talk back then – a lot of rotten talk – about change. Changing things. New world order … It damages, Bertie, and it cannot be allowed to stand.' His fist clenched. 'We fought for Britain – for the way she was, the way she is. I will not have you damaging this family now: damaging our name, our way of life. You have responsibilities.

39

'The war, I hoped, would teach you that. Clearly, it did not.'

And Bertie felt, then, for the first time, a cold stone in his abdomen: the certainty that having his happiness would actually hurt his father.

Bertie looked away, towards the huge heavy desk that dominated the room. There, next to the fountain pen and blotter, was a small piece of shrapnel. Bertie had been fascinated by it as a child, never dared touch it again after his father had once caught him poring over it, and had gone to hit him, before freezing, jerking and turning away. Bertie could still picture the heaves that went through his father's back. It had been the only time he'd ever seen him lose his composure. The only time, too, his father had ever even come close to striking him.

There'd been no beatings in Farley Hall. And when Bertie had once returned home for Christmas with a slender scar on his palm, he found himself discreetly moved out of that schoolmaster's class the following term.

Bertie had always thought this sat oddly with his father's martial attitude. Now, he thought he understood. Pain. Harold didn't want anyone — and certainly not his own son — to feel pain.

And yet if you'd suffered like that, it had to matter.

Bertie's power felt different in his hands, suddenly: destructive. Hammer-like. Too absolute.

'Love passes, son. Infatuation … you're young. Your mother's right, for once: this is the rest of your life.'

But it was just exactly the wrong thing to say, and Bertie burned again. He wanted Letty. He would have her — whatever pain that caused.

'Then I will spend the rest of my life with her.'

His father sighed, and shut his eyes.

'This won't pass, Father. I won't let it. I will love her forever. And if you want to me to take your place in the Lords, to take on Farley Hall, to provide an heir – it will be with Violet. Otherwise, I'm sure everything can pass to Rose—'

Harold's eyes snapped opened, but Bertie found he couldn't hold his gaze this time.

'Get out.'

As Harold's voice broke, he dropped his head into one hand, and Bertie knew that, despite his banishment, he had won. They would not discuss it again like this, but a wedding would happen.

He trembled as he shut the door behind him and walked away; the polished floor of the corridor felt like it had turned into uneven rubble beneath his feet. Letty would be worth it. She meant more than money, or tradition. But he had never stood up to anybody like this, let alone his father. And Bertie did not feel the triumph he had expected.

Chapter 5

April 1948

The room roared. Bertie leapt to his feet with the rest of them – but it was almost involuntary, as if he'd been lifted by the crowd of men who'd packed into the drab hall in Tredegar, filling it with smoke and raised fists clutching papers. Onstage, Nye Bevan broke into a smile, seeing his vehemence pass out into the assembled masses like a flame through a field of dry grass.

Bertie broke into a grin of his own. Never had he heard such oration, never felt so certain about the country's bold, bright future. Bevan might speak with a light, high, rising voice, but the Labour MP's words about the need for a National Health Service thundered into their hearts with conviction. The men around Bertie blazed, and he caught the eye of Geraint, Letty's brother, who had turned around – checking on him, Bertie supposed, although he couldn't imagine that anyone could remain unmoved by such passion.

Geraint clapped him, hard, on the shoulder; his great hairy paws had a span the size of dinner plates and it was hard to believe he could be related to Letty.

'Yes, Bert, yes!' he fairly bellowed, and then Evan, stood next to his son, looked around too. It was the first time, Bertie thought, he'd seen Letty's father appear actually happy, his face like a dim, sooty lamp prised open to reveal a light. He was ruddy, singing along to the chorus of the 'Red Flag' that swelled through the hall, with an almost delirious shine in his eyes.

'It's the most marvellous thing!' Bertie couldn't help the words leaping from his mouth as he leaned forward towards them both, hearing how odd his accent sounded here.

Evan's good bass voice continued to churn heartily, but a single nod at Bertie contained volumes. And it momentarily stilled his nerves, gave him hope.

Then the men – and the women, although fewer of them – streamed out of the hall towards the pub. The Black Mountains, where the Lewises lived, weren't true mining country, but Tredegar was only a valley away. As the Lewises and Bertie entered The Gradon Arms, several members of the male voice choir were already warming up with a burst of 'Sospan Fach', and the tangled vowels and soft intonations of the Welsh enchanted Bertie.

'What are they singing about?' he asked.

'A little saucepan on a fire, and a cat scratching a child,' replied David, Letty's other brother. Bertie assumed he was being teased, and fumbled in his wallet to pay for the first round of pints.

He noticed a small group of women by the door, in apparently urgent conversation – struggling over the singing with much additional hand-waving – with several men, including the leader of the Brecon Labour branch he'd been introduced to on the bus journey over. And Bertie experienced a shiver of guilt.

Letty had wanted to come but Evan forbad it. 'I don't believe that politics is a nice place for a young unmarried woman, and that's the end of it.'

The fight had broken out over tea (Bertie was slowly remembering to call it that, not dinner, although he could never get used to it happening so early). The fiery altercation between

Letty and her parents — escalating from her angrily sawing the loaf to Evan's finger wagging and fist pounding the table hard enough to make the crockery jump — was so different to the chilly, silent resentments that glacially spread in his own house, Bertie hadn't been sure where to look. He focused, mostly, on counting the knitted checks on the tea cosy, which covered an enormous brown enamel teapot, and only afterwards wondered if he shouldn't have challenged Evan, insisted that, these days, politics was *exactly* the right place for a young woman — especially one as determined and quick thinking as his daughter.

When they'd set off, Letty had stood on the doorstep next to Mrs Lewis; her mother waved, but Letty kept her arms folded. She was pleased — she'd told him as much — that Bertie had been invited along with her father and brothers. But she was furious that Evan wouldn't allow her to join the local Labour women's section so she could attend such events too. Especially on this occasion.

The Labour meeting was the biggest of the year for the local branch, bussed to Tredegar specially to attend the glorious homecoming for Bevan. This was the easiest of all the easy crowds to win over to the National Health Service. Nye, so often reliant on sarcastic humour, had dipped instead into a well of deep sincerity as he spoke about his upbringing in the town, his father's death from pneumoconiosis, and how it was Tredegar's own medical aid society that had inspired him to create a new national one.

Bertie kept hearing about the injuries suffered in the pits; nationalising them was one thing, but health care would be the real saviour. Then again, you didn't need to work underground to suffer. Bertie was astonished at the stories that swirled round Abergavenny too, as if talk of the incipient NHS had uncorked a bottle of desperation long kept stoppered. How Old Davy had

44

passed away because he was too proud to let anyone else pay for the operation to cut the cancer out. How Letty's schoolfriend Llinos died in childbirth, unable to call the doctor out as far as Merthyr Cynog in time. How Gareth worked on the railways alongside Evan in agony because he could neither afford the surgery on his hip nor the unpaid days off to recover. And now, all the soldiers and all their visible, and invisible, injuries.

Bertie had known about the privations of poverty in the abstract, and in long, elegantly argued discussions about the welfare state, turned over during dinner in hall or with cocktails at parties, had always argued that the NHS must be supported on moral grounds before anything else. But here he saw the actual, physical suffering.

The nation was limping – but it was also beginning to get to its feet. Even in the months he'd been visiting Letty, Bertie could physically feel the rush and rise among her community, alongside all he read in the papers. The new optimism. They had so little, but things were changing, and the appetite was sharp as a knife. For something better.

He still felt he had something to prove, however, with her family. It hadn't been easy, getting to know them. The first time that he'd gone round to visit, Bertie had watched Letty's eyes darting as she brought him into their sitting room, and he tried to restrain his own from doing similar, so she wouldn't think he was judging her home. A neat terrace of grey stone and dark slate, with its *ty bach* in the back yard still (they didn't speak Welsh, but that term for the toilet had somehow been held onto). Bible verses and framed cross-stitch on the walls, frilled and crocheted covers of all sizes spread over chairs and sofas whose patterns were long since worn or bleached out. An ugly green-edged tea set ('Mam got the best out for you'), and the huge pot, snug in its cosy.

Bertie had been seized by a clumsy claustrophobia: the room felt far too small for all the people it must hold and all the functions it must fill. There was barely a space to fold himself into, between the tea table – which he later realised was got out and put away for every meal – and the sofas, and the three substantial men of Letty's family, who for all their loose-jawed friendliness in the pub, seemed stiff and hemmed as Mrs Lewis fussed around them.

Letty had been a marvel. She kept the conversation going, drawing out her parents and brothers with questions about their day, like so many tugs on threads until the conversations pulled into a shape they were comfortable with. It wasn't that Bertie was incapable of talking to them – indeed, he put all his charm to work – but more that her family seemed uncertain at answering even the most ordinary of his questions. He noticed how Letty swiftly cut them with her own, as if only she could stitch together the conversation correctly.

He could tell she was pained, and Bertie had wanted to tell her – to silently send the thought right into her brain – that she needn't be, need never be. Later, when they stepped out for an evening stroll, he tried to find the words for it, and failed, Letty cutting off his rambling abruptly.

'Don't. You don't have to be nice about it, about them.'

Bertie had tried to protest, but she just said *isht*, a Welsh word he recognised was deployed for extra finality.

Over the months since that first meeting, the Lewises had begun to outwardly embrace him, taking him to the pub, to chapel, and to Labour meetings. But Bertie still wasn't sure they would actually want him for a son-in-law. This visit felt charged by the need to win them round, definitively. Because Bertie couldn't wait any longer. He had sworn to himself that this would be this weekend that he would summon his courage, finally, to ask Evan for Letty's hand.

The next day, after the Lewises trooped home from chapel and gathered round the table for Sunday dinner, Bertie felt pleased when the conversation turned to socialism, and specifically the merits or otherwise of the incumbent Labour prime minister. He sensed an opportunity.

'The question, really, is whether Attlee will have the brass to go far enough,' said David.

'He's a bloody sheep he is,' replied Geraint.

'Language,' shrilled Angharad, mock-striking her son's knuckles with the serving spoon.

'Exactly, Mrs Lewis: we won't have Churchill quoted in this household!' rumbled Evan, only the twitch of his moustache indicating he was joking. 'War-mongering—'

'Never mind about him anyway now, Dad, he's finished, gone – it's Attlee who you've got to worry about it is. Will he fumble it or not?' said David.

'Well, we won't have a truly free and fair democracy until the workers have a *say*, as well as a stake, in how their industries are run,' interjected Bertie rather too fast, alarmed at his voice's fluting tone. 'But the nationalisation of the industries and utilities is, well … it's a jolly good start.'

There was a pause. Geraint looked at his father, a light smirk on his face. David held still.

Evan grunted, nodded, ate a potato.

And Bertie felt Letty's hand lightly press upwards on the underside of his thigh beneath the tablecloth.

'And, uh, Evan, how do you find things now, on the railways? Busy spot, isn't it, Abergavenny – three stations!' Bertie stumbled on, fearing he sounded supercilious. 'Has nationalisation changed things much for you, day to day, actually in the, ah, the railway shed?'

'Not much, to be honest with you. Cleaning engines is cleaning engines, isn't it? Whatever name they paint on the side of the trains.'

'It's not got any easier to clean the coal dust out his clothes, I will say that, coal dust is coal—' chimed in Angharad eagerly, before Evan cut her off, raising a large hand with weary finality.

'Lad's not interested in laundry, now, is he.'

Angharad busied herself cutting up her last potato very small.

'Well you did get a little bit of a pay rise too, didn't you?' interjected Letty, fiercely, the question somehow a sideways statement of support for her mam.

Then it was Evan's turn to become absorbed by his food, and Letty looked immediately wretched, presumably for mentioning money.

'This isn't about the in-di-*vid*-u-al, Letty,' said Geraint, condescendingly. He picked through his words in just the same way she did, noticed Bertie.

'Geraint's right. But to answer your question, Bertie: no, for the working man it hasn't made much difference, day to day.' Evan paused, regaining control of the narrative. 'But it's the *principle* of thing. The Labour Party has finally done what it said it ought to do. Bring about the common ownership of—'

'*The means of production*,' joined in Bertie, grinning. 'And about time too.'

The corners of Evan's mouth turned up just a fraction.

That evening, Evan gruffly assented when Bertie asked for 'a word'. As he wound his way around to the topic, Bertie's hand inside his pocket tore his handkerchief into rags.

'What I want to say – all I mean to say is – Mr Lewis, I care so much for your daughter... I love her, and I would like to

ask you if I can, if I may, possibly, ask for her hand in marriage?'
Bertie stood towering over Evan, holding very still.

'You may,' was all Evan said, after a pause.

But then, in the midst of Bertie's effusive, exhaling thanks,
his whole body going limp as a puppet, Evan muttered quietly,
'You must love her, to put up with us.'

And it silenced Bertie. All his training in affability left him; he
had no idea how to respond to this display of self-deprecation
that contained – didn't it? – an actual shard of inferiority in the
face of Bertie's standing in the world.

At that moment, Bertie finally reckoned with the discomfort
his mere presence in their house brought. Would always bring.
Bertie didn't mention this wincing insight to Letty – to do so
would be to bring that discomfort to their own relationship;
better for them both to pretend it didn't exist, or to at least
pretend they didn't know the other knew about it. But he felt
her father's wound in the same way he felt his own father's.

Then Evan clapped Bertie on the shoulder and managed a
smile and offered him a drink to steady his nerves, and Bertie
gulped down the bad whisky while Evan went to send Letty
in. The proposal itself was brief – 'Will you—?' 'Yes' – and he
collapsed into a sort of exhausted relief. Bertie tried to hide his
tears in her hair; she felt them, wetting the nape of her neck,
but pretended she didn't.

Chapter 6

June 1948

A firework bloomed over the lake, and Worcester College glowed gold. A string quartet filled the warm evening air with soft, obliging music, and the sound of talk and laughter seemed to flow with it, the counterpoint melody of a summer ball.

Tonight, Bertie's home had at last truly invited Letty in. The college grounds, their preening crenulations and hulking gateways, twinkled with lights. The dark wood of the imposing quad door had disappeared behind a great bower of flowers in cream and mauve and a powdery pink, and there was a woman on the arm of all the scholars. Their rustling taffeta gowns softened the place, she thought.

'Letty! How lovely to see you. The old college doesn't scrub up too bad, eh?' It was Thoby, one of the very few of Bertie's college friends that he had seemed comfortable introducing Letty to during her visits to Oxford over the previous year. And no wonder: Thoby had a gossipy, conspiratorial manner most unlike the stuck-up awkwardness of many of the scholars.

'It's beautiful, Thoby!' Letty leaned in, letting him kiss her cheek. 'Tell me, the flowery entrance — that was your doing, wasn't it?'

'It was indeed. What can I say — I've an aesthete's eye for

colour...' Thoby's dark eyes twinkled as he patted his rather glossy hair, worn just long enough to reveal a natural wave.

'Well I only wish you'd told me beforehand, you know, I would've matched my frock.'

'But you look divine in violet, Violet: wouldn't have it any other way.'

Letty gave an elaborate twirl, and noticed Bertie – politely talking to Thoby's bored-looking date – watching her. She felt a zip through the middle of her body, and for just a second wished everything about the ball would disappear and leave them entirely alone.

This feeling of seeing yourself through another's eyes had turned out to be one of the most unexpected pleasures of falling in love. Letty had noticed basic lust swamping up the vision of men at home or at dances during the war, but this was different: when she saw how Bertie looked at her on these occasions, direct as a dart but somehow also liquid and gathering, she felt like the most special person in a room, the most beautiful, the most interesting. It was vain, she thought, to revel in it, but she did. It made her feel powerful.

'Now, Letty, my dear, on the subject of flowers you must tell me what you're doing for the wedding.' Thoby took her arm, handing her a glass of Champagne as they passed a waiter as effortlessly as if picking her a daisy.

'Oh, I haven't given it much thought yet, to be honest.'

'I'm thinking freesias...' Thoby's eyes glazed, his hands raised and spread, as he began setting the scene. Letty smiled to herself, brushing away the memory of how shocked, embarrassed even, she'd been when she first heard the whispered revelation about him. Silly thing to mind about, and she liked that neither Bertie nor Rose *did* mind. The four of them had formed quite the cosy quartet, and spent Easter weekend together at Merriweather, Thoby's family's sprawling home in the Chilterns.

Bertie came back over to collect her – 'Fine! Take away my favourite if you must!' huffed Thoby – and together they whirled round the gardens, Letty hellooing Bertie's college friends with dimpling smiles, and making pretty small talk with the girls they'd all found from somewhere for the evening. She could register, every single time, their surprise at her accent. With each introduction, there was a little tear in the fabric of the night, almost immediately and imperceptibly mended by the invisible stitching of their good manners.

'That's finishing school for you,' Bertie said with an eyeroll when Letty commented on it. But she didn't really mind – that evening, in her dress with its neat waist and frothing dark blue fabric, a dress that Bertie had bought for her with an excitable pleasure, she felt absolutely correct.

As Bertie politely answered questions about Farley Hall from an ageing don who'd known Bertie's grandfather before he died, Letty twizzled away lightly on her ankle, tilted her head back. She considered the college once more.

Why shouldn't this sort of place be hers?

'Hullo there, Leticia.' Her thoughts were interrupted by Tolly, a man with greasy, slick hair and too-fleshy features, who looked middle aged at twenty-one. 'Has he made an honest woman of you yet?'

'Wedding's next month,' she replied curtly, suddenly remembering all the reasons she worried she'd never fit in Bertie's world after all. 'What's next for you now then?'

'Back up to Scotland actually. Be at the family pile for the summer, deer season before too long. Do you hunt, Leticia?' He sucked on the pipe he smoked, grotesquely.

'It's Letty, actually' – she knew he knew this – 'and I must say I am partial to taking a shot at wild bores.'

Bertie arrived, and smoothly manoeuvred her away from the drunk undergraduate.

'Do they call him Tolly because he's so intolerable?' she muttered.

Bertie stopped her, put his hands on her almost bare shoulders, cool now as night descended. 'Is it too hideous, darling?'

'Don't be daft,' Letty leaned forward and popped a tiny kiss on his lips. 'I'm having a lovely time. I enjoy being rude about people you don't actually like anyway.'

'There do seem to be an awful lot of them ...'

'Well, that's because you've got me, and no one else can hold a candle now, can they? I've ruined life for you, sorry, love, every other conversation will always be disappointing.'

Bertie beamed at her, indulgently. And her heart expanded, looking at how his smile was just slightly higher on the left, how he managed to make even tails look a little rumpled. Soppy, adorable creature, thought Letty.

'I fear, Miss Lewis, that you are, in fact, exactly correct in your estimation of the situation.'

That was another thing: how verbose he became when he was tipsy. Letty couldn't help herself – despite all his tutors milling about, no matter who might see, she had to lean forward and kiss him fully, the familiar urge to merge with him completely feeling hotter and more vital than ever.

Bertie fought the desire to swing her round and back her against a tree, as he would do in secluded spots on their long walks; unsatisfying as it was, there was at least some shred of relief in feeling her body firm beneath him. Bertie would never tell Letty this, but he thought it unfair that she had spent the past several months scolding him for not doing enough work when the main reason he hadn't been able concentrate on cramming for finals was that he was being driven steadily insane by his inability to have her.

That Bertie had not only insisted on going to Worcester College, rather than following his father and grandfather to Magdalen, was bad enough in Harold's mind; that he'd then squandered the opportunity by only getting a 2:2 was a further embarrassment. Bertie knew his father blamed Letty.

And, he supposed, she was to blame even if she was utterly without fault; he found his studies, which he'd never been wildly excited by to begin with, staggering irrelevant and boring compared to Letty. Compared to kissing her and holding her, yes, but also compared to her conversation, her mind. How they could talk and talk, conversations springing off in tangents before being brought spiralling back, always too much to say in the time they had.

Her take on the world delighted him, whether he took her to see the London Symphony Orchestra ('I don't see why I got tutted at just for moving my head around a bit. If Shostakovich doesn't move you, that's the real problem, isn't it?') or a student production of *Troilus and Cressida* in a college quad ('What I reckon is, Shakespeare got his heart broken, and he's taking it out on a woman he's made up. It's petty, is all').

Her certainty in her instinctive opinion was quite unlike that of young men in tutorials, their languid assumption of intellectual authority and their silkily regurgitated learning. Letty's analysis was quick, stubborn, and deeply felt. Bertie began to view the world with some of the freshness of her perspective.

This, however, did not help his essays. Original thought, he'd gloomily moan into her neck or down a telephone receiver, was not valued.

'Bertie, get off the telephone and do your work,' Letty would chide, speaking from the box at the end of her street.

'But it's tedious and pointless. Translating the farce in *Ecclesiazusae*? Honestly, I'd rather hear about your interactions in the post office. I'm certain they're funnier. Is Mad Sal still trying to pay for stamps with yew berries?'

'Oh no you don't. Don't try to get me on a story, Bertie – go and do your work,' her voice stern, despite sounding far away. He groaned, but she didn't say anything. There was a long pause, where she listened to his breathing.

'You know, Bertie, you're a bloody lucky so-and-so, and you don't even realise it,' she burst out, eventually. 'I'd *love* to know about Aristophanes. Instead, I've got to weigh parcels all day. The only challenge for my mind is how to most gently break the news to someone that they don't have even a ha'penny left in their savings book. I would be *wallowing* in all those words, if I had the chance.'

Bertie was shamed, briefly. And a little surprised. Letty usually spoke of the post office with satisfaction: she'd been promoted again, to post mistress, a senior role that previously only a man might've had.

Privately, he'd always thought the day-to-day activity of the job as she described it sounded extraordinarily tedious. It had never occurred to him that she could be proud of having a job, and yet still actually be … *bored*.

The other thing seriously demoting his studies in Bertie's life had been politics – which he also joked was down to Letty, and the conversations he'd had with her father and brothers and friends. 'My political awakening is your fault, darling – couldn't you have left me sleepwalking through life like the rest of them? Then I might have got a First!'

Really, it was less an awakening than a distilling: Bertie's sympathies with the left wing long predated Letty. People spoke about war being a great leveller, but while serving in Italy, Bertie had been clear-eyed enough to see it wasn't, really; despite his inexperience, he was the one giving orders. Why? Because some distant relative had once pleased a royal and been given land and a title. It seemed a fatally foolish way to organise things.

But getting to know Letty, and her family, had certainly sharpened his thinking. They had a lived wisdom that he valued, in contrast to the pontificating of privileged students. Although Bertie noticed Evan never used examples from his own life, but rather spoke of the malnutrition of a neighbour's children during the '30s, of a friend's fight with 'bloody management' after injury on the tracks, of foully cramped housing 'over the way' in the pit villages.

In Oxford, Bertie had joined the Labour Party, and soon became secretary for the student group. They gave out pamphlets, held well-attended, sparky debates, and raised money. But Bertie's favourite bit was writing articles for *Cherwell*; he won great acclaim for one defending the nationalisation of the railways, even quoting Evan directly. He could dash off his student newspaper articles in half the time an essay took, and through adopting the warm, easy tone of a highly reasonable man, his pieces formed a contrast to the often tiresomely po-faced, rigid diatribes written by many of the radical left at the university.

His best reader was Letty: she would always praise any article generously, before gently pointing out a place where the writing lapsed into cliché or ugliness, or – much less gently – sticking a finger into a gaping hole in his argument.

'It's better to hear it from me, isn't it, love, than someone else? Then you can practise fighting back...'

'Or I can just change it so that it says what you think, and make it much, much better.'

'Or you can do that, yes.' Letty would preen, swishing up her chin and her hair, and he'd kiss her for her showing off, and for her cleverness.

Continuing to write such political commentary seemed to Bertie like the best way to go about changing the world, as a man with a 2:2 from Oxford and no great personal ambition. But his father had insisted that if Bertie wanted to be provided with a residence in London, he had to start looking for a 'proper job' on graduation. Bertie had no intention of remaining at Farley Hall with Harold — and besides, he'd seen how Letty's eyes shone when he'd mentioned moving back to the city.

He'd take any job to make her happy. But first, he would finally marry her.

'Do you know the best thing about this ball?' he asked Letty, as the string quartet began a Vivaldi sonata with a flurry and a girl shrieked as she nearly fell into the lake.

'The Champagne?'

'No.'

'My dress?'

'Close, but no.' He paused. 'The best thing about this ball is that it marks the end of being a student. And that means it's very nearly time to get married.'

Letty pressed her whole face into his chest, and he thought he could feel how big her smile was. It gave him such a flush of simple happiness that she was able to enjoy the ball. A reassurance that their lives might be plaited together in public as easily and naturally as when they were alone.

Bertie took one of her hands in his, and they began to sway to the music, moving together, very softly. And Letty felt so close to him, it was as if she might be able to push herself inside his ribcage, and shut it tight around her.

Another firework went off, and Bertie felt a pain in his abdomen, a cramp of disbelief that life had been so good to him.

Chapter 7

July 1948

Rose tucked the end of a spray of orange blossom behind a strand of Letty's dark hair, and stepped back. From below came the faint rumble of the car, waiting in the sweeping driveway of Farley Hall to take them to the church.

'Look at you,' Rose said, with a sigh, as her plump bottom lip wobbled. 'Just... the most *beautiful*.'

Letty bit her own lip, and tried not to jump up and down. Her arms and legs felt full of a squiggling energy, a fizzy excitement that she didn't know what to do with.

Today was her wedding day. Today, she became Bertie's.

And today was the day that Bertie became hers, too – that she would finally know all of him. Her stomach kept turning upside down at the thought. And then the thought that today was also the day when her parents and his – her world and his – would finally meet seemed to cause her stomach to drop to somewhere down around her knees.

Attempting not to let all that show, even to Rose, Letty set a smile on her face and smoothed her hands down her ivory gown.

At least Rose was with her. Had been, every step of the way: helping choose the dress, in a hushed, heart-stoppingly expensive shop in York, and helping her actually get into the thing that morning when her shoulders were shaking with nerves, and calling for endless cups of tea. Rose's round face was pink and damp as a peony in the rain from alternately beaming and crying all day.

'Well now, look at *you!*' Letty laughed, noticing Rose's eyes were wet once more. 'Honestly, Rose, I had no idea you were such a romantic.'

'Well of course, what on earth do you expect – I *adore* a wedding, and you're my best friend, marrying my only sod of a brother? It's just...' But Rose couldn't quite keep her jovial tone afloat, as if her words were being choked in salt water. 'It's just wonderful to see you both so *in love.*'

Letty felt touched that Rose was so touched, and tried to ignore the undertow of sadness in her words. It had been obvious Rose loved having them both around Farley Hall, even if their wedding planning must have formed a constant, bruising reminder of her own unmarried state. And now to be left there, in Harold and Amelia's permafrost, while she and Bertie moved to London, losing both friend and brother at exactly the same moment...

But there was no time to add all that to the stomach churning – it was her wedding day, and it was time to go. Rose handed Letty her posy and lifted the back of her dress as she walked down the stairs. And then there was her father, his own eyes springing damp as he watched her descend.

Evan squeezed Letty's hand tightly all the way to the church as they sat in silence in the back of the grand black car, moving slow and smooth as oil. Letty knew his grip contained all the love he couldn't say out loud, but she worried, too, that it was Evan's way of trying to keep a grasp on an event that had been taken so wholly out of his hands.

The decision to marry in the north had really been made so that their reception could be held at Farley Hall, and paid for by the Brinkhursts. Letty had always imagined getting married in her little local chapel, but she knew this plan made more sense: Farley Hall had beautiful grounds, staff on hand, and the means to provide a spread, from stockpiling the estate's eggs, butter and cream to throwing money at delicacies, drinks, and a live band. Thoby had been badgering the gardeners about what blooms he could use to decorate both house and church every time he came to visit. Taking advantage of all those resources did seem logical – a simple economic necessity. Until they had to tell her parents.

Evan and Angharad had gone very quiet, their eyes dropping to the well-scrubbed floor of their kitchen. Letty loathed herself as she stuttered on about Brinkhurst family tradition, as if she really believed that should override the only tradition her mam and dad knew: that the bride's family gave her away, and paid for the pleasure. It wasn't until Bertie stepped in, spinning elaborate, spurious stories of ancient aristocratic rituals, that she could see they grudgingly accepted it.

So they were to be married in the Brinkhurst's church in Knaresborough, by the Brinkhurst's doddering, deferential vicar – the same man who had christened Bertie and Rose. Which might have been charming, Bertie had joked privately after they visited him a month before the ceremony, if it weren't for the fact that he was so old, his presence threatened to turn the day into a funeral and complete the trilogy . . .

There was a hypocrisy nestled inside Bertie's willingness to be married by a man he didn't respect that Letty didn't find very appealing. And it was a quiet source of irritation, too, that she would have to say her vows in a building that – although just a provincial Anglican church, nothing especially elaborate – was so large and cold and set to be full of fancily dressed folk she'd never met and who Bertie barely cared about, compared to her cosy chapel at home, the congregation she'd known intimately since birth, all tucked in at elbows and knees.

Bertie was bemused by Letty's faith, and she could tell he liked to try to neatly box it down to simply a love of community, and ritual, and singing – things he could rationalise and anthropologise. What he didn't seem to understand was how talking to God made her feel: the sense of lightness inside her body, the way her edges blurred out, the merging with something vast and eternal and good. Talk of God embarrassed Bertie.

Please, God, Letty whispered silently to herself, *please let today go well*. She didn't usually attempt to bargain with Him – that wasn't how she conceived of God, not really – but there seemed, suddenly, so much that could go wrong.

'It's time, then, Letty my love,' Evan looked at her, his eyes serious and heavy. He put out his arm, and it felt so firm under Letty's thin grasp, that suddenly it was like she was the one clinging on for dear life. The door to the church opened, and Evan's chest swelled out as he steered her down the aisle – towards her new life. Her new family.

The organ surged, sounding too loud to Letty's ears, as a divided thicket of faces turned towards them.

Last to turn was Bertie. He wanted the moment to be somehow his own. Over all the months of wrangling with their families, of organising the church and the guest list and the reception, the wedding itself had come to feel more and more of a public show, put on for the sake of other people.

But he didn't want it to just be that. He wanted their wedding to mean something in his and Letty's private understanding of each other, too.

And there she was. Advancing towards him slowly, slim and pale and as polished, somehow, as a statue, with her smooth dress and hair – and yet when their eyes met, the same spirit sprang from them that he had first seen by the fire in the little pub in Brecon.

A moment in time. A moment out of time. When their eyes could say *I love you* in a crowded room, and nobody heard but each other.

And all the nerves that had flooded Bertie while he waited for her – watching the two sides of the church eye each other with curiosity, and concern – evaporated. It had not been easy getting to this point; it had already cost their families a lot. But it would be worth it.

Then time sped up, and the ceremony passed in a series of flashes, that he tried to keep hold of, to set in memory. Evan's booming 'I do' when asked 'who gives this woman away', practically vibrating the stained-glass windows. The vicar stumbling over the pronunciation of Peregrine, Bertie's loathed middle name, prompting an amused incline in Letty's sharp dark eyebrows. Her side drowning out his in singing 'Calon Lan', a Welsh hymn Letty had insisted on, even if the vicar didn't approve. The smile on Thoby's face as he brought forward the rings. And the cold, smooth weight of the band.

'To love, honour and obey...'

'Till death do us part...'

Yes, thought Bertie.

The ring slid on her finger, the fit as correct and secure as a key and a lock.

Oh golly, thought Letty.

But then she was being kissed, and it was Bertie, her Bertie, and the rest of the room disappeared entirely. And when she stepped out of the church into a new life, the bells pealed and pealed and pealed for them.

Chapter 8

October 1948

Letty stood in the kitchen, her body paralysed. The house was hushed. She was gripped with a physical indecision, whether to go out into the garden to pick the flowers, or upstairs to ... to do what?

She stood, held in the silence. Only it wasn't really silence: above her, the maid Clara moved around, doing the bedroom, or the library.

Letty didn't know how to speak to the maid. She had never minded it so much at Farley Hall, or at Merriweather with Thoby – but then, those visits always seemed like flights away from real life. Now there was a stranger, who was their age, and who lived with them, moved around them, and yet never properly talked to them. Was not their equal.

In fact, it was Letty who moved around Clara. She spent much of her days listening for her tread coming so she could escape to another room in time. Yet it was this act of listening itself that made her so stuck, stiff and unsure.

The grandfather clock in the hall began to softly chime. She disliked the way it relentlessly parcelled out the time, dividing and subdividing the day into not just hours but half and even quarter hours. But the grandfather clock had literally belonged to Bertie's grandfather, and Bertie would not hear a word against it.

A tread on the stair, and Letty hurried towards the back door, and quickly out. Their townhouse was tall and thin, backing on to a narrow garden. The slanted autumn light gave everything a honeyed hue, as if seen through a glass of sweet wine: the lawn, the neat beds, the small vegetable patch that had been put in by tenants during the war, and was still needed. Letty liked the abundance in the humble cauliflower and cabbage: fat, ruffled round things, just sat there, squatting in her garden.

It was still mild enough to step out without a coat – it was always, it seemed, so mild in London. But a thin whisper of chill round her legs reminded her that the seasons were changing. A plum tree had dropped its fruit, and waved only a few rusting leaves. Letty picked the last blooming flowers among the otherwise bare stems. A couple of brave peachy-yellow roses, crinkled crimson at their edges like the very end of a sunset. The garden she had so loved over the summer was fading to brown.

Still, it had been a blissful summer – beginning with their wedding, which had gone as smoothly as she'd prayed for, really. Bertie's well-bred friends had put all their best manners to work welcoming her family; even so, she was sure there were silent judgements and tickled whispers, on both sides. And when it came to the longed-for wedding night, in a hotel in York – Letty happy but exhausted after the strained performance of the long day; Bertie excited, fumbling and clumsy – the actual event couldn't help but disappoint. A short sharp pain, and a new fullness, and then Bertie's wet, finishing groans. For her, it was as though an itch she wanted scratched instead just got gently punched.

The next day they travelled to Burgh Island for their honeymoon. And it seemed like the right word for it: sweet and half-lit and mysterious. Over the following days and nights in a sumptuous hotel suite, amid the cloying warmth of an unusually sticky July, their bodies found one another. Sex overwhelmed Letty, crashing in over her whole body, leaving her with a sense of heavy, swollen well-being. Thin and quick of movement, she'd never previously felt voluptuous; now she luxuriated in what her body could do, could give and receive.

This headiness lessened when they were 'back on dry land', as they called it, with secret smiles. But nonetheless, the magical thing they had discovered between them – a thing that surely no one else had ever truly felt as they did, because if they did why would they ever do anything else with their time? – put the rest of life into second place. Letty wandered around London with a dopey expression she saw matched on Bertie's face.

Bertie had agitated to be allowed to do up and live in the townhouse on Matilda Street in Islington, which had been in the family for years but unused by them since the area had become too 'unfashionable'. Harold, as his father before him had done, preferred Knightsbridge when in town; reason enough, for Bertie, not to live there. Besides, with its pale, well-proportioned Georgian houses, Matilda Street was one of a few still moderately genteel addresses in the now overcrowded borough, and 'quite good enough for us,' Bertie said, convincing himself he was being a good socialist.

Letty didn't care what part of town they lived in – she was just thrilled to be back in London. And to have a four-storey house, to themselves, which they could decorate from scratch – able to point at something in a shop, not even looking at the price tag – felt almost surreal. The memory of darning the curtain that had separated her side of the room from her brothers' bubbled up once, when she was in the midst of discussing the merits of velvet versus brocade with a shop assistant, leaving Letty momentarily breathless.

In the summer months before Bertie had found a job, the two of them had indulged in long, decadent mornings in their new bed, and when they finally roused themselves, explored London arm in arm – walks around Hampstead Heath and Regent's Park, boating on the Serpentine, fiercely debating whatever they'd seen at the opera, the theatre, or the Proms the night before. Letty knew she ought to use the time to get to know Bertie's friends, many of whom also now lived in the city, but neither she nor Bertie could somehow be bothered. For the first time, they were able to spend all day and all night together, and they simply didn't want to share.

But then, quite suddenly, it was autumn, and everything was different. Bertie had got a job with Newby & Ball, a highly esteemed small publisher. One of their authors, a poet, was the father of one of Bertie's Oxford lot, and put in a word.

'So you get to read all day?' asked Letty, when he told her, incredulous at how easily Bertie had come by such an offer.

'It seems so!' he'd cried, picking her up and whirling her around the drawing room after he'd got the news.

Now the house felt large and empty without him coming up behind her and putting his hands under her blouse, or clattering up and down the staircases, endlessly forgetting what he went up for. Letty would wander around the finished rooms, slowly; she might have chosen the green velvet armchair or the rosewood dining table, but she felt like she was in someone else's house. A small child, visiting a little-known relative, unsure what they're allowed to touch.

She took the flowers back inside and arranged her harvest in a yellow china vase. Then the grandfather clock chimed again, chimed longer: half past the hour.

It seemed silly that it was half past eleven and she had already done the only pressing task of the day. It seemed silly that choosing what someone else should cook for you could be your only pressing task.

Letty went over to the telephone. She ought to call one of Bertie's friends' wives, arrange to go out for the afternoon. They were always so effusively friendly when Letty met them during an interval or at a drinks party. But as soon as Bertie turned away to talk politics with their husbands, it was as if all the words vanished from her mouth. Letty scolded herself internally – she never found it hard to chatter to neighbours in Aber, coming in and out the kitchen all day, and hadn't she found it perfectly simple talk to Rose and Bertie? Yet she couldn't help feeling there was an invisible glass plate between her and other women she met in London, a barrier everyone pretended not to see but was somehow quite impossible for her to cross.

She could call Rose. But then, since the wedding, things hadn't been quite the same between them either.

It felt wrong to admit her slight, whispered misgivings to Rose, about the tedium of domesticity within the home paid for by Rose's parents, or the posh world – Rose's world – that Letty now was expected to fully inhabit. She feared that if she let Rose see her shiver of dissatisfaction with married life, it might look like ingratitude. A failure to appreciate the very thing that she knew Rose yearned for, and did not yet have herself.

Letty felt sometimes that in gaining a husband she'd lost her best friend.

She turned abruptly away from the telephone and went up to their library-cum-study, her favourite room. To have a room just for books, and writing – that really was something, Letty reminded herself. On the mantelpiece, in pride of place, was the copy of *Sons and Lovers* that Bertie had given her, that they'd enjoyed such a happy afternoon on the punt in Oxford discussing together. They'd spent much of the summer reading the rest of DH Lawrence's books in tandem, arguing during long walks about which characters deserved the most sympathy, and which went too far.

Now she had a new project. Rose had given them, as a wedding present, scores of beautifully bound classics, which Letty had decided to read, in alphabetical order, from Austen to Zola. Not that Bertie had time to join her, anymore. Too many books to read for work. But at least it would keep her busy.

Letty called to Clara for tea, hearing still the note of uncertainty in her voice at giving orders, and then curled up in the armchair – there was no velvet in the world so good you couldn't tuck your feet up on it. She tried to settle to reading *Northanger Abbey*, telling herself that to be able to spend all morning reading was a delicious treat.

Clara opening the door caused the stacks of papers on Bertie's desk to sigh and flutter. He had had just a few pieces published in the *New Statesman* and would often squirrel himself away in the library after dinner, and scribble late into the night. Seeing these pieces actually in print always made Letty feel a hot pride in Bertie, somewhere between her ribs and her belly.

Bertie was not, however, very good at getting up in time for work the morning after a late-night write – and it was her that had to disentangle his long, limpetting limbs from her body. Even though she really wanted to curl into his hair-speckled chest and stay there all day. Wanted him to touch her in the way he did, his gaze firm with intent but also with an infinite softness that made her melt and pool.

'Get off me, you lazy bugger. You'll be late again,' she'd reprimand, eventually, as the faint chimes spoke of time's slip. But she knew there was also a touch of crunchy irritation growing in her voice – because he had a job to go to, a job he had got so easily, and took so lightly. While she had no choice but to give hers up. *Forever.*

Letty demanded Bertie bring home as many manuscripts as possible, and he needed little persuading. She was a quick reader, and he found her instincts on which submission should be passed on to his bosses ('it's very good') and which ditched ('load of rubbish') reassuring: where Bertie dithered, Letty was always so sure of her taste.

It gave Letty great satisfaction to help; she was warmed to see how much sway her opinion held with her husband. And the chance to actually shape what words got printed and put out in the world seemed like a grave responsibility – one that she took upon herself, she thought, with rather more diligence than Bertie, who was becoming a touch blasé.

Of course, she said nothing. Her job was to support her husband, not question. Her mother had impressed this on her especially.

'That's your role, now, it is,' Angharad had said one evening a few weeks before the wedding, when they were washing up the tea things. 'He's going to be an important man, I can tell, Letty, love, and you have to look after him. And keep the house nice for him.'

'Yes, Mam.'

'I'm serious, Letty.'

'I know, Mam! I never said you weren't serious, did I?'

There had been a pause as Angharad scrubbed at a plate, although Letty was sure the patches of egg yolk on it would have been dislodged already.

'It's just I know things are different for you, *cariad*. I've seen …

Well, I hope we haven't spoiled you is all. With school, and London, and that job and everything.'

Letty tried not to scoff. With all she'd seen of the women in Bertie's world, the idea that she could have been 'spoiled' by the limited education she'd had off the well-meaning but essentially ignorant Mrs Ketterick, or the mindless work she'd done all her adult life, seemed absurd.

'No, Mam. I know what a wife does, don't I? I've been watching you, learned from the best, I have.' Focusing on the dish she was drying, she had gently knocked her hip towards her mam's, trying to reassure her.

But now Letty wondered if Angharad hadn't had a point after all. Perhaps she had expected too much.

Because she had never in her life been so bored.

Chapter 9

December 1948

The doorbell kept ringing, a chime that itself seemed festive. The fire roared so ferociously Letty worried the boughs of holly and ivy hanging over it might catch.

Farley Hall suited Christmas: all that wood and dark heavy furnishing seemed cosy rather than oppressive in candlelight, keeping out the winds that yawned off the Dales. And at least some of the tension she always felt when she stepped into the house – the invisible wire that seemed stretched between all the Brinkhursts, vibrating with a just-out-of-earshot hum of anxiety – was slackened by bustle, and the presence of other people.

Letty had been surprised, watching Bertie pack a case (so badly Clara had had to come in and refold everything), at how bright he seemed about going home; usually visits to Farley Hall were reluctant.

'It's tradition. The Christmas Eve party was always my favourite – I make no promises, darling, that I'll be this cheerful on Christmas morning, when there's just a day of drinking with Ma and Pa ahead.'

'I hope you will be.'

He looked at her, concerned by the ice in her voice. That certain tone, somehow simultaneously both wounded and haughty, that he had heard with increasing frequency in recent weeks.

'Well it's our first proper Christmas, isn't it?'

'Of course! Of course I'm happy to be with *you* – it shall be infinitely, a hundred times better than any previous year. You can't imagine how delighted Rosie is to have you about, too.'

She could imagine, because Rose had sent her long letters in anticipation of their arrival. But in these letters, too, Letty noticed there was no question of whether or not they'd come to Farley Hall.

Letty loved Christmas at home. If it snowed, she and her brothers would sneak out and grab handfuls and wake their mam and dad by stuffing it in their bed, a prank endured on that day only. Letty wore the same knitted cardigan, with a wonky-legged reindeer on the back, that she'd worn every year since her (now departed) nanna had made it for her at fourteen; her dad would make the same joke he made every year, that the reindeer looked like it had been getting at nanna's gin. Children would knock and sing carols, collecting for the chapel that opened its doors to the poor on Christmas Day. The whole family would join in, Evan drowning everyone out with tears swelling in his eyes, and all the Lewis children would give half their Christmas money to the collection.

When she'd gone very quiet after he told her he'd booked their train to Knaresborough, Bertie had paused, and then said in a rush, 'Oh, Letty darling, you didn't think...? You didn't think we'd go to...? I mean, it's Christmas. And after all, you know, my parents have...'

They had. It was true. They owed his family. Were, in a way, owned by them.

They had to be grateful, and they were grateful, but this

gratitude, Letty thought, was always going to be expected of her in particular.

Her parents must have known this would happen, Letty thought as she wrote to them about Christmas (including three pound notes in the envelope, to add to the chapel's collection on her behalf, a donation that would dwarf any the Lewises had even managed before). But the silences afterwards suggested they had not. Or even if they had, they still wanted to punish her. If she'd got married to someone local, Christmases would have just grown larger and fatter and happier, not lop-sided.

So there she was, in Farley Hall's cinnamon-smelling drawing room, being talked at by Bertie's 'highly strung' grandmother, who insisted in a nasal tone how, unpopular as it might be to acknowledge today, all the best yule traditions came from Germany.

'I must steal her a moment, sorry, Grandmama.' It was Rose, dragging at Letty's elbow, a rescue mission.

'Sorry you got stuck with her, she's a dreadful old trout.'

'She had some very interesting things to say about Germanic folklore, actually...'

'Oh lordy. Never mind: I want you to come and meet someone. His name's Jeremy, and he's just returned from working in America for several years.' Rose puffed at her bob, a gesture Letty thought was most unlike her. 'I rather want your opinion on him.'

They snaked through the room, Rose exclaiming at everyone they passed, even if she'd spent several hours in their company already, until they reached a tall, broad man whose jaw appeared to have caught something in America, so un-English was its square shape.

'Delighted to meet you,' said Letty. She flashed her most engaging smile, trying to impress Jeremy for Rose's sake.

'Likewise.' All of Jeremy's broad body seemed inclined away from Letty, leaning against a mantelpiece.

'I hear you've been in America?' Letty asked.

'That's right, just back from the Big Apple for Christmas.'

'Oh, you aren't back for good now?'

Letty winced at how quickly Rose asked the question.

'Not if I can help it…'

And then at how her tremulous laugh lasted just a fraction too long.

'No, it looks like I am back – but I'd rather not be. Everything is so much bigger and better over there,' drawled Jeremy.

'Even the people?' asked Letty.

'Certainly.'

'Well, I suppose you fit right in then.' Letty frowned and tilted her chin up towards him, and his smirk. It turned into a frown.

'Oh don't say cruel things, the pair of you!' Rose laughed again, an unusually tinkly peal. 'Are you really not happy, even a little, to be home, among all of… us?'

Jeremy gave a shrug. A curl of rage rolled up inside Letty at his refusal to play along with their feminine efforts, his refusal to compliment her friend. If this man was the best available… She was gripped by the compulsion to press her fingers into Rose's arm, to tell her straight: you're better off without a man than with one like this. And that getting married wouldn't necessarily be the answer Rose so clearly believed it would be.

Not that she *could* tell Rose such things. To do so would mean confessing that marriage with even her brother could be a disappointment, at times. Would make Letty look like an ungrateful wretch, despite all her good fortune.

A waiter in a red-and-green waistcoat walked past and Letty pounced on a mince pie, allowing the boozy ooze of the

mincemeat to fill her mouth and stop her saying anything else
to Jeremy. She thought she saw a wrinkle of distaste on his face
at her apparent appetite, but Letty also wondered if she was just
seeing the worst in them all now.

Was it the war that had turned the remaining men into
brutes – or simply their scarcity? The knowledge they didn't
have to try anymore? She looked around for her own, and there
Bertie was, talking to a man Letty vaguely recognised.

Bertie felt sure he could feel Letty's eyes on him, and con-
gratulated himself when he turned his head and found they
were. Then a rush of very light, pure gratitude came over him
– that they had found each other, had fought their battles, had
got married. And that what they had now was so good, and so
straightforward. For there was poor Rose, struggling on with
the arrogant bore she'd peculiarly attached herself to. Bertie
flicked back to his conversation; he didn't like to think about
what might happen to Rose.

Jeremy excused himself, and Letty was unable to stop the
judgment creeping into her voice as they watched him stroll away.

'Well.'

Rose groaned, and bent till her forehead clonked onto the
mantelpiece.

'He can be interesting, I promise you.' Rose sounded
defensive.

'But ... Rose! He ...'

There was nothing to say. Nothing that wouldn't cause more
embarrassment if spoken out loud. How clear it was that Jeremy
wasn't interested in Rose. Letty wanted to find a way, without
acknowledging that fact, to also dispute it – to reassure Rose
that she was the most interesting woman in the room, that he
must be a fool and an idiot ...

'He's shockingly dull. I can't imagine why you wanted me to

meet him. Please tell me you won't have to spend all Christmas with him?' *It wasn't right, she hadn't got it right*, Letty knew it as the words came out.

'Oh no – his family are over towards Halifax, they'll just be at parties, you know. New Year.'

'Well, so will I. So don't waste your time on … *people* like him.'

Rose looked at her feet and for a moment Letty could feel how her edges were all shaky, as if the solid woman she'd always rested upon had been rubbled by an earthquake. Don't wobble, thought Letty, not you. And don't let it just be about marriage, or men – not Rose, not independent Rose, brought low by something so stupid!

'Love, how is it, here? With your mam and dad. Is it OK? Sometimes, your letters have me worried…'

Letty *was* worried about Rose's life at Farley Hall. But asking about that was also a deliberate change of emphasis. A vulnerability she knew she could better bear to hear acknowledged and spoken of, could maybe even help with.

'Oh well, you know. It is rather *strange* being here without Bertie.' Rose looked up, a deliberate smile belying the wet brightness of her eyes. 'Mother and Father and I mostly cheerfully ignore one another, to be honest, darling. And I get out on an awful lot of long walks. I'm doing the garden too. Just planning at the moment really – but they're big plans!'

'Really? With whatshisname, the gardener?'

'Yes, he's been doing it so many years he hasn't a single new thought, seems quite happy for me to sweep in. I want to re-do a lot of the beds for the spring, but also some proper landscaping. Change the hedges to frame the view better. Maybe a small copse of trees by the summerhouse. I find it all rather satisfying. Something to … think about. To make.'

'Something that's yours?'

'Yes, I suppose so. My dominion!'

'You should *always* have your own dominion. You're good at being in charge, remember? I think you should probably be in charge of the whole bloody country. Or Yorkshire, at the very least.'

'Oh, my darling Letty – I think that ought to be your job, actually. Now do tell me: you *have* joined a women's Labour group in London, like you swore you would the minute you could – or the Fabians, or some other earnest lot of agitators—'

But a screeching interrupted them as two of Rose's oldest friends descended in a whirl of furs and kisses and ribbony presents. Both women were crashing snobs, and on every occasion Letty had met them a finely calibrated combination of faux friendly condescension ('What a dear little brooch! Wherever did you get it?') and gradual physical snubbing left her feeling carefully edged out.

This time, she was rather relieved at their arrival. For Letty didn't want to admit to Rose that she'd joined no groups in London. She had genuinely intended to devote herself to socialism as avidly as Bertie did – endlessly attending meetings and talks – but the few times he'd taken her with him, she'd grown frustrated at the way the men spoke over her, assuming she was merely a pretty accessory to her husband. And the memory of the only women's Labour meeting she'd been to still made her shudder.

The closed-off group talked in intimidating acronyms and intellectual jargon – the sort of thing Letty always tried to cut from Bertie's articles. And when she introduced herself, she could tell they couldn't make sense of her: sounding like a working-class prole, dressed like a society wife (Amelia's wedding present to Letty had been a whole new wardrobe, professionally fitted in London). Despite knowing that these women at least claimed to believe in equality and opportunity for all, Letty felt gripped by the same fear that came over her when trying to talk to Bertie and Rose's upper-crust friends.

She'd felt hot and itchy, under their gaze, and unexpectedly unsure how to hold herself, as if her silk blouse and tightly waisted jacket were a badly-fitting costume. The thought came again, that increasingly insistent thought, that *she didn't fit in anywhere, anymore.*

Letty drifted away silently from Rose and her awful friends, one of them patting a baby bump with a pride that bordered on insensitivity. There was no obvious group to join, and the Brinkhurst's set were all so loud and braying, Letty found she wanted to retreat altogether. Oh to be able to lie on the cool sheets upstairs, alone ...

Funny how she spent her empty days yearning for company and yet now she had it, she only craved solitude. But then, it was really activity she yearned for. Something to do, not this idle purposeless chatter, which mustn't touch on politics or religion or the war – mustn't touch on anything real, even with her best friend – lest it be bad manners, lest it ruin Christmas.

Letty tucked herself into a corner by a window, beside the vast Christmas tree, hung with baubles, bells and bows in matching gold and red. It looked nothing like the bushy little fir they'd squeeze in the front room at home, with garlands of dried apple and orange.

She watched Bertie, and Rose: how they moved so eagerly around friends and family and people they quietly despised, how their tall frames physically lacked grace yet somehow conveyed a fluidity and warmth that Letty admired all the more because she knew she'd never manage it. Where had that social ability come from, she wondered. It wasn't their father, a post of stiff reserve. Perhaps Amelia had been more like them when she was young. But Letty could never see her social charms as anything more than a veneer, like a glittering frost that makes something cold appear beautiful.

'For you.'

As if she'd silently summoned her, there was Amelia, proffering a cognac in a fine crystal glass. Letty had a strange urge to flick it, to see if it would hum, or shatter.

'Thank you.'

Amelia lowered herself down on the low velvet chaise Letty was perched on with a languid movement of one well-oiled but still in control. It took an awful lot for Amelia to lose her composure, although not much for the fangs to come out.

Usually she ignored Letty. Even this intimacy was unnerving.

'Enjoying yourself?' There was something acid in the question, and Letty didn't know how to neutralise it.

'Yes, thank you. It's … all this, it's very beautiful.'

Amelia gave her low laugh. 'Nothing to do with me, my dear. I stopped being interested in *decorating* long ago.'

Amelia let her awkwardness hang in the air, like a bauble turning in the light.

Finally she sighed. 'And how are you finding it, then? Married life, with my son? In that wretched house?'

The image of Bertie naked in bed flashed unhelpfully into Letty's head. A flickering summer montage of them giggling about the house, *their* house, her eating dinner sat on his lap one night just because they could, or staying up just talking till two a.m. in the garden, under a big old moon.

But now. Winter. The grey London light that barely penetrated the rooms, the luxurious weight of all that velvet and silence. The strange disconnect between the wealth inside their four walls, and the scrabbling poverty only a street or two away.

The thick fogs, and the cotton wool in her head, that seemed to stop her being able to reach out to anyone.

'Oh yes, very good, thank you.'

Amelia laughed again.

'Really.'

And was it a door, opening? Was it an invitation? Or was it just that Amelia was drunk.

'Yes, I mean London's ... exciting. And I do love our house, actually. But I'm ...' Letty faltered, wondering whether to say something real.

Amelia stretched back over the seat, eyes half closed, looking elegantly bored. Letty hated herself, at that moment, not for being unworthy but for being unable to say anything expect polite platitudes. Dull.

'It's very dull.'

Amelia's eyes flicked first, and it was as if the rest of her body caught up with deliberate slowness, like a snake who clocks their prey and then slithers silently towards it. She raised her glass almost to her lips, and raised her eyebrows to match.

'Isn't it just?' she drawled, before taking a large draught.

Letty blushed.

'I don't mean to sound ungrateful, I know I'm the luckiest—'

'Rubbish. All women are born unlucky, but all wives are unlucky in their own way.'

The air was filled with laughter, but Letty felt they were sat outside it, looking in through a cool glass.

'I just don't know what I'm supposed to *do* all day,' she burst out. 'And when I do spend time with Bertie and his friends in the evenings, they only really want to talk to him – I'm meant to just pass them a drink.'

'Married men can be frightfully dreary, it's true.' Amelia still didn't look at her, but instead lit a cigarette.

'So, you miss your little job, is that it? Well I can't say I ever had such a thing—'

'But didn't you *want* one? Didn't you want to *do* something, make yourself useful?' Letty found herself ardently reaching towards Amelia, trying to meet her eye, needing to draw her. Instead, Amelia withdrew further, recoiling, coiling up.

'Well my job was to have children.' Amelia retreated into her usual tone, so arch it was practically pointed. She flicked her cigarette ash deliberately. 'And didn't I do a fine job?'

'Yes. Yes, you did, actually. They're the ... the very best people.'

They both watched Rose and Bertie, then, their goofy grins, the way they'd attracted clusters of people to them. The source of their goodness was a mystery to Letty. She wondered if it was to Amelia too.

'Well, you're one of the lucky ones then, Violet. If you can stand the sight of him, night after night, you're truly blessed.'

'But why? Why does that have to be all I get?'

Letty's hand flipped to her mouth. She'd managed to shock even herself. Amelia turned sharply to look at her, a smile threatening to raise the corners of her mouth.

'Well!'

'I didn't mean ...'

'I know.' Amelia swirled the little that remained of her cognac. 'Best not to think of it. The limitations. The miserable limits of our sad little lives, it's like ...' She struggled for the image, her lips gurning lightly. 'Medusa.'

'I'm sorry ...?'

'You mustn't look right at it – the disappointment. You mustn't face it, look it in the eye. Or you'll get turned to *stone*.' Amelia looked, instead, at the bottom of the glass. Letty put hers down on a long side cabinet. Its burn had lost its appeal.

'How do you kill it then?'

'You don't. You live with it. It does the killing.' Amelia looked pleased with herself, even if Letty thought she'd lost control of her metaphor. 'Or you find a distraction. I suppose you'll have children, soon?'

It wasn't asked in the tone Letty had always expected the grandmother of her children might adopt.

'Yes. I expect so.'

'Well there you go then, that'll keep you busy. Give you ... *purpose*. All that *meaning* you're pining for. Motherhood!'

Perhaps it would, thought Letty. All her life she had simply assumed she would have a family when she married; it hadn't really seemed optional. Yet something far down inside Letty had begun to balk at the idea that that was now all she was expected to do. That having children had indeed become the only way for her life to *mean* anything.

But it was a nasty jolt, to find herself more aligned with Amelia's ironic disdain than with the cooing wives of Bertie's social circle, or her aunties and cousins in Wales, all blandly assuming it was *only a matter of time*.

Amelia waved at a waiter, who knew to fetch the cognac. Letty fluttered her hand over her glass to refuse a top-up.

Bertie saw them, and sent a questioning look across the room, but Letty didn't signal for help. He felt a flash of the old fear that had stalked him all through his adolescence, of what his mother might say, how she might give herself away. The constant jumpiness that accompanied the dread of other people realising the truth about her, a truth it was his job to hide. To protect his mother.

'How did you find having children, then?' Letty asked the question in a very soft voice, as if scared of frightening Amelia out of her confessional mode.

After a long pause, Amelia replied, almost to herself, 'Shall I tell you? It came quick. I was young. Younger even than you. And Harold was older of course. It seemed we'd barely begun when – everything changed. My body—

'As a young woman my body was the only thing about me that mattered, you understand that. My mother knew how to dress me: demure, of course, but like a man-killer too' – Amelia gave a low chuckle, pleased with herself, faintly repulsive to Letty. 'Enough to ... tease. Even when I was too young to understand what it was I was teasing. I was quite the desirable young thing! And then you learn that you must keep a check on it: offer just so much, never more.'

Her voice dripped in scorn as her long, hard body stretched out, as if showing off its former glories in a clinging, wine-coloured gown. She had out-dressed every other woman in the room.

'And then – *pregnancy*.' The word tremored like the title of an American horror movie, advertised at the pictures. 'That carefully preserved body, taken over. Changing without my permission. And I was terribly sick. The whole time with Rose, and most of the time with Bertie too. Of course, *he* didn't take it seriously. Nine months of being ... belittled. And suddenly you see yourself for what you are: a brutish animal, swollen and-and lowing, with a great pair of—'

Amelia turned again to Letty, eyes struggling to re-focus on her face as if just remembering who she was talking to.

'Oh, am I scaring you? It's not the pain, dear girl. You can manage the pain. It's everything else. You're never the same.'

Letty tried to hold her gaze. She knew the right thing to do would be to stop Amelia, to fetch her a glass of water, but Letty also knew she would fetch Amelia another brandy herself if she'd only keep talking.

'I'm not scared.'

Amelia peered at her.

'No, you're not, are you? Don't know why. You ought to be.'

'I have Bertie.'

Amelia snorted, and stubbed out the remaining glow of her cigarette.

'He's not the cause of your strength, my dear. Hah!' She laughed, her eyes following her son across the room. He was hanging – with, it seemed to Letty, unconsciously cruel timing – on the arm of the doughy woman who had really raised him.

Nanny was perhaps a little younger than Amelia and might have been chosen all those years ago for her lack of physical threat: she was stout, with pudged cheeks and a long nose that called to mind a hedgehog. Her bosom, contained within the stretched fabric of a very red, high-necked dress, resembled some piece of well-upholstered furniture. Each cushiony breast was probably wider than Amelia's whole head or thigh, thought Letty.

The way Bertie had gushingly introduced the woman earlier to her as 'my dearest darlingest bestest lovely Nanny' had made Letty feel lightly revolted. It was like seeing an adult on a potty.

Bertie sipped at his port, and looked over Nanny's shoulder. And he felt a familiar sting of relief: that he'd married a woman who was absolutely nothing like his mother. A woman who was calmly happy with her lot, not twisted with venom.

Although Letty didn't look exactly overjoyed at being here. Bertie tried to let the port, and Nanny's gentle reminiscences, fog over the intruding thoughts of Letty's recent sniping. Her petulance at not being with her family at Christmas. Lord knows, his certainly weren't appealing – but as if they could have gone to Abergavenny! Where would they have even slept?

'That was the worst of it.' Amelia started again, as if further inspired by the sight of her son dandling round Nanny. 'I'd given him – them – my whole body, my life, and they'd taken it all, eating me up. And you'd think they'd be grateful – you'd think – well, thank God for *Nanny.* I didn't know how to hold them. Cried whenever I held them, cried till they were handed back to her.'

Amelia's head drooped, as if she'd used up the resentment that had been keeping her upright.

'Would you like – can I get you—'

'If you dare say water I'll have you thrown out of this house.'

Letty sat very still.

She had thought the women of her village were honest about life, but their stories were always plumped with jokes and euphemisms. She'd never heard anyone talk about their husbands or children or their body like Amelia had just done, tearing her life apart like a carcass, with bloody nails.

And yet. Still she spoke to Letty like she had no right to be there. Perhaps, Letty reflected, shooting a look now to Bertie to help her, to help her *now* (and he saw it and was on his way, he would save her), perhaps that was why Amelia felt able to share in the first place. Letty simply did not matter.

Chapter 10

March 1950

She was asleep when he pushed open the door – cringed it open, fearful of waking her, but still hoping she might turn. Smile a sleepy and inviting smile. One he hadn't seen for a while.

Bertie had intended to have one swift half, and be home for supper, to be able to talk to Letty – and take her to bed. They had agreed they would 'start trying', even if Letty had gone peculiarly quiet when he raised the subject.

But when it came to it, ravenous after a heated meeting about Labour's disastrous election results, Bertie hadn't been able to refuse the offer of 'just a quick bite'. Then his friends got onto the question of how this might halt plans to nationalise further industries, which put such a flame under Bertie it was gone midnight before he left his club.

Bertie trod slowly across the floor, the stealthy cartoonish creep of the half-drunk. Through a gap in the curtain came a pale cut-out triangle of moonlight. Letty's shoulder was illuminated. Ridiculous cliché, to compare a sleeping beautiful moonlit woman to marble, but as he approached the bed, taking off his clothes as soundlessly as he could manage, that's what she reminded him of. Might her skin be cool to the touch?

It felt like Letty had begun to cool towards him, recently. He wasn't sure when it had started. After a year of marriage? Maybe sooner, even. Bertie acknowledged to himself that he'd been so caught up in his own busyness and excitement – around the political groups he was involved in, in his blossoming writing career – that he hadn't noticed Letty slowly withdrawing. He tried to encourage her to come to dinners with him, to forge her own friendships. But there was something proud, something stubborn, in her that seemed resistant to his attempts to help.

Since moving to London, Bertie's life had really taken off. His brain was constantly frothing, making connections and grand plans. Words gushed over his lips in spurts of enthusiasm in meetings; his desk was strewn with half-finished pages of ideas for articles, or actions. And some of those words now got heard, and read, by other people.

A journalist, Stephen Slender, who Bertie had met at a Labour rally and discovered was also a Worcester Old Member, had come into some money and set up his own fortnightly review: lengthy, in-depth literary criticism and left-leaning essays. Bertie began accepting pitiful fees in exchange for several pages over which to spread himself and his ideas. His ego swelled with his word count – but his spare time shrank.

The *New Left Journal* made a minor splash, with punchy pieces suggesting private education should be abolished (despite Slender having met his co-editor at Eton), or critiquing the newly formed NATO as an imperialist project. Bertie's father was irate at his son's involvement, and unafraid to publicly condemn 'the rot'. The papers enjoyed fanning a brief public spat between them, after they publicly expressed opposing opinions on Windrush immigration in the pages of the *NLJ* and in the House of Lords respectively.

The articles – and his rising public profile – made Bertie freshly attractive to Newby & Ball, and he had been promoted, given a secretary. Without any extra graft (in fact, he had woefully neglected many of his duties), he had been rewarded. And become even busier.

Now every evening there was some work event or social occasion or political meeting which he was obliged to go to or speak at. But it was no chore: Bertie relished moving in a world of people on his intellectual level – here was conversation as duel, as chemistry experiment, as tango. And for a purpose: here were people who wanted to change the way the entire country – the entire world – was actually run.

Plus, everyone liked him. They listened to him. It was a little like when Bertie had been in the army, except now it wasn't a survival technique: it was pure fun. There was delicious pleasure in the gossipy in-jokes, the sneering at stuffy old fools, the youthful arrogance and ideas and conviction. Before, the only person who had ever really been *impressed* by him was Letty – an unfathomable, inexplicable piece of good luck. But now, Bertie sometimes caught his own brilliance reflected in the convex, candle-lit mirrors of other men's eyes. And what he saw there was a man who finally meant something. The very things that made him a failure in his father's eyes were, to them, the things that made him a success.

But if Bertie had found warmth in his new London circle, Letty had grown colder, and bewilderingly hard to reach some evenings. Her silence was a weapon she now wielded against him, as if punishing him for not understanding. But how could he understand what was wrong if she wouldn't tell him?

He lowered himself onto the mattress and reached towards her. Waking her was cruel, he knew, but something in the stiffness of her pose made him wonder if she wasn't awake after all.

Bertie nestled himself to fit her curled shape, feeling his wine-breath warm on her neck. He softly kissed the patch of skin behind her ear, revealed where her hair was pinned into rollers.

No movement. Totally still.

She was awake, then, surely.

He ran his hands up and down over her illuminated shoulder. It bloomed with small, unignorable goosebumps. Letty shifted and snuffled a little, to turn herself further away from him.

And Bertie's heart sank, at not being able to kiss her, or to hold her at least, their bodies warm and sleepy together. A bruised, hurt confusion in the thought that she no longer welcomed his touch.

He waited a moment, trying to breathe gently, wondering if she might soften, hoping she might turn ...

Letty felt a swell of relief when Bertie rolled away from her. But she made sure to stay curled up. Frigid. Turned to stone.

Silence was the only refusal Letty had. Sex was, after all, her duty, a husband's right. But she could make sure he absolutely knew that she did not want it.

She *wanted* to want Bertie. But when he leaned in in the silence of the night, it was as if some creeping, needy creature was on her, and she was repulsed by the tentativeness of the touch.

It hadn't started with revulsion, however. It had started with irritation: at the way *he'd* frozen *her* out.

There was the promotion – which he didn't deserve – and all the extra work it meant. And there was the journalistic success – which she supposed he did deserve – and all the extra work that meant. One or the other might have been fine, but together they meant there was no space or time for her.

In the first year of their marriage, Bertie pulled her into him on the settee, put a manuscript in her hand and asked her opinion, or paced his long legs about as she sat at his desk and tore through his own first drafts with a pencil. That was her skill, she knew: finding the best in his words – which tended to billow when he became too pleased with them – and folding them down into cleaner lines. Now, he rarely had time for such things, his evenings and weekends stuffed with engagements.

How hungry she was for conversation with him after the stretched-thin days. But although she would often join Bertie in restaurants, it wasn't the same as when it was just the two of them. She still somehow couldn't relax among his set. Letty felt certain that she was viewed by them as little more than a well-trained pet parrot, even by the few bluestocking women who managed to keep up with the men.

At a late supper (as she was learning to call it) after a production of *The Tempest* the week before, one of these women, Jennifer, had rather condescendingly made a point of interrupting the men to ask Letty her opinion, as if she'd never manage to contribute otherwise. Which, Letty acknowledged reluctantly to herself, was probably true.

'Well, I did like the lady who played Miranda. I thought there was just a hint of... resistance to her, wasn't there?'

'Resistance? Good Lord, whatever are you talking about? She couldn't have looked more smitten with young Ferdinand if she tried!' Paul, one of Bertie's colleagues at Newby & Ball, chortled over her.

'She'd never seen any other man in her life except her dad, had she!' Letty replied, feeling her face grow warm. 'And it's Prospero that controls her, really, passing her on in marriage. But when she has her eyes opened at the end – when she sees all the other men – "oh brave new world!" – well, I thought the actress gave us a *hint* that Miranda might actually not be satisfied with—'

'Poor old Miranda, eh, set to marry her prince and become Queen of Naples! True love and untold riches: tough luck!' Paul actually slapped his leg as he laughed heartily. 'Bertie, you really must stop feeding poor Letty revolutionary theories – she's applying them even to the Romances...'

But Bertie was so absorbed in discussing McCarthy with an editor from the *TLS* that he merely grinned before turning back to his own conversation. There was a time when he would have leapt to defend her and her ideas; would have told the whole table that she was the cleverest person he'd ever met, Letty thought. Now he was too busy advancing his career and talking dazzlingly about his own ideas to notice her, or hers.

On the way home, Letty folded herself into the corner of a cab and stared out the window, while Bertie pretended not to notice her mood, speaking in a voice so bright it was as maddening as if he were rubbing a balloon.

'Isn't Paul interesting? I thought his thoughts on the play were so... insightful.'

'Evidently.'

'Didn't you?'

'He's very sure of himself.'

'Well, you don't get to edit books without some confidence in your opinions...'

'No, indeed.'

'And what did *you* think about his opinion?'

'Does it matter?'

'Well of course—'

'Didn't matter when he interrupted me.'

'Oh, come on, that's just the rough and tumble of conversation – what do you want, to be given an allotted time as if you're in a debating team?'

'Well I've never been part of a "debating team" so I'm sure I wouldn't know, would I? Sorry that I didn't go to university, like Jennifer.'

'Letty... Jennifer is – is a fine conversationalist.'

'She is when she's talking to you.'

'Not to you?'

'Not really.'

'Do you not like *any* of my friends?'

Night and silence, apart from the cab's soft rumble.

But if Letty found the meals and parties dispiriting, they were better than the other option, really. One gilt-edged plate, one folded napkin, one glass. Clara hovering. *Smirking,* Letty sometimes suspected, with a shudder. Bosomy, loose-lipped Clara, who giggled with the chimneysweep and milkman, and had three children already, and surely never struggled to keep her husband satisfied. Who surely never had quavering doubts about being married, or whether she even wanted those children.

Letty pulled a blanket up over her face and shut her eyes tight. She swallowed the small sob that had gathered in her throat, trying to be silent but giving instead a strangled kind of hiccup.

Bertie heard her, and opened his mouth to speak. But nothing came out.

Chapter 11

August 1950

It had been late spring, or maybe early summer, when Letty noticed that Bertie kept mentioning the name 'Margot Bond'. Stephen Slender had taken Bertie to one of her openings: Margot had set up her own gallery – 'not actually on Bond Street, that would be too absurd' – with the wealth she'd inherited when her husband died, shot two weeks before the end of the war.

Letty wasn't especially worried; Bertie did get his enthusiasms for clever new friends. But then she saw, at a reception at the Royal Academy one evening, how Bertie's eyes kept sliding from the speakers to a red-haired woman, maybe fifteen or twenty years their senior, with the swollen hips and breasts of a woman who eats well in middle age.

And after that, Letty noticed how the oft-spoken words 'Margot Bond' always sounded simultaneously too light and too heavy in her husband's mouth. 'There've been very good reviews for the new show at Margot Bond's gallery'; 'Margot Bond was there last night too, interesting take on that Rattigan play.'

She was almost amused by it – it was such a stupid thing, to voluntarily, needlessly mention someone he was clearly a little taken with! It seemed he couldn't help himself, like toying with a sore, loose tooth with your tongue.

But if Letty couldn't remember when exactly she had started hearing Margot Bond's name, she certainly noticed when Bertie stopped saying it. His silence was so much louder.

Yet somehow, still, she hadn't believed it. Not Bertie; he wouldn't.

Now, she felt quite sure that he had.

It was a humid August evening, and something in the lingering, damp heat of the day's end had given Letty the desire to get out of the house. She decided, last minute, to join Bertie at a dinner, organised by Stephen Slender, in one of his set's favoured restaurants.

His friends, who spoke so incessantly loudly and rapidly at each other, went very quiet when Margot Bond arrived, very late, and sat at the only remaining seat. Opposite Letty.

As she settled down, and raised a glass supposedly in general greeting to the table, Letty noticed Margot's eyes meet Bertie's across the long table, and she saw something pass between them – a look exchanged like a promise, a present. And then Margot's eyes flicked towards Letty. They locked into one another for a still second.

And then it felt like the walls of restaurant had suddenly grown very high, or that Letty alone was at the bottom of a deep well, everyone's chatter sounding distant and echoey.

Margot half stood to top up everyone else's wine glasses, extravagantly. Letty thought the action might be flustered or culpable, but then she noticed how well it allowed Margot to show off her cleavage. Her fuchsia-coloured dress was cut so low it produced creamy swells of flesh under her armpits as well as over the neckline.

Still, she didn't meet Letty's eyes again as she filled up her glass, instead murmuring to the young man sat next to her about what she was going to order for dessert.

The heavy, spicy red wine seemed transformed into a cup of acid at Letty's lips.

Bertie's features were working overtime in the conversation he was half having with a friend sat next to him about Aldous Huxley, as if captivated. Actually, he barely heard a word: his attention was really all on Letty. Her gaze seemed to be boring into the decimated chicken carcass that occupied the centre of the table, its grey bones making a fragile, brittle arc.

Had she noticed?

Bertie said 'yes, I see' to some observation about dystopias and utopias, but really he moved to trying to catch Margot's eye again, only without letting Letty see.

It was impossible – the three of them made almost a triangle around the table.

Bertie was sure his heart hadn't returned to anything like a normal rate since Margot walked in. Actually, his heart hadn't been at its normal rate since Letty had announced that she rather thought she would join him for dinner that evening, after all.

When Bertie first met Margot, he assumed she was entirely caught in the orbit of Stephen Slender. Stephen was one of those lighthouse men, that seem only to have to direct the beam of their attention onto a woman to quickly draw her towards him – shop girls, secretaries, a ballerina, the wife of a cabinet minister... all came willingly, and all were dropped rapidly.

But one night Margot met Bertie's eye across a concert hall during the aching sarabande in Bach's cello suite no. 5. And when Margot fixed you with a look, you couldn't miss it. There was something sensual about her heavy eyelids, her large eyes, and the way her skin pouched below their steady gaze.

Bertie found that every time he met Margot over the following weeks – which was surely more often than coincidence could account for – the invitation of her held eye contact, or the trail of her fingers on his arm after laying a hand for emphasis, gave him instant, embarrassing erections. Her maturity – she had a low laugh, firm opinions and expensive tastes – made him feel younger than he was. Nervous, even. His hair seemed to constantly fall in his eyes when she talked to him.

And Stephen made it worse by nudging Bertie whenever Margot arrived anywhere, finding it all highly amusing. At last – Bertie had a pash! His friends had long laughed at him for his 'lofty morality' when it came to the opposite sex.

For all their speechifying about the rights of women, the men of his circle were often to be found pulling waitresses onto their laps or chasing other people's wives. Bertie maintained an air of detached amusement about it, but really this was a polite cover up of his disapproval. He believed that, before you could change the world, you had to consider your own behaviour. And that you ought not to simply pick up and put down other human beings for your own pleasure. Or give up on a faithful union just because things were hard.

But things had been hard for a long time, now. In fact, they felt like they'd gone from hard to impossible. The Letty that Bertie had fallen in love with had disappeared inside a dull cloud; a kind of grey despair crawled off her and over him, soporific and deadening. He clung to the fact of their love, but remembering their early tenderness, and giddiness, was almost too painful.

Bertie felt withered and shrivelled by Letty's clouded indifference. He wanted to feel the sun of Margot's desire and admiration full on his face, to let it warm him, bring him back to life.

'I've got a new exhibition I simply don't know what to do with,' Margot had purred one evening some months earlier, as they strolled after dinner in the night air, lagging behind their friends. 'Fantastic colours. Very ... vivid. But I just don't know what order to hang them in ...'

'Well, I don't know all that much about art, but I'd gladly give you a second opinion?' Bertie spoke lightly, and it was only when the words were out of his mouth and hanging in the air between then that they seemed to acquire a heavy, saturated weight.

Margot let the pause stretch, as if to make sure he recognised his entry into the game, to confirm that he definitely wanted to play. Then she took his arm, murmured, 'Well, that'd be *marvellous*,' and detoured them down a side street towards her galley.

They stayed there past midnight, circling each other as much as the paintings. In the end Bertie left, trembling on the doorstep at goodbye, a moment of almost unbearable anticipation ... before finally hurrying away down the street, without having touched any part of her body.

This delicious restraint established the steps for a dance that they continued to perform almost nightly, in public. Margot found Bertie at every party, and he slipped gratefully into her company like it was a hot bath. It was Margot that initiated every conversation, any touch, Bertie told himself, on long walks home when the guilt crept in round his collar and cuffs. It was Margot who leaned towards him at the opera, her soft thigh so warm against his that he couldn't follow the Italian. Margot who needed him to light her cigarettes, their faces close enough that Bertie had to hold his breath.

But the guilt wasn't bad enough to make him stop. In fact, Bertie admitted to himself in moments of agonising honesty, knowing that wanting Margot was bad only made the feeling more horribly thrilling. He was hooked, too, on the adrenaline that came from it all playing out in public, where the opportunity to go any further was excruciatingly, thankfully denied.

He found he even *liked* the thought of people gossiping: *Have they or haven't they? Surely they must have, by now!*

Because he liked how she changed him in the eyes of others. Margot Bond openly wanting him gave him new power.

But now, as she sat opposite his wife at the restaurant table, Bertie felt sick. The game he and Margot had been playing turned out to be real after all.

Bertie stared at Letty down the table, willing her to make eye contact. And then she turned, and – thank God! – it was as if the old channel between then opened up, the direct line of intimate understanding. Bertie let his eyes go soft, to telegraph that there was nothing really to worry about. Then he reached forward, and gently picked a flower off an arrangement in front of him and – holding Letty's gaze, feeling her anticipation – he stood up, hoping the jellied feeling in his legs wasn't too obvious, and walked round behind her chair.

Bertie bent down and tucked the pink carnation behind her ear, placing a reassuring, loving kiss on her head, before stumbling towards the bathroom to cool his overheated face with splashes of water.

That was that then, thought Letty, smiling sweetly while burning up inside. The fury she felt at the public display of guilt Bertie had just implicated her in went white hot, all through her body.

Margot Bond graciously turned away to redo her lipstick in a hand mirror.

The flower stem was damp and scratchy at the nape of Letty's neck. She wanted to tear at it, to throw it down on the table or the floor or at Margot's stupid red hair. But as painful as it was to have to pretend to be taken in by Bertie's romantic display, to publicly refuse it would be to acknowledge the truth of the situation, in front of everyone. That she now knew for certain that she was losing her husband.

Her lemon mousse wobbled on its plate. She'd never liked creamy, heavy desserts. She flushed it down with more red wine, the combination making a thick, sour slurry in the back of her mouth. It reminded her of vomit.

Chapter 12

April 1951

'But do you even want one?' Rose finally looked up at her, directly.

Letty didn't say anything, but began to pick the squeaky, certain stems from the luxurious bed of hyacinths, choosing the pinks over the blues.

'Just a girl then?' asked Rose, trying to nudge her friend into a reply with forced jollity.

It was good to see that enthusiasm back, though, thought Letty. Rose had been cheerfully brandishing secateurs when Letty arrived at Merriweather, mud freckling one half of her face and streaked across her gardening dungarees, while three red setters loped about in their glossy coats. Desperate to leave Farley Hall, Rose had moved to Merriweather to assist Thoby in remodelling the grounds there following his father's death, and they worked so well together they'd decided to make the situation permanent – and to set up their own garden-design partnership. Rose had even, she announced with a huge grin, enrolled to study on the nearby horticultural course at Reading University come autumn.

Rose and Thoby seemed entirely relaxed in each other's company, like a weight of expectation had been lifted from both their shoulders by embracing their unconventional arrangement.

Even at dinner, Rose had come down in staunchly sensible trousers, lightly matted with fine gingery dog hairs, while it was Thoby who garnished his pristine dinner jacket with a brilliant deep-red rose buttonhole, picking up on the rubies and emeralds of his several rings. They made a faintly ridiculous pair. But their almost child-like gusto for their plans proved infectious.

Yet while Letty was pleased to see Rose more like her confident old self again, she could tell it made her own despondency all the more obvious. She'd tried not to let on how much she was struggling in her intermittent letters. But when Rose and Thoby had come to visit Letty and Bertie for their twenty-fourth birthdays that January, Letty hadn't been able to shake the black cloud she was under even at her own party (a birthday party Bertie had had the gall to invite Margot Bond to). When Rose said goodbye, she had hugged Letty very tight indeed.

It was not long after that Rose sent a note.

Darling girl,

I insist you come to Merriweather At Once. Or at the very least, when the weather picks up. March? April? Don't say May.

I think you must leave that city and my brother – (it isn't Bertie, is it? Has he done something? If he has you can tell me, you do know you can?) – and come bound around with Thoby and the dogs and me. We'd all love to have you.

Your friend – absent no longer –

Rose

Over the last three days at Merriweather, Letty had begun to feel the weight that hung around her own shoulders begin to lift too. She spent most of her time outside with Rose, even in the splashy spring rain, and her continual upbeat chatter as she strode around the grounds was a balm to Letty.

But now here it was, here was the questioning. The questions everyone seemed to ask her: about babies, about children. About their absence, her failure, almost three years into a marriage.

'Has there been...?' Rose's voice was soft.

'No. No – nothing.'

'But you are...?'

'Yes!' Letty wondered if she'd been too quick in answering, hoped it sounded simply like embarrassment.

Rose began to pull up some rogue weeds as if her industriousness might make it easier for Letty to talk.

Since being at Merriweather, Letty had tried to open up about what her life in London was really like. How busy Bertie was! He was writing a book, about socialism and community, which meant he had to travel round the country, and had even less time for Letty than usual. She began to let on to Rose, too, how few friends she had made of her own, and how all the women she was expected to spend her time with only seemed to care about children.

She did not mention Margot Bond.

'Is everything all right with Bertie?' Rose asked, trying to sound unintrusive, making brisk little movements with her trowel. 'Have things... changed, between you?'

'Well, yes, I suppose they have changed. But that's just – life, isn't it?' Letty tried to sound vague. 'I'm well looked after. We don't fight, if that's what you mean.'

Rose insisted on eye contact. 'That isn't just what I mean, and you know it.'

Letty found it hard to swallow suddenly, but wondered if it was time for the words to come out. It was Rose, after all. Rose who now seemed strong, rooted again.

'I...' she began, but she couldn't. A red setter – possibly Scarlet, it was hard to tell – bounded over and pushed its damp nose under Letty's armpit three times till she gave in and fondled its silky head. Not looking up, Letty continued, words tumbling out even though she knew some part of the truth had to stay bricked up.

'I suppose I just feel bored, all of the time, and I know that you'll think me monstrously ungrateful – that anyone would.' Letty felt the usual stab of guilt: here she was, complaining to Rose, when she knew Rose would have loved to get married. Letty had had that chance, and she'd ruined it.

'I just – I just don't know that Bertie *likes* me very much anymore...'

The tear swelled from nowhere and dropped straight down in a line into her lap before she even had time to realise she was crying. But then, this happened quite often now – sudden tears would catch Letty off-guard. She found it embarrassing, and rubbed her eye fiercely, hoping Rose hadn't noticed.

'I thought my life with Bertie was the greatest, most surprising gift, more than I could ever have hoped for. And yet I'm so much... *sadder,* now, than I ever was before.'

'Oh, Letty, I'm so—'

'No, don't. I don't want – *anything*. Anything more from you. I know I have no right.'

'Everyone has a right to pursue happiness!'

'What are you – American?' Letty's old sharpness returned for a second. 'I'm well-off, and comfortable, with access to books and fine dining and theatre, I can buy a new dress whenever I like – that's not something anyone in my family has ever experienced, Rose! And not only that, but I caused you and Bertie and our parents all that... *trouble*. How dare I turn out not even to be worth it. How dare I be such a disappointment to him, to you—'

Rose tried to grasp her hand, but Letty snatched it away. Ruby (for she'd seen on her collar it was Ruby, not Scarlet) turned in circles between the women, then dropped to the ground and put her head on her paws.

'Might ... might a child help?'

'Perhaps ...' Letty knew that, if Rose was in her position, she'd have rushed headlong into motherhood. Knew, too, of wives of men who'd grown distant or neglectful, who'd poured themselves into raising their children, and found their purpose and joy there.

But Letty also knew that, if she had Bertie's baby, that would mean she would be tied to Bertie forever. Tied, just at the moment he replaced her with someone else – someone more interesting, and clever, and lively. Someone more like how she used to be, before this fog in her head and fear in her heart.

She couldn't forget Amelia's words. *It's not the pain, dear girl. You can manage the pain. It's everything else. You're never the same.*

When she'd been back home in Abergavenny a few months ago (funny, how she still thought of Aber as home), Letty had seen Bethan, who lived next door, crying as she scrubbed the back step. Bethan had a baby girl and a toddler, and a husband everyone knew drank his pay packet and took it out on her. Her knees were raw as red meat, her breasts hanging heavy, and tears were dripping off the end of her nose. Inside, the baby made a noise like the ambulances used to in the war. Off-white nappies snapped on the line, refusing to dry in an icy wind.

'Oh sorry, love,' Bethan said, wiping her eyes when she looked up and saw Letty, cracking a smile wide with apology. 'We're in the bit where I've got to leave her to cry. I know she sounds like a little banshee, though.' And Letty shook her curls and retreated and didn't know how to speak to the suffering that was really behind Bethan's bared teeth.

There were times when Letty thought she stopped herself getting pregnant by the sheer force of her will alone.

'No. I don't want a baby,' said Letty. It was the first time Letty had even spoken the thought aloud. She was still unable to meet her sister-in-law's gaze, but the words came out feeling oddly solid and correct. 'I don't want one at all.'

Rose stood up and stuck out her hand to Letty. 'Get up. We're going for a walk.' As if with supernatural hearing, the two other red setters, Scarlet and Madder, bounded across the lawn, leaping and circling.

Letty allowed Rose to lift her to standing, realising how damp her skirt had become. Rose didn't say anything, but kept hold of her hand as she strode towards the house, Letty trotting to keep up.

'Thoby! We're off up the hill, you're not invited!' Rose grabbed apples and her flask of water, slung her knapsack over her shoulder, and was out the gate and up the path.

Letty's heart fluttered, then pounded, as she struggled to match Rose's vigorous strides across the countryside and up a hill. The bracken's acid-green fronds were still mostly curled up tight, but a few were just beginning to reach into the world. High white clouds raced across the sky, in as much of a hurry as Rose seemed to be.

At the top, gasping and blood pumping through her body, Letty felt an unexpected burst of triumph. The spread of the Chilterns swayed away from them, and everything man-made was reduced to toy-town size. Miniature cars trundling on little roads; prim hedgerows boxing in neatly shrunken farmhouses and barns. But then, around and above it all, the infinite greens and blue that came before and after and beyond.

It was a feeling she'd not had in a long time. Her edges blurring, the pressure of something bigger behind things, pushing out through her body, that temporary vessel. It was the feeling Letty had a tremor of when her voice melded in song with others in chapel; when Bertie's fingers and mouth had made her disappear at the top of a frenzied bliss. It was the vast, soft feeling she used to get, in the days when she still prayed to God.

Letty wondered if she might cry again, but instead she just let her lungs burn and her arms lift on the breeze. Something inside her had come unstuck, by their conversation, at her admission. Released.

The friends watched the clouds' shadows run over the landscape, how the light came and went capriciously, illuminating a pale field or dimming a woodland to smoky indigo. Eventually, Rose turned to Letty. She put both hands squarely, firmly, on Letty's narrow shoulders and made her meet her gaze.

'It isn't inevitable. It isn't the only way. Look at me – I'm going to university soon, Letty! A new start. A new home. And never mind about marriage. Thoby does me just fine for company.'

Letty breathed in deep, as the wind whipped round them. It felt like fresh air had finally reached her lungs.

'I might be your sister-in-law. But remember: I was your friend, first.' Rose squeezed Letty's shoulders, firmly. 'I know things are hard. But if you ever need… Just come to me.'

Chapter 13

June 1951

Bertie's hand ran down into the dip of Letty's waist, the body heat coming through the coolness of light silk, and he moved in closer to her. The mattress creaked.

She stayed turned away from him. Her shoulders closed in towards one another, like wings, protecting her breasts from his hand that ran up and over her still, taut body. Bertie continued to caress her, beginning to nudge at the hard, pressed seam of her legs. His breath became ragged in her ear as he moved down again, prying and pushing into her; there was something wretched in how loud his breathing sounded next to her tight silence.

Self-loathing shuddered through Bertie even at the very moment he finished inside Letty's passive body.

That he should encourage his wife into conjugal relations, even if she 'seems reluctant', had been the advice of a doctor friend named Andrew Upshort. Trying to keep his tone off-hand as they smoked a cigar after dinner one evening, Bertie had mentioned Letty's ongoing ... *malaise*. Her listlessness. How changed she seemed, as a person. Bertie knew he had been ignoring the problem – so busy, finishing up his book; so distracted, by the attentions of Margot Bond – but things had gone on long enough, and something needed to be done.

He had to get back to Letty. Had to get his Letty back.

In the strained darkness of their bedroom, Bertie silently repeated Andrew's medical advice to himself – that the 'normal rhythms of marriage should be maintained', that 'pregnancy and motherhood would likely jolt her out of it'. He was doing this to help her.

Some weeks later, on a bright, clear July day, it was confirmed that Letty was pregnant. And Bertie was slightly surprised to discover just how extremely pleased he felt about the news. He couldn't help but swing Letty's hand as they walked home, longing to touch her belly – still looking so ordinary, but containing inside it something he hadn't known he wanted badly until that moment.

From then on, the dewy thought of his new family was enough to make Bertie hurry home from the office most nights. To put a stop to things, finally, with Margot.

He had agonised over the letter to her, crafting its tone so she might understand just how serious he was.

Margot – you know my feelings for you. But this has to stop. You're a marvellous woman – but I can't see you anymore, and I ask you to please ignore me if we meet in public. I'm sorry for any pain this may cause. But I believe it is the only way.

Margot's reply had been excruciatingly casual. *I quite understand. No need to worry so much, darling!*

And Bertie had felt like a chump, for thinking any of it had mattered at all.

He turned all his attention instead to Andrew Upshort's other piece of, rather pointed, advice: 'Women like to feel fussed, in my professional experience, especially once they're expecting. I'm sure being the focus of your attention will perk Letty back up.'

Bertie took to buying her little presents (lavender bath salts; a new silk slip), lavishing her hands with feathery kisses, and fussing about what she wanted to eat. And he found it was much easier to prattle on, even when she was quiet, because a whole vast new topic of mutual conversation had opened up: their own child! What school they might send it to, which of their friends' children would it be friends with, whether it'd have her eyes or his legs or his mother's hair...

Afterwards, Bertie felt like even more of an idiot for not noticing sooner. For being so wrapped up in his own fantasy version of their life that he hadn't noticed her reality.

Letty did not cheer up when she got pregnant. Letty started to cry. Quietly at night, when she probably thought he was asleep, then in the bath – when she must have known he'd likely hear – and then over breakfast. Just openly weeping into her half-eaten boiled egg, not even caring that Clara could see too.

It seemed as if Letty loathed him more when he was trying to be a good, attentive husband than when he'd allowed himself to be an absent one. Bertie began to wonder if she didn't want a baby after all. Or if it was simply that she no longer wanted *him?* He couldn't bear the thought, tried to ignore it, but nonetheless a dread moved coldly through his veins, slowing his blood.

And then one evening, he ran into Margot at an extravagant party thrown for a visiting American painter. Without discussing it, they silently left together. The warm, sultry air of late summer seemed to drape itself softly over the city, over their shoulders. Lovers, young or otherwise, kissed in shadows as Margot led the way to the next bar. When that closed, she led the way to a club.

It was a seedy place in Soho with simmering jazz and lingering blue smoke. There was an air of decided abandon to the place, everyone sliding drunkenly around as the trombonist slung up and down the scales. It was a place one of Margot's bohemian younger artists had introduced her to, not somewhere their circle would ever visit. This anonymity had surely been intentional, Bertie reflected hazily.

But it meant that none of his friends were able to get hold of him when Letty was taken to hospital, and only Stephen Slender kept trying, guessing – when the usual places drew a blank – that he might be found at a Margot Bond haunt.

As he ran through the too-bright, bleach-smelling hospital corridor, Bertie was quite certain that Letty was dying, as punishment. Or maybe, he'd thought, she would survive and the baby would die— and then he stopped to throw up burning whisky and bile into a mop bucket.

She was pallid but clean when he arrived. White face, white gown, white room, as if the whole scene had had the colour drained out of it.

She didn't ask him where he'd been. Or who he'd been with. And so Bertie couldn't insist that it was a one-off, a mistake, that he'd put all that behind him, he really had – and besides ...

Doctor Glass, a man whose large rectangular head made him look like a cartoon dog, appeared pleased when he looked over Letty, and discharged her the following day. Outside in the corridor, over a cigarette and much gesturing, he assured Bertie that the 'incident' was actually very common at that early stage.

'Nothing to worry about – she'll be right as rain within a fortnight.' Some rest, then fresh air, gentle exercise, and plenty to eat. 'She's a little thing. You might want to fatten her up.'

While she recuperated in bed at home, Bertie tried to force Letty to drink glasses of milk, to eat coddled eggs, and jam roly-poly. The milk left a stain on their forget-me-not sprigged wallpaper.

After a little longer, he tried to encourage her to get out of bed. What about the fresh air, and the exercise? Maybe … she'd like to go to church? Letty barely responded, rolling over to face the wall.

When Bertie called Doctor Glass, and tentatively told him his wife still wasn't 'feeling well – in herself', the doctor breathed his out concern loudly down the receiver. 'It can be that ladies take it to heart. I expect all her friends have already had babies, and she's a little worried? No need. The very best thing you can do is get on with trying for another. Put it out of her head.'

Bertie believed he was, once more, doing his duty. Letty recoiled as if she'd been bitten. She flung herself out of their bed, and almost ran across the room, the greatest display of energy he'd seen from her in months. She turned back, eyes blazing, hands held out by her side, half-clenched.

'My love, I'm sorry—'

'*Don't,* Bertie. Just … don't.'

'I didn't mean to upset you, I just thought—'

Her eyebrows jumped upwards.

'The doctor … he said it was perfectly safe …'

'Really?' Letty's voice sounded high-pitched, strained. 'After what happened? What *just happened*?'

'It was more than three weeks ago—'

'Three weeks! Three weeks. That's long enough to forget the *death* of our child, is it?'

'No, of course not. But, Letty, there's no need— I talked to Doctor Glass and he said that, in these early days, it's actually very normal, very common. It happens to most women at some point …'

Letty turned and placed her forehead against the wall. Bertie stopped talking.

When she spun back around, her fists were clenched properly.

'Why didn't he tell me? Why didn't he tell *me*?'

Bertie didn't know what to say. He had assumed she'd have known all this, that the doctor would have told her too, or that it was something women would talk about among themselves. But then, she had refused to see anyone except Rose since that horrible night, and was it possible his sexless sister didn't know about such things either?

She began to walk in circles.

'Letty, darling, calm down—' he tried, tentatively.

'Oh shut *up*, Bertie.'

It was almost a relief to hear her voice raised like this, after so long in dampened, muted tones.

'I'm just trying to explain – I just wanted to explain to you why I thought it was safe – the doctor said the right thing was just to try again...' Bertie was stuttering and stumbling, but somehow he couldn't help trying to exonerate himself. To prove he wasn't a bad man. 'He said it won't have done any damage, it won't be any harder – we can make another baby—'

'I don't want another baby!' Letty roared, stopping and facing him. 'You didn't see the blood, Bertie, and the— How could that be "normal"?'

She doubled over, as if still in pain, clutching her belly, frantic and babbling.

'I don't want a baby. I don't want a baby. I didn't want the baby. It wasn't normal. I killed it, Bertie, *I* killed it, I didn't want it and I *killed* it...'

A cold sweat flew over his entire body then, and his throat constricted. The walls of the room seemed to contract inwards, sharply.

Letty dropped to her knees and put her forehead to floor.

Bertie felt suddenly afraid of his wife, and who she might have become. *Could she really have...?* He couldn't even form the words to ask; and anyway, he couldn't bear to know more, of what exactly she'd done, he had no idea even *how* such a thing could be done, and he felt nauseous.

Bertie stuffed his legs into the nearest pair of trousers, ran down the stairs, flew a great coat round his shoulders, and fumbled with the door. Outside, the wind was up, and it howled for him and shook the plane trees, the branches rebelling and resisting – or were they urging him on? – as Bertie walked and walked through the night to the front door of Margot Bond.

His hand paused, fingers hovering just above the knocker.

Chapter 14

December 1951

'And of course, I must thank my wife, Letty. Not only for her unwavering support while I pored over *A Time to Rise* – and she poured the brandy' – Bertie paused to let the laugh ripple through the room, avoiding Letty's face in favour of all the other, friendlier ones that had gathered for his book launch – 'which was, I should say, large measures for her, not for me, and very justifiable, when you've got a writer in the house!' – the second lick of laughter, and this time his glance did catch on her, and her eyes were like cold blue stones above a forced, lipsticked smile.

Bertie felt warm, as if under hot stage lamps rather than the dim lighting of a room at the top of the Coach and Horses. He ran his fingers through his fine hair, and smiled into the deliberate pause, and tried not to look in the direction of Margot Bond.

'But really, I have a lot more to thank her for. Because without Letty – Violet – I would never have met my first subject for this book. I've been very privileged to get to know her family from south Wales. Her father's here tonight: *shwmae*, Evan!' – his nosy London friends let their glasses tilt as they craned for a glimpse of Letty's real-life working-class Welsh father – 'don't worry, I'm just showing off, Evan barely speaks Welsh himself!' – more gentle laughter. Bertie had perfected his rhythm over years of public speaking.

'But to be serious for a moment... It was through being welcomed by Evan that I, a socialist, have come to truly understand what socialism means' – and there was Evan, looking grave, but his eyes shining, filling with tears – 'don't worry! I know you've heard quite enough about socialism, and my book, from me already in this speech!' – Bertie threw up his hands, trying to keep up a jolly tone, against the undercurrent of sadness in the room, at his publishing a book on the successes of the welfare state when its architects had so recently been defeated in the election.

'But I really must conclude by extending my heartfelt thanks to Evan and his sons and the other men of south Wales' – Bertie couldn't help but notice one of Margot's thick eyebrow rise – 'and *the women!* For showing me socialism in action, for proving we really are stronger together, no matter how class might seem to divide us. For making my own spirits rise.'

A slight nod from Margot, and Bertie felt furious. At himself, for somehow being unable to stop addressing his speech to her; at her, for daring to turn up uninvited like this in the first place (and wearing *that* green dress).

Her presence at his book launch was surely no accident: Margot Bond always knew exactly what she was doing. But Bertie agonised over how it looked to everyone: as if things were back on between them. Not least, Bertie groaned inwardly, to Letty. It was deeply unfair that even when he was doing his absolute best, it looked like he was a complete monster.

The reputation that his presumed relations with Margot Bond had given him had long since lost its lustre: notoriety dulled, and now only weighed him down. Just another rotten husband; as bad as all of his friends, with their laughingly acquisitive, dismissive attitude towards women. While the gossiping whispers had, at first, been exciting – indulged, even, to burnish his sad little ego – now Bertie merely felt unjustly tarnished.

Because he and Margot had never slept together. They had never even kissed.

Oh, their lips had hovered, close; he'd pressed his whole body into hers, breath hot and desperate, and then pulled away, agonisingly unsatisfied. Wanting dreadfully, but never actually having.

Never having, because he was married. Because his wife was Letty. Because however bad things had got – and however tempting Margot had been – he still loved Letty, and he had sworn to a god that she believed in that he would be faithful to her until they died. Because he knew that it was false to think you could just have absolutely everything you wanted, without consequences.

And because, this way, he'd convinced himself, he could enjoy Margot and still be a good husband. A decent man, who lived by proper principles. Bertie had tried to cling on to the idea that Letty knew him well enough to intuit that nothing had *really* happened. The thought that she would be able to think badly enough of him to believe the gossip was too painful to contemplate, even now.

He gulped, hard, and attempted to direct his attention back to Letty, and her father.

'So I must conclude by saying thank you to Evan – and to Letty – for allowing me to begin *A Time to Rise* with a portrait of a rural community transformed by the welfare state. I only hope I have done you proud.'

And then his heart jumped, because Letty was looking up at him and her eyes were bright now too, and she *did* look proud.

When had he last seen her looking at him like that? Before the pregnancy. Before their terrible fight.

After it, Letty had taken to sleeping in the narrow single bed in the peach-coloured spare bedroom, and Bertie decided to think of her as an invalid: a sickly creature he had a responsibility to look after. What he didn't do was ever mention, or even allow himself to think about, what she had said that night and how true it might be. How a woman might go about terminating her own pregnancy.

It had been very early days, he told himself. It was *very common* to lose a baby, the doctor had said. Perhaps she was just delusional. These thoughts were like lids, he allowed himself to think them in order to press the other thoughts down.

But it was clear that there would be no children. No more marriage bed. And Bertie grieved not only for their lost child, but for the dream of the happy family that bled out with it.

Now here she was, smiling up at him. A real smile?

It was real, because Letty did love *A Time to Rise*: as a pen portrait of her family, her town and her community, she thought it was beautiful, and righteous. It felt, almost, like Bertie's parting gift to her. But for all that she was proud of Bertie, it was also hard to stand there and watch a man she'd lost speak about the community she'd given up, for him.

When she read the proofs, Letty had realised he didn't need her anymore. He had Margot to bounce ideas off, she'd thought at first, wounding herself with the notion. But as she read on, she decided that wasn't quite true either: there was no stamp of anyone else's voice in it. It was pure Bertie, it was just that his voice had matured, into something angry, honest, and persuasive – not above an occasional rhetorical flourish, but without the youthful excess she had once had to prune out for him.

He'd do just fine without her, she thought, watching him

look around the room as friends and colleagues applauded, and her dad wiped his eyes. Whatever happened next, Letty had wanted her father to be able to enjoy that moment. Wanted to be there for Bertie, too, at the point when his passion for politics and his hard work on his writing came together in their finest, fullest form.

Evan put an arm around her shoulder, and Letty found herself in a tight squeeze.

'Never thought I'd see the like,' he said. 'Me, in a book.'

'He's done well, hasn't he?'

'That he has. I'll be taking back as many copies as I can carry on that train now.'

'Are you sure you won't stay, Dad?'

'No, I best be getting back. Wouldn't have missed this for the world, though.'

Letty's smile was a little watery, her dimples shallow. Then her eye snagged on Margot Bond, laughing on the other side of the room, unignorable in a low-cut emerald-green dress. And the cold despair flooded her veins once more, and the certainty of her decision hardened.

She had wondered if Margot would dare come to the book launch. It had seemed too grotesque to really consider, yet here she was. Presumably Bertie just couldn't bear for her not to witness his big night, Letty thought. Or maybe Margot *had* half written the book, after all.

She would leave him to her. The marriage had been over between her and Bertie since the fight, really.

When the pain had started, and then all the blood and the clots, and Bertie couldn't be found (must have been trying *not* to be found), and she didn't know what was happening, and no one in the hospital explained... Letty had been so sure it must be her fault. That hating being pregnant and not wanting the baby so much had caused it to actually disintegrate and run right out of her.

She was such a bad mother she'd ejected her own baby.

Now, Letty wished she'd never confessed these fears to Bertie. She knew she had been irrational and emotional while he was calmly trying to explain the medical reality. She knew that she had also, in that instant, confessed to her husband that she did not want his child, and that that was a truly monstrous thing to admit...

Yet she still couldn't believe that Bertie, her Bertie – no matter how bad things had got – could be so uncaring as to see that distress and walk away from it. To see how broken and sore and ashamed she was, and to go to his other woman instead. The selfishness of that choice floored her. When she heard the front door slam, it felt very final.

But what he had given her in that same fight was a gift: a gift of knowledge, that let the cloud of superstitious guilt dissipate a little once she had calmed down enough to properly absorb it. What had happened to her – she hadn't even known the word for it – was *normal*. Happened to lots of women. Was nothing to be ashamed of.

Letty had telephoned her mother, whom she hadn't told about the baby or about losing it, the following day. Angharad was sympathetic, but the real comfort came from how un- surprised she was. 'Oh, *cariad,* I'm sorry. I had a miscarriage myself, one between the boys. And your aunty Nell had four over the years, poor lamb. You have a good cry now then – but try not to worry too much.'

Letty thought about going home for a while, but she didn't want to concern her family: she knew she looked unwell, too thin. She hadn't told them about things with Bertie. They wouldn't understand, she thought; they really would think she was ungrateful. Impossible to please. And they would have been proved right: vindicated in their suspicion that it didn't make sense to marry someone so different.

'Join me outside for a cigarette now, would you, Letty?'

Letty noticed that her father's expression had turned serious, his voice oddly formal. And she realised Evan had seen how her eyes were drawn across the room, towards Margot Bond.

Letty trailed after him, down an uneven wooden staircase and into the cooler night air. A light drizzle instantly peppered her set curls. Her father allowed the cigarette to burn down half its length, crackling as he drew lungfuls in and sighed them out, before he spoke. He kept his head lowered, as if worried someone might overhear.

'I don't know what's been going on here then and I don't need to know. Everyone tonight seems to be implying you've been ... unwell. And you look—'

'Dad ...' began Letty weakly.

'No, Letty, listen to me now.' Her father held a finger up, his old gesture of authority. 'Listen.'

He struggled.

'If you ever want to come home – ever, Letty, I mean that – and for whatever reason – the door is always open. They'll be no questions from me. And no deferring to your ... husband's rights, neither.'

Letty hugged her father then. She couldn't let him see her cry, and instead let the tears soak into the big collar of his best jacket.

When they went back inside, they found Bertie in a sentimental mood. He told Evan that his presence meant the world to him, even made up for his own father's absence. Evan busied himself filling a thick canvas bag with an excessive number of copies of *A Time to Rise*, and Bertie beamed. *He doesn't see that anything's different*, thought Letty.

Then her father said his goodbyes. He didn't want to talk to Bertie's 'well-to-do' friends – as he called them to Letty – all night. She couldn't blame him: Letty had heard two of them earlier making embarrassing small talk at him, probably hoping to be brushed with coal dust.

Seeing Bertie's friends through her father's eyes, Letty felt weary of them herself – even the fine, kind ones that she could feel loyally shielding her from Margot; even the ones who genuinely campaigned hard for the greater good, who didn't deserve to be scorned for what they were not. But she knew, suddenly and strongly, that they were not and never could be her people.

After waving her father off, she went to look for Bertie. To say her own goodbye.

All night, Margot had been just out of Bertie's reach, or couching herself safely in large groups. Finally, he'd got a moment to accost her alone in a corner, allowing his fingernails to dig into the soft white flesh of her arm.

'What the bloody hell are you doing here, Margot? You have to go.'

'Well, darling, I've missed you too ...' Her voice was breathily nonchalant, as if she was talking about merely missing the last post.

'I told you to leave me alone.'

'I know. Very cruel!' Her laugh was fluffy, and then she pouted extravagantly, as if sending up even the idea of the neglected lover. 'But after all those conversations about what you should or shouldn't write, and all those chapters I read ... Really, I couldn't not be here for the birth of your little book. We made it together, darling.'

Bertie wasn't sure if he was more revolted by the sentiment, or the imagery. How dare she try to take credit for his work. If anyone deserved credit...

And then he glimpsed something pathetic welling in Margot's hooded, heavy eyes. A need to be recognised, to matter. With a jolt, Bertie realised that the breezy note she'd sent him hadn't been real, that her usual rock-hard performance of amused disinterest wasn't real either. Bertie saw that it might be possible to hurt someone as magnificent as Margot Bond after all.

Then her eyes shot over his head to the door, and Bertie's followed their direction and met Letty's. His hands twitched; he dropped cigarette ash on Margot's luscious green dress. She slid away, lightly squeezing his left arm as she did so, a gesture of possession she had absolutely no right to.

Letty made her way over to Bertie slowly. She looked very beautiful, he thought: there was some high colour in her cheeks. She seemed more upright, more present, than he'd got used to seeing her. More like the old Letty.

Perhaps, he thought, in a tumbling rush, they could make it work again? Perhaps his book, his own small tribute to where she came from, had jump-started her heart, re-ignited the old affection?

'I'm going now, Bertie.'

She gave him a soft, dry kiss on the cheek, almost papery. As she leaned in, she pressed his right arm. Even after she'd released him, and gathered her coat, and disappeared down the stairs, Bertie could feel the ghost of the pressure.

Resisting Margot's later attentions, amid constantly topped-up glasses and the free-flowing compliments, Bertie walked home, alone, at the end of the evening.

The street was hushed, the night air thick with moisture, settling in a dew on the felted shoulders of his tan overcoat and chilling Bertie's hands as he fiddled with the key at the door.

The hallway was dark, but his eyes had adjusted to the relative gloom of the front step. And so he quickly noticed the envelope, a bright white rectangle, calling out from the dimness. Thick, and heavy, with just one word written on the front, in neat handwriting.

Bertie slid his finger into its corner, and the envelope opened with a tear.

21 January, 1947

The clock reads 7.31 a.m. as Amelia Brinkforth concludes a sixteen-hour labour, lying on her back on a gleaming ward in York, and a long, pinkish-red baby slides into the world without a sound. The midwife picks up Albert, who pouts at her in silent fury, until she gives him a brisk, gentle, enlivening slap, and he mewls. And at 7.31 a.m. in her bed in Abergavenny, Angharad Lewis shreds her face and crushes her mam's hand as her daughter Violet comes out of her in a tearing rush, and screams and screams and screams her arrival.

Chapter 1

January 1967

The doorbell rang

'Your turn,' said Max, giving Violet a kiss. She reluctantly raised herself off the faded, cabbage-green floor cushion, which had once been part of a sofa they'd found abandoned on the street. The bell went again, but Violet refused to increase her pace as she picked her way through mattresses, limbs, and ashtrays.

The door opened and – standing on the other side of it – Al felt a jolt when he saw her face, as if he were knocked briefly out of time. She was framed by its dark, damp-stained wood, and looked like some Frida Kahlo portrait – a stark gaze, no smile of welcome. Her eyes were underlined with heavy kohl, and framed by two long, wispy dark plaits; a full length, once-white dress came up in an old-fashioned lacy collar round her neck, making her pale face look practically chalky.

Tamsin and Johnny behind him were eager to get in, but Al felt stuck, as if his feet were magnetised to the doorstep.

'Jen told us to come here! Number ninety-two, right?' Johnny edged his curls over Al's unmoving shoulder and grinned at the girl. 'Come on, buddy,' he muttered in Al's ear, pushing to get inside.

'Come in,' said Violet, still not smiling; these were the fourth set of friends either Jen or Max had invited back. 'We're in Max's room.'

Al tried to smile at her, but she had turned to walk back down the corridor. The Welsh accent was a surprise, although it shouldn't have been. It had been one of the many small, slightly disorienting pleasures of starting university for Al – so many different voices! He'd been in halls with a man who actually sounded like Paul McCartney, who refused to believe Al could be from Yorkshire at all. 'Maybe a silver spoon factory,' he'd joked. And Al suspected that Johnny exaggerated his Mancunian accent in order to sound less thoroughly middle class.

It had been their very first night in Sheffield that Johnny had walked up to Al in the student's union and demanded to know whether or not he liked Jimi Hendrix, and when Al gave the right answer, uttered 'thank fuck'. Johnny had only been on campus a few hours, yet was furious with how 'straight' everyone was. 'Someone actually told me their favourite singer is *Rod Stewart*.'

Johnny had a wild bush of very light brown curls, and prioritised cigarettes so far over food that he was even slimmer than Al, if several inches shorter. It was the way Tamsin smoked, with apparent contempt for her own cigarette, that caused Johnny to decide to 'collect' her as a friend too.

When Johnny had introduced Al to Tamsin as they were waiting to go into a Politics lecture, it was lust at first sight: the thick wavy dark brown hair, the straight gaze, the stretch of solid thigh visible between her tall purple suede boots and a fluffy treacle-coloured coat. But Tamsin immediately made it clear that she had a boyfriend in London who was actually a professional photographer, and fully twenty-nine.

Yet while it might look as if this haughty creature merely tolerated Al and Johnny, the three formed a union of unspoken mutual admiration. Tamsin's friendship was a revelation to Al – having both been to elite, single-sex schools, it felt quite new to have such an intimate, equal, but utterly unsexual relationship with a member of the opposite gender. (Tamsin and Johnny were very good at pretending that their relationship was the same, when in fact Al suspected that they slept together on an occasional basis.)

Despite their initial tight loyalty, the trio also soon found others to befriend, their social circle rippling out, until it included people like Max, whom Al only saw being loud at Socialist Society meetings or at concerts in halls occasionally. Al didn't recognise this dark-haired Welsh girl though – and she didn't seem to recognise him either. His circle had swooped in to take control of the student union's ENTS committee in second year, wrestling Saturday night discos into more progressive territory, and Al usually took the end-of-the-night slot – achieving some notoriety for his divisive closing numbers, which ranged from Sun Ra to Sibelius. Between that and manning the table distributing copies of *Peace News* in the union most lunchtimes, he was something of a 'face' on campus. Al felt slightly disappointed that there'd not even been a flicker of recognition from her.

The way she moved as she led them down the corridor to Max's room was a surprise too. Upright, trim, almost a little trot. Her dress – a bit too long for her – swished around the dirty tiles as she walked, like an animal's tail.

'Johnny! Al! Tamsin... Welcome!' Max folded Al into a hug as the girl disappeared down into the gloom of bodies, cushions and record sleeves.

'Al, you've met Violet before. Have you?'

Al made a non-committal noise as he tried to parcel his limbs into a small patch of floor next to Max. But he felt sure that if he had met Violet before, he would have remembered.

Ah, but was she Max's? Yes, she was; a small light public kiss, before Max turned back and started a rambling monologue about how good the drummer had been.

'But I'm yammering on without offering you any refreshment, man,' laughed Max eventually. 'Violet, get another brew going, won't you?'

Violet lifted her head languidly from where she'd rested it in Jen's lap. Violet liked Jen, because although she seemed to do everything and know everyone, in herself she was quiet, tending to fade to the back of a room. It was soothing, among all these people trying so hard to find their personalities through forcefully performing different versions of them in public. With a calm symmetry to her oval face, long hair the colour of milky tea, and the light, grey-brown of her eyes, Jen reminded Violet of the illustrations of the pious Beth in the copy of *Little Women* she read endlessly as a child. Not that she'd ever tell her that: nobody wanted to be a Beth.

'Ceylon, lapsang, or half and half?' asked Violet as she began to gather assorted grotty cups, her movements quick and neat.

'Oh, uh. Well—'

'Half and half, Violet!' said Max, with certainty. 'It's the best, honestly, Al, the only way.'

Max never faded into the background. Max knew his own mind – so well that he presumed to know everyone else's too. She should insist that this Al choose what he wanted, resist Max getting his own way always, thought Violet, but she didn't.

A murky light came in through the dirty window, the moon too pale to illuminate the little kitchen fully, but casting grey beams enough for Violet to fill the kettle by. She was glad to have a role, really, at these gatherings, happy to do what Max told her to do, even if something inside her resisted the telling itself.

Doing what Max told her to do had changed her life. Her time at Sheffield had been colourless until he had seen something in her, plucked her as his own.

Even getting to Sheffield felt like it had been the will of other people. Violet noticed how many of her fellow working-class students – of which there were not many, not really – were there because of a single inspirational teacher. For her, that had been Miss Ketterick, whom everyone in Abergavenny considered 'eccentric' for her short hair and round little glasses. It was Miss Ketterick who had given her full marks in her essay on Wordsworth and the Sublime. It was Miss Ketterick who made sure Violet stayed on for sixth form rather than taking the job at Watt's, the clothes shop in town, and it was Miss Ketterick who paid for her train fare to Oxford.

'Oxford,' mouthed her mam, when Violet told her just two days before the interview.

The next day, Angharad had met Violet at the school gates. 'We'd better get you togged up proper, then, hadn't we,' she said as she steered them to Watt's and picked her out a neat lavender-coloured dress with a belted waist. Her mother, it transpired, had long kept her own 'emergency money' in a honey pot at the back of the cupboards.

Violet never wore the dress again. Magdalen College's yellow buildings had loomed, and she'd shrunk, and felt disorientated when girls asked her 'where do you go?' as if they'd have ever heard of her school. She felt stupid when they asked why she hadn't applied to Jesus, the Welsh college, as if she should've known about such things. When she tried to read a passage from *Doctor Faustus* under the gaze of a corpulent, whiskery professor, the lines swam and merged and failed to mean anything at all.

Then another letter came through offering her a place to read English at Sheffield, and her mam was so thrilled at this opportunity for her to 'get on', that Violet didn't know how to turn it down.

But the first night, when Violet tried to talk to the other girls she was sharing a corridor with in the glowering block of Sorby Halls, she found them to be as intimidating as those at her Oxford interview, if not worse – just as confident, but more stylish. City girls. She felt dowdy and dull and, as the weeks went by, more and more left behind, as if she'd missed out on some secret induction lecture that explained exactly *how* to be a student.

Sheffield itself was dour in the autumn gloom, but there was something familiar about the countryside around it. When feeling especially wobbly, Violet would take a bus or train out into the Peaks, which welcomed her with their wide, wild beauty, the copper ferns and muddy mauve of the heather. Sometimes, on those days, she would be able to fall asleep without crying.

After the Christmas holidays, Violet came back to university armed with a new determination: 1966 was going to be different. She had a new seminar group; she would start afresh. Reinvent herself.

'And so, let's turn our attention to Caliban. Any thoughts?' asked their tutor, a stooped elderly man named Dr Spearpoint.

Violet had said nothing, yet. *She would; she must. The Tempest* was one of the few plays she'd actually seen, nervously taking herself to an RSC production the previous term. But her throat felt sore whenever she tried to speak.

A male student with a lounging, spread-legged posture spoke up, again. 'He's the id – the darker side of human nature, the counterbalance to Ariel as pure superego.'

'Ah, thank you, Professor Freud,' murmured Dr Spearpoint. 'Caliban certainly is the classical counterbalance to Ariel, that gives the play its satisfying structure. But I'm not sure I'd agree that they are both parts of our *humanity* – Caliban is essentially monstrous—'

'Is he though? Or has he just been treated monstrously?'

Dr Spearpoint looked at her, sharply. So did everyone else in the class. Violet's face got very hot, and her heart rolled like someone was playing timpani inside her ribcage.

'Go on, please – Miss Lewis, isn't it? I've yet to hear any … analysis.'

She tugged at her turquoise tunic. She'd spent all her Christmas money on clothes, to shore up the reinvention with high boots and higher hemlines. Now she was embarrassed at how much pasty thigh was on display.

'Well Caliban's life was fine on the island – it was his island! – until he was enslaved, and now it's so bad, he can only find happiness in *dreams*: "when I waked, I cried to dream again". He's like … a brutalised underclass, beaten down till they can only wish for freedom. And revenge.'

Violet looked up, and caught the eye of a wolfish man, leaning forward with his elbows on his knees, smiling.

'It's a very pretty theory, Miss Lewis.' Dr Spearpoint's smile was smeary with condescension. 'But quite wrong, I'm afraid. Shakespeare's villains can often spin speeches; that doesn't mean we are to identify with them. And Prospero tells us he has tried to teach Caliban, but he remains uncivilisable.'

'Well he would say that now, wouldn't he? He wants him to chop wood for his fires!'

There was some laughter in the class, and Violet felt buoyed. 'And anyway, if you've got a good actor playing him, of course we'll feel for him.'

'Ah, you've seen a production where some actor moved you, is that it? Well, let me tell you – this goes for all of you actually – theatrical productions are an easy way to get a handle on

Shakespeare, but they are no substitute for the text. How about we consider the language *Shakespeare* chooses rather than what emotions an actor might stir up, hm?'

Violet was almost shaking. He was an idiot. Maybe they were all idiots. She would write a paper on *The Tempest* and she would argue so well and with so little emotion that he'd have to give her a good mark. And she would speak up whenever she had any thoughts at all. Because if that one was 'wrong', there was clearly no real right or wrong anyway.

'Way-out theory, blue.' It was the man with the grin, catching up with her as they left the classroom. Violet dragged down her dress again.

'Oh, really? Thanks. He didn't seem too keen...'

'Ah, he's just old-fashioned. Don't mind him.' The man looked at the floor, then back up at her, with what she could tell was staged uncertainty. 'Would you like a coffee?'

'Yes, please.' She'd answered too fast; this was dreadful.

'I'm Max, by the way.'

Max ran a hand through a mop-top of black hair, and his eyes crinkled over a big, easy smile. He was stocky, with broad shoulders and big hands given to eager gestures, clearing pathways. It wasn't far to the coffee bar in the union, but on the way they stopped five times for Max to speak to extremely interesting-looking people.

'Sorry,' he said to Violet, sounding earnest but with an unreadable grin, after an intense redhead only looked at Max while talking about a Freedom from Hunger fundraiser.

Violet demurred. In her head, she was already planning how to keep hold of him. He would be a passport.

And he had been. Violet was his girlfriend by Easter, and allowed him to sleep with her the first night they were reunited for summer term. It was not the revelation she had been led to expect. But the general cloud of uncertainty had lifted, and that was what really mattered. She had a role: she was Max's girl.

When she returned to university at the start of second year, her place there felt much more correct – like she had won the right to be there. And if Violet ever didn't feel like talking – and she often didn't; everyone else seemed to know so much more than her about everything that was important – it didn't matter. Max could certainly talk for them both.

'It has to be nurture—'

The men's voices were rising as she delivered the teapot and sat back down among them.

'But there's no way to tell, man!'

'Well that's a problem, but it's also *convenient* for a corrupt society.'

'Yes – go on...'

'Well it's really *convenient*, isn't it, if it's nature that makes some people stupid or poor or less, less, less capable of achieving – whatever "achieving" means, that's another matter – but what I'm saying is, we don't have to work to level the playing field if we can blame it on *nature*.' The curly-haired one, Johnny, spoke fast, words stumbling out of him.

'Well what are we talking about here? Give me some examples.'

Max loved asking questions of other people: demanding they persuade him, and throwing pebbles in the way of an argument.

'OK, crude example. Consider race: well, we know it can be a factor in predicting how someone does in education, how much they'll earn, how long they'll live and so on in Britain today. Obviously, we know that's not because of nature – it's not coded in... in anyone's DNA. It's about opportunity and, and, and *prejudice*—'

Max nodded along with performative earnestness, but Violet

couldn't help but wonder if he – or this Johnny – even knew anyone who wasn't white.

'So, is prejudice the same as "nurture"?' Max rolled the words around slowly, genuinely considering the question.

'It kind of is, yeah. It's a heavy word for the dark side of it – what you get from society, not just from your parents.' The posher boy – Al, was it? – spoke with a smoother, calmer tone than his jumpy friend.

'The role of the parents is grossly over-exaggerated, I reckon,' interrupted Johnny again. 'I mean it's important, but how you're taught to *be* is not as important in determining how your life will *go* as how *society* sees you—'

'And therein lies the problem! I dig you.' Max nodded sagely.

'Same goes for class, or, or, or – for women.'

Violet noticed Jen's head flick round. Jen was one of only four women in their year studying biology; she was used to hearing the theorising of the eighty-odd men who dominated her course.

'So, men and women, biologically different, yes?' Johnny continued. 'But does that mean their differences in behaviour and attitude come down to that biology, or to the expectations society puts on them from the moment they're born? Are we programmed to behave differently, hunter-gatherer or home-maker, or is that all just ... *bollocks*?' His hands were working overtime.

'I mean in that case, surely it *is* nature too?' Max began gently stroking Violet's lower back and she wondered how deliberate the timing was. 'Obviously skin colour is just that – pigmenta-tion – but women's bodies are actually made differently, for different functions?'

'Aha! Their bodies – yes – but their *minds*?'

'Well, yeah! I mean, nature has made it so that women's

desires support their biology. So they want to play with dolls because they're hardwired to care for babies.' Max threw up his hands in jokey defence as Jen abruptly stood up, as if driven to extract herself. 'I'm not saying they can't also be astrophysicists or run a bank! They're just perhaps less likely to want to because at some point the urge to make a family kicks in, right?'

His hands returned to caress her bottom. Violet thought she saw Al's head follow the movement, and look quickly away.

'You mean *nature* makes them generally more *nurturing*?' asked Johnny.

'Yes! I mean, that's not a controversial thing to say, is it? Women are, in general, more caring, better at looking after things – people—'

'Well, that *is* a heavy thing to say, man,' Al interrupted, although his voice remained soft, as if keen to distance himself from his friend's sparring, Violet thought. 'It's pretty controversial to assume that it's genetically hardwired—'

'Stop being so polite to him, Al, it's fucking *bollocks* is what it is!' Johnny laughed and pulled hard on a cigarette; it crackled, as if for emphasis. 'This is exactly what we're talking about, Max my friend: lazy assumptions and taught behaviour that are used to oppress whole swathes of society. What would it do to your ambition or belief in *what you could be good at* if you were told from the day you were born that you were only good for cleaning, and looking after babies?'

Al didn't doubt Johnny's commitment to female emancipation, but he had also seen first-hand, on several occasions, how his dressing down a less radical male was a tactic that impressed surrounding females. Not that many seemed to be listening to them here, apart from the silent, watchful Violet. Was she bored, or stoned, or vacuous? Or was it just hard to get a word in edgeways with Max?

Dear God, he was pleased with himself, thought Violet, as Johnny continued to educate Max in the myriad ways women were oppressed.

'But true equality must also allow for, well, biological difference!' cut in Max. 'Women can rule the world – and still be more inherently *nurturing* and *caring* than we are. In fact, wouldn't that be better?'

'Well why don't you start by asking one about it?' Al spoke his frustration towards the carpet.

A silence seemed to whip around the group like a little wind.

Violet sat very still, staring at Al's bent head, his fine, tousled hair. Max's caressing hand froze, hovering at her waist.

Then the moment shifted; the door to Max's bedroom was opening very slowly, and there was a cake full of candles, carried in by Jen.

'Happy birthday to you …' Her low voice led the singing as the rest of the room craned round and started to join in.

Violet dipped her head with a smile, trying – ineffectually – to hide behind her long plaits.

'It's just gone midnight! Which means you are now officially twenty years old, baby blue,' said Max, putting a warm arm around Violet's shoulder and bringing her in to kiss her head, a movement that felt just a little more possessive than Violet would have liked at that moment.

Al was still looking at her. A curious, slightly uneven smile played over his face.

Violet cocked her head.

'It's my birthday too,' said Al, with a shrug.

'Never!'

As the straggled rendition of 'Happy Birthday' came to its conclusion, Jen picked her way towards Violet, proffering the cake. Violet stood up, and then reached down for Al's hand. His fingers were long, warm and dry to the touch. *A good fit,* she thought, as she pulled him up, and then let go quickly.

'We've got a double birthday, everyone!' Violet announced, with shy pleasure.

'You too, Al? No way!' said Jen. 'Well, I think there's enough candles for you both.'

Al and Violet faced each other across the cake, and blew out the flames.

As the smoke from the candles rose like a wish, Al shook his fringe off his face, and looked up at Violet. He met her eyes, which looked somehow very dark and very bright at the same time. Their gazes locked, like two halves of a magnet meeting, with an irresistible, silent click.

Time stopped again, and this time, it stopped for Violet as well.

Chapter 2

February 1967

The moment Violet came through the door that Saturday night, and met his eyes across the room, Al knew that something would happen between them. The gooey, psychedelic lamps Johnny and his mate Ginger had fundraised for were going, jade green and orange and purple drooling down the walls of the hall that was used for the student union's parties. 'Sunshine Superman' was strutting over the sound system, and Al was in his groove.

'Tamsin,' Al whispered urgently in Tamsin's ear on the dance-floor. 'She's here.'

'Yes, but so is Max,' Tamsin hissed back, after a glance over her shoulder.

Al gave her a mournful look.

'Leave it to me.'

Tamsin and Johnny had laughed at Al for weeks after he first met Violet at Max's, teasing him for the way he constantly craned around in Graves bar or outside lectures, hoping for a sight of her. They'd expected him to get distracted before too long, as with his previous crushes. But not this time.

Al could not stop thinking about Violet. 'It's meant to be!' he would insist, moonily, in reference to their shared birthday.

'Well, maybe you could ask her boyfriend where she is,'

Tamsin would say, scooting away before he could get her in a headlock.

And the minute Violet walked into the union, and saw Al looking at her, the knowledge that she would be going home with him flashed across the room so certainly, she was surprised Max didn't sense it too. But then, Max was busy: scanning the dancefloor, catching the eye of a group of girls at the back, by the bar.

Recently, Violet had noticed a jingling restlessness in Max. The arm he used to sling across her shoulder, the hand that dropped casually onto her chest – a gesture of ownership that she hadn't minded, had been proud of even – now roamed through his own hair, hung out in his back pocket. He wandered off at parties, only to be found in the kitchen talking loudly at pretty freshers. Violet had shouted at him about it once when they got home.

'I'm sorry, baby blue. It was only a party.' He looked into her face with an impression of seriousness – but his voice was too light, flyaway, and something still danced in his rich brown eyes. Violet had shrugged on her threadbare wool coat with as much hauteur as she could manage, and was disappointed at how the front door of number 92 barely slammed in its spongy damp frame.

But walking along the Ecclesall Road back to her own house in the jelly-like bright blue between darkness and dawn, Violet became wrapped in a new fear. She mustn't give Max any reason to leave her. Worst were the nights where he stayed out, but she felt like she had to go home to study. Max often good-humouredly tried to point out to Violet that her panics over work were unnecessary: since the start of second year, she'd shot miles ahead of not only him, but most of their year. 'I think you might actually be the top girl, you know?'

She didn't know. She hadn't ever thought to separate the top results into men and women.

Her anxiety was manageable when she was absorbed in her reading, but as soon as she put her head to the pillow the panic started. The parading images of Max, getting with some prettier, taller, sexier girl. Of Max leaving her, lost and alone, to a sea of pitying looks. Because where would Violet belong at university without Max?

She hadn't expected to find an answer so quickly.

Max squeezed her arm. 'I'll go get us some drinks.'

'Just a lemonade for me, please,' said Violet. Something told her that she wanted to keep a clear head tonight.

Tamsin and Al watched as Max made his way over to the bar. With a slight raise of her eyebrows, Tamsin swirled away, weaving through the crowd to arrive just behind Max. Seizing the moment, Al looked back to where Violet had been – only to find she'd disappeared. Somehow, he wasn't worried. He knew he'd find her.

Al began pushing his way onto the dance floor, uninteresting bodies clouding his view. Then a man swayed to the right, and – ah! There she was. Standing alone, a clear path between them. As if spot lit, ready, and waiting.

Their eyes met again, and Al danced towards Violet, head bobbing and body twizzling slowly across the space. Halfway there, the song shifted into 'Subterranean Homesick Blues', and Violet was laughing by the time he reached her.

'I think you've got too many limbs for this song,' she yelled in his ear.

Al looked down at himself. He knew what she meant. The tempo was unforgiving. But she wasn't faring much better: while he thought she looked cute in a short, strangely rigid patterned mini dress, her bopping movements were pretty stiff.

'What cruel bastard put this on just as I have to try to impress you?' he shouted back at her.

'You don't have to impress me.'

A laugh escaped Al, at the easiness of it. He somehow knew he'd feel like this with her. They danced, badly, together for the remaining minute of Dylan. Then the DJ fumbled the record and the room hissed into unnerving quiet.

'Hello,' he said, looking her dead in the eye.

'Hello,' she replied.

'That's a nice dress.'

The crowd booed the DJ.

'Why thank you. I made it myself.'

'Far out! Talented too.'

'Broke more like.'

Violet looked past Al, to check on Max. He was immersed in conversation with a dark-headed woman standing too close to him, next to the bar. Violet's drink forgotten, presumably.

'Ah, yes. Is it ...' Al felt sure that Violet was the most perfect woman in the world and that he must know every single one of her thoughts, but he also didn't really know how to start that process. 'Is it, uh, cheaper to make your own clothes?'

'Course. This is an old curtain! Found it cut price. Nice pattern, and bob's your uncle.'

Bob's your uncle? Jesus Christ. Thank God the music was back, thought Violet as The Kinks chugged in to fill the stretching gap.

'Did you say ... curtains?' Al shouted again, into her ear.

'Yes! Well if it's good enough for the von Trapps ...'

Al had no idea what she was talking about.

'Oh come on. *The Sound of Music.* You must've seen it? I went three times, just with my mam!'

'Ah, yeah. Singing nuns, and Nazis, and Julie Andrews and – curtains?'

Violet stuck out her hand, and he twirled her so she could show off said curtains, and then there were shallow breaths, shuffling feet. For the next several songs, they danced around each other, occasionally breaking into secret little smiles, directed down at the floor, as if seeing the feeling on the other's face was all too much.

And then the DJ put on 'Light My Fire', and they were facing each other and suddenly barely moving at all. A tiny hip sway in on her part, then on his, and as their sweating palms met, their fingers spread like two leaves unfurling in slow sun. Al closed his fist, binding their fingers tight together. The tiniest tug of her body in to his, and the lightest brush of lips.

And Al hadn't known kisses could feel like that, and Violet hadn't known kisses could feel like that either. The first touch seemed to send crushed glass round her bloodstream, opening out all the blood vessels, everything suddenly racing and flooding and dangerous. She drew away, looked around, panicked.

Max hadn't even noticed. The woman was leaning in close now, her hair tumbling perfectly like some lustrous velvety curtain, a hand resting on Max's shoulder; his head was dipped, and he had the concerted, concentrating expression he pulled when he wanted to make someone feel special.

Al followed her gaze. He beamed with gratitude, and when Violet looked back, she thought the smile was for her.

They left without saying goodbye to anyone.

It wasn't far to Al's house, and they hurried back, hands thrust in pockets to keep them from touching each other, in case they couldn't stop, in case anyone saw.

He led her straight to his room, closed the door, turned, and there was a pause — chests rising and falling, words seeming empty and insufficient — and then Violet wasn't sure who'd lunged first, but there were hands everywhere and clothes dropping and a descent to the bed and kissing and kissing and kissing...

Al drew back, and took a moment, looking down at her, his eyes swollen with a kind of tenderness. He reached down, very softly, and began to touch her.

Violet's throat opened but the sounds seemed to come from somewhere else; she'd never made sounds like that before, it was her and it wasn't. And he kept going, the pressure – *yet not quite enough* – and the muscles she didn't know she had, tightening and everything crushed, the boundaries dissolving between her body and his and everything else in the whole entire world.

And yet still he held eye contact, a look in his eyes that was hopeful and expectant, a look that asked 'yes?' (*Yesnearlysonearly*) but also more than that, a look that somehow bound him to her, right inside of the annihilating electric everythingness that his fingers – *just his fingers* – were somehow bringing to her *yesyesyes*—

Violet's eyes snapped shut, and she went very stiff, then very floppy, then curled so hard into Al that she effectively head-butted his chest. He gently slid his hand out, and attempted to wipe it surreptitiously on the sheet behind him so he could take her face in his hand.

'Hey, hey now, Violet...' He tried to reinstate the eye contact which had been held by them both for so long – ferociously, almost like a dare.

Al tried to think if he had ever really made eye contact with anyone while touching them before. He didn't think so. But he also hadn't had anyone react like that before.

Violet pushed her nose into the small triangle of blonde hair on his skinny ribcage. He smelled faintly of oranges, and she wondered why, trying to give her brain something to focus on, so that maybe her body would stop twitching. It felt like a wind-up toy, that she'd lost control of. Allowed someone else to wind.

'Come here, come on,' Al coaxed her out gently. She looked very small, and embarrassed, and her eye make-up had run all over her cheekbones. He kissed her forehead, then her pointy, bobbly nose, then her mouth, softly. A little sheepish smile gave her dimples. He tried to push his tongue into one.

'What the hell are you doing now then?'

He liked her accent best when she was indignant.

'Ah ... just your dimples. Thought they needed a bit of attention too.'

'With your tongue?'

'...yes?'

'Well there's other places could use it more, I think.'

Violet had no idea where such sauce came from. She felt lightheaded, untethered.

Al disappeared under the duvet, despite Violet wriggling and saying no, he didn't have to, she was joking, oh God yes—

Perhaps it *was* the eye contact though, because although she enjoyed it, it was less like her body and all known dimensions had been turned inside out the second time. But when Al moved on top – and just gently pressed the side of her face with his thumb at the same moment he moved inside her, and they gasped at the same time, watching each other's face changing as they felt their own do so – it was as if everything had moved into place, exactly as it should.

Afterwards, as she lay with her head in a nook of Al's arm, Violet let her gaze wander around his room; she'd been too busy to notice anything except him before. There were Indian drapes pinned up for curtains, and teetering piles of books – novels and poetry collections as well as cópies of *Resurgence* and his politics textbooks. A painting of a Pre-Raphaelite woman with a sulky mouth, in a surprisingly good frame, and a battered but clearly once grand red armchair. Violet wondered what sort of house it came from; perhaps one like Max's, a London townhouse, somehow both rickety and imposing.

Max. The concept of 'Max' passed through her brain, and she felt nothing, and then felt guilt for feeling nothing, which was at least better than really feeling *nothing*-nothing.

They lay silently, Al stroking her shoulder very gently. Bodies were so strange, he thought to himself, looking at the perfect, alien bones beneath her pearly skin, and wondering why no one had ever told him that humans were capable of doing what they had just done. A calmness settled over him, a thick sense of satisfaction and rightness.

'Imagine if you never—'

He stopped. Perhaps it would sound silly out loud. And what if – his eyes flicked down to her dreamy face – what if it was always like that for her? With Max too? Perhaps it was just *her* that was special.

'Never experienced *that,* in your whole entire life? I know. It would be …' Her voice was small, but contented, all sighs and feathery edges. 'It would be an actual *tragedy.*'

'That was exactly what I was thinking.'

'Maybe that's why people don't talk about it, not proper like – you wouldn't want to upset all the people only having just ordinary, fine sex. Wouldn't be fair.'

And then Al couldn't stop grinning, and she twisted her head to look at him, and the grin jumped to her face too. Good God, this was all entirely ridiculous, he thought, but it must – *surely it must* – be the very start of love.

Chapter 3

July 1968

It was always shortly after asserting that nothing was happening that Violet realised everything was happening.

Al was stroking the back of her head and now it felt like he had a lot more fingers than was really probable, as if each stroke left a ghost finger behind. Then he turned towards her, and smiled, a process that seemed to take a long time.

The bongo player from Tyrannosaurus Rex seemed to play directly into Al's right foot, which jiggled of its own accord. He took in the crowd, mostly sprawled, like him and his friends, on the grass in Hyde Park, although a bank of vertical bodies further away were bobbing gently in front of the stage in time with the music.

'You OK?' he murmured, leaning in to Violet, hoping her trip was starting gently too. She had a warm smell, a mix of buttery toast, incense, stale tobacco – maybe coming from her dress, a pale green diaphanous thing with a drawstring made of cowrie shells.

'Mm–hm.'

'Feeling something?'

Her eyes ran over the scene, friends and strangers that all seemed to be connected somehow to the music, as if the sounds were strung together on invisible delicate fine threads, like spiders' webs.

'Yeah, I think so.'

'Far out.' Al's smile got even wider.

'I suppose,' Violet found herself saying, 'music doesn't really exist – or isn't really finished, anyway – until it's heard by someone? We make the music too. In our minds?'

'If a tree falls in a forest,' shouted Ginger, who was lying topless on his back, his freckled skin already turning a brilliant red in the fierce sunshine. 'Profound, man!'

Violet quickly blushed to match him.

'Shut up, Ginger,' said Clara, prodding him with her bare big toe, around which she'd tied a daisy, already crushed and bruised. 'Violet is still a novice. *Be nice.*'

It was Ginger who had orchestrated their gang's great decampment from Sheffield to London after they graduated. His father had a run-down place in Highbury that needed doing up; Al and Violet, Jen, Tamsin and Johnny, plus Clara whom they knew from the student newspaper, had all moved in, rent-free, to 'help' for a month or so.

The house buzzed with people, and activity. They'd spend hours sewing political banners in the garden or preparing a piece of street theatre supporting the Biafra protest against the sale of arms, then all go up Primrose Hill together at sunset to watch the lights twinkle on over the city, or stay up to greet the dawn by jumping up and down on the sofa to 'Good Day Sunshine'. But the new living situation was also hectic – there were people everywhere, all the time, with guests dropping in and out for days or weeks at a stretch, hopping between beds as they did so. And so far, the only repainting done was a mural of a naked woman in space, in the style of The Fool. Al had bought all the multicoloured paints, even though he was supposedly running perilously low on cash: Harold had frozen his account, 'until you get a proper job'.

Material things were overrated, Al declared to Harold and anyone else who'd listen, adding that poverty was a price worth paying for freedom. When he announced this to Violet – admittedly after four pints in the pub that he was somehow still able to pay for – she'd snorted. 'Have you ever met someone who genuinely doesn't know where their next meal is coming from?' she asked tartly as she steered him home down the road.

The fluid chaos of the house was also fuelled by acid: since they had moved to London, some of their group seemed to take it all the time. But it was true that Violet was a novice, compared to the rest of them; she'd only done LSD twice before, with some trepidation. She didn't want to miss out on anything that was important to Al, and their other friends, but she had also been afraid. Al assured her acid was 'the most connecting, spiritual experience' he'd ever had, and she trusted him on that – what she was really nervous about was her brain.

'I've only just discovered I've got one worth bothering about,' Violet joked to Al when he wheedled at her to join in. She knew it was a distinctly straight position to take. But she had got the highest mark of anyone on a single paper in finals, and came third in the year overall.

After Violet got her marks, Al had been so proud he'd walked into every party for weeks using the news as a greeting, even though she told him to *isht*. And when she found out that she'd got a place on the literature MA at King's that autumn, he'd bought her a handsome, leather-bound copy of *The Rainbow* as a present; she'd got one of her best marks writing about *Sons and Lovers*. He wrote inside the cover: 'For the cleverest woman I've ever met. Here's to your next brilliant essay – and to our next chapter'. Violet's eyes had filled with tears, and she'd clutched the book to her chest very tightly and given him a fierce, biting kiss.

At her graduation, her head of department had sought her out, pumping her hand in fulsome congratulation. Violet's parents, looking small and stiff in clothes they usually only wore to funerals, addressed the professor with such soft-voiced bobbing it made Violet's toes curl inside their flat velvet slippers, shoes her mam scolded her for wearing once she'd sufficiently recovered from the ceremony with a vodka and orange in the Broomhill Tavern.

Al hadn't been there, and Violet felt a shameful bubble of relief that she hadn't had to introduce her parents to him, like that. Because this shrunken version wasn't who they really were. She thought of her mam, really, as bustling and cheerful, clucking with friends and aunties at the back door; of her dad, really, as so proud, of his job on the railways (even if he was only a signalman) and his work for the union.

Al had been in Provence with his parents the week of graduation; they'd been less than bothered about marking his 2:2, especially in the shadow of his sister Rose's infamous double-first in Classics from Oxford. Before they left, he'd presented his parents with the final double-issue of the student paper, which he edited – very brilliantly, Violet thought – telling them that was where his energy had gone, and where his future lay. It included the special report Al had made, from Paris, on the student protests, plus an in-depth analysis of how the university was failing to sufficiently boycott South Africa, and a cartoon supplement called *The Breadheads*, owing a significant debt to Gilbert Shelton and Robert Crumb.

His father had immediately made a great show of stuffing it in the bin. But later, when Al had stolen into Harold's study on the hunt for some matches, he found the paper, uncrumpled and pressed flat between two heavy books. When he'd told Violet about this – on a woefully expensive call from a phone box in a village over three miles away from their villa – she pretended to agree it just proved that Harold was, in fact, a massive hypocrite. And wondered if maybe she had it easier with her parents, after all.

A high-pitched shriek cut through Violet's reverie. Ginger had grabbed at Clara's prodding toe, and made to put it in his mouth. Now she was pretending to kick him in the head.

'Woah, loud scenes,' said a stranger with a long sandy beard sitting near them, whom Violet had noticed watching first Tamsin, then Clara, waiting for a chance.

'He tried to suck my toe,' announced Clara to the stranger, pointing at Ginger and pouching her plump mouth into a petulant 'o'.

'Well, who can blame him,' the stranger said admiringly.

Clara preened, shamelessly.

When she first met Clara through Al, who edited her gushing music reviews for the paper, Violet had had one of those rare moments of recognition. Here was someone else like her, someone else whose dad had a normal job rather than running the country, someone else who had to work in a shop over the Christmas holidays rather than going skiing. Thereafter, there was a silent solidarity of glances between them, at the lack of awareness of their privileged friends.

But since they'd moved to London – Clara's hometown – Violet felt outstripped by her. She was a little overwhelmed by the capital's noise and its dirt, but Clara suited summer in the city. She understood the buses and tube, and took control of the group, asserting the quickest way to get to all the best places. And she managed to make a certain sweaty dishevelment look casual and sexy – whereas Violet felt perpetually flustered, her pale skin prickling from heat and pollution.

Violet watched now as Clara leaned lazily back on one elbow, and declared loudly how hot it was. Then, making sure that everyone – but particularly Johnny, and the bearded stranger – was watching, she began to unfasten her badly made crochet top, releasing a pair of splayed, tanned breasts.

Tamsin quickly followed suit, and after a while, Al nudged Violet, encouragingly.

Violet shook her head, slightly, and then Al bent his head over her, nosing towards the V-shaped opening of her dress, his somewhat sparse new beard tickling her skin.

'Stop it,' she hissed, in a whisper.

'Oh go on,' Al murmured into a gap that wasn't quite cleavage. 'Why not, when it's so sunny?'

'I don't know – I just feel… I don't know if I want people to look. People other than you.' Violet's head felt too swimmy to make much of coherent argument, but she knew what she *felt*. Going topless just didn't feel *equal*.

'I don't mind.'

Violet sighed. 'I know *you* don't mind.'

'What I mean is, don't feel you have to save them for me!'

'I don't!' Violet dropped her voice again, not wanting the rest of the group to hear. 'Jesus Christ, it's not all about you.'

Al lifted his head, and pulled back, to look down at her seriously.

'Of course not. It's your body. But in a truly liberated society, wouldn't all bodies be free? From shame?' He gestured down to his own chest, bare and lightly tanned, with a smile.

Violet twizzled a long strand of hair reflectively as Tyrannosaurus Rex finished their set to distant applause.

'But the thing is, I don't know that it does feel free – yet.

They're not just any old body parts, are they? When you look at breasts, they're not *neutral*. You're admiring them.'

'I've got eyes for no one but you, and you know that's true.'

Violet did know it, actually. And she was grateful. Their friends all seemed to be going a little crazy: whether it was because '68 was their summer of love – 'blown over from the West Coast a year late' as Johnny constantly claimed – or because of the thrilling panic of finishing university, almost everyone seemed to be coupling up and then swapping frantically. Freedom: the thing they all said they wanted and yet now it was upon them, it was terrifying. At times, there was a manic edge to the fun, like a fairground ride going that bit too fast.

But when Al looked across the table at her during their long, ramshackle dinners, Violet felt strong, and centred. In the middle of an all-nighter at the Roundhouse, he'd bend his head, look properly into her eyes, and a slow smile would curl across his face. It felt like a secret gift: while everyone else ran about, they could stand still with each other.

'I know you only have eyes for me,' Violet said, softly, taking Al's hand and tracing a pattern on it with a long blade of grass she'd picked. 'But … that's not the point. You admit a bare chest is not the same as, I dunno, a naked elbow?'

'Why not? Why should it be any different? It could be the same!'

'Yes, but currently it *isn't*.' Violet could feel the irritation rise in her. She started pulling apart the blade of grass. 'It's sexual. I see the way some people look – a load of chicks lost in music, a load of men running their eyes along chest height like they're trying to choose the ripest fruit at the market.'

'Well you'd have the sweetest plums of all,' said Al, leaning and kissing down her neck towards her breasts again.

'Oh get off,' she laughed, swatting him.

Then she sat upright, and considered him for a few seconds.

'OK then: I'll do you a bargain. I'll go topless – when you get your cock out.'

'Come on, that's different – that actually is sexual! And... private.'

'Well so are breasts, in our current society. So fair's fair.'

Violet felt something shift in the energy of their little group, and looked round. Clara was kissing the bearded man, with gusto. Johnny, whom she had definitely shared a bed with for some of the last fortnight, was watching, but smiling. Was it a smile for Clara, being free to enjoy herself? Or a smile for the benefit of the rest of the group (and Tamsin especially, who was still also with Johnny on other nights, after all), to prove what a gas the whole open arrangement really was?

Things happened so fast now. It was like a whole layer of permission and protocol had simply been lifted away. All that stuffy, uptight old rubbish – the woo and the chase, women pretending not to want it and protecting their 'virtue', the man as pursuer and then provider. Violet worried that some of her friends' feelings were getting hurt by all this freedom. But to destigmatise sex, and pleasure; to accept that love could flow between different people in different ways; to just chill out and *enjoy* this one brief life ... *Well, bring on the revolution,* Violet thought, tipping her head back to the sky and letting the sun and the music drench her, letting herself soften.

It was possibly a long time later or maybe very soon afterwards that Al was dancing with Tamsin and Violet in the crowd, making their way down nearer towards the stage, where Pink Floyd had started playing. Everything sounded exceptionally loud.

His lungs expanded with the guitars, and his arms raised of their own accord. Let there be more light.

Violet's arms were wavering back and forth in front her face like snakes. Watching Violet dance was perhaps his favourite thing in the world, Al thought, with a sudden clarity that he needed to share this fact with her, but lacked quite the right words.

'Words are very inadequate!'

'What?' She couldn't hear over a spiral of guitar, ascending into the air.

'They just can't say – can't fit – enough for you.'

'For me?'

'To describe you.'

She threw her arms up again. 'I am uncontainable! I contain multitudes!'

Al saw Tamsin behind her roll her eyes. But Violet did, he thought.

The speaker stack squalled into ear-shredding feedback, and then retreated. Across the park, the trees and the people all waved as the music began rising and building inside Al's body.

His eyes telescoped onto the drummer, holding drumsticks like a conductor, holding it all together. And that was a bit like what God did, Violet thought, not control everything but just provide the rhythm, set our hearts beating and our time running, the great conductor—

Someone spilled a lukewarm can of beer down the back of Violet's dress, and she flinched, and then turned and stroked the stranger's face and felt like she knew him, too. Violet understood then why Al and the others were so into blowing open these doors—

And Al knew that the boundaries between him and Violet and the music and the earth were mere shimmering membranes, and Violet thought how the love she had for Al was love like

Jesus knew, not controlled or limited but in everything and everyone, all the time and everywhere, and—

But then, quite abruptly, the band was over. The absence of music hung in the air, like it had its own weight. People were leaving, everyone pushing against her body, the wrong way. But Violet just wanted to stand still and hold Al's hand. She felt like she'd just learned to stand up.

Chapter 4

February 1969

'No condemnation now I dread, Jesus and all in Him is mine—'

Evan's voice boomed in Al's left ear. Violet's father had surely deliberately sat between them on the chapel's narrow pew. But Evan's positioning was something of a relief: his strong bass obliterated Al's own voice – wobbling over his hymnbook, with tiny pages that were so soft he worried just holding them might reduce them to dust.

It was his first visit to Violet's home town, and Al thought he could perhaps see why she'd been putting it off. Abergavenny was stuck in something of a time warp. People still wore hats here. Stiff suits. Al's feet were freezing inside the only smart pair of shoes he had in London, which he'd dug out specially, and which were now spittled with mud.

'Alive in Him, my living Head, and clothed in righteousness divine—'

Righteousness was right. Every head held high and facing front, in neat little rows; every mouth trapping open and shut in sync. It was quite unlike the Anglican church Al had been raised in, with dwindling attendance, droning sermons and muttered singing.

'Bold I approach th'eternal throne, And claim the crown, through Christ my own.'

Yet despite these hymns' triumphal lyrics, they all still ended on a dying fall, a sighing, sagging sort of conclusion. Al hated hymns: making a tune so dully predictable that anyone could sing along first time was not a musical merit.

A final prayer and a fumbled donation and they were released. Outside, a bright acidic sunlight hit Al's eyes, and he squinted at the various middle-aged women who gave him a good look as they passed, nodding at Evan or stopping to talk to Angharad, presumably passing judgement on his long hair and wide-legged trousers, in some kind of code.

Violet finished talking to a cousin in a peach twin-set, and made her way over to Al with a smile that caused his shoulders to drop about two inches.

'You all right?' she whispered as she squeezed his hand. Violet suspected Al didn't realise he was rocking lightly on his heels, that his eyes were darting around the churchyard.

'Yes. Yep. Yes. Great service.'

Violet snorted.

'You loathed it, and that's fine.'

'I didn't, I … Well yes, I loathed it.' He pulled her round so he was only looking at her, not all those hats, those wary eyes. 'I can't sing. And I don't do the bearded old guy, you know that. But …' He paused, his body finally stilling. 'I got to find out more about your life here by going, and I would sit through any number of moans about the body of Christ if it means understanding you better.'

Violet let her head knock into his chest, her forehead at his heart. She breathed in his usual smell – that indefinable Al smell, that always reminded her how much he was other, not of her, and yet was now also the smell of familiarity, of reassurance. Of home.

Al was the bedrock of her new life – the one she'd made

for herself. London, academia, and living with friends; protest politics, parties, and mind-expansion. Being back in Abergavenny with him stirred strange feelings up in Violet. There was the pleasure at returning to the countryside, and the friendly chit-chat of everyone knowing each other. But that brought with it an oppressive claustrophobia: Violet could just feel the judgment swirling around Al, with his beard and beads and shaggy sheepskin coat. *Why's a posh toff dressed like that? Like a weirdo. A hippie. A poof.*

Seeing Al in Aber reminded Violet of all the things about her hometown she'd been keen to escape from – and revealed sharply how far she'd already travelled. *I can never come back*, Violet realised with a jolt. She simply wouldn't be able to make herself fit anymore.

'I'm not sure I made a very good impression back there,' said Al as they walked back to Violet's house through the town, which looked charming now the sun was finally out. 'Sorry.'

'Don't be daft. You just … maybe you just aren't what they were expecting, that's all.'

Violet hadn't known exactly how to describe Al to her family or friends. She had said things were 'quite serious' when they both moved to London after university finished – although her parents obviously didn't know that they had moved in together, in their unmarried state. As far as her mam and dad were concerned, she now shared a rented house in Ladbroke Grove only with Clara, Tamsin and Jen. She hadn't corrected her parents when they assumed they were Masters students too; Violet didn't know how to explain that most of her housemates signed on or worked part-time menial jobs, proudly considering themselves artists, activists, and drop-outs.

She had, however, warned her family that Al was 'a bit posh'; Violet felt she ought to manage expectations before they met, although she hadn't quite been able to be honest about the extent of Al's privileged circumstances. Her brothers had teased her shamelessly, anyway, even from the little she told them. 'She's going out with an English toff,' Geraint had told the whole pub with a laugh one evening. 'Likes of us not good enough for you anymore, is it?' a lad she'd known at school had shouted.

But that all changed at Christmas.

As early as October, Al had been arguing that Christmas had become no more than a capitalist wheeze, and they should both remain in London. 'We could stay in bed all day, give each other the meaningful yet free gift of oral sex, and eat nut roast.' 'And who's going to make the nut roast if we stay in bed all day?' laughed Violet, before refusing to even consider it.

'My mam would kill me if I didn't come home. And anyway, I love Christmas! It's not capitalist round our way – it's about sharing your good fortune, and getting together with your loved ones.'

'Could that include me?' beseeched Al.

'Yes, of course – you'd be very welcome. And they should probably all meet you at some point.'

But although Al was demonstrably excited about the visit all winter, he had changed his plans last minute and returned to Farley Hall with his sister instead.

When he had first mentioned that he might go to Wales for Christmas, Rose had been comically outraged. Once it became clear he was serious, she turned up on their doorstep in Ladbroke Grove one damp Sunday evening and, after a pot of jasmine tea and some small talk, finally begged Al not to leave her and her husband Peter alone with their family.

'You know what it's like,' Rose had said, reaching across the kitchen table, with its veins of spilt candle wax and paint stains, to take Al's hand.

Al squeezed it, remembering the previous year's booze-sodden Christmas lunch. Amelia had laid into 'your pathetic, spoilt generation' while banging the best silver cutlery like a gavel, joined by their semi-senile, harrumphing grandfather who lavished particular attention on how Peter had never served in a war. Rather unfairly, given there hadn't been one in his lifetime, Al tried to point out in defence of his blushing brother-in-law.

'But you have Peter, the two of you will be fine,' Al said, unconvincingly.

'It's Mummy. Three glasses of wine and the claws come out.' Rose retracted her hand, and looked down at the table, a nail picking at some of the wax. 'I did my very best and I'm still a disappointment to her – never mind Peter!'

Amelia had long made it clear that Al's way of living was odious to her – but perhaps she found Rose converting her double-first from Oxford into simply a life of comfortable suburban servitude with a nobody husband almost as bad.

Sometimes, Al had thought he could actually see the weight of all his mother's own thwarted ambition, plonked like sand-bags on his poor sister's shoulders. The summer after Rose had graduated, two years ahead of him, Amelia had paraded her around charity balls and functions, shamelessly introducing her as 'my absurdly clever daughter, Rose' – hoping to find her a job opportunity, a husband, or ideally both. Al wasn't sure if Rose had buckled under that weight of expectation, or bravely thrown it off, in choosing to marry Peter – a mild-mannered son of an accountant who did something in the Department for Transport. Not at all like the glittering lawyers or inbred landowners Amelia constantly tried to set her up with.

'If Rose isn't going to pursue her own career, she should at least have given it up for someone *worth* it,' Amelia had a tendency to sigh poisonously after a few drinks, even when rather too close to Rose's (or Peter's) hearing.

Rose had eyeballed Al over her mug of tea. 'Don't leave us to her. It's *Christmas*. Besides, you know, darling, I can't even match her and get sloshed myself this year.'

Al groaned, and put his forehead on his table.

'Can't you go to Peter's family, and leave our lot to pickle in their own sourness?' he said into the grain.

'Mummy dearest threatened to cut the allowance if we didn't go, and we need it for baby things. And the roof repairs. Civil servant salaries aren't exactly all that.'

'You need to free yourself from this acquisitive mindframe, Rosie,' said Al, looking up at his sister, only somewhat mischievously. 'Once you renounce stuff – and recognise you don't absolutely *have* to have five bedrooms and a Chelsea-worthy garden – they can no longer threaten you. It's the big secret that will set you free: *money doesn't matter.*'

Al remembered his father, speechless with rage, slamming the door when Al said those exact words to him some months earlier, insisting with a provoking smile he was 'perfectly happy' living on the dole, and continuing to renounce his inheritance.

Rose scoffed. 'I mean, if you're actually happy living in squalor, then—'

'Living by my principles!'

'Oh come on, what principle? That getting a job is selling out?'

'Well ... yes?'

'Look, if you can manage without their money, congratulations. But if I tried to raise a baby in a place like this, I'd probably be arrested,' she said in her firm voice, looking exaggeratedly over each shoulder around the grimy kitchen. 'So Christmas must be gritted through. And I'd really, really hoped you'd be there with me.' Rose rubbed her just-starting-to-show baby bump, rather manipulatively, Al thought.

When Violet told her mam in clipped tones that Al wouldn't be coming for Christmas after all, she was met with much exclaimed disappointment. But that twisted, and slipped into something else altogether once the thick, creamy envelope arrived.

'Well!'

There was something stagey in the exclamation, something designed to attract attention. Violet brought the eggs through to the tea table in the pan, and saw her mam holding a large Christmas card at arm's length, looking at it as if it might be written in Mandarin. A photograph: an ornate fireplace, a crest, a family – a maid – several maids – dogs – and there was Al. Violet wanted to snatch at it; the pan felt suddenly heavy. In the hot oil, the eggs hissed and spat.

'To Miss Lewis, and family, Wishing you a merry Christmas from Lord and Lady Brinkhurst, and all at Farley Hall.'

There was a trembling pause, like the moment when an object is thrown up in the air and seems to hover at the top of its arc.

'Well!' exclaimed Angharad again, and everything in the room crashed back down to earth, David and Geraint scrabbling for the card, the words 'lord' and 'lady' and 'hall' bouncing around the four walls of their terrace as Violet tried to focus on serving the slippery eggs between jeers and elbows. Only her dad remained still, head down, diligently cutting up a sausage.

'Bloo-dy he-ll, sis!' said David, stretching out and adding syllables incredulously, grabbing at the card and turning it over and over as if it were a puzzle that needed solving. 'You didn't say you were dating an actual bloody *aristocrat*!'

She didn't know what to say. She hadn't really meant to

keep it from them, but in the moment, she felt caught out, and exposed, by the revelation. That her boyfriend lived in a *hall*. Had maids. *Staff*. Would one day be ... Lord Al? *It was all too absurd.*

But Violet completely failing to answer back or make a joke out of it caused her brothers' mocking to quickly fizzle out. Because this wasn't indignant, proud Violet, deserving the best, but rather someone uneasy and wincing. In the face of her embarrassment, they stiffened too.

Angharad carefully placed the card behind others on the mantlepiece so you couldn't really see it.

So when Al finally came to visit Abergavenny with her – the pair of them arriving on the Friday afternoon, Violet in a velvet cape and Al in his sheepskin jacket – he was met with a certain amount of expectation. And then confusion. Her family just didn't know how to behave with someone so different to them.

Her mam had got her hair done specially, and couldn't stop touching it with a small, fluttery gesture, but her little nods at anything Al said rapidly dwindled during the visit. All the aunts and cousins and even the usually indomitable Granny Grey who just happened to 'drop by', desperate to see the actual *lord* their Violet was dating, ended up gawping, stumped by his bohemian appearance. Her brothers reacted to Al's strangeness in the only way they knew how: shut down. Don't engage. If they didn't recognise something, they would attack – or retreat. At least it had been the latter, Violet reflected.

They'd not had a moment to themselves since arriving. Maybe now was a chance.

'Shall we change our shoes, and go up the hill before dinner?' said Violet to Al, hanging back as they approached her house after church. 'While it's not raining for a minute.'

It had been miserable since they'd got to Abergavenny, a fine, almost sideways perpetual rain boxing them indoors. And it got dark so early, Al noticed, a deep grey dark, rolling away and muffled into silence by the sleeping, velvety hills. But even in the gloomy daylight, everything looked grey – the sky, the slate roofs, the damp pavements. The people. It was an uncharitable thought, Al recognised, but being there made Violet seem like a greater mystery than ever. Thank God for higher education grants, he had thought the previous afternoon with a stab of cutting clarity, as he watched her lunking brothers slumped on a too-small sofa, staring at a rugby match on the tiny black and white TV, while her mother made tedious, fussy small talk at Violet about other people's marriages and babies.

'Mam! We're going up the hill!' bellowed Violet from the doorway as Al struggled out of the tight, smart shoes into mucky walking boots, wrapping his trousers around his leg almost twice and stuffing them in at the ankle.

'When are you?' Angharad shouted back down, already half-way upstairs to change out of Sunday best.

'Now in a minute!'

'Well who's going to help me get the dinner?'

'The boys can!'

'Violet!'

But Violet was yanking Al back out the door before he'd got his coat done up. Her shoulders, now cased in a grubby old green jacket, were set back with determination. And Al was gripped with a love that was also a terror of getting things wrong for her.

At the top of the Sugar Loaf, Al doubled over, panting and red-cheeked. Violet, who hadn't broken into a sweat, looked at him triumphantly.

'Too many ciggies,' gasped Al. 'I used to be able to yomp up the hills round us at home without feeling it at all.'

She just tossed her head, like a proud little mountain goat.

'Show off!' he cried, and picked her up and spun her around, her legs seeming almost to fly off into the wild horizon. Violet screamed as loud as she could, and some stuck, solid thing inside was freed into the freezing wind.

'I bloody love it up here,' she said, in a smaller, earnest voice when she'd recovered her stumbling footing, and swayed her body in towards his. *So long; so lovely*, she thought, and wrapped her arms very tight sideways around his trunk.

Al wanted to ask her something, but he didn't really want to hear her answer.

He swallowed, and tried to think of something else to say. But all the small things had vanished in the face of the wide expanse of earth below them, illuminated by the wintery sun and the thin blue brilliance of sky they had climbed into. Now, even the sleeping fields shifted restless in brown and muddy purple, dark green and straw-yellow, the monochrome dullness of the rainy days all but erased.

Maybe it didn't matter what her parents thought, or the people she'd grown up with. Maybe *this* was what mattered, this direct line to nature, and the direct line between them. Something swelled up inside him. Sublime or psychedelic, it was all getting at the same thing.

'Of course you love it up here,' he said. 'It's all so ... *vast*. And free.'

'Isn't it? I forget how much I miss it when I'm in London ... I know there's other ways, but walking up a hill has still got to be the quickest way to enlightenment, I reckon.' She laughed, but she also meant it.

'Do you still believe any of that heavy stuff?' Al asked, grabbing her hand and kissing it quickly.

'Church stuff?'

Al nodded, and felt Violet go still next to him, as she did when she was contemplating something serious.

'Not really. I mean, I still like the singing, and the coming together. But do I actually believe there's a god you can pray to, that meddles in things, and that sent his son to die for our sins ... no. It just – it just doesn't make much sense now, does it?'

'Not a minute of sense. I mean, sin really is the worst lie seized on by the powerful, just such a brilliantly effective way of keeping the masses—'

'All right, Karl Marx, save your speech.' She smiled, and swung his hand, before resuming. 'I suppose the thing is, well, I don't feel like I *have* rejected the core bit: a belief that there is something bigger, more mysterious than us in this universe. You feel it, don't you, when you look at this view? Or when you take a tab. It's just that that doesn't need ... hymns. Or sermons. Or us telling people they're wrong to have desires, or be gay, or whatever.'

'Amen,' said Al cheerfully, kissing the top of her head. 'You took the words practically out of my mouth.'

And Violet felt pleased, and then suddenly strangely resistant. She dropped his hand, and pulled up an old crackling stem of terracotta-coloured bracken, and used it to swipe at the air as they walked.

'But then – I don't think chapel *was* like that, not really. I don't like it when people just ... dismiss it.' Al went quiet, opening up the space for her. And then she softened, recognising that he did that even – perhaps especially – when he didn't agree with her. And that that was rare in men, and she loved him for it.

'I do still miss that ... *collectiveness*. The community of it,' she said, looking a little mournful.

Al nodded, and put his arm around her and held her close.

'That's my house – can you see it? Chimney's going,' Violet said, breaking away and pointing down toward the town, and Al's attention zoomed along her outstretched finger, right down the chimney pot. Her tiny cramped home. Her family.

He didn't know quite how to make sense of them. Whenever he answered Angharad's questions, it was like the words were wrong, or came out in the wrong order, and he could physically feel the silence created by the wrongness. And then Angharad would rush in with a half-comprehending answer or a total non-sequitur, or Violet would try to steer the conversation back to safety, and round and around they went, never quite meeting.

At first, the men had been all puffed up, firm handshakes and back slaps, and when they tried to talk to Al it was like the volume had been turned up needlessly. But every conversation they tried – what team did he support, what car did he drive – he couldn't respond in a way they expected. Al had been excited to discuss politics with Violet's father, but even there they never managed to quite run on the same track.

'You're a union man, I hear, Evan?' Al had asked in their first conversation, while Angharad fussed around pulling out a series of ever tinier nested coffee tables, draping them in doilies, and finally bringing in plates of biscuits and an ugly, squarish orange-patterned tea set.

'That's right. More important than ever now. What union are you part of then?'

'Oh, well, actually I don't at the moment have a ...' Al felt for the first time a shimmer of shame at deliberately being on the dole. 'But of course I stand strong with unions and their right to strike. Wilson's coming for them now, with Barbara Castle leading the charge!'

'Maybe.' Evan paused. 'Not a fan of Harold Wilson then?'

'Well, his government's done some sterling work on social

issues – doing away with the death penalty, the Race Relations
Act, decriminalising abortions and homosexuality—' Al had
been trotting out his usual rapid-fire assessment of the prime
minister, before he noticed with a jolt how Violet's face had
gone even paler than usual. Evan, David, and Geraint were all
looking very closely at their tea cups, which appeared absurd in
their large hands, palms almost as big as the saucers Angharad
had got out specially.

'Ah, but, on economic matters – the unions – um...' Al
gulped down some tea, and it was too hot, and he tried not to
show how it was burning him all the way down his oesophagus.
'I mean, you have to support the workers, or how are you truly
a Labour government?'

There was a grunt in assent, but he suspected he'd lost them.

The question was back on the tip of his tongue, and he knew
he must let it out, if he didn't want the worry to feed and grow
on itself like a cancer.

'Do... do you think your family are disappointed by me,
Violet?' he asked, his heart beating like he'd just climbed the
hill again.

Violet's head flipped up and round to look at him.
Disappointed? Was he mad?

They'd never tried so hard to impress someone, never failed
so comprehensively to just be themselves.

'What? No. They just...'

They're not like you, Violet thought, and she started to shred
the bracken spear. During the weekend, Violet hadn't been able
to quite work out who she was most embarrassed of, or for.

Al softly touched her shoulder, turned her to look at him,
and in his eyes she saw the need. Oh God, he needed reassuring
too! The awkwardness had got to him, even to him.

'Oh, my love, you're not a *disappointment*. It's more ... it's more ...'

He genuinely doesn't know, she thought, looking into his searching eyes, flicking across her face.

'They're intimidated by you!'

A twitching frown.

'Your world! *Our* world, even. It's when you casually mention "the ballet" or "the opera". When they saw that picture of the bloody mansion you grew up in! And yet, half a year after graduating, you also actively choose to not have any money or a job or a nice house or proper clothes ... they don't understand it! Either of it. *Any* of it.'

She barrelled into him again, a reassuring hug, and Al let his hands drop round her shoulders, a little limp. He had thought (although he wasn't proud of the thought) that his upbringing and education might help, really, might impress them. Hadn't considered how confusing his rejection of all that comfort, all that opportunity, might seem to people with so much less.

Al blinked his eyes hard in shame.

'They just never thought I'd be with someone like you, is all. It doesn't mean they're not thrilled,' she lied. 'But I think you just give them a window onto how my life has changed?'

Al pulled her away, and then kissed her softly, thoughtfully, on the forehead.

'You know, it's like your parents too,' she continued. 'They all lived through the war – all their generation wanted afterwards was respectability, and stability, and safety, I suppose. A "good life" for my mam and dad meant a secure job for him and a nice little house for her with nice cushion covers and ... all the *stuff* you could so easily have, with your background and connections and that! All that bourgeois rubbish that you – *we* – don't even want!

'But maybe my mam and dad don't quite realise that I don't want it yet.' Violet groaned lightly, leaning into his chest again. 'You know, I think they really thought I might come back to Aber after I finished the MA. And I suppose seeing how different you – *we* – are … well, it's hard for them.'

Al nodded, and rested his chin a little sadly on her forehead. She was good. She was kinder to her parents than he ever managed to be to his. He found Harold and Amelia's obsession with appearances and status, with hoarding their own power and influence, exhausting and hollow. And although their strict expectations for what he would do with his life – the few kinds of prestigious jobs that were acceptable, the tiny selection of titled women he must choose a wife from – might be worlds away from the expectations of Violet's family for her, both paths were equally prescribed and narrow.

'It's all really changed for you, hasn't it?' Al said, and felt her nodding. 'But it's changed for me too. It's changing for all of us. Like a great, big …' He sliced his hand out, across the spread landscape. 'A great big crack, between the generations. Whether you come from money or not.'

Only a person who comes from money would think of it like that, thought Violet. But still, when she looked out past his hand, she could see the crack snaking down the land, the fields coming apart along the seams of their hedgerows, trees ripping up into the air, an uncrossable dark chasm spreading.

Chapter 5

October 1969

'Well it's a bit different to last year.' Tamsin pulled on a cigarette, drawing in the chill in the air too. The chants had already begun, and Vietnamese flags waved in scarlet folds. But the crowds at the protest were a fraction of those that had pulsated towards Grosvenor Square the previous March, whipped up and high on injustice.

'Yes. Shocking turn-out, really, considering the scale of what's planned in the States today,' said Al as they walked towards the embassy. 'Do you think people were put off after the violence last time?'

'Could be.' Tamsin linked her arm through his and pumped a sign reading *Withdrawal works!* 'Cowards. It's not like things in Vietnam have got any less terrible.'

The previous March, when they were still students in Sheffield, Violet and Al had helped organise coaches to bus people down to the demo. Things had turned ugly after the police moved in, and was declared 'The Battle of Grosvenor Square' in reports the following day.

As the crowd had grown jumpier, as the chants grew faster, and as he watched Johnny baiting and dodging out of the grip of a policeman, Al had felt something rise in him too. But then Violet had taken his hand, tight, and he had seen the small frown on her face. *Hold still*, it seemed to say. *Stay true.* He admired how she moved away from conflict and cockiness, when everyone else was drawn towards it.

'Well it's not peace, is it,' she said, when they talked on the coach home afterwards. 'It's ... male rage. Protesting is *so* important – but those few protesters wanting to smash things or punch a policeman, they're giving in to the same urge as the people we're meant to be protesting *against*. They're just using a good cause as a way of showing how strong and tough they are, instead of a war.'

She had planned to come to the protest today – Violet was as fervent as any of their friends in her anti-war stance. But Rose and Peter were in town that afternoon for a friend's birthday, and were planning on coming round afterwards with baby Susan. As Tamsin, Al and Violet, the last of the housemates to leave for Grosvenor Square, began to wrap up, Violet had looked around their kitchen with dismay.

'Oh bloody hell, look at the state of this place!' Crusted dishes piled in the sink, on a mulchy bed of soggy tea leaves; dead flowers were turning a jam jar green. Multiple saucers were heaped with little snowy mountains of soft ash, and escaped papery skins of garlic rustled in the cracks of the tiled floor.

Violet had put her embroidered leather saddle bag down, heavily.

'I better stay and tidy up, then.'

'No way – leave it. We can do the washing up when we get back.' Al tried to sound breezy. 'It's much more important that you exercise your democratic right as a citizen to refuse imperialist—'

'Al – please, you don't need to lecture *me* about democracy—'

'Well it doesn't matter if things are a bit grubby – it's only Rosie!'

'It's not you who'll be judged by the state of the place, though, is it. It's me. And we promised them food, so one of us had better cook. And do the washing up, so we have something to bloody eat off.'

Rose and Violet had met several times, and while Al could count on Rose — unlike his parents — to always be friendly to Violet, they were not close. He suspected that Rose considered her merely a symptom of Al's peculiar lifestyle, regarding Violet, in her long scarves and ratty maxi dresses, with the same tolerant bemusement she had for all his friends. It was true that their shared house felt a world away from Rose and Peter's home in St Albans, with its curving driveway and matching apricot towel sets and stunning garden. But still, there was no need for Violet to try to impress her by pretending to be straight, pretending to care about the *cleaning*, thought Al.

Violet had begun picking up dishes from the table and putting them down next to the sink as if they had personally insulted her. Tamsin had silently taken Al's arm, and engineered a swift exit.

The mist that had hung, hiding the tops of buildings as they'd taken the freezing bus through town, was beginning to clear as Al and Tamsin entered Grosvenor Square. As they approached the crowd they spotted their friends, and a few new additions: Clara snuggling performatively with a handsome student from Kenya named Bryton; Johnny with his new crowd of friends from art school, unfurling a structurally unsound appliqued banner.

Tamsin gave a low sigh of annoyance.

'Is she one of them?' asked Al. He had yet to meet Johnny's girlfriend, whom he'd got so wrapped up in since starting at Goldsmiths.

'Yes. The little blonde one. *Jilly.* Pale as a snowflake, and just as *precious.*'

Al squeezed Tamsin's arm, her fur coat silky beneath his fingers.

Johnny gave Al such an enthusiastic smack on the lips that he nearly dropped his banner in a muddy puddle; he'd moved to student digs on the other side of London, and they missed each other's daily presence. Tamsin stayed warily away, and re-joined Al next to Ginger once all greetings had been concluded.

As the time passed, they stamped their feet to keep warm, intermittently joining in with, and getting bored by, the chants that waved through the sparse crowd. A guy with two long plaits in his beard started playing 'Masters of War' on an acoustic and a security guard outside the embassy checked his watch. All the while, Al could feel Tamsin staring at Jilly.

He tried, every now and then, to distract her with questions, which she answered monosyllabically. It was strange to see her bothered like this. Tamsin and Johnny had moved in and out of each other's beds so easily for so long, they had seemed almost more solid than many conventional couples. They'd even hang out with each other's latest conquests without any stress; there was a foundation of understanding between them that no newcomer could ever threaten.

Except now Johnny had chosen someone else, all the time.

'I don't need him to myself,' Tamsin eventually declared, turning her head deliberately towards Al, as if continuing a conversation.

'What's that?' Al looked down at her sulky face, and a rush of affection ran down the back of his legs.

'I don't have to have him to myself, it isn't that!' Tamsin said, irate, as if Al was arguing with her.

'No?'

'No! We've been sharing for... *ages*. We're *good* at that. It's *fine*.' Tamsin lit yet another cigarette, and Al wondered if maybe they all needed to cut down. 'It's that now I don't get to have him at all. Ever.'

He wrapped her up in a big hug then, and felt her waft her cigarette tip away from his coat, and his hair.

'I know.'

It was important, Al thought, that he make Tamsin feel better but it was also important that he didn't have to see her crying. He didn't know how he would be able to be friends with Johnny if he had made Tamsin cry, although he also recognised that Johnny hadn't technically done anything wrong.

'I didn't think I'd care – I *hate* caring!'

'Tamsin: you're a human. It would be very weird if you didn't care. Christ, *I* feel a bit abandoned by him even!'

He could feel her nodding her head.

'You might be the worst hippie I've ever met, do you know that?' Al continued to press Tamsin to him, aware of the irony of not being able to look his friend in the face while he told her what he was about to tell her. 'All this peace and love chat – look at you, here to protest war – and yet you won't even admit to yourself that you care about someone—'

'I don't *love* him!' Tamsin pushed away furiously, looking up at Al like an angry cat, arching its back. Her thick hair was sticking up where it had rubbed against the curly fluff of sheepskin. Then she looked around, as if worried someone had heard, flicked away her cigarette butt and hurriedly smoothed her hair down.

'Look, let's just go home,' offered Al. 'We really ought to help with the cooking, at least.'

Tamsin nodded, mutely, and strode off across the green while

Al quickly said his goodbyes. He ignored the subtle twist of Johnny's face, pretending he hadn't seen the question in it.

'Will you be writing about today for the *Standard* at all?' asked Tamsin as they waited, interminably, for a bus, Al feeling guiltier the longer it was delayed.

'Fat chance,' Al snorted. 'They barely let me touch a type-writer.'

Al had been excited, at first, by the opportunity to become tea boy and general dogsbody at the *Evening Standard*. An old school pal had introduced him to a chum who was assistant news editor there, and he'd started within a fortnight. Violet had laughed at the way he was able to get a job so easily, once he finally decided he needed one.

But the role was dull: Al took down copy, searched for cut-tings, sorted the post … and only got to write the shortest, driest news-in-brief stories. It seemed like a step down, really, not only from editing the student newspaper but also the writing and activism he'd dedicated himself to since they graduated.

Al had consciously prioritised passion over a pay packet. He'd spend days cranking out 'Stop the Seventy Tour' flyers for anti-apartheid protest on a Gestetner printing machine Ginger had liberated from somewhere, or dedicate weeks to organising anti-NATO protests, featuring the ceremonial drowning of flags in buckets of red paint. But he also wrote with zeal – mostly free-form screeds for zines run by friends, although he'd been elated when Gandalf's Garden had printed his article explaining, at considerable length, why pacifists had a moral duty to be vegetarians.

Swapping all that for long hours helping other people write stories that only served to prop up the establishment rather than working towards dismantling it did not delight Al. Still, there was no money in promoting revolution, and getting some money had – for the first time in his life – become important.

He had been perfectly happy scraping by on the dole, until there'd been two months where he had failed to make the rent, and the landlord, Nick – an obnoxious thick-necked Cockney with permanently bloodshot eyes – had come round with a baseball bat and used it to gently nudge Clara's crockery teapot to the floor. This sent her into a fit of hysterics Al thought she really rather enjoyed.

What he had not enjoyed was the way Violet had turned her back to him that night in bed, the ridge of her spine seeming to bar his touch.

'I'd *never* be in debt like that. My family has never owed anyone any money, wouldn't even get a washing machine on tick,' she'd said quietly, into the wall, and quick shame had licked through Al's body.

Violet had started earning the minute she finished her Masters, in order to save up for the PhD she was desperate to do. Even though she was told she was bound to get funding, Violet still insisted on getting herself a little financial cushion before starting such a long project, and accepted the offer of paid work with a professor she loathed. At least he was an expert in her field, looking at gender in Shakespeare; she was to index his new book, *The Fickle Female in Troilus and Cressida, Hamlet, and King Lear*. Violet soon grumbled about how dire and sexist his arguments were, and about how gross Professor Andover himself was. The image of this old man leaning too close over her as she worked – 'it's disgusting, I can see all bits of dandruff in his greasy hair' – made Al's stomach turn.

If he could earn some money, perhaps Violet would feel able to just get on with her studies. And, before that, perhaps they could go travelling, or at least on holiday together. It felt like all their friends had been having adventures abroad: backpacking round Nepal, taking the Magic Bus to Afghanistan, living the hippie dream on the West Coast. The latter, at least, seemed doable: Professor Andover might prove useful yet, having mentioned his sister had a flat in San Francisco they could stay in sometime. They'd only have to save enough for the air fare.

By the time Al and Tamsin got back to the house in Ladbroke Grove, Rose, Peter and Violet were already sat round the kitchen table. Jewelled yellow light from the Moroccan lampshade and the smell of the stew simmering on the stove and the sight of Violet holding baby Susan's chubby-jointed little body all combined to ambush Al with a sudden sense of cosy gratitude.

Baby Susan frowned at him, then held out a tiny hand demandingly. Al bent to one knee, and kissed it lavishly till she gurgled with amusement.

Nothing had prepared Al for how he'd felt the first time he held his niece, in the hospital; he'd had no particular interest in children, but the minute she opened her eyes and scowled at him, it was as if he had been knighted. Given a new purpose in this life.

While kissing his sister's cheek and shaking Peter's fleshy hand and refreshing the gigantic communal teapot he'd bought to replace Clara's, Al continued to steal glances at Violet and Susan. Little smiles broke and receded like tiny waves on Violet's lips as she in turn watched every flickering change in emotion run across Susan's face. Seeing them together was almost too tender for him to bear.

He allowed himself to picture Violet holding a tiny, downy body of their own making. As he bent over the teapot to refill it, Al beamed a crazy big secret grin into the steam.

'How was your friend's birthday?' Al asked Rose, bringing

the pot to the table and then turning to tickle Susan under her rolls of chin.

'Very nice. Saw Jeremy, do you remember him? He's living in London now too and doing really rather well for himself...'

Violet watched Al simultaneously politely nodding along and wryly smiling in amused judgement as Rose nattered on about old acquaintances that Al clearly had zero interest in. But it didn't matter: even if each found the other faintly ridiculous – which they evidently did – there was a bond between the siblings, a sort of affection that Violet could feel beneath all their conversations, that didn't have anything to do with what they were actually saying.

Violet liked Rose: sure of herself and her thoughts, she also came across as just uncomplicatedly *satisfied* with her life, bouncing Susan or affectionately patting Peter's hand or talking for far too long, really, about the new rockery she was planning.

But she was bewilderingly different to Al. It was like Rose had just missed a train, Violet thought, the train that Al and she and their friends had leapt on, taking a whole generation somewhere new. What a difference a few years in age could make! Rose had been left behind – and she didn't even seem to mind.

She was just so *straight*. It wasn't just the big, spotless, blandly tasteful house. It was that she bought *The Times* and was 'concerned' about politics, but had never been to a demo. She listened to Verdi and Puccini, not Beefheart or The Byrds; preferred Virginia Woolf to Tom Wolfe. The only thing Violet had ever felt she truly connected with her over was Shakespeare – Rose clapping her hands together and quoting chunks of *Othello* at Violet when she revealed she was doing her Masters dissertation on the physical expression of masculine jealousy in his plays.

Al – who had enraged his parents by choosing Sheffield University over Oxford, on the basis of its lefty reputation – had a tendency to talk about Rose's time at Magdalen dismissively, as if spending the Sixties in the library was a disgrace when you could have been out on the streets. 'All she did at Oxford was study very boring old books, very hard, and then find a man to marry,' he once commented dismissively. Violet had defended a woman's right to be very interested in old books and accused Al of being almost as judgmental as his mother.

But perhaps they both had a point, Violet thought, watching Rose try to hush an over-tired Susan. Because what use was that impressive degree when you only talked to a baby all day?

Baby Susan's grizzling turned to screaming, and Rose went to put her to sleep in Violet and Al's room. When she came back down, they were all discussing women's lib – or rather, Peter had expressed some slight interest in the topic, and Al, Violet and Tamsin had held forth at great length, until Tamsin hotly concluded that marriage was a prison for women, and housework and babies were 'its manacles and chains'.

Violet hastily steered the conversation around to her plans for her PhD – 'on the disruptive physical potential of women's onstage silence at the end of Shakespeare's plays' – and she couldn't stop her face glowing as she talked about how much she'd loved her Masters at King's, how she couldn't wait to get back into her own research again. 'It's just such an … immense *pleasure* to feel your brain being stretched like that – I swear, when I'm working out my arguments on the page, I can actually *feel* my synapses crackling,' Violet said.

But when Rose got up, insisting on doing the washing up, her back turned to the table, Violet worried that perhaps both conversational topics had felt somehow pointed.

So when Rose went creeping upstairs to retrieve baby Susan,

Violet followed. In silence, they gazed down into the carry cot, nestled on the bed, and the soft pink bundle curled within. The existence of perfectly formed miniature humans suddenly seemed so implausible to Violet, it was like magic.

It was then that Rose spoke, almost whispering. 'She's my job now. And what could be more important than making this human the best human she can be? She's the most interesting thing I've ever studied.'

Susan snuffled in her sleep, and something in the gentle movement of her mouth reminded Violet of Al's face in rest. The sudden urge to stroke her little face, to gather up and squeeze Susan's tiny body tight, came over Violet in a wave of almost painful sweetness.

I do want one, Violet thought, a stab of sudden certainty in her solar plexus. Then the thought butted in, sharply: *But not yet*.

First, there were books to read and arguments to be made and papers to publish. Places to go – Indian beaches, Greek islands, Moroccan souks; Istanbul, Kathmandu, San Francisco. To see how far she could get from south Wales, and who she might be when she got there.

A baby would have to wait.

Chapter 6

July 1970

The first impression of San Francisco was a disappointment. But it was also the only time Al had ever felt the urge to photograph a street sign. Two little words. *Haight. Ashbury.* Al clicked the shutter quickly, then let the camera drop to his chest, as if he'd never taken a picture at all.

Cloudy with jet-lag after their first ever long-haul flight, he and Violet kicked off their holiday by heading straight to the infamous neighbourhood – the birthplace of the hippie movement and the summer of love, their counter-culture mecca, that they'd both been desperate to visit for so long. And yet there it was, full of dogshit and junkies.

It was as if the film reel Al had imagined – freaks sat around singing 'Hey Mr Tambourine Man'; head shops and thrift stores blasting music into sunshine; tanned girls with actual flowers in their hair – was water-damaged: everything seemed grimier, gloomier. A hamburger packet rustled around their feet, and the sky above was ominous with amassing, bulky clouds. A woman with vacant eyes swerved towards them, and then snarled away when she saw their blanching expressions. A man in a headband with a paunch beneath his fringed waistcoat grinned as he approached, but then just shouted at Violet 'watch your purse, little lady!'

'It's a bit … *dirtier* than I was expecting,' Violet said, sounding uncertain.

'I think we might be too late,' said Al, pressing her hand in recognition that the scene had moved on. They'd missed the moment.

It was an anti-climax, especially given how long they'd been saving up for the flights, for a trip abroad together. Their antici-pation for San Fran, in particular, had been brewing for months – ever since Professor Andover revealed his sister's apartment in the Russian Hill district would, in fact, be free for the entire summer. It seemed like the perfect moment for an extended break: Violet had finished her work indexing Andover's book, but wouldn't start her PhD till the autumn, assuming she did get the expected funding for it. Al, meanwhile, was at a loose end, career-wise: he'd recently quit his job at *the Evening Standard* in pursuit of a promised job at a new radical left-wing publication, which had folded before it even managed to launch, to his enormous frustration.

But it did mean the summer was theirs – long, free, and set to be spent in a new city, a whole new country. And as their jet lag and the city's fog both lifted, so too did Violet and Al's initial misgivings. The rest of San Francisco proved as enchanting as they'd dared hope, and they were happy to play tourists for a while: walking its hills, cycling the Golden Gate bridge, and being shocked at how cold the sea was to swim in.

It was while browsing a hip bookshop that Al picked up a copy of the city's *RiZe* magazine, a notorious underground publication often spoken about as America's best, that he'd been on the lookout for. All the rest of the day, he couldn't stop reading bits of it aloud to Violet.

'The politics are right-on, the culture writing is sharp, the

illustrations are great – it just has this energy, this urgency...'
he enthused, waving the copy in Violet's face.

'Well, why don't you go and introduce yourself, while we're
here?' she suggested eventually. 'Pitch them an idea or two. You'd
be a good fit for it, I reckon.'

And so it was that Al steeled himself to go back to Haight-
Ashbury – where the office of *RiZe* was based, just off the
main intersection. The magazine had been founded there by
one Micky Mountain as a DIY venture during the neighbourhood's hippie explosion, and grown steadily more legitimate,
recently netting financial backing from *Rolling Stone* founder
Jann Wenner.

The building was decorated with a mural of the caterpillar
from *Alice in Wonderland*, the name 'RiZe' painted in swirly,
smoke-like writing around the doorway, emanating from the
caterpillar's hookah. Al knocked, his hand perspiring into a page
of notes of ideas for articles he'd brought with him.

'What? We're in the middle of an editorial meeting – make
it quick,' a man with huge aviator shades, a walrus moustache
and a cowboy hat opened the door and bellowed in his face.

'Uh, hello – I'm – um, my name's Al, and I wanted to, uh,
speak to someone about writing for the – the magazine...?'

'You English?'

'Ah, yes, in fact, I am. Very English indeed.' Being in America
had for some reason made Al start speaking like he worked for
the BBC.

'Huh.' The man rubbed his moustache. 'Weird. We were just
talking about this Edward Heath cat. Your recent elections?'

Al's brain whirred.

'Actually, I was *just* going to suggest an article about *exactly*
that. How, ah ... that is, what the unexpected Conservative
victory means for Britain's leftwing... um—'

The aviator shades didn't look impressed. Al could feel sweat accumulating behind his neck.

'And, ah, did you know – the pollsters think it was partly down to the World Cup?' Al continued, with a slightly desperate rise to his voice. 'It affected national mood, voter turnout, that sort of thing. I could, uh, write a piece on that: How Football— I mean, How Soccer Killed Socialism . . . ?'

The moustache twitched. 'Hm. You better come in and talk to Micky.'

Introducing himself as Jonjo, the man ushered Al into a small office, filled with mismatched chairs, typewriters, ashtrays, and gig flyers. Six men were sat around a large central table, looking weary, in the midst of an ideas meeting which, it seemed, was seriously short on ideas. A few thoughts were scrawled on a blackboard, mostly struck through or with large question marks next to them. In front of it sat the famous Micky Mountain. He had surprisingly terrible teeth for an American, and a conspicuously large bulge in his tight white cotton loons.

'This is Al, he's English, he wants to pitch you, Micky. Which seeing as no one else seems to have any fucking suggestions this week might be worth a shot,' said Jonjo, sitting down heavily next to Micky, and gesturing almost dismissively towards Al. 'Shoot, kiddo.'

Micky Mountain met Al's gaze for a moment, his pale blue eyes exerting the draw of a deep, strong current. Here, then, was the man to impress, the still centre of power.

Al swallowed, hard, and started to reiterate his hasty pitch about the election. As he trailed off, Micky Mountain sighed, slightly, and Jonjo threw up his hands in frustration, and Al felt so awkward at being thrust into their impasse that he simply carried on, rattling through his list of other, better planned-out ideas for articles.

He was speaking at speed about an insider look at British boarding schools – their screwed-up psychology and bullying traditions, and how these were replicated at the top of every powerful institution in England – when Micky raised a hand.

'Stop – Al, was it? I like that one. Psychology stuff is going down well at the moment. You have your own experience you can bring into it, I assume? Open those wounds.'

'Yes, right, absolutely. Glad you—'

'You can file by Friday?'

'Of course.'

When Al hand-delivered the piece three days later, Micky read it immediately in front of him, and gave a slight nod. 'You have a light touch,' he said softly, turning the sheets (copied out in Violet's neater hand) back over. Al couldn't stop his grin – he'd worked over the article endlessly, Violet reading and noting several drafts, and banning him from attending a Quicksilver gig at the Fillmore until he'd finished it.

'Thank you. Actually, I have some more suggestions for other articles? I wondered if—'

Micky held up a hand, gravely. 'Come back Tuesday. Our next editorial meeting, midday. Till then.'

Al turned up to the meeting with more pages of suggestions, pitched with a dry mouth but such springy enthusiasm that he could feel the team warming to him. He was commissioned to write an insider portrait of the British Black Panthers (Al slightly exaggerated how well he knew a founder, Darcus Howe), and an explainer on the significance of south London to David Bowie, offering a flavour of Bromley and Beckenham for the clueless American reader.

And Al thought he sniffed a longer-term opportunity. They were clearly interested in running international stories; why not angle himself as an informal London correspondent? He and Violet still had almost two months of holiday left – surely time enough to prove himself as a writer and endear himself to *RiZe*'s team, and perhaps ultimately persuade them to continue to commission him occasionally once he was back home. No more jobs as tea boy – instead writing the sorts of journalism he'd always dreamed of, long and loose articles, about radical politics and progressive culture, about music and mysticism and whatever else he was able to convince Micky was worth the wordcount.

During the next few weeks, Al made sure he buttered up *RiZe*'s staff outside of the office as well as at ideas meetings, buying beers for their lead interviewer, Perry, when he just happened to bump into him at gigs, or wangling himself an invitation to Jonjo's self-proclaimed 'legendary' beachside barbeque, and eating so many ribs and wings that he vomited in the toilet immediately after getting home. 'So much for vegetarianism,' Violet muttered, holding Al's hair back.

Micky was the exception: Al did not approach him. People buzzed around Micky like flies, and Al didn't want to get swatted.

It was only at the start of September, when Micky came and stood next to *him* at The Lighthouse and they nodded in silence to a jazz quintet's lengthy set, that Al felt secure enough to put his plan into action – to suggest to Micky that he might become something of a roaming, London-based contributor.

They had a date set for their return now: 1 October, just a few days before Violet's first meeting with her PhD supervisor at King's. She'd finally heard, after a series of inexplicable admin delays, that she had indeed got her funding; a brief, long-distance phone call from her mam met with squeals and hugs.

Al had booked a fancy seafront restaurant for a special celebratory dinner, that they couldn't really afford. He hoped to be able to bring his own good news to it, too – to offer Violet the reassurance that he'd have some employment, however sporadic, once home. They could both toast their future together in London: her a brilliant academic, he an international freelance journalist...

On the day of their dinner, he went to *RiZe*'s office early in the morning, to try to catch Micky alone. He was bent over some proofs and indicated for Al to sit at the large table, and wait.

'What did you think of that piece we ran last week on Anaïs Nin?' Micky looked up, abruptly, neatening his pages.

Al's brain raced. It had been a coup to get the journalist, who usually wrote for *Oz*. But he'd thought the final piece was unpenetrating, and Violet had hated it. 'It is *ty*-pi-cal' – her accent had picked through the word crossly – 'of a male journalist: he is more interested in her screwing another famous man than he is in *her*, all that stuff about Henry bloody Miller. She's interesting because of how *she* writes about women's desire – not just because of who she sleeps with.'

'Well... it was a good hire,' Al replied to Micky, and then paused. As the pause stretched, Al thought he sensed that the question might be a test – of his honesty, and of his journalistic instincts.

'It was disappointing, to be honest, Micky. I mean, the writer seems more interested in Henry Miller than Nin for half the piece. But her writing is interesting because it's so unflinching on *women's* desire – *that's* what we should have really gone in deep on.'

Micky nodded, and simply said, 'Yes. That's it.' When he asked a moment later what it was Al wanted – and Al began his spiel, asking if he could continue write for them, from London, somehow – Micky began to smile and held up a hand.

'Al. I don't want you to go back to England. I want you to stay here, and work for us.'

Al's insides jumped.

'I know it's a big change, and a big commitment' – Micky raised his hands as if anticipating Al's refusal, then paused, and slowly smiled his charismatic, snaggle-toothed grin as he spread those hands, turning the defensive gesture into that of a generous offer.

'But, Al, my friend, this is also an opportunity. A very big opportunity. You'd be one of us. On the inside, writing, editing, coming up with ideas for other folks too. I've been impressed by how quickly you understood the magazine, the local scene as well as its international outlook. I want you to help shape the direction – *the future* – of *RiZe*.'

Al couldn't quite believe it: Micky Mountain was pitching *him*, not the other way round.

'Say yes.'

How could he say no, to that offer – that career-transforming, life-changing offer? And how could he say no – to *RiZe*, to Micky Mountain?

'Yes.' The word seemed to speak itself, true and certain, but even as Micky was slapping Al on the shoulder and steering him towards 'his' desk, somewhere in the dark shadowy cavern at back of Al's skull another voice was shouting *No no no*, was howling, *But what about Violet what about London what about Violet Violet Violet—*

That evening, Al waited until after they'd toasted her funding, raising a glass of good Russian River chardonnay to 'the future Doctor Lewis' as she proudly tossed her long hair, lightly curling in the thick salty air of the sea breeze.

Then he took a deep breath. 'So, I finally had the chat with Micky this morning.'

Violet's eyes widened, brightening. 'How did it go ...?'

'Well. Really really well.' Al didn't know how to phrase it, and as he struggled to find the words, it became harder and harder to hold onto the idea that he had, in fact, made the right decision in the moment.

Al took a rather large slug of the wine.

'It was your doing, actually – the thing that swung it was your opinion on that Nin piece, I reckon, which I parroted back at Micky. And yes, I am very aware of the irony of that ...' Al laughed, deflecting, putting the moment off.

The moment when he had to say: *I'm not coming home with you.*

'Oh, don't be daft,' replied Violet lightly. 'They like *you* – who you are, your ideas.'

He avoided her eager gaze.

'So – go on? What did he say? Are you going to be *RiZe's* chief London correspondent then, or what?'

'He said ...' Al fiddled with a loose thread on the edge of his embroidered sleeve. 'He offered me a job. A proper one, member of staff. Helping shape the magazine. And I, um ... I said yes.'

Al finally looked up. Violet's face was radiant, and her hand shot across the table to grip his in delight.

'Oh, Al! That's incredible – that's just incredible!' For a second Al was stunned, by how generous she was, to give him such instant, unflinching support, when this job was only going to make things so much harder for her, for them.

Then he realised he hadn't been clear.

'It's, um, it's here. In San Francisco. The role, I mean ... I'll be in the office. Writing, and editing, and, um ...'

Violet tried to control her expression, but she felt like everything behind the skin of her face was crumbling, disintegrating, falling down inside her.

'And you've said … you'll take it? You already said yes?' She kept her face very still, very tight, eyes still widened and mouth frozen in her previous smile of congratulation, as if she couldn't let her features move at all or they might collapse completely and betray her.

Al nodded, glumly, and although he began to tell her what an exciting opportunity it was and how he really had just *had* to say yes, his triumph was actually fast evaporating at the thought of what the job really meant for him and Violet. Of only having another few weeks together in San Francisco. And then being apart, for God knows how long … But somehow, he couldn't speak his doubt or give voice to those fears; instead, Al could hear himself at a distance, prattling on, as if desperately trying to shore up his own belief in the correctness of his hasty acceptance.

Violet couldn't bear to look at him anymore. She half turned on her wicker chair to stare instead at the ocean as Al ran out of words. The smile still stuck tightly on her lips, she tried to let the rage inside her ebb away, rather than roar over her.

She wanted to ask the question, the question he hadn't yet raised. *How long—?*

How long will we be apart – how long will I have to live without you in London?

She took a deep breath, in and out, determined not to show how devasted she felt. Somehow, she couldn't be the one to ask. *How long how long—*

Let him have this, Violet told herself sternly. She didn't want to spoil his moment. It *was* a great opportunity, after all. He had been doing his best writing for *RiZe*; she could see how well he and Micky clicked. If Al had asked her, she would have had to tell him to seize the opportunity, would have reassured him that they could make it work.

But he *hadn't* asked her, a small internal voice said. And now, announcing the plan, he hadn't even mentioned the distance. Did he not even care – did their relationship really mean so much less than his career? Or had he just not even stopped to think about it...?

Al watched Violet watching the sea. The water was beginning to darken as the sun inched down behind it, the sky bleaching to the palest shell-pink and stone-washed blue. Somehow, she was still smiling. *Putting on a brave face, surely.*

Perhaps, thought Al in a sudden rush, perhaps there was a different way – perhaps they *didn't* have to be apart? Violet loved San Francisco too, after all – she was always going on about how much she liked the lifestyle, the sunshine, the open-minded people, swimming in the ocean, and in other people's pools. Couldn't she stay with him, for a little longer at least...?

Their food arrived, Al opting for celebratory lobster, while Violet pointedly stuck to a vegetarian pizza. As Al started eating, the thoughts continued to tumble through his mind. Maybe this was a solution! Maybe Violet could just push back her start date – Shakespeare could wait a few more months, or another year, after all. She could get work in a bar easily enough, they'd met plenty of other British and Australian and French girls doing just that... Or – or she could just get a head start on her reading, but from the beach!

'So, do you have to take the funding... right now?' asked Al, cracking a lobster claw.

'What do you mean?' Violet spoke through a mouthful of dough.

'Well... can you, you know, delay the start time?'

'Of my PhD?'

Al looked expectant, made some vague gesture with his hands.

Violet put down her slice, and crossed her legs, deliberately, under the table. Her denim cut-offs dug into her flesh, still white despite all the sun.

'Why ... why would I want to do that, Al?'

'I just suddenly thought – if you could – and of course maybe you can't – but if you *could*, you could stay here for a bit?'

'And why would I want to do that?'

She saw him floundering for words, but she felt merciless. *Let him say it.* She would give him all the rope he needed. *How fucking dare—*

'Well, *obviously* I don't want us to be apart – but now I've got this job – and you love San Francisco – so it just occurred to me that, maybe, you might be able to push things back, and stay here for a while ...'

'And not do my PhD, is that what you mean?'

She saw him swallow, and press on.

'Of course I don't mean—'

'Not do the PhD I just heard I got full funding for? The one that I've been saving for, for ages, indexing that bloody book? The one that was on the cards way before we even decided to come here, for what was only really meant to be a *holiday.*'

She picked up a crust again, but before it reached her mouth, found herself almost shouting, 'I have my own work to do, Al!'

He had the grace to blush, then, but a cold growing chill was already creeping steadily over Violet's body.

'No, no no no no, obviously I'm not saying *don't* do your PhD ... I just thought maybe, maybe you could just push it back a year, or not even a year—'

'Jesus Christ, Al! What the hell?' Violet pushed back her chair, with a crunching scraping sound. 'First you take a life-changing job – without even *talking* to me about it, without even *thinking* about what it might mean for me, for *us*. And then – then!

– you genuinely suggest that I should give up my studies, my career, my work to – what? Follow you around Haight-Ashbury sniffing out stories? Straightening out your arguments for pieces that only have your name on? No fucking thanks.'

Violet grasped at her own throat, shocked at words coming out like darts, that she could see were finding their target. Somehow, at some point, she had stood up.

'That's – woah, OK. That's unfair.'

'Unfair! Unfair is you not even stopping to think, for one little minute now, what *I* might want. That you might perhaps support me in *my* career.'

'Well Shakespeare isn't fucking going anywhere, is he? This magazine's time is now – *my* time is *now!*'

Violet's pulse raced, but all her words vanished. It was like she had dropped into a deep, white, roaring sea, and was incapable of opening her mouth lest saltwater flooded in.

Seeing a worried-looking waitress moving towards her, an awareness of where they were – and of how loudly she'd shouted – came crashing back over Violet. She grabbed her satchel from under the table, and walked out of the restaurant with as much dignity as she could manage, holding her chin high as if that might prevent the tears from spilling out of her eye sockets. Down the road, at a bus stop, she finally let them fall, bawling and crumpling in on herself, missing three buses in a row and scaring a toddler whose mother silently passed Violet a packet of Kleenex.

Al stayed in his seat at the table, grimly drinking the rest of the bottle of wine as if it were medicine, until the sun had set completely and everything went dark. He felt tilted, unsure quite how he'd ended up in this situation.

This disoriented feeling – of something having shifted be-tween them – continued throughout their last weeks together

196

in San Francisco, until suddenly it was the first morning in October and Al wasn't sure he knew how to bear it. He sat blankly at his desk at *RiZe*, unable to get anything done.

He tried to hold on to the fact that he had got what he wanted – the job was all official; he had his own chair, his own typewriter. But all he could really think about was the arc an aeroplane was taking at that very moment, across the curve of their planet, away from him. Taking Violet back to London. Five thousand miles away.

The clouds kept puffing past like something from a children's cartoon. They were ridiculous; chewable, clutchable. But watching California and its coast below shrinking rapidly felt symbolic now to Violet, infused with significance.

She and Al had made up, after their terrible fight, with first stiff and then soft apologies. The need to make the most of their last few weeks together outweighed any simmering resentments. But now, as the aeroplane reached its cruising altitude, the reality of being apart from Al – the thought of not rolling into him, half-asleep, for spongy morning kisses; of not being able to throw down her battered bag and tell him what her new supervisor was like – made Violet's head feel light and empty. She continued staring out of the little windows, counting clouds, trying to pretend to herself that her eyes didn't keep blurring with tears at the thought of all the miles, stretching out behind her, separating them.

For a second, Violet remembered the uncertainty she had felt when trying to imagine, at nineteen, who she would be in the world without Max. But she'd been young then. *And shy, and silly, and a totally different person.*

Maybe it all seemed unreal because aeroplanes were so unreal. The air was already dry, and stale. The flight attendants, lips slathered in a waxy, orangeish regulation lipstick and calves taut in navy heels, trotted up and down the aisle like well-trained show dogs. She'd been charmed, on the journey out, by the dinky foil-covered tray, the miniature compartments of food, until she'd tried it. The bread roll was like a dried face sponge; the pat of butter solid and slippery as soap.

Violet reached into her satchel and unfolded the latest copy of *RiZe*. She was proud of Al. It was good. Well, mostly; some of the writers had more bravado than insight, and she thought Perry's interviews were too much about Perry (Perry, whom Al admired so much that she hadn't told him about the time he'd felt her up at a gig at the Winterland when Al left her alone with him).

Al's pieces were often among the funniest and freshest, she thought – and then he would land a political point (often honed through conversation with her) in the final lines. It was that flair for a serious-minded sucker-punch that had been noticed by Micky. And now, he was on the inside, 'learning how they really do it,' Al had said, repeatedly.

How long the learning process would be had been left unclear.

Violet said yes to the stewardess's offer of a drink, sipping greedily at the slightly flat gin and tonic even though it was still the morning. And she began to turn her thoughts to her new life in London.

After a few scrabbling phone calls, she had found a place to move into: a commune, in a condemned property on Matilda Street in Islington. Lily Jamieson, one of the few women she'd met at an academic conference earlier in the year, had let her know that there was a room going spare in the squat and Violet had quickly said yes.

A few years ahead of Violet, Lily had an impressive career already, her research focusing on the 'erotic confusion' of cross-dressing in Elizabethan drama. She had insisted, in a brilliant, provocative paper titled 'Olivia Liked Viola', that at the end of *Twelfth Night*, Olivia would rather marry Viola than her male twin. At the conference, she'd cited Violet's first published paper on the potential meanings of Olivia's silence towards him in the final scene, and Violet had experienced a warm pleasure at hearing her words coming out of Lily's mouth. Even better, Lily had made a beeline for her at the end and insisted that Violet come for dinner with her at a vegetarian restaurant down the road.

Over the phone, Lily had described the commune as a 'radical feminist living space' and Violet felt a flicker of excitement at joining their fold when she arrived back in London.

It had been a revelation watching Lily talk to male academics at the conferences. She was exceptionally pretty in a way that they seemingly couldn't help but make assumptions about: she had very blonde curly hair, an upturned little nose and an equally upturned upper lip, which made her look perpetually eager. As men approached Lily during the coffee breaks, clearly intending to flirt with her rather than talk about her work, she'd icily reiterate facts and theories until they talked to her in the same way they would a man. Or until they walked away, fuming.

Violet, on the other hand, often found herself tongue-tied during small talk, conscious of how out-of-place her Welsh accent sounded. The first time she'd delivered a paper, nervously fast, a male lecturer had jokingly shouted 'Speak English!' Violet felt sure people looked on her as a special case; afterwards, they often asked about her background, not about her work.

'Ignore them,' Lily had insisted, vehemently, when Violet once confessed her fears about never being accepted into their world. 'And then prove them wrong. But it won't be easy – a working-class Welsh woman, talking about Shakespeare? You're going to have to work twice as hard as someone like ... well, someone like your Al.'

It was true, thought Violet, staring out of the little plane window, crystalised with ice. She had her own work to do.

Violet rolled up *RiZe* and put it back in her satchel. She drew out her copy of *Measure for Measure*, and a pencil, and opened it at act V.

Chapter 7

September 1971

Al watched the naked bodies writhing on the mattresses beneath him. It was as if he was in a strange wildlife documentary, looking down onto a forest floor, limbs like centipedes flowing over one another.

Actually, they weren't flowing. Flowing was what you wanted; flowing was what you had been told to expect of an orgy. Instead it was all elbows and shuffling. Visible tan lines and flabby pale bottoms. 'Are you ...?' 'Can I just ...?' Shuffle-shuffle. Admittedly, the low blue light, a sheet of cellophane taped around the main bulb, helped the vibe. But they were all just bodies. It was about as erotic as visiting a greengrocer.

Al squeezed himself back out of the door, just as a man grunted into a loud, abandoned orgasm, and he tried not to think about Violet. He also tried not to think about how on earth he was going to write an insightful piece for *RiZe*, his first as deputy editor, on the sexual politics of free love, orgies, and long-distance relationships when really all he wanted was to be on the other side of the world with just one woman.

Al was still loving working for *RiZe*, and his recent promotion felt like a significant recognition. He had finally found his groove and, thanks to his deepening friendship with Micky, he'd been introduced to all the most interesting people in San Fran.

Weekends were spent travelling breathlessly beautiful stretches of coast to Big Sur and Carmel, or going to parties at the cottages of rock stars in Laurel Canyon. But it all came at a cost. He missed Violet painfully, a physical ache for her, right inside his bone marrow.

And as the months had gone, long-distance had proved difficult. Their nightly calls, rigidly scheduled because of the time difference (a luxury only afforded to them by Amelia becoming sentimental after too many glasses of wine and agreeing to pay all of Al's eye-watering phone bills), had lost the lustre of the first few weeks, full of yearning and eager updates. The distance stretched between them and neither really had enough to say, night after night. The sense of obligation grew dull and heavy, and they ended up bickering – or worse, allowing gaps and silences to expand down the line.

So, one night in April, tired after a long day and horny without Violet, he said it.

'How would you feel about trying an open relationship?'

Later, he wondered if he'd asked the question merely to provoke a response, fed up of the strained, empty conversation that seemed to be all they had in them.

Or maybe he said it because of Cassandra. The tall, deeply earnest illustrator had been visiting *RiZe* almost weekly lately, and always came over and perched on Al's desk. She gave off a faint body heat and with it a gentle whiff of some kind of warm, spicy wood. Her very long legs were shapely but strong, and her syrupy brown eyes held his gaze without embarrassment as she told him how much she loved his accent.

'It's just I was reading this thing, by a feminist who called monogamy "the last corset", um...' – Al felt less sure about what he'd said to Violet, with every word – 'and I was also talking to someone who's done it long-distance and, now that I'm going to be out here a bit longer, maybe it is time to talk about, er...'

Violet didn't say anything.

Al held his breath. She must be furious with him, he thought, for even daring to suggest such a thing. And he was surprised to feel a sudden push of relief. Maybe the answer wasn't to be found in other people, after all. Maybe the answer was between them.

'Yes,' Violet said, carefully, her voice sounding as far away as it ever had. 'Yes, I do think that might be wise, actually.'

Violet dragged the phone into her room, and perched on the end of the bed, the cord stretched tight round the doorframe. She didn't want this conversation to be overheard until she understood it herself, and there was always someone coming or going in the soot-blackened, squatted townhouse on Matilda Street. She kicked the door to her bedroom shut, and cradled the receiver to her ear, feeling a little light-headed.

Because it was a relief, a shockingly huge relief, to hear him suggest an open relationship.

'Thank you, Al. For having the ... bravery, to bring it up.'

'Oh! Well, no, sure.' Al tried to smile down the phone, but his lips were wobbling in different directions, and he thanked God they'd had this conversation a whole continent apart. 'And only if, you know, you're actually sure – I don't want to be the patriarchal man, forcing you into—'

'No, Al. I do want it, I think ... Well, women have needs too!' Violet laughed, and it sounded tinny and cheap even to her own ears. 'We've seen our friends open up, and have a lovely time, haven't we? And we've talked about jealousy before, and how that's just not our thing. As long as we're loving, and honest, and open-hearted ... I think it will be all right?'

'Yes. Love is the main thing, isn't it? And I do love you, Violet—'

I love you so so much, Al wanted to say. *You have no idea how much, how completely and utterly I fucking love you,* but there was a fat lump in his throat and he knew if he said it he'd start crying, and he couldn't quite bear for her to hear that when she wasn't able to reach out and touch him and make things right.

He hadn't seen Violet since she'd flown back out to San Francisco for a few weeks in January, to celebrate their twenty-fourth birthdays (an indulgence also funded by his parents, which Al hated asking for, but would grit his teeth over if it meant he got to see Violet).

Violet heard the swallow and struggle, and wanted to wrap her arms around Al. But a kernel of annoyance also hardened inside her. Because, really, *how* was their relationship ever going to work if he could barely manage even the most basic 'I love you' down the phone?

And anyway, a different thought kept intruding.

'There isn't ... there isn't anyone else already – is there?'

Violet felt like she was playing a very accelerated game of chess, as if with each utterance she moved in and out of power, or danger, like a poor pawn.

'No! God, no!'

Nothing had happened with Cass, Al thought. No need to tell Violet yet. But now it could, without any guilt. And yet suddenly, all he really wanted was Violet.

He should just get on a plane and see her, this was absurd.

'And there's not anyone for you either?'

'No! No,' said Violet.

There genuinely wasn't, and there was also everyone. Any swiftly passed stranger could set off an explicit train of thoughts. Violet found herself thinking about sex in the library (with that man in the glasses, hard, against the shelves), in the theatre (clenching in her seat at an alarmingly erotic *Taming of the Shrew*), on the bus (staring at the back of a stranger's head). It was like an itch she couldn't reach.

'And this ... "agreement" – it's just in the interim. A practical thing,' Al said.

He sounds forced, Violet thought. Hesitating, almost upset. *But it had been his suggestion. It was his idea.*

'It was Al's idea' became a justification that Violet clung on to, tightly. She whispered it to herself, when she went home with someone within an hour of meeting them, or when she let a much older, married professor take her over his desk because the desperation of his desire made her feel powerful. Because even now she could scratch the itch, it never stopped itching.

In the two months that followed the agreement, Violet became intoxicated, high on her body's ability to give her pleasure – and her ability to persuade seemingly any man she wanted to help her find it. *With zero risks!* she smiled, popping the pill and reaching for a glass of water. *And guilt free!* she thought, gleefully hugging her bare legs as she waited for a stranger to come back from the shared bathroom in Matilda Street, refusing to feel any guilt when he picked up and flicked through the Aldous Huxley novel Al had bought her on their birthday from the bedside table.

So when Al said he had hooked up with a girl from work – 'but it doesn't mean anything' – it was actually another relief. More than a relief: Violet felt a small seam of pleasure at the thought that they were both making it work. That they were successfully living by their principles, and transforming the rules of their love.

She would tell anyone who would listen that she truly believed their generation had unlocked the biggest secret of all:

HOLLY WILLIAMS

sex was joyful, not sinful. Why wouldn't you share that intense spiritual and physical connection with as many beautiful people as possible, instead of jealously hoarding it? She would not feel shame simply because her church, her community, her family, had brought her up that way. She would not feel shame simply because she was a *woman*.

And anyway, it had been Al's idea.

'Look, Violet. You know there's no judgement in this household.' Chris looked up from laying out a feeble potato crop from Matilda's garden on the kitchen windowsill. 'It's just... is all this running around with strangers really making you happy?'

Violet frowned, lifted the spoon grandly into the air from the large pan where she was making jam, and turned to face Chris with it. The radical living arrangement at Matilda Street was non-hierarchical, naturally, but some people are also just natural leaders – and Chris was theirs. She was in her late thirties, with a short crop of straw-like hair that she usually covered with colourful headscarves, and had worked as a civil servant, before quitting and taking a series of steps 'down and left'. By the time Violet met her, she was running a shelter for battered women in Finchley.

'I mean, sure,' Chris continued, not put off by Violet's spoon wielding, 'I dig all this finely honed ideological theory. But can you really claim that letting a guy you barely know shove his knob up your bum after getting you to sniff amyl nitrate is a "spiritual connection"?'

'I don't "let" anyone do anything to me, Christine Conolly. You see, this is the problem, even in our choice of language, we're still reflecting a patriarchal system where men *do* and women just receive—'

'Uh-uh, stop right there. You've got a cheek lecturing me

on language use – when you're using my name wrong!' She chucked a particularly stunted tuber at Violet's bum. Violet dodged it, stuck out her tongue, and then kicked the offending potato across the filthy tiled floor towards the overflowing compost bin. 'All I mean is, *is* it really joyful and respectful, and all those things you said it could be, or are you just frustrated being trapped in a relationship—'

'Did Lily tell you to "have a chat" with me?' Violet tried to look sternly at Chris. 'Because you know she just wants to convert me ...'

It was a lazy deflection, she knew, even if Lily and Chris did reliably try to persuade Violet of the merits of political lesbianism whenever they got onto a second bottle of red.

'Well we all want *that* darling,' laughed Chris, despite having made it very clear within weeks of Violet moving in that she was not at all her type ('no meat on your little bones').

'Anyway, I'm not trapped, I want to be with Al—'

Chris held up her large palms. 'No, I know! Sorry! *Language.* But before the – what is it you call it, the arrangement?'

'The agreement.'

'Before the agreement, when you moved in, you were frustrated. Right? And you had grand ideals for what free love could be. But now, well, maybe you don't seem so frustrated, but you do seem ... a little manic?'

Violet stirred the pan aggressively. What did Chris and Lily know, about her needs, her pleasure? Chris hadn't had a serious relationship for ages, while Lily apparently had whatever woman she wanted whenever she wanted them.

'I have a good time!' Violet said to Chris, but her voice sounded smaller than she'd expected it to. 'I've told you this before, it works for me: I find it easy to, *you know*. Anyway, I don't need romance or soppy stuff; I've got that with Al.'

'Well, sure.' Chris had turned away, washing her hands in a sink still half full of poster paints from the children's workshop they'd run at their big kitchen table that morning. 'But isn't it the *connection* the bit that you always evangelise about? Just sex might be easy, but is it worth it? Because it looks like it's become a ... compulsion, maybe, rather than a beautiful magical thing?'

Violet decided the jam needed her entire attention. The fruit bubbled furiously away beneath her, gone bright and glossy, as the red crept up the large brass thermometer. It was true, she thought, that since the agreement, her way of moving through the world had changed. She used to lose herself in music, in the fuzzy high of the weed, and the circle of Al's arms – and occasionally thought it might be nice to just slide easily into someone else's, like Tamsin and Johnny allowed each other to do. But now she *was* allowed to do that, it wasn't occasional, it was constant: the looking around at all-nighters and concerts, wondering who it would be, greedily seeking eye contact. Trying to dance so she looked alluring, to make her hips suggest sex; choosing dresses that emphasised her tiny waist or her neat shoulders, rather than just whatever let her move easiest. It all took up so much space in her brain.

The next morning, there'd be awkward conversations with nice guys who thought she wanted to start something, and she'd feel a brush of uncertainty – *not guilt*, just uncertainty – about whether she was hurting their feelings. Or worse: the ones that really didn't care, eyes blank, getting out of bed without a touch. The ones that had used her. *As I used them*, became Violet's chanted mantra, then.

'Maybe you're right.' Violet turned off the heat. She tried to turn around, but it was too hard to meet the gaze of her sensible, loving friend.

Loving. Love. That was, after all, what was missing in all these rash, fleeting encounters. Her love was all tightly tied up and sent across the ocean. It would come back to her, she was sure, but right now she didn't have possession of it.

'But wouldn't letting love in with other people be ... *more* of a betrayal?' She began to line up the assortment of empty jars

'Would it?' asked Chris. 'Or would it mean just valuing yourself properly?'

'And valuing the other person, maybe,' said Violet gloomily. 'Maybe it's not nice to use people.'

'Maybe not. It does all sound a bit ... transactional, to be honest. "Violet Lewis: The great orgasm collector"!' Chris laughed heartily, and wagged a joking finger. 'And just because it's men's bodies you're using doesn't make it OK, you know ...'

'Oh, bloody hell now, Chris, go easy on me,' laughed Violet, spinning round, and spreading her arms to demand a hug. 'If *you're* feeling sorry for the guys, I better start being worried,' she mumbled into Chris's lumpy, homemade knitted jumper.

But although she brushed it off, the conversation shifted something in Violet. She stopped going out so much, and deliberately poured herself into her studies, as well as the communal spirit of Matilda, as the house was known.

The seven women living there shared all the chores, and the cooking, and their entire incomes. Violet even had to help look after two other women's children, Annie and Tallulah, a development that had made Al moony about the idea of kids for a week, until he asked where their dads were. Violet had explained over the phone that men were only allowed at Matilda if they also shared the childcare and their salaries too – a necessary societal revolution and '*the* thing that would make men and women truly equal'. They hadn't stayed long.

When Al pointed out that if they couldn't even get a couple

of hippie dads signed up, it was going to be a long slow revolution, she hung up the phone in fury. Because the more Violet
invested her time and energy in Matilda, the more passionate
she became about the women's way of living.

She helped little Annie and Tallulah stage silly, much-abridged
Shakespeare plays with cardboard swords and painted fairy
wings, and taught Chris and Lily how to make proper curtains
to replace Matilda's makeshift boards and sacks. They, in turn,
helped Violet master public speaking, and the cooking of vast
vats of chickpea and vegetable curries to feed the groups of
women who'd often end up staying for dinner. Matilda was
becoming a community hub, every day hosting a tenants' asso-
ciation meeting in the basement, a consciousness raising group
around the kitchen table, or a self-defence session in the garden.

Violet's involvement in her housemates' activism deepened
too. Simply to live differently wasn't enough; they had to change
the material conditions of their less fortunate sisters too (as
Chris was fond of saying). Still, Violet inwardly recognised that
political work also gave her the same adrenalised rush and self-
congratulatory satisfaction at *doing things differently* that she'd
previously got from her hook-ups. The heady triumph of preventing developers from closing a women's refuge in Hackney.
The intensity of the 'womyns'' poetry group in Brixton, where
people shared experiences of abuse and trauma under her guid-
ance. Protesting, marching, raising her voice in council meetings;
the voice that the women around her had helped Violet to find
inside her.

And then, as the months passed and she got deeper in, the
shine began to wear off, just a little. Occasionally – just occasionally – Violet felt herself recoiling from the more radical
portions of the movement.

At one especially heated meeting about how to attack men

going into a newly opened Soho strip club (*eggs? Glue? Pig's blood – wait, could they collect enough menstrual blood?*), Violet was plagued by flashes of the violence she'd witnessed from men at protests: furious faces, swearing and spitting at the fuzz, or smashing shop windows on May Day.

Sometimes, the women's hatred of men was as bad as men's hatred of women. As bad as any hatred. But she had expected women to be different.

The feeling crystallised at a protest on Fleet Street. It was unusually hot for September; the closed road seemed to shimmer, the policemen looked thunderous, and Violet could feel the sweat begin to trickle down the inside of her thighs. A woman started shouting that all men were rapists, all men should be castrated.

'God, I might head off if it's going to be like this,' she whispered to Lily.

'Stay! Stay. We need moderate voices!' Lily implored, absently bopping a 'Sexism Kills Women' placard.

'No, we don't, we need radical voices,' interrupted their other housemate, Mabel, the most militant Matilda resident, who had her usual 'Kill All Men Now, Ask Me How' badge pinned to her shirt. 'Be more radical than you need to be, and the movement might just shift the mainstream an inch. Ask for something you think they might go for, and they'll not recognise the need to budge at all.'

'I get that,' said Violet wearily, familiar with the argument. 'But why does it have to be so ... aggressive?'

'Men *are* aggressive – it's all they understand.'

'But then aren't we stooping to their level?'

'What, you'd rather use your feminine charm to win them round?' Mabel sneered, all curled up at her edges. *She would*

say that, because she has no shred of feminine charm about her at all,
Violet found herself thinking, and quickly felt bad.

'That's just playing by the system they've put in place for
us – it's like trying to fight while wearing the straightjacket
they sewed,' Mabel continued.

'Well, maybe. But I don't want to try to put on their clothing
either, thanks, to make *their* way fit *me*. We should be doing it
our own way – peacefully, femininely, not embracing violence
and anger.'

Mabel snorted at the word 'femininely'. Violet felt shamed,
noticing Lily looking at her with what she assumed was disappointment, and then realised was something else.

When they went to the pub afterwards, because Violet did
of course stay for the rest of the protest, she wondered if Lily's
leg – bare below her cut-off dungarees, and soft with long
downy hairs – was brushing against her own more than it might
really need to.

There was a dress code in the movement, especially among
the lesbians – but although Violet never dared say it to anyone,
she didn't really understand why, if they hated men so much,
they wanted to look like them. Violet's attire – the floaty dresses
and floppy-brimmed hats, the beads and baskets – tended to
attract smirks.

She had started wearing less make-up, recognising that beauty
products were a capitalist trick, and that false beauty standards
were a burden placed on women by men. But sometimes she
wondered why should she change her appearance for women
either – wasn't there an irony there too? Violet liked how her
eyes appeared rimmed in kohl and mascara. This was the face
she had chosen for herself: her own transformation from country
mouse to city girl. And she didn't want to look different when

Al came home. She didn't want to suddenly have dark, hairy legs. She kept her razor hidden in a box of tampons.

But Lily's leg hair felt very, very soft, and much later when the other women were going to bed and Lily looked at Violet for just a fraction too long before asking 'bed – or another bottle of wine?', Violet's heart gave a small but definite kick. And when their legs began to mix together as they spoke and sprawled and curled up on the sofa till late into the night, she felt the old itch return once more.

The kiss was very soft, and it started small and slow – unlike many of the random men, who'd leapt and plunged, so frantic it was like trying to kiss an alarm clock while it was going off. Then Lily pulled back, and the question – *is this OK?* – was asked so gently just with her eyes, and Violet had answered with so wide a smile, such a big yes, they moved back together with an inevitability, a rightness that Violet realised she hadn't experienced since she'd last seen Al.

And when Lily moved down to kiss her neck it felt like tiny bubbles were rising in all of Violet's limbs, rising into the very crown of her head where they popped and fizzed. And they slid to the floor and their limbs flowed over each other's so smoothly—

And Al tried again to lie down among the bodies at the orgy, taking off his top and kissing a woman with large, loose lips, and letting her inch down towards his groin, trying to keep an erection even though he thought the movement made her look like a caterpillar. Come on, he told himself, he must be able to enjoy this. And anyway, he needed something to write about. He let his gaze run over all the flesh in the room as the woman very adequately began to blow him off with her soft lips, and he knew it should feel erotic and wild – he told himself it was erotic and wild – but he felt a little numb from the coke the drummer in some band had given him, and they were all just bodies, rubbery and mechanical and crucially not hers—

And Lily's touch on Violet was so slow and tender, but light, just the very pads, the tips of the fingertips, circling. There was the familiar pleasure of the unfamiliar touch – always so different to the predictable satisfaction of her own hand – but there was something else too. It was Lily. Her friend. A thousand tiny threads connected her to Lily; they were just pulling in a different way now. And then hearing the sigh, right in her ear, a sigh of soft pleasure at finding her so wet as those fingertips pushed inside, and another sigh at the way Violet's lower back couldn't help but jut and rise to meet the exploring touch as it found its home, made Violet contract involuntarily and everything pushed inwards and upwards—

And Al came, half in the woman's mouth, half on her cheek and shoulder, and he saw her face looking up at him, and glitching into disappointment, presumably because she had noticed that he looked sad rather than ecstatic, or at least a little grateful, and something shrivelled inside him, and out.

He had to get back to Violet.

Chapter 8

February 1972

Since Al announced he'd be coming back to London in February, Violet swore to herself before every one of their (now weekly) phone conversations that this time she would tell him about Lily. Tell him that she'd been sleeping with her housemate for the past five months. Tell him that, on his return, he'd be moving in not only with Violet, but with a woman who had been her lover.

Then his return got so close Violet decided she might as well do it in person. More honest that way.

With one week to go before Al's return, Chris came into Violet's room and handed her what felt like a lifeline. She sat on the bed rather heavily, her finger tracing the patterns of the crocheted bedspread Angharad had made Violet years ago.

'I'm really sorry to have to say this – but I've been talking to the other housemates, and we just don't feel we want a man living here, even one as absolutely lovely as Al no doubt is. We think Matilda needs to be a women-only space.'

'Right.' Bells were ringing somewhere in Violet's head.

'I can't wait to meet him, by the way! And I know this is last minute, so of course it's fine if he stays a few weeks until you two find your own place—'

'Oh...' Violet felt her mouth fall. 'I thought – I mean if it's about a man – couldn't I stay?'

Chris's face went through a series of hurdles.

'Well, yes, I suppose—'

'I just feel so *settled* here, so committed to Matilda and its – its *mission*. I really— well, I just don't want to move.' Violet could hear the panic spiking in her voice – but the opportunity she thought she had spotted seemed to be slipping instantly through her fingers, and she mustn't let it.

Chris had looked down at the bedspread, her finger still swirling, around and around.

'I just want – need – to live with *women* right now.'

'OK. Well. If you're really sure that's what you want – I mean, we love you being here, of course. We love *you*. But...'

Violet gave her an innocent look, and Chris raised her hands, in a gesture of acceptance that was a little less enthusiastic than Violet thought her idea deserved.

It was two days later that Lily addressed Violet's plans.

'Right, you,' she said, after Violet interrupted her by wriggling onto her lap. 'I can see I'm going to get precisely nothing done when you're in a mood like this. Let's go for a walk.'

'Well, you've been working too hard anyway lately.' Violet drew back, tilted her chin down, widening her eyes up babyishly at Lily.

Lily's recent total absorption in her work – she was on a deadline to submit her first academic book – had made Violet turn petulant: she'd wanted more of her in their final weeks before Al came back from San Francisco.

'A walk wasn't quite what I had in mind...' Violet continued, coyly. 'And anyway, look how windy it is!'

'It'll do us good. Blow the cobwebs away. Come on.'

They took a bus to the Heath, and headed in amongst its oaks, the wind snatching at any last dried leaves still clinging on.

Lily put her arm through Violet's, more firmly than affectionately.

'Now, Violet. You can't make me feel like I'm your naughty treat before you go back to normal life – that's not fair. On me, or on Al actually.'

Violet tried to wrap herself around Lily's arm, as if to help buffer against the gusts of wind but really because she was greedy for physical closeness. 'I know! It's just ... It'll all be different once he's back. And I'm scared I'll be different around you when he's around too?'

'Oh, you will.' Lily put a small, quick, understanding kiss on her temple. 'I won't be though.'

'No,' said Violet, almost to herself. 'I'm sure you won't.'

That was the ideal state, Violet thought: being absolutely yourself and absolutely honest with everyone. Not to constantly change and bend, giving some people this side of yourself, some people that.

But then, wasn't it simply that a different person brought out different aspects of you? With Lily, Violet often felt like a little girl – perhaps because she knew their situation was temporary, their romance like a bubble, light and floating. Where she would get irritated at Al for not taking her seriously or feel the need to push back against his assumptions, with Lily she had no resistance: she wanted to roll over, like a puppy playing for attention. All her intellectual fight – all the determination she had to find within herself in order to be listened to professionally, politically, or even down the pub – dissolved. Partly it was because Lily knew she was clever, Lily *chose* her because she was clever; with Lily, she didn't have to prove herself.

When alone – walking to the library under bitter skies, or

riding the bus to visit Jen – Violet's thoughts all flooded to Al's return. His arrival couldn't come soon enough: she was impatient for him, hungry. It was more than a year since she'd last visited him. Things had been going well at *RiZe* – well enough that Al had persuaded Micky, who he'd become very close to, to trust him to set up a London version of the magazine. *RiZe:LDN* would largely use American content, but with a smattering of more specifically British features; Al was, of course, to be editor. It was a promotion – but more importantly, it was a plan that would get him back home.

But Violet's longing for him rose up in her only when she was alone. Whenever she was with Lily, Al faded, and she just wanted to curl up in Lily's lap and be petted and forget about everything else.

How this was going to work when Al was in the same room was unclear. Violet tried to imagine the three of them in the house, but it was a smudged composite image that she simply couldn't hold in her head.

Lily tried gently saying – and then tried loudly shouting over the wind – that she thought that Violet's decision to stay living at Matilda, without Al, was very likely to be misconstrued.

'This ... *thing* between us has been so great!' she said, squeezing Violet's arm. 'But I always knew it had an expiry date on it. I don't want to get in the way of you and Al – and I think if you stay living at Matilda, I ... will?'

'I just don't want to leave the house!' insisted Violet.

'But won't it be hard,' said Lily, stopping, and forcing Violet to face her and look properly into her streaming blue eyes, 'won't it be hard for us to live together and not ... carry on? You always said you'd stop all that once you and Al were in the same place again. Won't he see continuing to live with me as a pretty significant ... choice?'

Violet rubbed the toes of her boots against the muddy path of the Heath, and finally looked up at Lily from under her eyelashes, with a beseeching curve of her lips.

'I thought me and Al might, you know, re-negotiate?'

Lily rolled her eyes, and pulled Violet in towards her. 'You,' she said into her ear with a bad smile, 'are a proper little menace.'

There'd been no such smiles on the actual day of Al's arrival. Lily's expression had been tight, and Violet's own insides felt as if they were being pulled in many different directions, like stretched, sticky chewing gum.

Finally the doorbell rang, and there he was. Looking tanned, his hair golden-tinged even in the fading light of the winter's afternoon. *Was he even taller than she remembered?*

Violet charged headfirst into Al, burrowing into him, her eyes squeezed tight as he wrapped his arms around her and held her close. *Home.*

For a second, nothing else existed.

Al had dreamed about their reunion for weeks, and wanted to capture and preserve the moment. But then everything seemed to just whizz by, too fast. 'You must be freezing,' Violet exclaimed, bundling him inside. There was a hasty tour of Matilda, leaving an impression somehow both intense and nebulous to eyes yawning with jet lag. Al liked the organised chaos of the place, the outsized piles of communal towels and sheets and jumpers squidged into vast shelves in the utility room, the giant pans and teetering over-stuffed vegetable rack. The whole house was filthy, though, which took Al by surprise until he remembered Violet complaining over the phone that communal chores didn't really work when half the inhabitants considered any kind of housework to be 'patriarchal oppression'.

The residents of Matilda each embraced him in big, welcoming hugs, and Al was relieved by their openness towards him. He could see shining on Violet's face a certain pride in them all as they sat him down at the massive kitchen table and grilled him cheerfully about his time in San Francisco. And they seemed genuinely impressed when Violet opened her slightly belated birthday present, that Al had wanted to wait to deliver in person: a copy of *Blue*, the record sleeve addressed 'To Violet – my fellow blue woman' and signed by Joni Mitchell herself. 'Now that is pretty special,' breathed Chris, unusually starry-eyed at Al's tales of hanging out with the singer-songwriter.

But the one housemate Al really felt drawn to was Lily: radiantly pretty but somewhat cool, she was the most arms-length of the group. He kept catching her looking at him, and then looking away, as if bored, when he met her eye. Al was gripped with an immediate, strong desire to impress her.

That night, Violet and Al got little sleep. And when Violet sat very neat and upright in bed the next morning, and said she had to 'explain about Lily', Al's attitude was considerably more relaxed than either she, or he, had expected.

Al had long suspected something must be going on between Violet and either someone in the house, or one of their good, old friends. He'd tried to ask her directly on the phone, but found the words impossible to formulate. So he'd written a long letter, asking outright, and then explaining in excruciating detail how much he regretted ever suggesting they have an open relationship. Reading back over it, Al was embarrassed by his inability to choose the right words – it sounded whiny, paranoid and pitiful. He'd tossed the letter in the bin, and continued to imagine the worst instead.

During his last few mad weeks in San Francisco, Al had trodden his fear around the city like it was a stone in his shoe, brought it onto the plane and found it had become a sharp rock by the time he'd reached Islington. But now here it was, out in the light, and turning out to be something glittering – and really rather appealing.

'I mean, she's gorgeous. Really – very – pretty. I can't blame you!' was all he'd managed to say. Somehow, this little pert blonde Lily just couldn't seem like a … threat? And, in a head that was disorientated and sleep-deprived and relieved, the most insistent thought was just what the two of them must look like together, naked, a thought which he tried hard to push down, convinced his male-gaze guilt must be streaked across his face like paint.

Violet had wondered if that mental image might just help matters, and decided that, on balance, she was happy to let it, for now. She muttered a few reassuring platitudes, and fell back into kissing Al. And when they had sex again, she was confused to find herself getting wet at the thought that Al was turned on by the thought of her having sex with Lily.

Despite this revelation being received so well, Violet decided to leave the news to settle somewhat before also telling Al that he needed to move out. And that she was staying put. But as the days passed, she could feel Chris becoming antsy. When Al went out to scout for offices for *RiZe:LDN* one morning, Chris said, 'Today, please,' and gave Violet a look.

When the doorbell went, Violet felt like she might be sick in her mouth.

'You've got to get me those keys cut, love,' said Al, barely chastising really as he bent down to kiss her full on the mouth, a slight slip of tongue, smiling a little as he felt her respond by sharply pressing herself into him.

Every passing kiss was full now; a week back, and Al still wanted all of her, all the time, the heat and generosity of her body. Had it changed just a little, he wondered, the curve of the belly a little more pronounced, the hips a little more padded.

He couldn't stop sticking his fingers into her dimples – how had he forgotten them?

Violet saw Lily coming down the stairs just as Al kissed her at the door, and seized up briefly, before pushing her body firmly into his, as if to block it all out.

Had Lily made the barest fraction of a pause before she continued into the utility room?

The house was unusually quiet – the others had gone with the kids to a puppet theatre, all except Lily who had promised to catch up with the laundry she hadn't done for weeks while finishing a chapter of her book.

'Tea?'

'Of course.' Al followed Violet into the kitchen, almost tripping over the wholesale sacks of brown basmati rice piled by the doorway.

'Al, um. There's something I need to tell you.' She had her back to him, putting the kettle on.

'Oh God, not another thing?' He beamed at her back, so she could hear in his voice how he wasn't serious, how well he really was taking everything.

Violet *was* different now, though, he thought, watching her. Especially when Lily was around. He did find it strange to see flashes of their intimacy – the glances, the way they passed plates and cutlery to each other like a dance, the shorthand they fell into when discussing political actions and their academic research.

But then, he told himself, he saw those flashes between Violet and Jen, Violet and Tamsin: friendships where subterranean rivers of understanding ran between them, that he had only partial access to. What partner would ever begrudge such a thing? Sure, the intimacy between Violet and Lily had gone a little further, but it was only sharing more skin, he tried to tell himself, and got the beginnings of a hard-on.

And anyway, he was just so glad to be back. Nothing felt insurmountable now he could just touch her.

Violet put down the mugs and sat opposite him at the table, a heavy mahogany heirloom Mabel had inherited from her grandmother. It looked out of place in their kitchen really, and had to be covered with a tablecloth to protect its long glossy surface. The cloth needed a wash, stained with spreading contours of spilt tea and a few crusted, yellow globules of egg yolk.

'You can't stay here.'

The words were more blunt than Violet had intended. Al looked blank.

'I wanted to say it in person rather than over the phone, and also Chris only told me just before you came back anyway. They've decided they don't want any men. In Matilda – in the house. It's part of the whole – *project*. A women-only space.'

'Right.'

She sighed, cross with herself for not explaining it with more kindness, more gentleness, for not helping Al feel OK about this. She could hear now how bewildering it sounded, out in the open air.

Sighing. Was she impatient, he thought, with him? For not anticipating this?

'And... wait, I have to leave? But you – you have no plans to?'

'No.'

Violet wanted to say more, to say *sorry sorry sorry* and *I know this wasn't what we planned*. But saying sorry would be like admitting the wrongness, the selfishness, and to do that would mean admitting that it wasn't fair to ask for what she wanted.

And something stubborn inside her just wanted it. Wanted both lives.

Had she always been this cold, thought Al, staring in disbelief as she cast her gaze down, onto a wonky, hand-thrown mug.

'Right. Really? OK, great. Thanks a lot.'

'Al, I'd have you here, you know that, it's just I can't really argue with the collective decision, I'm sorry but I can't, it's a collective!' She looked up then, all beseeching.

'No, I see that.' And Al's eyes seemed to have clouded over, and she felt a zap of fear. She'd rarely seen him angry; it was one of the things she loved about him, how he never used even the threat of that force.

'I know you can understand, Al, you will understand when you've been back a bit, and I'm sorry if it seems ... rubbish. But it's just I'm so settled here, I love it, and it's about the only way I could afford to live in London, with my grant as it is—'

'That's bollocks, Violet, and you know it!' he interrupted her, his large hands flicking in accusative gestures across the table. 'I already told you – my parents have given me my money again now I've got this job. I mean I don't particularly want the stupid money' – Al squeezed his eyes shut tight, briefly – 'but if that's what matters to you, we can get somewhere really nice, we can even *buy* a fucking house if that's what you want—'

'Al! Don't shout at me! You know that's not the stuff I care about—' Violet waved vaguely around her at the grubby chaos of Matilda.

'Well don't try to blindside me with crap then! I'm not an idiot, just because I've been away for a few months.'

'More than a *year*.'

'For fuck's sake,' Al muttered, putting his head in his hands and trying to breathe.

Violet wondered how much Lily could hear in the utility

room, folding the dried washing. If she'd think Violet was full of crap too.

'Al. Listen. Please.' She took a deep, wobbly breath. 'You're right. That sounded like an excuse. The thing is, I really truly honestly believe in this place, this way of living – and it works. *We* work: as a house, as a family, as a part of a wider community making daily change. And I have become part of that.'

She could feel herself trying to speak simultaneously to Al and to Lily, to make everything she said to him make her sound better to his ears, but also to Lily's.

'And I can't go back to just living how we were, and partying all the time, Al, that isn't what I want anymore. There's got to be some ... *purpose.*'

Al could feel gritty crumbs, pressing and popping beneath his left elbow. He regretted, then, all the breathless stories about his last few months in San Francisco, telling Violet about the late nights dancing, or the time on the boat with the mescal, the lost weekends down in LA. Because that *partying* was only to fill the time, to pass all the sodding *time* he had to get through before he could get back to her.

He was ready to make a home with her; he wanted to have a family with her. He had thought that starting all that was part of the purpose of his return.

'A purpose. And what exactly is the purpose here, in "*Matilda*" – except keeping men out?'

'Oh, Al,' said Violet gravely, trying not to feel too pleased. 'I can't discuss this properly if you're going to be a child about it.'

She sighed, and continued, the words sounding like they were coming from Chris, or Mabel, or Lily's mouths. 'You've got to try to understand: women *need* our own safe space, away from men. You've got the entire rest of the world! Everywhere you go is a man's space! Surely you can see how important this is to me?'

'Well, clearly. Clearly it's more important than ...' Tears pricked in his eyes, and Al twisted to look out the back window, to the tangle of pale, dead creeper that had once grasped its way over the wooden fencing. The raised beds were brown and empty, except for a few bare sprout plants, sticking up like still-loyal sentinels.

The utility door softly thudded, and Lily came in, eyes averted, to drop a wodge of greying tea towels on the corner of the table. At the very edge of his vision, Al saw the look that passed between them, as Violet extended an arm toward Lily, who turned and left. What was in Lily's big pretty eyes then – *I told you so? What did you expect?*

Something like that, something knowing.

'Is it so you can still screw her?'

Violet's face went very hot then very cold, like all her blood was rushing about in different directions, betraying her.

'No!' she said.

She had thought about that, of course she had. And she had been sure – really sure – that that wasn't just what it was about. But now ... Violet felt caught out, shaky and flushing: signs of guilt, as if her body had chosen the worst possible moment to reveal her true feelings to herself, too.

'No, honestly, it's just about the living arrangements—'

'Don't lie to me! Do you want—' The air that whooshed in and out of Al's lungs sounded very loud in his ears. 'Do you want to carry on being in an open relationship? Ideally, if you had your own way, would you carry on sleeping with her too – with us both?'

'Yes. But it really is about more than that, *more* than just—'

There was no moment when it felt like a conscious choice,

but Al did sweep his mug off the table, did pull at the tablecloth so that Violet's mug and the little china milk jug did career off too, seeming suspended in the air for a brief horrible moment before cackling on the tiled floor, spinning in pieces into every corner of the kitchen, and one of the chairs did get flung over too, and afterwards Al really wasn't sure what he had shouted as he banged and banged on the glossy table. But he would always remember the silence afterwards, and Lily's face as she reappeared in the doorway, and Violet's face as she cringed away from him, curled in her chair. Afraid.

Meeting him off the tube with a fag in hand and a vehement kiss, Tamsin immediately offered that Al could move in with her and Johnny and their housemates in Notting Hill. 'Johnny's in my room so much you may as well have his,' she insisted breezily. 'Makes rent cheaper for us all anyway.'

'Not that that's actually a problem anymore,' Al said, with a gloominess that belied the fact that – ever since Harold accepted that 'London editor' was a real job, even if he loathed everything *RiZe* stood for – Al had more money at his disposal than in his entire adult life, if he wanted it.

The first night of his exile, Al was bundled into the double bed with Tamsin and Johnny. His sleep was fitful; once he woke and was comforted by the old familiar smell of his friends, another time he jolted out of a guilty, disturbing dream where their limbs belonged to hostile strangers in the middle of an orgy. In the morning, for a second he went to hug Violet, before finding Johnny's bonier frame. The bed seemed to crash through the floor as he remembered what had happened.

Tamsin brought a whole teapot back to bed, and muttered 'well this is nice, it's like the old days'. She stroked Al's hair, and made him tell them exactly what had gone on, finally.

'Oh, Al, you bloody idiot. That's not like you,' she said when he'd finished his wretched retelling, twisting the seam of the duvet cover in his hands when it got to the bit about the smashed crockery and the yelling.

'I know.'

'But she knows that too. It will be fine.'

'I'm going to, ah, make us some toast?' Johnny stepped out of bed and put on some stretchy striped trousers. He wasn't good at talking about feelings until after he'd had three pints, when you couldn't get him to shut up. 'Do we have any bread? Maybe I'll just…' He threw a big holey orange jumper over his curls and scooted out the door.

Tamsin's room was like a cocoon, swathed in heavy velvet curtains and lit by red and orange lamps. A fern billowed out of a fireplace. Perhaps he could stay in her bed, sinking into the saggy crushed velvet cushions, forever, Al thought. He pulled the duvet over his head.

'Look, you're entirely allowed to wallow – but not like this, in guilt,' said Tamsin, sternly. 'Now you've actually explained yourself, I really, really don't think you've done anything that bad. It was an entirely reasonable reaction to being kicked out of a house she's sharing with someone she wants to carry on sleeping with!'

But Al's guilt was like a fortress, and nothing could get through it.

After all, they had agreed to do things differently, to be different. To be different to their parents' unhappy, rigid generation – stuck in loveless or sexless marriages, putting up with sexist rubbish because that was just 'the way things were', the tedious and corrosive obsession with respectability… To be open was to be free.

But then, jealousy, that low, creeping thing, had come crawling in. And had turned him into a monster.

'It was my idea! What did I expect, Tamsin, when I said we could try an open relationship? I must've known one option could be that she'd *like* it!' Al groaned.

'That wasn't the agreement, though, was it? It was all meant to stop when you came back?'

'Well yes, but … Life happens, doesn't it? And maybe if we can be honest, and open …'

'Well you have been honest and open.' Tamsin took his hand, and patted it. 'You've been honest and open that you don't want this.'

Al pulled his hand away, and tried to cover his face with it. 'I was such a prick.'

'Al, you were a prick, but you were a highly provoked one. I can't believe Violet is playing the wronged party! It's only because she lives with all those po-faced, righteous little witches—'

'No no no, Tamsin. Less of that. Don't demonise your sisters!'

Tamsin let out an exasperated raspberry. 'You've internalised all their shit! You know what, *I'm* gonna cast a hex on *them*.'

A few days later, there was a 'summit' back at Violet's house. *Matilda*. To reckon with what had happened, and whether Al would even be allowed back in their space as a visitor.

All the housemates were sat, waiting, around the table as Al walked in, unsure of how to hold his hands, or even his head. They all looked very severe. He lurched towards the waiting, empty chair.

The next half hour seemed to last most of a day, and yet was also almost impossible to take in. It felt as if a solid weight of disapproval was pushing towards him, like a cement roller. The women spoke very articulately about male violence and penile imperialism and the negative energy he'd brought into their female space, how if their relationship was going to continue, in any form, he would need to 'work on himself' and 'earn back their trust'.

Al was quite sure that Lily was stroking Violet's leg under the table as Violet did that face, that tight, puckered face she did when she was trying not to cry.

Violet wasn't exactly sure why she so badly wanted to howl and bawl and beat her fists on the table. Lily had told her, before they went into the kitchen, that she was being 'brave' facing Al again. But now he was sat in front of her, Violet wondered if she wanted to cry because of what they were doing to him. The way they were diminishing him, every earnest, judgemental utterance shaving a little off the man she loved. *He doesn't deserve this*, she thought.

She tried to squash down that thought, but it would not be submerged. After two restless, uneasy days, Violet couldn't stand it anymore, and set off to Notting Hill. She didn't know what, exactly, she was going to say to Al – but she knew she had to do *something*. To acknowledge, at least, the injustice of the situation.

Tamsin answered the front door, her face immediately drawing down into a scowl below her heavy fringe.

'Is Al here?'

Tamsin held her gaze, cold as iron. Violet's toes clenched inside her Doc Martens. It was perfectly clear where Tamsin's allegiances lay, then.

'No,' she said eventually, and allowed another excruciating pause, before a tiny sigh. 'He went to his sister's. And she's driving them to see their parents. In Yorkshire. *Sorry* – but you're too late.'

Was it possible to shut a door smugly? If so, Tamsin managed it.

Violet felt deflated, her gesture denied. Having prepared herself for a difficult conversation, being deprived of its resolution caused a panicky fear to surge within her. She *had* to see Al, thought Violet. She had to make things right.

As she collapsed onto a seat on the train to York, Violet told herself her heart was just racing because she'd had to run to the platform. But no matter how hard she tried to concentrate on a dense paper titled 'Silenced with a Kiss: How Benedick stops Beatrice's mouth' her heart continued to bump inside her. Violet gave up, and turned to a battered copy of *Persuasion*, but even Austen couldn't distract her from the drama of her own life.

Rose didn't look any friendlier than Tamsin had done when she opened the door at Farley Hall.

'Oh. Hello.'

Then there was a screeching, as Susan came running, on fat little legs, till she crashed into Rose's calves. Peeking out, she recognised Violet and ran forward for a hug.

'Golly, you've grown!' *Bland, pointless thing to say.* But Violet was working hard, to block out the thoughts trying to ram their way into her brain.

The last time she had seen Susan was the night she and Al babysat her, shortly before they went to San Francisco. After they'd put her to bed, their conversation turned to children, and they'd talked with a vague, milky dreaminess about having their own – some time far in the future, once they were proper adults, a future where Al was a respected political journalist and Violet was a leading academic and they'd travelled the world together, and also the world had become a better place to raise kids in and...

How naïve, thought Violet, trying not to squeeze Susan too hard, and wondering with a sickening jolt if the life choices she was in the middle of making might prevent her from having children with Al at all. And then: whether that vision of the future, with Al, was even one she wanted, anymore.

'Yes, I have grown,' said Susan, releasing Violet from her slightly sticky grip and lifting her arm above her head. 'I'm going to be tall as Mummy soon.'

'What have you got on yourself – what has Grandma been feeding you?' Rose looked distracted, momentarily, by the state of Susan's hands and mouth.

'Cake!' Susan announced with glee, performing a standing u-turn and running back in the direction of such banned delights.

Rose shook her head, as the sound of murmuring, fussing voices greeted Susan.

'Sorry, am I interrupting something ...?' asked Violet.

'Yes, but nothing to do with me. Or Bertie. It's a coffee morning – all the local ladies, plied with *extremely* sticky French patisserie, in exchange for donations to this charity Mummy's got involved in. She's on *quite* the mission – absolutely obsessed with helping "the little African girls" learn to read and write.'

'Oh. Well, that sounds like a worthy cause, at least? Better than, I dunno, helping retired show ponies or whatever.'

'Indeed. And it keeps her ... *occupied*.' Rose refused to soften, but Violet thought she detected something else below her display of indulgent weariness towards her mother. A lick of pride? Or simple relief?

'Anyway, I doubt you're here for an éclair. Bertie is out in the garden, keeping well away from them all. I'd go round the side too, if I were you.'

Violet nodded. At least she wouldn't have to come face to face with Amelia. They'd met on a few occasions, although Al preferred to have as little to do with his parents as possible. Violet had heard the stories; could feel the dread and humiliation Amelia's drinking had caused, dripping off even his memories. But while witnessing his mother's scorn for Al always made Violet's entire body clench in awkward sympathy, Amelia's attentions to her had never been so very bad. Violet suspected that was down to her doing a Masters and then a PhD; Amelia liked to ask a lot of questions about Violet's research, her career plans.

The gardens were almost bare, the ground hardened to a pale, minty green with the stubborn frost. Violet's crunching tread sounded conspicuously loud in the barren landscape.

She knew where he would be: the oak tree at the end of the garden. Its leafless branches spread broadly over the bench that curved around its trunk, as if they wanted to protect him.

'Hello.'

'Violet. What are you—' Al had a piece of paper and a pen in his hands. He hurriedly stuffed them into a coat pocket.

'I … I wanted to talk to you.'

Violet had thought they might just fall into each other's arms, that getting on a train was enough of a conciliatory gesture. But Al remained sat down, his eyes remote.

'Tamsin said— I got on a train—'

'Right.'

'Look, Al. I'm sorry, about the other day – it's been bothering me, I know that it came across like an ambush, and I just…'

Trying to move back towards him felt like wading through mud. Violet attempted to take a deep breath but her lungs seemed shallow, and clogged.

'I love you,' she managed, desperately.

Something flickered over Al's face. And Violet knew exactly what he was thinking about: the time they'd come over to Farley Hall from Sheffield as students, and sat under the leafy oak tree, so easily in love it felt like they were drunk on each other's smell, high on each other's words. Al had said it first, in a low, almost agonised voice, right into her ear, and then – with a great big happy laugh – he had flung an arm out towards the horizon and shouted it, shouted, 'I *love* you, Violet Lewis!' so loudly, it was like he wanted to wake the ancient landscape with the news.

And she'd said it back to him, over and over again, until the words frayed and splintered but the feeling remained.

Now, those same three words felt claggy in her mouth, hard to form.

'I really, really do ... love you, Al, and I want to make this work. If you still do. And I understand that – because of Lily – you might not want to.'

Was all this so difficult because it was worth it, because it would get them back to the easiness they'd always had? Or was this just what their relationship was like now? Violet curled inwardly at the thought that she might have spoiled it.

Violet sat down next to him on the curved iron bench. Not too close, not touching.

He fiddled with his scarf, unable to stop worrying at a loose thread. A scarf that Violet's granny had made for him, she recognised with a thump. How knitted together their lives were.

'Have you come here because you've changed your mind about living at Matilda?'

No, thought Violet, surprised at how clearly the answer came. How certain it felt. How resistant.

She didn't say it out loud, but as the pause lengthened, she really didn't have to. And she wondered why she *had* come, if she had so little, after all, to offer Al. Just a vacant apology.

'All I want is you, Violet,' Al said eventually, his voice sounding unexpectedly harsh. 'That's all I ever wanted—'

'Don't say it like that! That feels like an accusation.'

'OK, but it's true.' Al had become strangely aware of his breath going in and out. Everything around them felt slightly unreal, like he'd been dropped into a film set rather than his family home.

This was surely it.

'Is the only option, now, being open?' he asked. It was the question he'd been struggling to phrase in a letter to her, failing once more express himself, even in writing. To make the case, for it being just the two of them.

And Violet felt a surge of understanding then: that, despite her chasing him, it was still really she who held all the power. She felt the unfairness of what she was about to say, and the unfairness of how she had got that power by making him so angry that he'd behaved badly.

But she didn't know if she could go back to how it was before, or even if she wanted to go back. Here was the chance to have Al, and to have Lily, and to have anyone else she ever decided she needed, without judgement. Without it being her fault.

'Yes, I think so, Al.'

In the distance came the sound of Susan, running out into the garden, screaming with joy, and Al had a profound sense of having lost his grip on his life.

'I know it won't always be easy, it'll be a lot of work – from both of us – but I think we can do it.'

He still said nothing.

Inside his pocket, Al's hand was crumpling and tearing up the half-written letter.

'And, well, maybe we can see – just see how it goes! Maybe both our feelings will change. Maybe Lily's feelings will change! But if we just keep talking, and we keep being really honest with each other, I think it could work.'

And Al knew then that that was as good as he was going to get, and he knew that he wanted to believe her rather than actually did believe her, but there was nothing else to hold on to. And so he reached out for her gloved hand, and held it tightly, and said, OK, if that's what you want let's do it. We'll carry on being open. She'd live at Matilda, he'd stay with Tamsin and Johnny. They would make it work.

As they left the bench to go inside, the light was falling, darkening the hills far away in the distance. Al might have agreed to everything Violet had asked for, but she did not feel the triumph she had expected.

Chapter 9

June 1973

The sun was beginning to go down on the last day of their holiday, and the waves, too, crept in for the night. The patch of sand they'd dozed on was shrinking, almost breath by breath, and the thick air smelled faintly herby, a scrubby greenness mixed with the saline tang of the sea. The heat was nicest at this time, Violet thought. Gone was the sizzle and sweat of the day, the brightness that couldn't help but startle every time you left the shade; now the light was low, as if angled deliberately by a photographer to flatter. Even her pale legs, drenched in the pink-orange of early evening, looked golden.

She was hungry: they'd barely eaten since their late, lazy breakfast of torn bread and gritty soft white cheese, topped with local Greek honey. There was bad coffee, and sensational peaches, which filled her nose like none she'd ever eaten at home. Violet's stomach growled, but the insistent lapping sea seemed to demand one more dip.

'Come on,' she whispered, and tugged up an arm that had sprawled off the towel into the sand. 'One last splash in the sunset.'

The tiny waves that caressed her feet felt like nibbly little kisses as she picked her way into the shallows. Violet pushed past the cool slap at her thighs to duck her head under. Emerging, the light shook through water droplets, and she turned.

And there he was. Golden, too.

She was still getting used to the shorter hair, still unsure about the moustache. But in the sideways amber light, Al's face was struck by handsome shadows and planes of light. He looked good. Greece was good for both of them. They'd needed a holiday.

London had been a struggle that spring. Violet was finding it hard to find the motivation for the last push on her PhD, even, feeling sick of Hero and Helena and Hermione, itching to move on to a new topic. And London seemed overcrowded somehow, and perpetually mired in low-hanging drizzle, matching the increasingly morose mood of the nation.

Violet and Al had moved back in together the previous autumn, after Tamsin and Johnny had surprised everyone by announcing that they were engaged, and moving to a farmhouse in Devon ('We're sick of sharing – each other, but also our space. We're going all-in, finally'). With this news, Al had seized an opportunity, asking Harold for the money to buy a flat, from whence rose an obvious ultimatum: Violet could keep seeing other people, but she had to move in with him there, or it was over.

Violet thought she was ready. She still loved the Islington commune, the sharing and the work; she still truly believed in Matilda. But things had cooled with Lily. After the initial drama quickly subsided, the thrill and zip of having two people became something more ordinary: nourishing, often delightful, but also hard work.

By the time it finally came to the ultimatum, Violet found she couldn't quite remember why she had found Lily so irresistible anyway. Lily talked over people, and was not just confident but inflexible. She had become increasingly insistent that Violet should renounce her greedy bisexual ways and commit to lesbianism. But being told to dump her boyfriend because 'sleeping with the enemy actively upholds the patriarchy' only rubbed Violet's stubborn streak up to a gleam.

And the freedom Violet had ringfenced by staying at Matilda came at a cost to her relationship with Al, she recognised: they'd never got things quite back to how they had been before. She was living the life she'd wanted, that she'd fought for, and he never explicitly complained. But their time together was often punctured by tiny, cutting criticisms and simmering arguments about nothing in particular.

Moving in with him seemed like a sensible step. They settled on a charming but slightly shabby terraced house in Westbourne Park, with a half-rotted wooden deck that looked out onto the canal, and which Al and Johnny fixed up when the weather improved and Violet filled with plant pots and cheap hammocks.

But if moving back in together had eased some tensions, it hadn't solved them all, as Violet had rather blandly assumed it might. Six months in, and Violet had felt constrained somehow, as if some vital organ inside her was wrapped with fine metal wires.

It wasn't just her: she noticed the tension in Al's jaw too, a tiny clicking clenching, revealed now his hair no longer swung around his shoulders.

Besides, when he spent long days across town in the *RiZe:LDN* office – or went off on lengthy jaunts to interview groups or to 'embed' himself with counter-culture communities, for his much-acclaimed long features – Violet found the house too quiet. She was used to a perpetual low-boil hubbub: children in the garden, voices raised in debate; Lily playing Aretha too loud while cooking, or the singing group learning harmonies. And Violet started having strange flashes back to life in Aber: the teapot always on the go, someone always in for a chat, everyone helping with each other's kids. How it was women who were around, mostly. In a funny way, their little terrace in Aber had been closer to Matilda than the far more conventional set-up she'd agreed to with Al. An empty, lonely house.

But she'd promised never to bring anyone else back there, and she didn't.

Violet would go and spend the night with Lily at Matilda only very occasionally, and more out of strange inverted duty (*after all that fuss she'd made!*) than anything else. At conferences, she might try to take advantage of the private bed in a different city. And there was a gorgeous, butch woman who went to monthly abortion rights campaign meetings in Tottenham whom Violet often kissed greedily afterwards. But, comparatively, things were quiet.

Still, she recognised she was busy compared to Al. It was a mystery to her: he had so many more options than she did, really. At parties, she'd see girls – *women* – hanging on his words, or sometimes literally on his arm. Yet when they tried to slide in for a kiss, Al politely moved away. She'd watched it happen, unsure whether to feel pleased or guilty.

Maybe he does indulge when I'm not there, Violet told herself. But she somehow knew he didn't.

Once, at a gallery opening, he hadn't noticed her arriving, and it had been like watching an old home movie: there was the Al whose movements were loose and easy, confidence radiating from every sexless, affectionate shoulder pat and effusive head nod, the Al who could pass through a room of people making them feel better about themselves. Later, after she'd kissed him hello and went to talk to the artist, Violet had glanced back over at Al and caught him watching her, and it made her breath catch: he'd turned stiff, his limbs closed up and folded in. When they got home, she immediately ran a bath and insisted he join her. She sat behind him and wrapped her arms around his torso as the water bobbed around their conjoined bodies, silently trying to push love back into him from her chest.

It'd been a shock, because Violet had thought – had told herself – that they were doing better. Al seemed more settled, and if *RiZe:LDN* made no money, it still looked and felt like a success. Its launch party, in a warehouse near Kings Cross, had become legendary after a minor royal got so smashed they were photographed getting into a paddling pool. Other magazines wrote about them; Al was profiled in the *Guardian* and *Time Out*. He got automatic guest-list spots to every gig or exhibition he wanted, every launch party, any nightclub.

But the thought that Al was only able to truly be himself at these events when she wasn't around was planted that night, and had grown and twisted itself around Violet's insides for months.

She swam to close the distance between them, the water feeling warm now she was fully immersed, and smiled at him. Al broke into a grin, that big lovely lop-sided grin of his. But it was still her who reached out her arms, clasped them behind his neck, and swam her legs around his waist. He so rarely made the first move these days.

She was slippery as an eel, and Al let his hands travel over her buoyed body. Their eyes met, and there was so much now between them that even this weightless moment felt too much to hold.

Al drew her in, and squeezed her hard, but Violet gently pushed away, keeping her legs anchored round him while leaning back into the ocean, her hair fanning and falling behind her like seaweed. Her face bobbed just above its surface as she stared up into the sky.

'There's just one, very bright, star.'

Al pedalled his feet in the water hard to keep them both afloat, and held her steady, as she pointed up at it. But the movement made her groin jam into his low belly, and Violet experienced the usual stirrings. She pulled herself back up till they were kissing, and beginning to sink under the water, and laughing as their mouths got contaminated with a swell of sea water.

But by the time they'd got back to their house, the moment had passed. They were staying in a rustic whitewashed cottage, with a shower that was really just a spluttering tap spouting out of the wall outside, with a salt-encrusted wicker screen for modesty. Violet sluiced herself and stepped out quickly, without the inviting touch that had seemed promised in the sea.

Al realised he was too sad to mind. Then he caught her watching him as he dressed, and when their eyes met she gave him such a kind smile that Al felt a dread heaviness sink through him and settle somewhere inside his legs.

Al had wondered if a holiday might help. Might just make him change his mind.

Now the holiday was almost over.

They walked to the taverna in near silence. Halfway there, Violet very gently took his hand. It felt so correct in his: so small in his long fingers, yet also always just the right size. He swallowed, trying to keep the stinging tears at the back of his throat, behind his eyes. A nearly full moon shone an obligingly opalescent light on her long white dress and cicadas chimed in like they were in some old romantic movie, and somehow it was the happiest he'd been in years too, and Al just didn't know if he had enough space inside him for it all.

'You look beautiful,' he said, as they sat at what had become their usual table, and ordered their usual carafe of local wine: a lightly sedimented, darkly yellow liquid more like dry sherry than white wine. After giggling and insulting it extravagantly the first night, ordering it had by mutual silent agreement become an inviolable tradition.

'Oh, Al – thank you.' The compliment took Violet aback; it was too formal somehow, the sort of thing she imagined people said on dates.

When their food arrived, Violet wordlessly divided her grilled fish, and put it on Al's plate, as he slid across some of the salad and chips, the compromise they'd accepted was as close to vegetarianism as they could get on Crete. Two thin scraggy cats they'd become fond of trotted over and began to wind themselves around their legs; Violet had christened them Purdita and Pawlina ('must you bring Shakespeare into everything?' 'I can't help it!') on their first night. She slipped a few bites to the floor before she'd even tasted the fish herself.

Al watched her and wondered about this, this sharing of language and habits, this somehow automatic life they built together, that needed them both. That didn't – couldn't – exist outside of them being together.

A cat mewed at him plaintively.

Would he ever be able to build such a life with someone else? He wasn't sure which thought was worse: the idea that this was it, or the idea that something this special was in fact completely replicable.

'You're quiet.' He could tell it was meant to sound gentle, even if it actually sounded false, too sunny. 'Sad about the hols ending?'

Al put down his cutlery decisively.

'It's been a good holiday, hasn't it?'

'The best.' She smiled, generously. Her face was gently lit by the candle and the string of lights that looped through the rush-plaited roof. Vines curled perfectly around the electrical wires, like they were trimming a fairy-tale illustration.

'There's something I need to tell you, actually. Before we go back. They're closing the magazine.'

'What? Oh, Al – I'm so, so sorry.' Violet's hand shot across the table. 'Did you— I'm surprised you could enjoy yourself at all! You should've told me ... And, well, can we really afford all this?' Something fluttered inside Violet as she waved her fork.

Was it relief? The past few days, she'd thought she felt something advancing, something big. She had tried not to think about it, not to face it, but it was like the tide slowly coming in: you knew it was happening even if you couldn't see it moment by moment.

But it was just work. Money. Nothing more ominous than that.

Yes, what she was feeling *was* relief, trickling through her body like soft spring rain. She chased a few cubes of slippery cucumber and tomato around her plate with her fork. *In fact* – and then her brain raced, speeding to catch up – *maybe this was good!*

Maybe Al could come with her this time, to wherever she got her post-doc in the autumn.

Violet had already had a few conversations about 'opportunities' with department heads; her papers had been unusually well-received, and her PhD would be impeccable, even if it killed her. She would go wherever it took, and work as long and as hard as she needed, to have her books published, to have her books on the reading lists, to lecture rooms full of students and make sure that the people like her in those rooms knew that they could do it too.

She'd assumed she'd be doing all that alone, however, for a time at least. That Al would stay in London on *RiZe:LDN*. She had selfishly consoled herself with the thought that there would at least be her own room in whatever town she ended up in, and new men and women there to take back to it.

She assumed he'd had this thought too. But they didn't talk about it.

And yet now that thought had been swept away in a rush by a new one – one that surprised Violet in how welcomed it was. Because, oh, wouldn't it be easier and sweeter to start the next chapter with Al by her side! Wouldn't she feel stronger, more ready to take on that work? Maybe they could both start something new, somewhere new ... together. Maybe he could get a job with a local paper in Newcastle or Bristol or Edinburgh or wherever she ended up. Her thoughts whirred too fast, new ideas tripping over each other. *But perhaps – perhaps this really could be the solution!*

'Is the magazine closing soon?' she asked, keen to get a handle on the new situation.

'Er, yes. Next issue is the last.'

'What's happening to the American version?'

'It's continuing. But Micky's handing over editorship, some new young guy—'

'Not you?' Violet wouldn't want Al to go back to San Francisco, but it was still obviously outrageous they wouldn't automatically give him that job.

Al felt a warm rush of love; she'd always done this, always expected the best for him.

'Actually ...' Al swallowed. He couldn't eat any more; the few mouthfuls of fish he'd managed had been fibrous and dry in his mouth. 'Micky and I ... we've been making new plans, together.

Finding investors. To set up a new business – a small-scale, radical publisher. Rize Books. Non-fiction mostly.'

The waves sounded very loud in Violet's ear, coming closer to the taverna.

'Magazines are all very well, but we want to have a little more ... lasting impact. To change the world! It's a big step. But I think we're ready.'

And the waves throbbed and broke, or it might have been her blood in her ears. Something was boiling up in Violet, fuelled by the sense of déjà vu. Al *knew* she would have to take a first job at a British university after she finished her PhD, he *knew* it was a crucial moment in her career ...

'But *where* will you be setting this up? In *San Francisco*?'

When Al had first mooted Rize Books to Micky, a few months earlier, the biggest question mark was where they would be based. Because Al realised that if he had to go back to San Francisco, he would also have to call things off with Violet. He simply couldn't do long distance again. The relationship would be hard enough if Rize Books was established in London and then she got a job at a university in Glasgow or Cardiff; if it was in the States, it would be fully impossible.

'No, actually. Micky is moving to London. He loves the city, and he feels ready for a change. Serendipitous. But ...'

Al watched her face soften with relief, and his throat felt like it had been slashed repeatedly with a razor.

Because when Micky said he'd happily come to London to launch Rize Books, Al had been struck with a horrible realisation: that the idea of breaking up with Violet had actually felt more right than the idea of staying with her. He didn't really want to leave the UK, or their house, or his friends – but San Francisco had gleamed, briefly, as an escape route. A legitimate excuse, a way to end things.

Al had honestly hoped that he might get used to the open relationship, to sharing her. In the early months after he came back from San Francisco – after his outburst at Matilda had seen him solidly cast as the villain – he was too afraid to show any displeasure, any uncertainty in their agreement, in case she left him outright.

Then he thought that living together might solve the problem, would let him feel more secure.

But if anything, the jealousy just got worse: a sour vine that wound through everything, choking the pleasure out of life. When Violet came in, zesty after a march, he now wouldn't ask to hear all about it, he'd wonder if she was so pleased because she'd bumped into an old conquest. When she was excited about giving a paper, all he could think of was seedy hotel beds, creaking. Any party she came to was coloured by a gauze of paranoia, the tiniest, most innocent touch worried over, growing grotesque and enormous and erotic in his imagination till it was like every man and woman in the room was actively trying to fuck her there and then in front of him.

He pushed his possessiveness down, but it found a way to creep out and strangle their relationship anyway. Petty little remarks. Bickering over unimportant decisions. A slow, slow diminishing of physical affection.

They joked less.

She didn't make him laugh anymore.

He wasn't relaxed enough around her to laugh.

Al had known for several months that he had to leave her.

'But ...? What is it?' Violet's face was searching his, trying to understand why he looked distraught. 'I mean, this all sounds wonderful, Al, I'm incredibly proud of you!'

Al flinched, and shut his eyes.

'I just ... I wonder if it isn't time for a bigger change.' Al took a trembly breath in, and opened his eyes again to look at her, straight on. 'I don't think I can do this anymore, Violet. The relationship, the agreement. Especially not if you might have to go and work on the other side of the country...'

The tears seemed to spring into her eyes before her brain had even fully registered what Al was saying. She wanted to push back her chair and turn and run away into the olive hills, but she also felt frozen, in place and in time, as if she might be stuck on the taverna's wicker chair forever.

'I'm sorry...' Al reached across the table, but Violet wouldn't give him a hand, keeping them in her lap, her eyes looking down at the plate of half-eaten food as tears rolled steadily all over her face.

The waiter with the attractive wrinkles came waddling over, palms spread, to offer more wine, dessert, and halted abruptly as he saw Violet crying, the amount of food left, the nearly empty carafe. Al mimed for the bill, morosely.

'I just think... I don't think it works anymore. Does it?'

Am I wrong, Al wanted to say. *Have I got it wrong?*

He hoped he might have got it wrong.

'But... why? Is it just because of the *possibility* of long-distance?' asked Violet. 'Because I might get a job in London anyway, you know, and–and I can make sure I only even apply to universities in the south, maybe...'

Violet looked up at him, her eyes darting around his face again, the words spilling out before she took time to really consider what they might mean for her.

'Or is it... is it really because of the agreement?' Her voice had gone very small, and she looked back down at the tablecloth. One hand began steadily moving her wine glass around, making a complex interlocking pattern on the cheap paper tablecloth with its damp rim. Round and round and round.

'Violet, hey, come on.' Al tried to coax her back into eye contact, reaching for her face, but she whipped away, like a child who thinks the thing they've broken won't be broken anymore if they can't see it, her chin turned into her shoulder, her eyes shut tight.

'Just tell me.'

'Please, this isn't your fault. It's just … Well, it's both. I wouldn't ask you not to follow your work, wherever the best opportunity was. You're going to be an important woman, Violet Lewis. I know it.' She still didn't look up.

'But yes – really, it is more about the agreement. I don't want to share you anymore. Wherever we are. I'm sorry if that's not very groovy – I'm sorry I can't be cool about it – but I can't, Violet! And I have tried.'

Then it was Al who got up, and fled, throwing a fistful of notes on the table in gesture that would have seemed absurdly overdramatic if his heart didn't feel like it was actually tearing apart, and he stumbled down the uneven stone steps and onto the damp give and sink of the sand. For a moment, he was alone, facing the black boom of the ocean, only the nearest, lowest breaking waves catching the light from the taverna.

He really couldn't do it anymore. It was like there was acid inside him, that he had swallowed willingly but that corroded him every day – his sense of self, his sense of worth. Even his love for Violet.

Al thought he might have been able to deal with the agreement if it had just been about Lily. If it was a one-off. Despite it all, he had actually grown to quite like Lily – and he certainly understood the attraction. He could see that Lily possessed all the qualities that Violet would like to have in herself: the intellectual confidence, the self-assurance, her iced ability to manage her sexual and emotional affairs.

And besides, the infatuation had clearly faded. Lily was no longer much of a threat.

The problem – although Al had never actually told Violet this – was all the others.

There had been a conversation in a dimly lit pub near Highbury & Islington tube station, over a half-pint of mild and full pint of bitter, a few days after they'd come back from their apparent reconciliation at Farley Hall. Feeling raw and skinless and exhausted, Violet and Al had agreed the best thing to do was embrace 'total, loving honesty' in the relationship. It was as if they had found a strange new closeness in the crisis. They could say anything now, it had briefly, intoxicatingly felt like.

She'd wanted to know what had happened for him when they'd been apart, and he'd told her a little more about Cassandra, and how bad he felt about how frustrated she'd got with him ('why are men who say they're in open relationships never really emotionally available?'). They laughed together at his dreadful orgy experience and the abandoned article.

So it seemed only right to ask her too.

'Oh I can't list them!' Violet had deflected, smilingly, with a slight blush and a wave of the hand.

'God, how many were there?' laughed Al.

And then he saw that it actually was impossible for her to answer the question. And then he wanted to smash something again.

'Was it … mostly women? People like Lily, in the movement?'

'No, mostly men.' Violet dropped her voice to almost a whisper. 'This was before Lily – just, lots of strangers, no one important, nothing … ongoing.'

And then he wanted to smash himself up, to actually hammer off his own limbs.

Al had assumed his girlfriend being half in love with someone else was the worst thing that could possibly happen to him. But it turned out that the thought of fifteen, twenty, thirty penises – *what figure would be too many to count?* – moving inside of her, and the thought of that happening over the same months when he was speaking to her on the phone and not even knowing (*had they been waiting in her room, even, for her to finish the call?*) was much, much worse.

'But they didn't mean anything! Really, Al, it was all totally insignificant. And also, I should point out, it's what we've agreed we're allowed!'

A fruit machine, somewhere in the pub, paid out a gaudy clattering jackpot. Three men at the bar laughed too loud, and Al had wondered if they could tell somehow, if they were laughing at him.

He knew it shouldn't matter. And he could tell that she really didn't think about those encounters much, that she was a little bit proud but also a little bit embarrassed about her 'wild days', as she'd occasionally jokingly refer to them. Those experiences did not define Violet, and Al did a good impression of forgetting all about it.

But really, the brutish, pointless, meaningless sex she'd had lay between them, like a pile of dead bodies, festering.

Al heard her neat, light steps tapping down the stairs towards him. She stood by his side, and he could feel that she was looking dead ahead, at the sea, rather than at him.

Violet took his hand, and she wasn't sure if it was because she really wanted to keep him by her side, or if she was just too scared to let him go.

She felt like she was splitting in two. How could she want such different things? To be with Al forever and have children and grandchildren and grow old together and die – but also to be free, truly free, to go wherever she chose, to follow whatever opportunities she could make for herself, to discover all the versions of herself she could be with all the different people she might meet, in all the different places … The two paths diverged, here and now, and she realised with cold clarity that she really couldn't follow both.

Might have, in fact, already started down one path. Violet wondered if it was too late to turn back.

'What if we weren't open anymore? What if it was just … us?' she said, quietly.

But instantly, the thought of all that pressure — of Al being her all and her only; of both of them knowing she was sacrificing something she wanted; of the strain if she did then have to leave London for work — all of it felt like it was pulling the thin wires in her chest even tighter.

Al shook his head. 'I don't know. I don't think so. I think what we had … I think it's spoiled.'

'Spoiled. Oh, Al …'

He tried to find the words to explain what he meant, to bring the jealousy into the open air. But they just wouldn't come. And so when Al squeezed Violet's hand, and then let go and walked towards the sea, it felt like the end.

It wasn't really the end, because they had to fly back to London together, and slept several more nights in their bed, sadly and heavily together, and found they were able to be kinder and more generous than they'd been for months, making each other cups of tea and plates of toast, dividing their books and their records with occasional quiet queries over ownership, and taking it in turns to howl briefly while the other held them, and stroked their back, and then teared up too, until they both laughed at how covered in snot and mascara their T-shirts were getting.

The day before she moved out, Al slipped the letter into

one of her books, and then put it back into the cardboard box with the rest. Since they'd got home from Greece, he had been seized with a compulsion to put all of his love – and some of his pain – down on paper, finally. He wasn't trying to win her back; he just needed to write, with honesty, all that he felt.

So it was a deliberate choice to hide the letter in *The Rainbow*, the book he'd given Violet when they graduated, and one that he felt sure she would keep for the rest of her life.

What Al could not know was whether she might open it, sentimentally, in coming months, or if she might find it too painful to look at, leaving its pages (and his letter) to gather dust on a shelf for years. Perhaps even for decades.

21 January, 1967

The clock reads 8.09 a.m. The midwife in Abergavenny hospital laughs as the baby races out of her mother; *she's in a hurry to see the world, this one*. Angharad gasps in relief, and reaches for the kicking bundle of limbs, and the girl she's already promised to name Violet latches straight onto her breast and pulls, hungrily. And in a private room at a hospital in Leeds, exhausted and sodden, Amelia gives a low bellow as finally her reluctant son is pulled into the world with forceps, seeming to resist all the way. His tiny body is disturbingly red and mauve, and slick as offal, but his cry goes straight to her own guts and Amelia reaches out, too, to hold her child.

Chapter 1

December 1987

Did it smell of strawberries?

Albert moved into the tiny room, the lights flickering between yellow and a copper-sulphate blue, smudged by the clouds and jubilant hisses of dry ice that, yes, smelled of strawberries.

Already, people were moving, to the sort of music Gregsy had been playing him recently. The groove of disco but a more insistent beat. And there was a looseness, as if the nuts and bolts in knees and elbows had been loosened. Heads lolling back. And smiles. Just loads of... smiling.

The last time Albert had been to a club it had been a snotty place in the West End where women in crisp jackets looked at him like he might've been picked out of a nostril. He'd pretended to enjoy it, but really felt mostly bored. At the studied unbotheredness of it all.

No one looked unbothered here. They looked like they'd found the most incredible secret and were desperate to share it with you.

'Nice, eh?' said Gregsy, slinging an arm around Albert's shoulders and handing him a Lucozade.

Albert swallowed.

Just when he was beginning to suspect the pill wasn't going to work for him, the music started to sound incredible. Absolutely essential, in fact. As if it had been tailor made for his body. And then it was like a fountain rose up inside Albert: up his spinal column, up breathlessly through his chest, up pulsing through his limbs.

'Fuck!' he shouted at Gregsy, feeling his eyes widen.

Outside, the queue was moving slowly, and Vi was freezing. The wind rustled through her 'going out' coat, belted with wide lapels.

'I thought you said it was easy to get in.'

'Well it bloody was last time I came!' Mel dragged hard on her menthol and rolled her eyes. 'Madness.'

Mel had come back to Bristol after reading week bursting with stories about these new nights her south London pals were going mad over. Vi lied to her parents about when term ended so she could go with Mel before heading home for Christmas.

Mel passed her something that felt a little chalky, and a nervousness twisted in Vi's lower belly.

'Just a half. You'll be fine.'

She swallowed. Vi thought she probably actually would put her hand in a fire if Mel told her to.

By the time they got inside Vi was beginning to feel something shifting around the edges of her vision. The place was so small, she almost walked into the back wall without realising it was a mirror. A guy in a loose lilac vest top saved her, and started dancing with her. But Vi didn't know how to move to this music. Until, suddenly, she really did.

'Back in a sec.' Albert clapped Gregsy on the shoulder and went to find the toilets.

'Sorry, can I ...' He tried to move round a short girl with a dark head of hair, her hands coiling above her closed eyes. Then they suddenly snapped open.

The music crashed into the depths of the earth. A strobe

kicked in. She was frozen. Flickering, but frozen. Locked into eye contact. A strange jolt of recognition. *I know you.*

Then the warmth and the light flooded back.

'Sorry, were you trying to get to the loo?'

And she swerved elaborately, her arms indicating the way. When Albert came out, he couldn't quite remember where she had been. And he couldn't find Gregsy either. But he started dancing again, and then time didn't so much speed up as absent itself entirely.

Eventually, the overhead lights crashed on. Everyone panted, and laughed at each other's faces, laced with sweat in the too-bright yellow of it. The DJ put on 'All You Need is Love' as he waved the crowd out. And Albert thought that probably everything was going to be all right from now on.

Chapter 2

June 1989

It was one of Vi's favourite games, to imagine strangers' faces from behind. But when the man finally turned around, his face wasn't quite what she expected.

But it was gorgeous: a soft, wide mouth, a long nose and massive eyes. A little dopier than she'd expected. Actually, rather adorable.

Vi realised she was probably staring a little dopily herself and dropped her gaze to the ground, worried he'd caught her looking. The grass, dried out by the weeks of good weather, was already pressed and flattened in criss-crossed patterns into the dusty earth. The mass of bodies stepped to the beat coming from the sound system that loomed over them all from a makeshift stage, dripping with a camo net.

The early evening air was cooling, but she could already feel the beginning of the prickle, as if she had a lizardy kind of outer skin that had crackled in the sun. She had Jimmie's massive sweatshirt on, its sleeves flopping over the end of her hands, but this feeling of her own outline told her that it was starting. Maybe had already begun.

As she danced, Vi let her gaze slide near the good-looking man and past him. She could feel her brain speeding up, as she tried to work out if he was looking at her too, without him noticing she was looking at him again.

His legs were long, and seemed jellyfish-like in their limber, limp movements. Stretching out of a pale pink sweatshirt, his hand beat a metronomic time, occasionally reaching out and pulling back in, as if to scythe and gather the sound towards him.

No, he definitely *was* looking at her.

Vi met his gaze. *Those eyes!*

A big dreamy smile took Vi's face as she glanced back down at the ground again. She moved slightly closer to him, her feet almost floating, weightless, yet still felt faintly surprised that the rest of her body obediently followed.

And then there she was, looking up at him.

'I like your hair!' he said, stooping slightly.

Vi's hand involuntarily went up to it. She'd let Mel put what was meant to be a rainbow streak in her choppy bleached bob, but only the pink had really taken: the green was a sickly yellowish shade, the exact colour of grass that's been deprived of light under a tent.

'Really? I think it's pretty gross.'

'No, it's ... fun.'

'So are you, ah, having a good time?'

Vi wondered if she could really be bothered with chatting. The guy had the distinct accent of the guys at uni, the ones that pretended to be normal but turned out to have second homes in Tuscany. She was sure that she could feel Mel behind her, watching. Smirking, too, probably.

'Yeah, it's a decent site,' she said, non-committally, and then closed her eyes and let her shoulders go with it a bit.

But when she opened her eyes, she realised the man was definitely dancing *with* her, not just near her. And he'd tuned in surprisingly well, given he was about twice her size. She raised her hands to the beat. And he pulsed his large fingers towards hers.

And it was just perfectly timed, because that was when something began to multiply inside Vi. She felt as if there was helium being pumped under her clavicles, expanding upwards as if to meet him.

'BEHHHHZ!'

Another man leapt on his back, yelling. He was wearing a pair of round dark John Lennon glasses, and a constellation of small red pimples punctuated his jawline.

'I'm sorry... *what* did he just call you?' Vi asked.

'This is Bez, man! Bez! Who are you?' The man swung round and seemed to notice Vi for the first time.

'*Bez?* Are you for fucking real?'

Albert wanted the world to stop spinning, and in fact to rewind it and prevent the various innocuous events that had led to this nickname from having ever happened. He shrugged Pat off his shoulders.

'Yeah. I know. It predates the Mondays, honestly – my name's Albert, Bert, Bez? If you can believe that. This is Pat.' His mate bobbed around them both like a monkey looking for attention.

'Riiiight.' Vi enjoyed sniggering at him.

'Well what's your fuckin' name?' asked Pat, in a thick scouse accent.

'Vi.' She stuck out her hand, suddenly stiff and proud.

'Nice to meet you.' Albert's handshake was as floppy as his dance moves. But his hand was warm, and surprisingly soft.

'Vye? What's that short for anyway then?' asked Pat loudly, and Albert just wanted him to go away, because it was like there was a sort of circle growing around him and this Vi, her face seemed to be opening up to him like a flower, and he didn't want clumsy Pat to trample on it.

Like a flower. Fuck's sake.

'Short for Violet—'

Violet! Literally *a flower!*

'Ha! What a bloody pair! Were you born in the Victorian era or what?'

Albert tried to shoot Pat a glance, but Pat had been known to ignore very direct instructions to piss off, let alone glances. At dusk. While wearing shades.

'Actually, it was my granny's name? My mam promised to give it to me when my grandmother was on her deathbed – she died just a few weeks before I was born. Heartbroken, she was, not to see her first grandchild.'

'Oh, right, sound.' Even Pat was quelled by such a revelation. He muttered something about it being a pretty name, and then started dancing, hard, his forehead jutting in and out to the beat. He looked like a chicken, Vi thought.

Albert looked stricken.

'Don't worry, only the first part of that was true,' she whispered, leaning in towards him. Her words tickled his ear.

When she pulled away, there was an impish smile on her face. A face that looked really familiar, like maybe he'd actually known her forever? Then the beat got harder and both them couldn't help but respond, digging down into it.

After he didn't know how long, Albert realised he needed to talk to Vi again very urgently and bent down towards her once more. She smelled of cut grass and stale smoke.

'Sorry, where did you say you were from?' *Feeble.*

'I didn't. But we came from Bristol, so it wasn't too bad to get here. Waited ages for the address though.'

They had sat outside the Little Chef on the M4 for so long,

263

taking it in turns to fruitlessly try the number on the call box, that they'd eventually all gone in for egg and chips. A middle-aged waitress wearing too much bronzer had glared at them as she put down the grease-glistening plates. Finally, a phone call revealed the directions for how to get to the rave, and the six of them squeezed back into Mel's duck-egg blue Morris Minor and bumped along with a dreadful mix tape blasting out from Jimmie's boombox, till they found the site

'Yeah, it didn't look like the farmer was going to let us go ahead here for a while.'

He was nodding sagely and Vi realised that he was trying to impress her. She found she felt pleased. Which was strange. Usually she found that peculiarly male brand of showing off – of knowing certain records, or some particular weed or pill – crushingly boring.

'You're an organiser then?'

'I help out.'

Albert hoped the insouciance made it sound like he was being modest about how central he was, while not technically ruling out the truth – that he was barely involved at all.

An old school friend, Harry, was one of the main organisers. They'd bumped into each other at a warehouse party in Milton Keynes, and then a few weeks later at a charity ball at York racecourse that their mothers had insisted they attend. Both smirking at the contrast, they'd swapped numbers.

When Albert heard about the rave, he had called Harry, rather too persistently. He felt like he was standing at a door, and so eager to be let in that even if knocking loudly was uncool, it was worth it.

Eventually Harry had said there was a space in his car, if he helped with the set up. Albert had been jumped up for days, hazy but happy visions of his new life misting up his mind. But when they got to the field, Harry high-fived a load of guys much older than them, suddenly started speaking as if he might have grown up in Bethnal Green, and no longer met Albert's gaze. Albert had been relieved when Gregsy, Pat, and the others showed up.

'Are you a student at Bristol then?' Albert leant in, closer than really needed, and the coarseness of Vi's dyed hair brushed against his cheek.

'Yeah. Third year. Finish in a few weeks. I really ought to be writing an essay on DH Lawrence, not dancing in a field!'

'I've not read any Lawrence.'

'Oh he's very strange – a lot of … *feelings*. I'd start with *Sons and Lovers*, and then *The Rainbow* and *Women in Love* – you'll love it, I promise!' *Where had that come from*, Vi cringed. What if he wasn't even interested in literature?

'I've actually been meaning to read him. I love stuff from that sort of time – Woolf, Forster, Beckett, uh … Joyce—' *Don't push your luck*, thought Albert. His copy of *Ulysses* had had plenty of use as a bedside table next to his mattress on the floor, but he'd not got too far with actually reading it.

Vi smirked, and raised her eyebrows at him, sceptically. And then hated herself for refusing to be impressed. Here was a beautiful man, at a rave – and he also wanted to talk about *Modernism* – that was the dream, wasn't it?

'So you're studying English then?' Albert pressed on, before she could ask him any questions about Joyce. 'Isn't that, like, traitorous for a Welsh girl?'

'Fuck off.' She grinned, and poked him in the rib.

He wasn't that far off, mind, thought Vi, her mind traipsing backwards. Her mam and dad had been very keen she should go to university, but had assumed it would be in Wales. Cardiff or Swansea, like nearly everyone else from her school. But the new English teacher, whom they all laughed at for insisting she be addressed as *Ms* Ketterick, kept taking Vi aside and recommending extra books, and suggested she try for Oxford. Vi had snorted at the thought – not fucking likely she'd get in, and not fucking likely she'd enjoy being with all those poshos if she did. She'd felt a funny little tug inside her when she tried to hurry away from Ms Ketterick rather than really talking with her about it properly. But there were rumours about the short-haired teacher that Vi knew would get spread to her if she lingered too long after class.

When it finally came to choosing where to go, Vi simply put the decision off for a year, working in The Fountain to save some money. Which was so crushingly boring, she decided she couldn't bear to stare at the same faces for another three years. Bristol was the closest university where she wouldn't actually know anyone.

And when she came back for Christmas at the end of her first term, and her mam made her go to the candlelit service in the chapel, Vi gave her own small, fierce prayer of thanks to God for making the city of Bristol so obligingly near Abergavenny. She sent another little prayer up to the stars now, a few beginning to prickle across the night sky. Because thinking about how different her life might have been if she'd gone to uni with all her old friends from Aber made her throat feel briefly constricted. At this precise moment, she might be shouting along to Bon Jovi in a sticky-carpeted Swansea club with Llinos Price, and being chatted up by sleazy blokes, rather than raving in a field.

One of the things Vi loved most about the acid house scene was that no one was very bothered about appearing attractive to the opposite sex. It was a far cry from The Young Farmers' dances that she had gone to round Abergavenny, held in barns hung with strings of lights, all the girls dressed up in tight tube skirts and mini dresses, sparkly ruffly bits helping to draw the eyes to the flesh within. But it wasn't just the eyes: groping was rampant and indistinguishable, as much a normal part of any night out for the men as getting into fights and punching their own mates (which, looking back, was also a strange pastime). *Why did we put up with it*, wondered Vi, her brain far back in the memory, even as her hands stabbed upwards in time with the hissing rhythms of 'Strings of Life'.

She should thank God too, really, that she'd found Mel, who'd introduced her to this different world. Or that Mel had found her. Vi twisted round to see her friend, her hips swaying, completely unselfconsciously. Her eyes — a strikingly pale hazel colour that strangers often felt compelled to comment on — lit up when she saw Vi looking at her, and she danced over.

Mel didn't try to be sexy — that wasn't her vibe, wasn't anyone's vibe — but it was also simply a fact that everything Mel did looked vaguely hot. Even in a big tartan bomber jacket that obscured most of her shape. Some of her curly hair, an Afro loosened by mixed heritage, was bubbling out of a top-knot. Vi reached out and gave it a little play (something she was only allowed to do when Mel was high, and which she felt a bit guilty about afterwards) and Mel wrapped her arms around her friend's waist.

Vi had noticed Mel in lectures in the first week of their first year, because Mel wore thick magenta lipstick, and was one of the only girls to stick her hand up and ask questions. And because she was one of the only people who didn't have what Vi would learn was a 'home counties' accent. Mel was from Croydon, and proud.

The tap on the shoulder came some weeks later, when Vi was queueing for the toilet of a nightclub.

'Oi, you on my course?'

'Yeah. Hi.'

Mel was standing with her weight all in her left hip, arms folded, looking bored.

'I'm Mel.'

I know, Vi stopped herself from saying.

'I'm Vi.'

'God, it's good to hear someone who doesn't sound like they're felating a plum. How you finding it all? The course and that?' Mel's slanted eyes squinted as if they were judging everything, and her voice was low; it was like her confidence came from deep in her belly.

'Yeah, it's … all right.' Vi swallowed. 'And I dunno, I reckon seventy-five per cent of lectures are going over my head at the minute. I didn't expect it to be so much about Freud. And … *penises.*'

This was true, and Vi spoke dolefully. She'd chosen English because it had always seemed extremely obvious what a novel or a poem was on about. But their lecturers appeared to be fixated on uncovering dark complicated psychological urges in everything, and then covering them up again with dry, dull, impenetrable 'theory'.

Mel 'mm-*hmm*'ed approvingly. 'I do not envy no penis! Why the fuck would I want a penis? Barf-o-rama!' she laughed.

It was as if Vi had passed a test. Mel had got out her fags and lit one for her too, offering it with an eyebrow raise that was more expectation than question. Vi, who didn't smoke, had taken it – the start of a bad habit, and a firm friendship.

The memory reminded Vi that it must be about time for a toilet trip.

'I need to go to the loos,' she declared into Mel's ear.

'Mm, yeah, me too.'

'We're going for a wee,' Vi shouted at Albert, feeling Mel give her a mildly incredulous look.

'Oh right. I might come with you actually.' Albert knew that once this girl wandered off, he might see her again in five minutes, or never.

They wound through the crowd, better lit as they got closer to the big lights next to the stage. A laser moved up and down, bisecting the bodies in red and green lines.

Vi heart sank when she saw the queue for the portaloos.

'Why are you bothering, they'll be gross by now anyway,' said Albert.

'Yeah fuck it, I'm just going in the trees.' Mel started off.

'Mel!'

She turned round, and groaned as she clocked Vi's little chin-jutting look.

'*Fine.*'

Albert shrugged, and wondered if Vi wasn't a bit uptight after all. But at least he'd be able to find her again.

They were still queuing when he came back. He joined them, rolling cigarettes which Vi quietly smoked as Mel cheerfully grilled him about where he was from, what he did, and then why exactly he'd dropped out of a law degree at LSE to move into a squat.

'Yeah, fuck 'em – who wants to be the agent of the law? I'd rather be an agent of chaos. Especially this country, fucking state it's in.' Mel's lip curled and jutted as she spoke, and Vi could tell she was convinced by this Bez. *Albert.*

'Yeah exactly. I mean I just realised I didn't want to be on the side of the establishment, you know?'

'Amen.'

After finally getting to the front of the queue, Vi dashed towards a free portaloo. The plastic door slammed loosely in the frame. Vi wondered, as she hovered over a hole already filled up and tried to release some wee that just didn't want to come, if by the time she got out, Albert might prefer Mel.

Vi gave up on the wee. She pulled her tampon out and dropped it in the hole. She'd tucked another one in her bra earlier and as the paper wrapper fumbled and fiddled in her fingers, Vi found she had to concentrate very hard on both opening the packaging and not falling backwards. Once it was in, she breathed in deep to ready herself for returning to the outside world, and regretted it.

Back in the chilling air, it was as if a glittering golden light had settled on the outlines and edges of everything and everyone. Albert was beautiful, Mel was obviously beautiful, Amit had found them and was talking animatedly, his thin wrists flicking in the air, and he was beautiful. Something surged inside her, and Vi felt like her feet were skipping even as she tried to walk in a straight line over to them, almost stumbling in her chunky Kickers.

'Hi.' She didn't need to say anything else.

'Hi.' Albert looked at her very directly. Unafraid. He wanted to just crawl inside her heart, really, that was all.

Mel cynically raised her eyebrows at the pair of them, standing there dumbly smiling at each other, but she was grinning too.

They all stood around for a while, an incredible urgency in their chat about Amit's new admin job at the council and the intricacies of canteen politics, and then about what it was like living in London and signing on. And Albert's previous attempts to sound cool or impress Vi melted completely.

They all listened – really listened – as Albert told them about falling out with his dad, the actual Harold Brinkhust, Conservative MP, notorious architect of Thatcher's decimation of the trade unions. Really heard, as Albert told them about all the expectations that had always been put on him, and how those had fallen away after meeting a different kind of person at uni, that he could see it was all a load of crap, and he just didn't want to live like that.

His 'radicalisation', as Harold liked to call it, happened quickly. By Christmas of his first term at LSE, Albert was quietly picking holes in his father's off-hand pronouncements about privatisation and deregulation; by Easter, he was arguing with him about taxation. By the end of a summer, spent mostly at Gregsy's house in Wakefield – who had gone to study politics at LSE as a direct result of watching his dad and uncle strike for month after month – Albert hotly announced he wasn't going back to study law. That he was now, officially, 'anti-establishment'. And that he didn't need his dirty allowance anyway.

'Members of the ruling class, the fucked-up elites ... they don't – they genuinely don't – want what's good for this country or its people, right,' Albert said to the group, but really always keeping one eye on Vi and how she was reacting. 'They just want to stealthily keep all the wealth to themselves and for people exactly like them. And I know I'm part of that world but I just – I just don't *want* to be, like does that make any sense?'

Yeah of course, of course, they all chorused, and even though Vi and Mel laughed at boys like Albert at uni they were nodding here like they really felt for him. Vi was sure she could feel the seed of his pain sprouting inside her own chest.

'It's living by your values, mate – turning down his money. I respect that, you know?' said Amit, and Mel squeezed his shoulders, because they'd all heard the scenes when Amit's parents had come to visit unexpectedly and found a white girl half-dressed in his bed, all noticed that he'd had to get a job not long after that rather than flashing his usual cash about.

'Yeah, but you know what? It's events like this that make the difference.' Albert laughed, and put his arms round the group with floppy affection. 'People just getting on with it ... doing something different? Changing things? I want life to be like this!'

'Yes, matey!' laughed Mel.

It was true: Albert felt full of sudden optimism, and strangely close to this group of people he'd only just met. To this girl. He never normally told people who his father was – too much judgement, too much baggage. Even Pat didn't know. So it was weird that he'd told them – *told her* – so quickly.

Albert had had only loyalty towards his father as a teenager, although it was an unexamined one. When the hate mail arrived – and when he watched his father being pelted with eggs on the evening news – a fierce love burned in him, but somewhere in among that ferocity was embarrassment too. A desire not to have to see it, not to look.

Even away at his boarding school, where intellectual debate was boisterous, schoolboys deliberately taking the most obnoxiously extreme views – on both right and left – there was an awkward sense that it was better not to mention politics around Albert. Or at least not once things had got really nasty.

It was Harold's excessive joy when the miners went trudging back – he recorded the footage on a VCR, made Albert watch it over and over with him while he drank actual Champagne in front of the TV – that soured something inside his son. Albert wasn't used to seeing his father show much emotion. But it was more than that: there was something grotesque in his triumphalism. How he mocked the men on TV, affecting to find their audacity – walking back with heads held high, banners waving – absolutely hilarious, given that they had *lost*.

Amelia had stood in the doorway, sighing with frustration at Harold's lightly slurred, self-satisfied pleas to join him. 'I'm going to a *fucking* meeting,' she shouted as she left, and Harold scoffed.

At university, he didn't tell anyone who his father was. It wasn't meant to be a secret, but the more he didn't say, the more it inevitably became one. Because no one minced their words there – the political divisions were bitter, and while plenty of people on his law course were cut from the same cloth as the boys at school, the lads in Albert's halls were certainly not. It wasn't long till he heard someone slagging off 'that stupid stuffed-shirt cunt' and realised the cunt in question was his father.

He still didn't say anything. He couldn't untangle the two knots of fear inside him: that he was a bad person for not defending his own father. And that it might be his own father who was, in fact, the bad person.

The DJ started teasing that unmistakable, signature KLF bassline, prompting Mel to interrupt the chat, to insist they all went back to dancing nearer the speakers. Vi let her head rest on Albert's arm as they stumblingly followed Mel.

A cool breeze gusted over everyone, sending shivers tickling up and down Vi's spine; she thought a heavily sweating man they were passing actually raised his head and cheered the wind. And then Albert saw a group of guys he knew and stopped to speak to them.

Vi was torn, her body following Mel but her hand still in Albert's. She dropped it, and started walking slowly backwards away from him, unsteadily, grinning. *Surely he'd follow?*

Albert was drawn after her, as if connected by an invisible thread. She was waiting for him, her hands bunched up in her over-long sleeves. They stopped, facing each other. Enjoying the tantalising moment that seemed held and still and trembling even as the music powered onwards, its insistent hook tripling, rippling, repeating.

Vi swayed and twitched, small movements, drawing him in.

Drawing him.

Drawn.

Their bodies locked together, arms and knees and legs. His face an inch away. She could feel his breath on hers. She wanted him to kiss her. But she also wanted to keep the moment paused, in agonizing expectation, for as long as possible.

It was like the second before diving into a pool of water, and then finally the decision was made. And he thought he might actually drown.

For the rest of the night, Vi and Albert kept saying to each other that they ought to go back to the music, ought to find their friends. But all they wanted to do was kiss, and hug, and stroke all the soft bits of each other's bodies that they could find. And then stop kissing for a bit so they could talk, and find out absolutely everything about each other. And then start kissing again, until they had kissed each other down onto the damp, grassy floor, in a dark corner of the field. Still fully dressed. Still wishing they weren't. Him lying gently over her, stroking her hair and gazing down right into her eyes.

As the sun came up, Albert wrote his number on a torn filter pack and tucked it into the front pocket of Jimmie's sweatshirt, because of course they both wanted to see each other again.

Vi had never been particularly romantic. She didn't even believe in 'the one' – it was a concept she and Mel sneered at as mathematically implausible, if nothing else. 'Oh, oh, "the one" just *happened* to do the same uni course as you? Just *happened*, out of millions of people in the whole universe, to also stack shelves in the same branch of Bargain Booze on weekends? Yeah bloody right.'

But as she drove away from Albert that morning, the June sunshine drenching him in yellow light, it felt like the universe had broken its laws of probability to drop an extraordinary gift right into her lap. And while everyone else nodded off in the back seat, she stared out of the Morris Minor's wound-down windows, marvelling at how green the countryside was and how the blue of the sky looked like it had been scrubbed up specially for her. Everything was brand new, squeaky clean.

The midsummer day was warm before they even got home to Bristol, and their front room smelt stuffy and dusty. Vi stripped to just her long T-shirt and pants as she sprawled over the sofa, her jeans and Jimmie's jumper — grubby with grass stains and dirt — tossed on the floor. Finally, she slept, passing out on the couch after the spliffs and mugs of cheap red wine they'd had to 'take the edge off'.

When she woke up, her mouth parched and tanniny, sleep was swiped away in an almost sickening rise of excitement. She reached down for the sweatshirt, to find Albert's number. *Would he back in London yet?*

The jumper wasn't there.

In the kitchen, the washing machine rumbled.

Chapter 3

March 1991

The van groaned and rocked slightly as Albert swung his legs out of bed. There was a chill to the air, and he quickly pulled on the loose woven trousers he'd been living in for weeks, a T-shirt and an almost matted wool jumper, its stripes of maroon and purple seeming to merge into each other the longer he didn't wash it.

Albert had been in the woods since late January, in a camp designed to stop a bypass being built through the ancient forest. He'd become something of an expert in setting up camps over the past year and a half, an enthusiasm for self-organising that started with helping out at free parties but quickly tilted towards more political actions. Albert had been inspired by meeting people who didn't just drop out of conventional society to party, but to change the world: taking direct, non-violent, maximally disruptive action against banks, politicians, and corporations, environmental polluters and nuclear technologies. After long stints at peace camps outside power plants and nuclear bases, the latest movement was towards protecting forests from the Tories' insane new road-building plans.

When Albert came back from his piss, only a crown of dark hair was visible above the lumpy, too-thin duvet, its forget-me-not blue cotton cover so worn it was underbelly soft. The scratchy blanket thrown over the top, that they'd shiver without at night, was slowly sliding off her. She was still asleep.

This was good, because she hated being woken up. But it was bad, because he wanted a cup of tea.

Fuck it. He'd make her one too. The water gulped as it slopped heavily from the water box into the tiny, tarnished metal kettle. While waiting for it to boil, Albert raised his hand idly to the van's little window, so beaded with condensation it could have been designed to protect their modesty. He drew a heart in it, then glanced behind him.

He rubbed it out.

Albert took both cups – hers a righteous, vegan black – back to bed, and to the now snuffling shape beneath the duvet.

'So *early*.'

'Not really. It's gone nine.'

A snort.

'What happened to morning meditation walks?'

She sank her teeth into the giving flesh of his hand, which had been playing carelessly around her pointed little face, crinkled and sour with interrupted sleep.

'Ow!'

'It's still winter.'

'It might be spring.'

More snorting.

'There are green shoots, now. It'll get easier,' Albert said, almost to himself. 'When the weather's warmer—'

'All right, since when are you Mr Big Expert on surviving on site?'

Albert considered pointing out that that wasn't what he'd been trying to say, but it barely seemed worth it. There was no way round it: she'd always have more experience than him. Electra would always be the actual new-age traveller, the one whose mother quit her job after an epiphany during the 1976 solstice at Stonehenge and moved her three children into a double-decker bus belonging to a man named Peaceful Steven.

He once asked her why, of all the names in the world, she'd chosen Electra. She had shrugged her thin, almost knobbly shoulders and said she liked how Electra sounded like the feminine version of *electric*, which made him smile. He didn't ask if she'd read the Oresteia. He knew she'd stash knowledge of Greek tragedy as further evidence against him. His *elitism*.

Electra refused to tell him her birth name. But Albert kept secrets from her too – who his father really was being chief among them.

Albert rarely told people in the environmental movement. But a few days after he'd first hooked up with Electra – riding a wave of triumph because the man from Gloucestershire county council had told the diggers to turn around: there'd be no progress with the bypass that week – he had felt tempted to confess. Sitting around the campfire, their faces roasting in the flames but the night cool on their backs, Albert had been about to offer up his nugget of intimacy.

Then he remembered the time Electra had quite earnestly insisted that all members of Margaret Thatcher's cabinet should be charged in an international court of law for crimes against humanity.

Electra was utterly uncompromising in her moral view of the world. Anyone whose attempts to live well were less than absolutely perfect were likely to encounter the scorn of Electra's curled lip, her thick eyebrows pulling in. If she found you to be a let-down – as when Neil revealed he rented out a house he inherited to students despite believing that property was a root cause of inequality, or when Jenni admitted she actually preferred bottle-feeding, or when anyone who professed to be anti-capitalist also smoked – Electra was prone to take you to task so vigorously that *she'd* start crying. This combination of rigid rationality with overwhelming emotion left Albert floundering, feeling obscurely guilty.

What was in Electra's favour was the fact she was just continually *there*. They'd been at the site almost two months now, and even if they'd missed the worst of the January gales, the first fortnight of February had still been brutally frigid. A cold body was better than none at all. Even a cold body who, after sex, liked to sharply remind him that she didn't believe in monogamy; that structured relationships were a form of gendered oppression. They'd got into a fight the one time he'd complained, asking if she'd mind at least waiting till he'd taken his dick out of her before reminding him of her lack of interest, a remark that *she* claimed was 'insensitive'.

But there was very little else to do on site. The only other excitement had been the week when there were actually diggers to see off and pigs to swear at, when they all made chains round the oaks and the campervans and tipis. Then, the shared sense of purpose – and the more brutish force of pumped adrenaline – made Albert feel alive. Made them all feel alive, it was obvious, a brightness glinting off eyes and teeth.

He even quite liked climbing up and up the 'mega oak', as they called it, to sleep on the little platform in the tree. Swallowing the first sway of vertigo and settling in with a grainy sleeping bag and torch, knowing he'd wake numb in finger and toe every hour. But at least it was an event.

It also quietly filled Albert with a sense of duty, a word that seemed too square to use among this crowd, a mix of environmental activists, travellers, students, and a few excitable local ex-hippies. *Duty* became an idea that he held close to him, like a child clutching a beloved toy they think they might be too old for but don't want to give up. It was his duty – his responsibility – to protect these trees, this land. The lungs of the country; the roots of our identity.

Albert was reaching across the big communal table to pass the soy milk to Electra for her breakfast cereal when an unknown car pulled up at the site. Arrivals were routinely met with suspicion, but also hope: they'd been joined in the forest by everyone from a local MP to awkward teenagers dropped off by frowning parents for an afternoon. Local opinion seemed mostly on their side. Everyone hated the traffic in town, but the woods were the place where people walked their dogs, had first kisses, summer picnics. Where they went, in recent years, to forget about redundancies, and recession, to lose themselves in impressionist drifts of bluebells or the sugar-coated crunch of frosted leaves underfoot. People needed them.

Around the camp, everyone had risen to their feet at the sound of the car. Albert saw Electra glance towards her own tipi, as if scoping out how quickly she could leap back there if there was a threat.

'Pigs in blankets?' hissed Jenni, squinting at the two bodies getting out of the car as she wrapped a braid tight around her finger.

The man, broad in a black coat that must once have been smart, carried a big bag. The woman fussed with the belt of her thin-looking trench and rummaged in a handbag, a show of being busy.

'Nah, that'd be a feeble attempt to be undercover,' whispered Electra, with her usual certainty, as they walked over. 'They're press, bet you. Camera bag.'

They'd had press before. The local paper oscillated in its opinion: pro cancelling the bypass, then worried about the sorts of people the protest was attracting. There'd been stories of a nearby farmhouse being robbed, which turned out to have been by two local, unconnected teenagers.

Such developments prompted a couple of tabloids to come down, however, subsequent reports using the term 'ECO-WARRIORS' in capital letters, like it was a bad thing. Even the *Guardian's* report seemed as interested in lurid lifestyle details as in their environmental aims. Why was it relevant, Electra had railed afterwards, that some of them had dreadlocks or that Albert's van had flowers painted on her side? Privately, Albert thought that anything that helped drag attention to the issue was worth it. What mattered was saving the trees, and fighting against the disastrous plan to build more roads, for more cars – and if that meant that they as 'crusties' had to become the story, he was willing.

Then Albert's heart leapt up through his sternum into his throat, snatching away his breath, before dropping quickly to his belly where it seemed to spin around, like a dog chasing its tail. It was *her.*

Was it? Yes, surely it was! Her hair was dark, not blonde, now. But that bobbly nose, the pale skin. And surely, those eyes. Blue eyes that he had looked into so long, so soppily, that night. He'd never held eye contact like that with anyone. Might never have stopped had her friend not physically pulled her away into their funny little car. The image of it flashed in his mind, puttering and bumping down the track, her face watching despondently from the window.

Blue eyes, that he had thought so often about finding again. Every party. Every rave. His mates destroyed him for how much time he spent looking past them, over their shoulders. Completely sure that one day, he'd look up and there she would be. Coming over to him, like she had done that night in the field.

Like she was doing right now.

Oh God. She still hadn't seen him.

Had she ...?

Maybe she didn't remember—

Vi. Violet. Vi.

He'd turned her name over in his head too, endlessly. Obsessively, if he was honest. If he met anyone with a connection to Bristol or anywhere in Wales (he'd forgotten the name of her town), he would also ask if they knew a Vi – hopefully, lamely, pathetically! – and of course they never did. Vi. ViViViViVi. Vivid, vivacious, vital Vi. Violently fucking absent from his life.

And then time passed. The hope dimmed. The despair over why she hadn't called (boyfriend at home, lost the number, moved to Australia, *died*) also dimmed. Just a romantic story, the one that got away.

But there she very much was.

Vi walked gingerly towards the camp. There were some bits of rushy matting and thin planks of wood, saturated by the mud they were intended to cover. The dirt was already spattering her flesh-coloured tights; she could feel the pinpricks of wet tickling up her legs. Why on earth had she worn the cheap, high-shine heels her mum had got her on discount last month?

The protestors had all stood up. *Closing ranks?* She swallowed, her Adam's apple seeming unusually present.

They're just people like you, the sorts of people you'd have been friends with in Bristol, she'd kept telling herself on the drive over, staring out the window while Pete the Pics sang along, somewhat flat, to Radio 2. Maybe she'd even know someone there.

But she felt stiff in nylon, and all the tricks Derek – her editor at the *Western Mail* – had taught her for how to ask open-ended questions seemed to have left her brain, like a flock of startled birds. When she tried to think what to say, there was only a field of emptiness there.

Come on, she scolded herself. Pull yourself together. This was her chance: a chance to write her first double-page spread, to get a proper byline. *If it's good enough*, she heard Derek's voice saying, a promise she kept replaying too, along with the wink that accompanied it. A wink that turned it into a threat? Or an extra little vote of confidence? (Or just a reminder of Friday night?)

'All right?' Pete the Pics raised his hand in hello as they came to a stop at the edge of the rag-tag settlement. There were about twenty vans and tipis and tents, with various levels of Day-Glo decoration, while tarpaulins stretched over stoves and boxes and washing up bowls, dripping with red, blue and yellow Tibetan prayer flags. The soft, nonsensical clunk and clatter of wooden windchimes sounded from somewhere in the camp, and a set of bongos lay, in idle threat, next to the fire pit.

Pete the Pics nudged her.

'Hiya. We're, um, from the *Western Mail*?' Her voice sounded strangely high-pitched. She raised her hand in front of her eyes, squinting at them all, even though the sunlight really wasn't that bright. 'We wanted to write a piece on – I mean, we *will* be writing a piece on the, um, ongoing protests here and we were hoping to take some pics and have a little chat, like ...'

Vi swallowed again, heavily. Pete waved his camera, non-threateningly. He looked – as usual – a bit bored, and utterly unflustered.

When would she finally notice him? Albert wondered.

'Would any of you, um ...'

Silence, and a sea of faces: wary, hard. Hostile, even. Or was she imagining it?

If only they had a leader she could speak to, rather than this unfocused mass. One-on-ones she could manage. She was *good at*. It was just this audience that made her nervous. *Bloody non-hierarchical structures.* Even though the air was cool, she could feel a warm dampness spreading under her pits, and in the gusset of her stupid synthetic tights.

When will she see me?

Pete, perhaps actually being sensitive for once, swept in, and started asking what *exactly* he could take pictures of, as if the general principle of picture-taking had already been OK-ed. A man with an unlined face but frosted, greying hair and a woman in an enormous sheepskin coat stepped forward and started talking to him about practicalities.

Vi nodded as Pete talked, as if she was graciously letting him take charge of the situation. And her confidence – her sense of purpose – began to crawl back. She interjected suddenly, asking the woman in the coat if she could get a few quotes about life in the camp. The woman waved her hand behind her head and said, go talk to that lot, see who's up for it, I'm no spokesperson.

Several people had sat back down at a long, makeshift table – a piece of thin wood over palettes, lashed to crates. Vi picked her way over.

Albert remained standing, rooted to the spot.

His whole skin seemed to be about to burst.

Vi flicked a look at the tall man standing stock still next to the table. No, it couldn't be. And then her neck muscles seemed to freeze, stuck looking the other direction. Could she look again. No, she couldn't. Her feet kept taking her towards the table, but her mind was stuck a few steps backwards, wanting to turn, *desperate* to check.

It never was him, though. Over the last two years, so many messy heads of dirty-blonde hair in a crowded bar or on a station platform had turned around, to reveal tiny noses or chunky glasses. Overheard soft laughter that quickened her pulse never turned out to really belong to Albert.

Vi hadn't spoken to Jimmie for a full week after the incident with the washing machine. She knew it had been unfair. How was he supposed to know that she had Albert's number in the pocket? But the disappointment – the great fucking chasm opening up inside, a black hole of disbelief that sucked the rest of her in – was so overwhelming, she was completely inconsolable.

'Babe, you've got to get over it,' Mel had said, patting her leg beneath the duvet on the third day she'd refused to get up. 'He's just another bloke.'

But Albert had not been just another bloke. Albert had been *possibility*. Albert could have been life-changing, Vi was sure. What they had in those too-few hours had to be the start of something absolutely huge. It was as if the rising tide of change, and optimism, that had broken out in waves of ecstasy across the country over the previous two years, had found its finest form in this other person she'd somehow stumbled on.

'Vi?'

His voice was uncertain, but also like a sharp pull on a rope somewhere very deep inside her.

She turned. And then the trees seemed to shoot right up into the sky, and the ground beneath her dropped a few inches.

She caught herself, and then everything sped up, as if life was on fast-forward, the universe catching up for the lost time. But it had given her another gift, thought Vi, as an effervescent disbelief at her good luck surged through her.

'Oh my God!'

'It's—'

'Yes, it's—'

285

'Albert? How are—'

'I can't believe it—'

'I know!'

'It really is…?'

'How are you?'

'What are you—'

'This is crazy—'

And then they laughed, and Vi felt a little out of control, like she might not be able to ever stop. And they felt the people around them watching – keying in, curious, softening (or hardening, in the case of Electra, whom Albert was vaguely aware of, darkening as she watched). There was a funny little hug, awkward and too eager at the same time, Vi half-hurling herself into his arms, then going stiff, with the shock, and the audience.

Albert gestured to her to sit down at the table, but when Vi tried to follow, the heel of her shoe got stuck in the mud. She didn't notice that she'd fully walked out of it until the earth came as a cold slap and she yelped, falling clumsily onto the stool.

Albert leaned down and picked up the shoe and went to put it back on her foot. It was like bloody Cinderella. The hunt for the mysterious woman met while dancing, the sliding on of the shoe. But her foot didn't slip in easily, so she had to wriggle and he had to shove a bit.

Why was she wearing such stupid shoes anyway, Albert wondered. The squeak of patent leather. He couldn't remember the last time he looked twice at a woman in heels. Electra would have labelled them the uncomfortable tools of patriarchal oppression, signifiers of impracticality and a disconnect from the land and earth!

Vi winced. It was like she could see the thoughts ticking

through his head. The judgements forming. She was sure he wouldn't like what she'd become. She wanted to shout: I'm supporting my family! I'm not like this at weekends! I am political too – *I also love trees!*

'You guys... know each other then?' Jenni's eyebrows were raised, amused, as they both tried to settle at the table, despite practically humming with some kind of electrical charge.

'Right – yeah!' laughed Albert, nodding away.

He was still adorable, thought Vi. But he was also different. A terrible, patchy beard. Hair long enough to be tied back. He seemed bigger than she remembered, but maybe that was just the sheep-smelling jumper. And his voice had changed, surely. It would be harder, now, to guess at those posh roots.

'We met – God, couple of years ago, at a rave. Summer of '89, was it?' Albert framed it as a question, even though he knew for certain.

'A lifetime ago!' Vi said, too bright, suddenly feeling the need to protect herself. Maybe it wasn't a treasured memory for him? Maybe he'd barely even thought of it since!

A lifetime ago? Albert felt stung by the distance Vi put between then and now. His life had expanded in that time, but in line with those nights spent raving and dreaming. If each month had taken him further away from the path he was expected to follow, they were also steps along the path he was already on when he met Vi – a path that led very naturally towards this forest, these people. People who lived on the edges of society, or made their own idealistic alternative version of it.

A lifetime ago sounded like a break. Like she wanted nothing to do with any of it.

Well, of course not, Albert suddenly thought. Look at her: she was in uniform. The uniform of the working woman, handbags and high heels. Make-up and suits. She was the press. The fourth estate. The establishment.

'So the *Western Mail*? That's cool – I mean, how is—'

'What is the *Western Mail* – is that Welsh?' interrupted his friend Taz.

'Yeah,' Vi spoke in answer to the man's question, not Albert's. She didn't seem to be able to meet his gaze. 'Based in Cardiff, cover the whole country – though mostly focused on the south.'

'So why are you here then?' Her interrogator's brown eyes were sceptical as he flicked a roll-up into a black-and-white tin that had once housed No Frills baked beans.

Vi looked down momentarily, and decided to opt for honesty.

'It's been a very slow news week. Need to fill the pages. You're not far over the border – my editor thought the pictures, and a human-interest story, was what we needed.'

She thought there was a small ripple of respect, for being honest at least. Someone offered her a cup of tea, and she nodded gratefully, then got out her notepad.

'Look,' Vi said, a confidence charging through her veins suddenly – or was it just a desire to convey to Albert *this cheap smart coat and nylon skirt suit isn't me, not the real me, I'm the same girl I was in '89*. 'I'm gonna level with you all: I think what you're doing here is *bloo*-dy *brill-i-ant*.'

Her accent! It was just the same. The way she swore for gentle emphasis! The way she extended those vowels!

'But I'm not going to say "oh I'm on your side". Because it won't be an op-ed on why we need to save trees – it'll be a report on the camp, what it's like, how you're surviving the rain and the cold. Why you think it's worth it. And also, for balance, why some people think it's wrong. Councillor David Anderson—'

Snorts from Electra, head shakes from most of the table.

'Yes, I thought he'd be about as popular as a fart in a lift.' Vi smiled knowingly, pulling them slowly in towards her. Still not daring to look at Albert. 'He's got some *charming* things to say about you all, I must say!'

'I bet!' shouted a very young girl with a pretty face peeking out of her long Dr Who-style knitted scarf.

'But look: he has already given me some ... *robust* quotes. That we will be using. So. You can have his perspective, and a bunch of photos Pete has already taken. Or ...' she raised her chin, trying to look authoritative but appealing at the same time '...you can help him get the most persuasive images for your cause, and you can chat to me a bit about the brave action you're taking, and know that I will put the other side over as squarely as I can.'

'*Brave*' was going a bit far; sneaking towards flattery. *Shit.* Had she held them?

She glanced at Albert. He looked away quickly. She noticed the girl with very black, very curly hair noticing it too. Shit.

'Well of course I'm in!' Albert banged the table jovially. 'I can't quite believe Vi is a proper journalist now, but I can tell you we need more people like her writing things. You can trust her.'

And then their eyes locked in, and Albert knew for certain that what he had said was true. He did trust her.

Albert spent the morning manoeuvring her round the camp, introducing her to everyone. Vi's hand flew over her notebook in scrawls of shorthand. She nodded and smiled and smiled and smiled and asked faux-naive questions with widened eyes so they'd say more, give up more.

'We know people want to think we're just daft hippies, but what we're protecting goes way back,' said Neil, the grey-haired man, with measured intent. 'These trees are ancient – and they belong to all of us. They're part of our English heritage, as much as Stonehenge, or Buckingham Palace.'

Yes, thought Vi as she scribbled, *yes. That's it. That's the line.* That's how I can help you – not by repeating woo-woo statements about the need to protect the lungs of Gaia, but with an appeal to misty-eyed patriotism and old English myth-making.

Neil was nodding earnestly as she wrote it down, just the slightest smile dallying around his lips. Did he mean what he said, or did he know he was trotting out a palatable line? Did *he* know that *she* knew that this was the best way to persuade readers – or did he think he was playing her?

'You're going to be underestimated,' Derek had said to Vi on one of the first door-knocks he took her on after she started at the paper as an apprentice. 'It might not feel like it, but that's actually to your advantage. People will tell a pretty little young woman things they would never tell a middle-aged male reporter.'

This had proved true – but it had also got Vi stuck on soft news. She was desperate to write about politics, to use her disarming presence to uncover scandal and injustice; instead, she was sent to grieving relatives and charity fundraisers. But the bypass piece might just trip from fluff into something more serious if she could get juicy enough quotes.

The only problem was that, at any given moment, half her attention was on Albert. Her peripheral vision had become super-charged. Both her heart and her groin seemed to hiccup every few minutes, whenever she remembered that he was here, she was with him.

And he was always hovering around. Had she had enough tea? Would she stay for lunch? They were having dahl. Oh, she should speak to this person about having a baby at the camp, to that person about quitting their job for the cause.

Albert showed her inside his van, and while Vi was stood marvelling at all the clever little shelves and drawers, someone outside shouted for him.

'Back in a sec.'

As she looked around the van, absently, Vi's eyes hooked on the book by the side of the bed. *Women in Love.* A tatty paperback, much-thumbed. Her mind flashed back to their first shouted conversation, under the lasers.

'You'll love it, I promise!'

Before Vi had too long to ponder the significance of his reading the third book of the loose Lawrence trilogy she'd recommended to him, the short girl with the curly dark hair came inside the van.

She even looks a bit like me, Vi couldn't help but think.

'Oh, sorry. I'm Electra. He's giving you the tour, is he?'

'Um, yeah. I'm Vi.'

'I know.'

There was a pause, that got steadily more saturated, like a threatening raincloud.

'Don't mind me,' said Electra, and Vi couldn't gauge the irony level in her voice. 'I just wanted to grab my pants. Doing a wash, while it's not raining for once.'

She swiped various bits of clothing from a small pile by the bed, and Vi felt calcified with a quick-forming kind of shame, and resignation. It crept over her body, hardening it instantly.

When Albert came back, he was so bounding that Vi was sure he couldn't have seen Electra talking to her. Didn't know that she knew about the two of them.

At lunch, Pete the Pics looked bored. He picked up his cutlery like it might be infectious, and contemplated the splat and spread of the dahl like it might be diarrhoea. Which to be fair, it did resemble, thought Vi.

'Let's go then,' he said quietly to her after he handed back the wooden plate for washing up. 'Beat the traffic.'

'Yep, sure.'

She began to gather her things, then felt Albert's eyes on her. They looked all thick and gooey with − what? Longing?

No. He was someone else's.

Just nostalgia then, maybe. Or with wondering?

And he did deserve to know, didn't he? She hadn't managed to tell him yet. Panic rose in the back of Vi's legs as Pete began to twizzle the car key round his finger, impatient.

'I just… I just want to go up the treehouse, all right? Be good for the piece.'

A sigh. '*Fine.*'

The trunk of the biggest oak tree was broad, its bark cracked like a crusty baguette. Vi kicked off her shoes and began to climb up towards the little platform that wobbled near the top.

Albert had swung himself through the branches rather gallantly, but he didn't think Vi had seen. She seemed distracted.

There were handcuffs and bungee cords up there, as well as sleeping things. 'In case the police get someone up here to try to arrest the sleeper,' Albert explained. 'You can cuff yourself to the tree. Makes it harder for them.'

Standing in close proximity to Vi, and her trench coat, he was confused to find that the presence of handcuffs seemed suddenly suggestive. Albert prayed that his cock would stay soft; an erection was very obvious in these trousers, as Electra was fond of unsympathetically pointing out.

The forest around them was still mostly bare and brown, a few tall pines standing bold in blue-green needles further off. But the glossy shoots of bluebell plants splayed over the mulchy dark damp floor beneath, and patches of wild garlic were nosing out too.

'Never been up this high in a tree before.'

'You OK?' Albert asked, feeling his own stomach's turmoil at the slight swaying of the platform. He wondered if it felt worse than usual because he was worried on her behalf, or because of the butterflies that had taken up residence since her arrival.

She was fine. Climbing upwards into the spiralling city of reaching branches was a freeing thing. It seemed to pause the world below. A miniature, temporary escape.

He had gone a bit pale, mind.

'I lost your number.' The words burst out.

His head flicked up.

'If you were wondering. You probably weren't—'

And Albert didn't mean to reach out to her, but he did and it was maybe better than words anyway.

'Oh.' Vi smiled, and closed her eyes. Just a moment of it. Surely she was allowed that. 'You did wonder.'

'Of course.'

She sighed, hard. Squeezed his hand. He read the pain in it too. She opened her eyes, and retracted her hand, slapping it back on a branch. 'My housemate, Jimmie, went and ... well, it doesn't matter now anyway. But I am really sorry. That I never called.'

'So am I.'

Vi dropped her gaze, and then irritation at him scrunched through her veins. He had no right to flirt with her like this, up in a tree, away from the eyes – *literally over the head* – of his girlfriend.

She felt very certain that if she kissed Albert he would kiss her back. But something stopped her.

And then the irritation turned inwards. Why start caring

about that now? Her conscience didn't get in the way usually, when there was almost nothing of consequence even to gain. The occasional Friday nights with Derek, after he bought her pint after pint in the Black Horse, so that everything went fuzzy – including her morality. She knew bonking married men was bad; bonking your boss went all the way to sordid. But the fact that Derek thought she was worth the risk to his marriage – and to his job – made her feel momentarily feel powerful. Even if he held the power, really.

Sometimes, she felt a chill of guilt in the few minutes after he came on her belly or her bum, his lumpy semen cooling in the air of the unheated office or the back of his seven-seater Peugeot. But mostly, she didn't feel much at all. Just a brief respite from life's pervasive boredom.

Her job had its moments of excitement and terror – but the commute to Cardiff was tiring, her family were tense and sullen, and she gave them so much of her income she could barely afford any social life of her own. Vi had only meant to go back to living at home a few months, while she and Mel saved up to 'go travelling'. But then Mel had got the job as a runner at ITV. And then inflation happened. And then the mortgage on the four-bed bungalow, in a part of the town her mam always called 'smart', went up and up and up. And then her dad lost his job.

All through the miners' strikes it was as if a moral anger kept Evan inflated: he campaigned among his own union for railway-men to go out in support of them, co-ordinated food parcel deliveries for the upper valleys, and took Vi with him to picket lines. But once Thatcher won, all that righteous puff began to slowly escape. And then the railways began 'implementing efficiencies', and Abergavenny having both a station master and a ticket officer was deemed 'wasteful'. And when Evan started to sign on, it was like he signed his whole self away.

Then Angharad's hours at Watt's were cut too, and it all made Vi want to scream, but her wages were the only way the house wouldn't be taken away.

It was her brother Geraint who had first spotted the advertisement for the Peggy Southern Memorial Apprenticeship at the *Western Mail*, shortly before he gave up his own job hunt and joined the army. The three-month opportunity was only open to aspiring female news reporters, living in Wales, under the age of twenty-five.

Vi had vibrated with a thrumming sense of pride at getting the role, despite her unremarkable degree results and skimpy portfolio of the few student newspaper pieces she'd managed to fit in around their full schedule of partying. Then, two weeks after her apprenticeship had been converted into a proper job, Derek ran his hand up her thigh under the reflective copper gleam of the pub table, and the vibrations stopped. But the trips to the pub continued.

After all, Vi no longer went out much in Abergavenny. There'd been one night after moving back when she got very drunk on tequila shots in The Fountain, and snogged Becky Jones on the edge of the pool table. Walking home afterwards, Vi kept feeling her cheeks, which stayed hot. But the next time she went in, Becky wouldn't even meet Vi's eye, and the other staff and drinkers started sniggering. Humiliation surged through Vi's body, leaving her face prickled and hot, this time in an unpleasant way.

So at least Derek's intermittent interest provided a flicker of distraction. *Validation.*

Albert realised he was holding his breath.

She was gazing down through the tree. The big beautiful ancient oak that held them both, together, in this moment. He wanted to reach out and touch her hair, he wanted to reach out and forcibly pull her to him.

The relief that had spread through his body when she had at last explained why she hadn't called – *she liked him she liked him she'd felt it all too oh thank fuck thank Christ it really had been a thing* – had almost immediately converted into anticipation.

Gorgeous, delicious anticipation.

When she looked back up, that would be the moment. He would look into her eyes, and he would kiss her.

Vi began to climb down the tree.

Chapter 4

April 1991

Vi went down the high street in Abergavenny first thing on Sunday, the morning still wrapped in a tissue of mist but hinting at the brightness to come. Trees were finally reaching into green, and birds chattered frivolously from them.

'Yes, don't worry, I've got a flippin' bundle put aside for you by here,' said Gavin the News, making great ceremony of barely being able to lift the five copies of the *Independent on Sunday* onto the counter for her. One for her, one for her mam and dad, one for Granny Grey, one to be sent to Geraint, serving out in Belfast, and one for spare. Vi smiled doubly when Gavin wouldn't let her pay, and heaved the newsprint bundle into the sunshine.

She sat down on the furthest bench from the road in the gardens, aiming for privacy. Her fingers felt fat and clumsy as she flicked through the pages of the supplement magazine inside. *The New Review*. It might as well have been printed on gold leaf.

By Violet Lewis.

Small white print. Beneath, in bigger print, 'INTO THE WOODS'. Then, in middle-sized print, 'How the battle for Britain's trees turned ugly'. And then the blown-up shot that Pete had taken: a low angle of Jenni in a short flowery dress, her arms wrapping round a tree trunk. And bisecting the shot, the black uniform of a policeman advancing towards her, truncheon extended. And there, on the next page, was Albert – halfway up a tree, rising above a scene of devastation and chaos below.

They were great pictures. Pete's photographs caught the carnage. He'd been there at the right time – they both had.

Two weeks after they first visited the camp, Vi had received an anonymous tip-off at the *Western Mail*. Specially hired security forces were going to move in with the police the next morning, to clear the protestors from the woods. But Derek wasn't bothered anymore. Old news, he said.

'You've got to go,' Mel had insisted on the phone, when Vi chatted to her that evening. 'It could be a scoop! You can shop the piece around. And anyway … I know you've been dying for an excuse to see him again.'

'He's got a—'

'Yes, I know. But sometimes people are with the wrong people. Sometimes, nicking someone's boyfriend is actually an act of *charity*. When you're, like, seventy-two, you'll both sit around and laugh about it.'

Vi expected to have a hard time persuading Pete to come with her. But Derek had just formally refused him a pay rise that had long been in the offing; bunking off was the least he could do by way of rebellion. They arrived just in time, amid flashing blue lights and an absurd fleet of white GS vans, a looming cherrypicker and a sheriff officer droning on about an eviction order through a megaphone. And no other press.

Suddenly, Vi got a glimpse of the younger man Pete must once have been. He ducked and twisted through the lines of police, through the protesters, his camera coming through the trees, somehow everywhere at once.

Then she spotted Albert.

Vi ran towards him, waving, just as his arms were pulled back by a security guard and he couldn't reach out to her.

But their eyes clicked onto each other for a leaping second, and she knew that – whatever happened with the piece, whether any paper bought it and printed it or not – she had made the right decision to return to the camp. To *him*.

Then a policeman was moving towards her too, and Vi's attention flicked round.

'Reporter,' she snapped. He groaned, and shouted over his shoulder to a superior, by which time Vi had nipped away and climbed on top of a VW van to survey the scene.

It was like a wave – of heat, of air, of noise, something tangible – had hit her. The security forces, with their hard hats and high-vis jackets, were like the bulldozers they wanted to make way for: she watched as three of them smashed through the cooking station, pulling down the tarps and throwing things into boxes, whipping them away into vans. Whole tents full of possessions were lifted in their arms as their owners scrabbled and screamed, unsure whether to stay wrapped around the trees, to lie down in front of the police vehicles, or to try to stop their belongings being torn up and taken away.

Worse, though, was seeing bodies treated in the same fashion. Jenni's Doc Martens were kicking furiously as she tried to escape the arms of a policeman. The matronly woman who had made the dahl was being backed into a police van, even though her hands were lifted, her face blurring with tears. Taz's head kept rising from the dirt and being pushed back down by a security guard with a knee on his back, who couldn't keep the snarl off his face. Vi thumbed Pete towards him, and wanted to cheer when he snapped before the security guard realised there was even a camera there.

Anyone who could raced to get into trees – several more of

which had makeshift platforms and treehouses in now – clipping on harnesses and pulling on climbing ropes to winch themselves up. But not many were fast or strong enough, being dragged back down to the floor by their muddy boots. Some – including, yes, Albert, thank God, he'd got out of their clutches and up a tree – were merely balancing on boughs, lashing bungee cords and blue polyprop rope around their bodies to help them stay up as they embraced the trunks.

Oh, God, she wanted to put her arms around him.

It would also make for really strong visuals.

'Don't fucking touch her,' came a shout below the van. Vi had looked down to see Neil, the man who'd given her such eloquent quotes, his pale eyes bright with fear and fury, trying to stand in front of a white-blonde teenage girl with a nose ring, who had to be his daughter. The security guard hit at the sides of Neil's legs till he buckled and the girl began to cower and whimper as hands reached roughly for her.

'Ought to be in school,' came the gruff voice. 'Get over to those vans.'

Vi scribbled the quote down, and then felt guilty, and jumped to the ground, her own Docs – she'd dressed appropriately this time – landing in the mud with a squelch.

'Oi, fucking press here, mate. Don't put your hands on her unless you want the whole world to read about it.'

It was as if she had a cape flying behind her. The security guard spat at her feet, but turned around. 'Save the trees!' bellowed the girl at his back, lifting her fist weakly into the air. And Vi knew she had her opening paragraph.

Fourteen people were arrested, and all of them – with the exception of Electra – were happy to talk to Vi from the cells. Albert explained to her in furtive, exciting whispers what the real situation with Electra was, and relief charged through Vi's nervous system. They both became somewhat melodramatic, intoxicated with the parts they were getting to play in what was fast becoming a *significant national event*. She asked if she could include information about his dad in her article, and he'd said of course because he'd trust her with anything, and added wasn't that funny as he really barely knew her.

'But I do know you, Albert,' Vi found herself saying, earnestly. And he nodded – he felt it too.

Vi spent that night at what was left of the camp, helping the protesters that remained with the clear up. Broken sticks of furniture and smashed tree platforms were turned into a fire that they huddled round as darkness fell. And Vi also made sure she jotted down details about the healing circle, and the resulting fight over whether or not they should include policemen 'in the light'.

The following morning, she recorded the names of the group of distinctly un-crusty locals – including a schoolteacher, two councillors, a trio of earnest teenagers, and a nonagenarian holding a 'Bog Off with your Bypass' sign – who came up to stand with them, to bear witness to the first trees being felled. They brought candles, which struggled to stay alight in the fine grey spring drizzle, but also sandwiches and bags of Golden Wonder and flasks of tea.

And when they sang 'Jerusalem', in loud but breaking voices, as the first chainsaw started, Vi knew she had her final paragraph.

The editor insisted it should be the first. And he'd insisted that Albert's arrest – and the details of who his father was – must be bumped up to the second paragraph, along with the perfect quotes Albert had given Vi from the prison cell as he awaited bail. 'I'm doing my duty, as my father raised me to, it's just that different generations have different ideas about how duty is best done.'

Sitting on the park bench, with the magazine spread open on her lap, Vi felt consumed by a vast pillowy pleasure at seeing her words – and Albert's words – right there, in black and white. But a queasiness also churned, beneath it. What if Albert, and his activist friends, didn't like what she'd written? Perhaps he would be furious that he – and his father – were the top line, rather than the political message or the police brutality.

Well, she would know soon enough. He was due to pick her up in the van in just a couple of hours. Albert had rung her after his court appearance – which had resulted in a fine, which he only had to pay back in miniscule monthly instalments; he was calling it a moral victory – and asked if she was free that Sunday. For a trip, to the seaside, in the van. To celebrate his freedom, her piece running.

Vi tried not to let the thought that he might not want to see her anymore take root, and instead, hurried back to the bungalow, where her mam was waiting. Eager to read the piece – or really, just to show it off to all the neighbours.

Breakfast was ready, but the thought of the eggs her mam was frying in puddles of oil made Vi want to gag. She was too nervous to eat.

After managing half a slice of toast, Vi went to her room to pack a rucksack in anticipation of her reunion with Albert. She changed her outfit four times, deciding finally on her favourite loose, short denim dungarees over a royal blue belly top, a combination which flashed just a hint of skinny midriff at the sides, and quite a lot of leg. She stuck her hair into two stubby, jaunty bunches, and allowed herself a little eyeliner.

Eleven o'clock. Vi plonked her bag on the bench by the bus stop on the main road, not wanting to give her mam and dad the chance to get a look at Albert's flower-painted old van as it turned in their cul-de-sac.

11.12. Vi regretted her outfit choice. Her thighs were continuingly breaking into goosebumps. They looked practically *blue*. April in Wales was too bloody early for shorts.

11.19. A puttering sound. And, yes, it was unmistakably Alber's van. *He had come!* As the vehicle approached, Albert's face popped out the window, sunny and laughing and weather-beaten, his hair pirouetting in the wind.

'You, Violet Lewis, *Independent on Sunday* journalist, are a *miracle.*'

He came to a stop, lifted the paper out of the van's window, and waved it madly, shouting, 'Brilliant brilliant brilliant!'

And relief coursed through Vi's body again, and she dropped the bag, and leapt at Albert as he got out the van.

He whirled her around so her bare legs spun free in the air. But when they came to a stop, a shyness descended on them both for a minute. Albert kept his arms around her, though, until Vi finally peeked up at him, breath held, body tense.

And then, somehow, they were kissing, and it was just as she'd remembered.

'Hello, you,' said Vi, when they finally broke apart, with a deep-dimpling smile.

'Hello to you too,' Albert replied, before squeezing her back in towards him for more.

Finally, they stepped apart, and Vi picked up her rucksack to chuck in the back of the van, and they drove away. Albert put on a tape, and they shouted out the windows *'just what is it you want to do? well we wanna be free!'* at an alarmed pensioner walking a dachshund, and Vi got the giggles.

Eventually – for the van was not capable of high speed – they reached the sea. They drove around the Gower till they found a quiet spot and, without even discussing it, for it was so obviously inevitable, she clambered straight into the back of the van, where the small double bed was already made up.

Albert rummaged frantically for a condom as Vi fumbled with the metal fastening on her dungarees, feeling like all her blood had been urgently redirected to between her legs.

As Albert finally sank into her, Vi could hear the waves breaking outside, and they mingled with the sound of his hot breath in her ear. And then sensation rippled out and broke over and over her entire body, until they both crashed together in the release of it.

'Well that was a long time coming,' said Albert with a laugh afterwards. 'What'd we call it – two years of foreplay?'

'Bit stop and start for my liking,' teased Vi.

'Don't worry. I'll make it up to you,' said Albert, and started kissing her again. 'We've got all the time in the world now.'

Then he pulled back, and looked down into her eyes, and she knew they were both remembering the rave, the field, the high, held eye contact in the coming light of dawn. That sense of golden promise, now finally fulfilled.

Chapter 5

January 1992

'Happy birthday, darling.' Amelia kissed Albert's cheek, firmly, and pressed his shoulders, and then turned to Vi. 'And to you too, of course!' A similarly swift, deliberate pair of kisses. 'Isn't it a funny thing?' she murmured as she slid off her camel-coloured coat and handed it to the waiter without even looking his way, as if sure someone would always be right there.

'Let's do presents before we order, shall we?' Amelia dived into an elegant purple paper bag and brought out two parcels, handing one to Albert and a smaller one to Vi. 'It's only a little thing,' she said with a wave.

'Ah, thank you,' said Albert as he shook out a cashmere jumper, that was at least in the sort of sludgey green colour he liked to wear.

'It's lovely!' Vi chirruped as a hot pink scarf, made of some fine diaphanous material, fell out of the wrapping paper and into her hands.

'Well I'm not sure it's really your "thing" now I meet you, but you're very sweet to say so.'

Good manners were actually impossible to answer, thought Vi, as she tried to make her smile look real, which she suspected made it look fake. The wrapping paper slid off her lap and a waiter silently lifted it out of sight before she'd even realised it had fallen.

'And what can we get you to drink?'

'I'll have an Asahi, please.'

'Me too,' Vi said quickly after Albert.

Amelia seemed very absorbed in the long thin menu. They all waited for her answer. Suddenly, the air had changed.

Eventually the waiter gave a tiny cough. 'For madame?'

'Sorry, yes, maybe I'll have the tuna—'

'They're taking drinks?'

'Oh! Yes! Ah – a sparkling water then.'

And Vi felt Albert soften next to her as Amelia handed back the wine list without having opened it, and immediately began to tell Vi in great detail about the different kinds of tuna she could order.

Vi had actually been to a sushi restaurant before – she and Mel had gone to new 'it' restaurant ChopChop when Mel was celebrating her promotion from *late*-late-night TV presenting to a 10.30 p.m. slot that everyone their age seemed to watch. That restaurant had been loud and pleased with itself in neon and white, ostentatiously buzzy – whereas Ginza gleamed with taste and quiet discretion. Amelia matched, Vi thought, a glistening elegance in her satiny champagne-coloured shirt and caramel highlighted hair.

She wondered if Amelia had chosen Ginza as an act of generosity, or to deliberately intimidate the country girl her son was dating. Or to annoy Albert with its opulence (Vi noticed he was wearing his 'End Capitalism Now' badge). Or perhaps it was just completely normal, and Amelia had no thoughts at all a beyond those on the merits of yellow or blue fins.

Amelia ordered for herself, and for Vi. Albert wrestled his order back from her – 'Actually I'll have the calamari bento'

– while Amelia sighed at the waiter as if to apologise for a wilful toddler. Then she raised her fizzy water.

'May twenty-five be a very happy year for you both. Quarter of a century! My little baby, twenty-five years—'

'*Mother.*'

Vi grinned, and tapped her beer glass against Amelia's tumbler. After the little that Albert had shared with her about his parents, their arguments and bitter divorce and Amelia's struggles with drinking, she'd been expecting something of a gorgon. But here she was, as normally embarrassing as any parent.

'And I'm very glad to meet you too, Violet.'

'She's called Vi.'

'Fine, Vi! Although Violet is a very beautiful name, it seems a shame to shorten it. At least he's stopped with that ridiculous "Bez" business.'

'That was *years* ago—'

'It was awful though,' sighed Vi mock seriously, looking into Amelia's eyes only, attempting to establish a rapport with her.

'So did you do anything to celebrate your birthdays? Or birthday, collective?'

'Yeah, we had a little party,' Albert said, deliberately vaguely. 'It was fun, wasn't it?'

The night flashed in camera-bulb snapshots before Albert's eyes. His mates who ran the Sub-Mersion sound system throwing them a party in an empty office building in Willesden. Mel pulling the plug on the decks at midnight to make everyone sing a wheezing, lurching round of happy birthday. Vi, turning to him as she was coming up, and lifting her chin and demanding 'put your tongue in my mouth'. Wrapping his arms round her, and shoving his tongue into their hot kiss and then whispering *I love you* in her ear, *thank God I found you.*

'Yeah, it was really fun,' added Vi, unsure quite what else it was appropriate to add.

Amelia raised an eyebrow at Vi.

'Well, I can see I'm not going to get much more out of you than I am out of my son.'

Vi smiled her most ingratiating smile. She didn't want to say the wrong thing. But when Albert barely said anything, it was hard to know what the right thing was.

She took a large gulp of the special Japanese beer. It tasted like ordinary lager, really.

'What, um, what are you working on at the moment? I mean, Albert said you were going to Romania next week?'

'That's right. Glad he remembered something. It's with my charity, Education Action, I assume he's told you about it?'

Actually, Albert didn't talk about Education Action all that much. There was clearly a huge, shy pride in his mother, for setting up a charity from nothing, particularly in the aftermath of the divorce and her recovery. But Vi noticed that this pride always came laced with a certain ironic tone, at it being Amelia's connections, and her luxurious approach to fundraising (balls and auctions; mentions in both the House of Lords and *Tatler*), that got Education Action such spending power. As if charity didn't *quite* count if the funds came from wealthy people ostentatiously having a nice time.

Vi's opinion was that if the end result was good, it didn't matter where the money came from.

'Things are obviously still very, very grim there,' continued Amelia. 'We're trying to get education for girls on the map as they prepare for their first free and fair elections. Raise awareness, encourage some pledges. That sort of thing.'

'That sounds amazing.'

'Well, it will be if we manage anything, which is not a given.

Don't go into charity work, darling, especially advocating for girls – it's one part change to ninety-nine parts banging your ahead against walls built by idiotic and fearful men.' Amelia swept her grand hair off her face in glamorous frustration. 'But now tell me: how is life in *your* ghetto?'

'For fuck's sake,' muttered Albert.

'Sorry – I just can't help winding my son up,' Amelia said to Vi. 'But are you still in that dreadful place?'

'It's not dreadful.' Vi couldn't help a little fire creep into her voice. 'Brixton is a very ... *vibrant* area.'

'It's a dangerous area.'

'It's really not,' Albert sighed.

'We actually did a lot of work with teenage girls in deprived parts of south London last year, and let me tell you—'

'*Mother.* Please.'

'Well I don't see why I give you an allowance when you insist on endangering yourself with your choice of postcode anyway.'

While Harold still refused to allow Al any of his inheritance as long as he 'refused to get a real job', Amelia had insisted on giving him an allowance from the moment the divorce went through – more in order to differentiate herself from Harold than out of any particular desire to help fund her son's dedication to a life of activism, Albert suspected.

To offset the awkwardness he felt about this monthly cash injection, Albert usually gave most of his mother's money to whatever camp or cause he was involved in at the time. But then when Vi wanted to move to London, to pursue her career in journalism – and sternly asked him would he please come with her, because why would they ever want to be apart again – it became clear a financial cushion was going to be necessary. And he was happy to use it for that if it meant he got to live with Vi, and to help her feel able to pursue her dreams. At least it was Amelia's money, technically, not Harold's.

After a summer spending weekends travelling to festivals, camps and free parties in the van – hungry and greedy for each other's company, treading water in the week till they could be together again – both Vi and Albert had jumped at the chance to move in with each other, properly, when a room became free in a cramped terrace on Chaucer Road, sharing with Jimmie, Mel, Amit and his girlfriend, Anita. There was such sweetness, waking up next to each other every morning – and between them, Vi and Albert could actually cover the rent with their dole.

While Vi threw herself into trying to get freelance work or a job on a paper, Albert found no shortage of local activist groups to channel his energies into. He spent his time gluing up the doors of banks and corporations in Canary Wharf, running sessions in the squats springing up over south London on legal rights in the face of police raids, and volunteering for a homeless shelter in Vauxhall. Albert's non-threatening affability – his rare ability to connect with almost anyone – meant he even managed to make headway with the most of the paranoid, jittery heroin addicts who regularly stayed there.

But what their combined dole did not stretch to was helping cover the mortgage on Vi's parents' bungalow. In the weeks before she moved to London, Vi had confidently repeated to her mam and dad what Mel had insisted over the phone – that she'd be sure to get work after her big piece in the *Independent on Sunday*, that even freelance would be better paid than the pathetic regional starter wage she was still on at the *Western Mail*. But freelance riches had not yet materialised, and nor had a job.

So Albert dipped – quite willingly – into his allowance each month in order that Vi could send a contribution home. A contribution she allowed Angharad and Evan to believe she had made from writing. 'Consider it simply wealth redistribution,' Albert said, as lightly as he could, wanting to lessen the pain he knew Vi experienced at taking the unearned cash.

Looking at Amelia now, her ease and ooze as their sushi arrived, Vi wondered what she would say if she knew where her money really went. *A bungalow in Aberystwyth.* Actually, she'd probably be fantastically polite and airy about it. And then Vi felt a deep purple flush of shame, imagining how angry – how devastatedly quietly fucking *furious* – her parents would be if they knew that the money really came as a handout from this golden woman, not from Vi's honestly earned pay packet.

It was only temporary, Vi told herself. It was only until she'd clawed her way into a career. But she knew, really, that it was also to protect her own wounded pride: she didn't want to admit to her family how much she was struggling, in *that London.* 'Cardiff not good enough for you anymore, is it?' Evan had said, dimly, when she'd told them of her plans to move.

Vi speared a piece of cold, damp tuna. It occurred to her that this solitary mouthful probably cost the same as her mam's hourly wage in the clothes shop. She swallowed painfully, and Albert thought he could feel the lump going down his own throat.

'Have you seen Rosie lately?' he said to Amelia, in a bright attempt to change the subject.

'Yes, of course. She did the flowers for our fundraising luncheon on the boat just the other week. And did you know she's doing blooms for Jeremy's wedding to that minor royal from – oh where is it now – Denmark…?'

Albert gave a minor eye roll in Vi's direction while Amelia continued to gush about the many society events her daughter's extremely chi-chi floristry company, Rose Red Blooms, had or was about to provide displays for. Compared to Albert, Rose couldn't be a more perfect child to Amelia, Vi thought: an intimidatingly successful, impeccably groomed Oxford graduate, both crazily talented and hard-working, she also had a uncommonly smart, good-looking husband named Benjamin, who made a fortune at one of the banks Albert regularly protested against.

When Albert had taken Vi to meet his sister at her floristry shop and studio on Kensington Church Street, Vi had been prepared to smirk. Fancy, over-priced flowers for Sloane Ranger weddings and restaurant openings and product launches? *Gross.* The only red rose she was interested in belonged to the Labour party, she'd joked to Albert as they approached.

But she'd been caught off-guard: Rose's elaborate displays were over-the-top, for sure, opulent cascades of doubtless trendy blooms that Vi didn't know the name of. But they were also simply delicious, like a knickerbocker glory for the eyes: piles of plush pink petals spiked with cream sprays; delicate curlicues of long-stemmed orange and yellow blooms; great showy spears of waxy hot pink softened with feathery green ferns.

'Wow!' Vi said, feeling like her eyes were on stalks, and as if her mere presence was sullying the premises, with her tattered trainers and baggy, holey jumper. 'I've never seen anything like these before. They're ... *bloo*-dy *gor*-geous.'

'Oh, thank you, darling – that's very, very kind of you to say so.' Rose had swooped towards her, long legs lengthened further by high heels and elegantly cut black trousers. Then she ruined any impression of glamour by wrapping Vi in a huge and clumsy bear-hug.

'My God, I have been just *dying* to meet you! Albert hasn't been able to stop talking about how *wonderful* you are!'

She whisked them to a wine bar, where Vi initially felt even more awkward perching on a chrome stool. But her discomfort was soon washed away by the pricey Chardonnay Rose bought a bottle of, and her extreme warmth. She'd asked Vi question after question, and appeared fantastically interested in every single answer she gave. She was even discreet about her own successes – certainly not name-dropping wildly, as Amelia continued to do enthusiastically on her behalf, in her absence.

'Anyway, enough about Rose,' said Amelia finally, putting down her chopsticks deliberately on their small golden stand as if at last running out of boasts. 'How are things going for *you*, Vi? Albert doesn't tell me anything over the phone. Are you getting lots of lovely work now you're settled in London?'

'Well, some. Journalism is ... it's actually quite competitive. But I'm getting by, you know.' A piece of sushi, its seaweed surface slippery with soy, escaped Vi's chopsticks.

Amelia nodded slowly, arranging her face in a look of neutral optimism. Albert could see she was trying to work out if Vi was being charmingly modest or face-savingly euphemistic.

It always surprised him when Amelia was sensitive like that. On some level, he still expected the drunk's snap judgements and lack of filter. The memory of the moment when Amelia said 'you'd be pretty if it weren't for that nose' to his first girlfriend, a quivering sixteen-year-old who had arrived dangerously late to a garden party, hurried unwelcome into Albert's mind.

'That big piece on the tree protest thingummy was very good, I thought.' Amelia said slowly. 'Not like most of the rest of the tosh written about it. Yes! I did follow it!' That addressed to Albert. 'I do actually take an interest in his activities, you know, despite the impression he might give. I want to understand – and *he's* not going to tell me.'

Albert sighed, and wiped his mouth with the thick napkin.

He did actually try to tell her about the campaigns and protests and camps. But whenever they talked, she'd speak over him – as she was doing right now – or get fixated on idiotic questions like where they went to the loo. Or point out repeatedly that the road had gone ahead anyway, as if he didn't know.

'Well, thank you,' said Vi.

'Surely that must've got you a lot of work? Great big spread in the *New Review* like that?'

'I'd thought it would've been more useful, to be really honest with you…' confessed Vi to Amelia, dipping her gaze down as she fiddled a chopstick in the leftover slurry of wasabi on her plate. 'I guess I was naïve – I thought between the experience on the *Western Mail* and that big piece I could just walk into work here…'

'Well you have been getting work,' Albert said, placatingly.

'Not much of it, and not the sort of thing I actually want to be doing.'

Vi was still determined to be a political journalist, if only someone would give her a shot. She'd recently pitched investigations into child poverty in second-generation immigrant communities, and into why women didn't go into party politics, to the *Evening Standard*. She was commissioned to write a personal essay for the property pages about 'the reality of living in Brixton', which was given a headline she felt was borderline racist, and a piece on how female politicians' clothing still mattered in the run up to the election. Which, she raged at Albert, was such an 'imbecilic' commission she would have turned it down had she not urgently needed the cash, and the byline.

'Well, I guess any work is good work at the moment—' Albert said.

'No, it isn't! It's crap! It's total crap and we both know it! Don't pretend to be proud of me—'

'I'm just trying to be supportive.' Now Albert sounded tense.

'Well, *don't*. I want to write about the world, as it is, every-thing that's wrong with it – and I want to *change* it. I don't want to write rubbish about' – Vi exhaled her frustration through her teeth – 'about which nightclub is hardest to get into, or why some band of snotty art school boys are having a feud, or why sushi is so *in* right now!'

A waiter heading in their direction made a sudden swerve. The words had come out louder than Vi had intended, as if forcefully propelled by the build-up of pressure from trying to keep a lid on months of feeling frustrated and embarrassed at her own failure.

There was a pause, and then Amelia smiled, sardonically.

'No, I can't imagine why you would want to write about any of that. And nor should you have to.'

'Sorry,' Vi replied, all in a rush, shaking her head. 'I didn't mean to get— I think it's just my friend, and her friends, they've all done really well really quickly, they've got their media jobs, but they also have to properly sell themselves, you know? Be all fun and kooky and hot and–and *female*. And that's just … that's not why I want to be doing any of this. I want to cover meaty, political stuff – not lifestyle features or "women's issues".'

'Ah, but you *are* a woman. Bad luck, my dear.' Amelia gave Vi a long hard look. 'Still, it's a mystery to me why someone with your brains and fire hasn't been snapped up, really. I, too, seem to know umpteen overpromoted young people in the media. Did you know Sebastian Tollington is arts editor now at the *New Statesman*? No – the *Spectator*. And didn't he almost get sent down from Cambridge?'

'Who on earth is Sebastian Tollington?' replied Albert.

'Sebastian! Tolly! You know: Millicent's son.'

Albert nodded in vague recognition.

'Actually, Millicent was very generous at our most recent fundraiser – I'll ask her, shall I, if they have anything going at the *Spectator* for Vi. Annnnd' – Amelia stretched out the word as she flipped through a mental rolodex – 'we used to go to skiing with that dreadful little man who was something at the *Observer*. I'll find out if he still is. He's bound to know someone anyway. I imagine that'd be more up your street, hm?'

Amelia raised her glass as if to say that was the end of that, problem solved.

'Thank you. That's ...'

Once again, Vi really had no idea what to say.

'Totally unfair? Indeed. But it is how these things work. And I know Albert wants to reject everything that his father and I stand for, but I don't see why just because he has no ambition, yours should be stymied too.'

Albert looked at his mother, his face suggesting he was about to boil over, at being so belittled in front of Vi. She pressed her hand onto his leg under the table, trying to silently reassure him: *It's OK. I know you and the work that you do, I know what matters to you – I know you try to change the world every single day—*

But then Amelia shifted her gaze to Vi, giving her a slight smile, and a nod. And Vi felt as if Amelia had handed her a gift. A parcel of good fortune, and also of courage. One that needed to be passed, woman to woman.

One that Vi decided she would seize, with both hands.

Chapter 6

August 1993

The sun was baking the city. Vi could smell the tarmac as she walked through Brixton, the pavement itself gone tacky. A haze hung over London, almost gritty in its thickness, and the collar of her blouse was limp.

It was too hot to want to walk, really. She'd got on the bus at Westminster, but that had been even worse – airless in the rush-hour traffic, only brief gusts through the window as it lunged over Vauxhall Bridge, so Vi had decided to jump out at Brixton Academy. Her neighbourhood was good in summer.

The bubbling of the steel pans, which could infuriate her in her pre-coffee morning dash to the tube, now put a smile on her face. The market hummed as she swerved down Electric Avenue, a box of bright yellow mangos catching her eye. Two men were hunched over a game of dominoes, the board balanced on an upturned sunflower drum. A battered speaker next to them juddered with heavy, echoing dub.

She felt the bass in the soles of her shoes as she turned to head towards Herne Hill; Albert would already be waiting for her. You couldn't rush in this heat, though, and Vi let her hands trail through the bushes that reached out across crumbling walls onto her path as she strolled down streets of tatty terraced houses.

Vi stopped outside Rise! Books, tucked into a corner of the

curving road just before Herne Hill station. A box of curled, reduced paperbacks sat dusty in a basket in front of one window, while the other sported a pot of pink begonias, beginning to crisp in the fierce glare of the sun. Vi idly pressed their soil as she peered in the window, and thought she must remind Albert to water them.

She could see Albert inside, his head bent over a book as usual, a few wisps of sun-lightened hair sticking up from a rough bun. His oblivious absorption made something swell up inside her. A certain protectiveness, like she imagined parents must feel for their children. And the faintly terrifying reminder that he continued to exist even when she wasn't there.

Vi had been pleased when Albert started working for Rise! Books earlier that year – helping manage both the little bookshop and the tiny associated radical publisher. She'd begun to worry that their lives in London were diverging: although she couldn't fault the time (and money) he always generously committed to the causes he believed worthwhile, it was also true that the anti-capitalists, squatters and environmental activists he counted as comrades truly loved to party. Meetings, lectures, fund-raisers, actions and protests all tended to end in the pub, which often progressed into impromptu nights out, long lie-ins, and desolate suicide Tuesdays.

All of which had become less fun, and less sustainable, for Vi since she needed to be in the *Observer's* offices by nine a.m., and often worked evenings and weekends. Never mind all the extra hours she put in as a union rep, and as a volunteer at the local Labour branch. She couldn't deal with the come-downs anymore; she had shit to be getting on with. So Albert having to take on a little more responsibility, too, had helped things between them, evened up the relationship.

It was almost exactly a year ago, in the August of 1992, that she and Albert had first met Stewart Spring, the founder of Rise! Books. How transformative that chance encounter had proved, Vi reflected as she went to push open the door.

Stewart had been holding a workshop at a festival on a traveller's site in one of the remoter patches of Wiltshire, about how to run an anarchist business; he didn't yet own the bookshop, but had just set up Rise! Books as a small-scale indie press. Stewart's wide, square face was elongated by a curly black beard that stuck out like a shelf, and a receding hairline. His eyes were unusually round, which gave him a perpetually startled, mildly manic look, matched by flickering, pernickety hand gestures. But as the talk went on, Vi could feel Albert becoming steadily more impressed by him. He asked Stewart eager questions about what authors they published, and the session effectively dissolved as the pair nerded out, passing from Rise! Books' latest publication, *EcoFreeZone*, to Bakunin and Bookchin, *Shock Slogans* and *Steppenwolf*.

Albert volunteered to help at a book fair the following week, and a friendship flourished further via a Levellers gig and a stint joining road protesters at Twyford Down. So when Stewart inherited his grandmother's little terraced house in Herne Hill just after Christmas, and felt embarrassed and unsure what to do with it, Albert was confident enough in their ability to work together to suggest turning it into a radical bookshop. He could come on board as a partner, provide a little capital investment. Excited, Stewart suggested they both co-manage Rise! Books the publisher, and Rise! Books the shop, together – equally sharing the responsibility and the profits (if there were any).

Albert looked up at the tinkle of the bell. He was lost enough in his book – enjoying snorting at Francis Fukayama on a regular basis – that he had assumed it would be a customer.

It was always a pleasure to be surprised by her. That split

second of non-recognition, just a tiniest fraction of *who's this attractive*— before, ah! It was her, and she was his.

And of course it was Vi – it was 5.46 already, he saw, glancing at the grandfather clock that sat incongruously grandly in the corner of the bookshop (it had looked even more awkward squashed in their hallway in Chaucer Road after Albert brought it home following his grandfather's funeral; Vi had hated its constant chiming).

She leaned across the desk and kissed him, threatening the piles of books and sheaths of paper already billowing lightly under the breath of a cheap standing fan. Albert reached his hand up to her neck to pull her closer, and then recoiled. Vi laughed.

'Sorry! It's pretty hot out there. I am *sweat*-y.' She mimed flicking away droplets from her armpits and forehead.

'You are, aren't you,' said Albert, coming round the desk and rubbing his nose into the damp collar. 'Mmm, salty.'

'Get off!' she said crossly, delighted, as he manoeuvred her backwards to the desk while nosing down into her shirt and the slick space between her breasts.

Then Albert turned to flick the sign to Closed and to shunt a bolt home. He picked her up and carried her into the tiny stock room. Vi always felt she ought to object to the way he could just move her around, like an object or a pet, but she didn't because she actually liked how small it made her feel. And she definitely did not want to interrogate why that also made her feel sexy.

He put her down – tenderly and also clumsily – on the threadbare carpet.

'I really wouldn't,' she said with a grin as he pulled off her knickers.

'You just try to stop me.'

Vi squirmed as he spread her thighs decisively far apart and dropped his head over her. It was always a surprise when Albert became blunt and forthright in his desire. There was something unrefuseable about his movements. And she liked that too, although it was another thing she thought she maybe oughtn't.

Dust motes swirled in the air above them in a shaft of light from one small high window. Vi watched them twirl, and then everything inside her very quickly began to coil. And centre. Like water circling down a plughole.

'Oh fuck. Fuuuck. Yes. Yes. Oh ... *ye-e-e-e-s.*'

Albert pressed harder with his tongue and Vi had to dig into something. *Don't crush his head.* Her hands scrabbled at the floor. *Oh God.* Then her whole torso flicked right up with an unstoppable shout. Pushing right into his mouth. Held there, in the pulse and the incredible stillness of it. *Yes* ...

She collapsed back on the floor. Her legs flopping out again. Some book shoving into some other book.

Albert leaned over her and smiled. Then he kissed her mouth, tonguing her own taste into her. And the thought of that made something inside him go black and certain and urgent. He raised himself up and began to unzip his flies.

She lifted her hips up towards him, in eager invitation, then winced.

'Fucking carpet burns.'

'Do I need to go easy?'

'You need to fuck me immediately.'

A push. Steady, inwards. And then the rightness of being encased by her, the fit and holding, made him groan. And Vi clenched, to make him sigh and wilt again. He could see how much she was pleased with her power, and indulged it. But then the blank urgency returned and he had to move, in her, against her. The urge to come immediately competing with the urge to prolong the feeling, moving inside her, until nothing else existed—

This time, Albert collapsed on top of her. His chest heavy on Vi's lungs. The grandfather clock struck the hour and something trickled between her legs.

Albert finally rolled off, dislodging several paperback copies from a stack of Gramsci's prison notebooks, which briefly threatened his exposed penis. He lay back and sighed again. But Vi was getting up, tiptoeing, almost, into the tiny toilet.

Vi reached, with relief – for it was not always guaranteed that either Stewart or Albert had remembered to go to the shop – for the roll of loo paper, balanced on top of a crispy stack of *LRB*s. She mopped herself, squeezing out as much fluid as she could so it wouldn't ruin her knickers, and had a wee.

'We're going to be late,' said Albert, his voice coming through the partially open door. Somehow she could tell from its timbre that he was still lying down.

'Get up and put your clothes on them!'

'I am up,' came his jovially outraged reply.

'Liar!'

A scuffle, and then a hand waved round the door. It disappeared. Then Albert's penis waved round it instead. Vi laughed, and tried to grab at it but he retreated. His face – pleased with himself – finally peered round.

'Long wee.'

'Get dressed, you. And bring me my bag.'

Vi slipped into a flimsy, daisy-patterned cotton sundress, crinkled from spending all day in her work bag, then located her knickers under a fallen Gramsci. She stuffed her still-damp blouse and nasty synthetic skirt into her bag, happy to crumple that version of herself away for the evening.

'All right, Tufty McGee,' said Albert, tousling her hair. She kept cutting it shorter, and bits were sticking up after their brush with the carpet.

'That's your fault that is,' said Vi, smoothing it down with one hand as the other unbolted the door.

Albert thought her hair suited her better when it was longer (and more feminine) although he wouldn't dare say it to her. At least the crop meant there was more of her nice neck to kiss.

The heat outside was dimming to bearable, even if it still felt implausible for Britain. Vi grabbed Albert's hand as they started towards the park. Her usual trick for helping his stride slow to match hers.

'How was the briefing?'

Vi exhaled loudly. 'Frustrating. They're just all so ... *insufferable.* I mean, I know the Tories were always insufferable, but now they're useless and yet also complacent?'

'Well, undeserved victories and the end of a recession and a billion years in power will do that, I guess.'

'I dunno, I think health could be one of the things that takes them down. But even in the face of all those headlines about NHS waiting lists – a million people! – the Tory fuckers don't seem to give a fuck. And our darling secretary of state for health, Virginia bloody Bottomley, is a bottomless pit of not giving a fuck.'

Vi actually growled, her shoulders tensing up.

'That your headline, is it? I like it. Punchy.'

'I expect the headline will be one of the despairing quotes I got from those doctors yesterday. Did I tell you about the pics that came in from Shota Kawakama? He got this long one looking down a corridor just full – I mean really full – of people on trolleys. Shocking stuff. Might even be the splash; his photographs have certainly boosted my word count.'

'And how many of them will you use in tearing Ginny a new one?'

'Many. She deserves it! I've rarely met a politician so craven. I mean, some of them at least seem to actually *believe* in what they're doing… But she knows the NHS from the inside – and yet still wants to break it up? Doesn't make any sense!'

Vi stopped, rummaging in her bag crossly till she found a water bottle, taking a lukewarm sip. She sighed heavily.

'Sorry. Too nice an evening for such outbursts. But trying to ask her questions was like wrestling with a squid. And I just think this shit really *matters*.'

'I know. Channel it all into the words. You're doing essential work, my love.'

'Thank you.' She swung the nearly empty water bottle with agitation. 'But am I? Is it enough just to write about it – to point out that other people are doing a crap job? Sometimes I wish I could just take more… *action*. Make more of a tangible difference.'

'Well, maybe you should stand for Parliament yourself?'

Albert's tone was joking, and yet there was a tiny seed of seriousness inside it. Vi had become more and more involved in their local Labour group, and while Albert might often hold forth on the 'bullshit' of two-party politics, Vi had always been more pragmatic than him, more concerned with working within an imperfect system than taking it down. *She'd probably be a very good MP,* he thought.

'Don't be daft.' Vi's response took a moment too long to land. Maybe she *had* thought about it?

'I'm not being daft! You'd be great!'

The sun shot low into their eyes as they crossed the road into the park, and so Albert couldn't quite read the look Vi gave him. The light now had the thick, syrupy colour of apricot wine, and the dried-out grass was parched to fine pale silt along the edges of the paths.

'And how are you feeling about this weekend?' Albert asked very softly, taking her hand again.

'Yeah. I had another practice reciting that bloody daffodils poem in my lunch break—'

'"A flock! A host?"'

'That's the one. Nanna did really like daffodils, I suppose, although I think it was more nationalistic than out of love for Wordsworth.' Vi swung her arm. 'I'm more nervous about the eulogy, though, Jesus Christ. I just reckon they'll all expect me to be polished at public speaking now, some Moira Stuart shit.'

'Ah, you'll be grand. I know it.'

'Well it's not like anyone else in my family wants to get up. Happy to hold forth down the pub – but come a funeral...' Vi rolled her eyes, but with affection. 'I feel more worried for my dad than anything else, to be honest with you – he doesn't like big displays of emotion.'

They walked on in gentle silence, Albert suspecting there was more she needed to say.

'Actually, I mean he *used* to. Loved a good cry when the choir sang "Calon Lan". Used to get proper loved up with my mam, or with his mates even, after they had a few if Wales won. But then ... I dunno, I think he just shut down after—' *Why not just say 'the miners' strikes?'* 'Back in the day he'd have cried and sung his heart out at the funeral. But now ... I'm not sure how he'll cope.'

They stopped by a pond to watch the ducks and moorhens splashing and fluttering in its shallows. Frothy trees were a healthier green above the stagnant seaweed-coloured water, which emitted a faint rotten smell from its half-dried banks. Vi told Albert that she thought the moorhens looked like they were wearing plague masks, and he smiled as if this were the first time she'd made the observation.

'Anyway. Sure it'll be fine. Thanks for coming, and that.'

'Of course.'

'Are *you* feeling OK about it?'

'It's really not about me – I just want to be there for you.'

Actually Albert was a little worried about the trip to Abergavenny. He'd only met Vi's parents once, the previous May. It had not gone well.

Albert had long been keen to get to know her family, but Vi had always put it off, sheepishly confessing her nervousness, because of who his father was. 'My family tease me about it, you know – "how can you be dating a Tory", "class traitor", all that – and I tell them you're nothing like that, that you rejected all that. But I think they find it easier to tease me than to try to work out what an ... "environmental activist" might actually be like?'

They certainly hadn't intended for the first introduction to happen in the aftermath of a bender. Vi had planned a solo visit home during a week she had off work. But then Albert had heard about a rave on Castlemorton Common happening the same weekend; it wasn't *so* far from her parents' house, he could drop her off in the van afterwards, and then drive back to London alone.

When it came to it, Albert and Vi had both been completely strung out after spending days at the massive gathering, coming down off rollercoasting highs, not much sleep and only the odd falafel wrap for sustenance. Time had become irrelevant given music played almost round the clock, and so they stupidly hadn't anticipated that Albert dropping Vi off a little after five o'clock in the afternoon might mean a greeting party. She'd planned to sneak in the back door – but as the van pulled up, her parents both hurried onto the front patio to meet them.

'Can I please just have a shower, Mam?' Vi had said grouchily, but the Lewises insisted they both took a seat on the sofa immediately – even though Albert could see Angharad eyeing his harem pants with horror, no doubt fearing for the state of her cushions.

After spending so much time dancing, sitting and sleeping outdoors, being inside the Lewises' home felt fully surreal. Albert couldn't quite process how everything matched, patterns parading across floors and curtains and furniture. He was sure the faces of the staged, framed photographs around the room were laughing at him.

Albert and Vi hadn't realised, from inside, that Castlemorton had become the biggest story of the week. But Evan and Angharad were horrified that their daughter had been there: they had been watching the news, had seen all the reports about the 'UK's biggest ever illegal rave', had watched how the police had failed to be able to take control or shut it down. Evan tersely waved the *Mirror* in front of Vi and Albert, as if the headlines could express all the horror he couldn't quite find the words for.

He eventually managed a hissed 'how dare you corrupt my daughter like this', his finger actually raised and tense and thrust towards them. And while Albert felt a churning misery in his belly, the soap opera cliché of the stance and utterance also made a horrible laugh rise through his chest. He made a swift exit, waving mournfully out of the van's window to Vi as he headed back to London.

'The thing is,' Vi said when she phoned Albert late that night, whispering so her mam and dad wouldn't hear, 'the thing is, it really *was* a surprise to them, that I'd go to something like that. They didn't know what I got up to at uni. So it was just a bit of a ... shock, I think. And it's easiest to blame you, isn't it?'

Neither Albert nor Vi had been in any rush to repeat the encounter, but it felt strange, now, that he still didn't really know her family, given how serious the relationship was. And as a second meeting, a funeral hardly felt auspicious. Albert dreaded the thought that he might face any hostility from her relatives. That his presence might make a sad occasion even more difficult for Vi.

He wanted to say it to her: *I'm sorry, for putting a strain on your relationship with your family.* But it was too hard to acknowledge out loud.

Because it was also hard to have to apologise for who you were. Both the identity you chose – an activist, a drop-out, a raver – and the one you're given and can never escape. *Son of a titled Tory politician.*

As he got older, Albert had begun to feel almost more embarrassed that he so readily apologised for his father, than he was embarrassed at him being his father in the first place.

Involuntarily, Albert pressed Vi's hand hard, pained by it all. Vi looked over at him, and Albert smiled at her with a false reassurance.

She knew that smile. She could see he was covering something up. It was kind of him. But God! He must have so much contempt for her family. For their small-minded disapproval of him, and his father, when it was, after all, Albert and his inherited wealth who had paid their mortgage for years. Kept them afloat.

The scream of children on swings and slides gave way to the dim thunk-thunk of tennis balls as they walked, the park carved into its separate social functions by railing and net.

And then – their people. Albert felt himself relax at the sight of their friends, all gathered together.

'Albert! Vi!'

Stewart got up off the blanket and gave them both one of his very tight hugs.

'Happy birthday! Sorry we're late.'

'Enjoy your day off? You couldn't have chosen a better day for it, pal,' smiled Albert, getting a balloon out of the back pocket of his shorts, blowing it up and bopping Stewart on the head.

'Come here, now,' demanded Mel, refusing to get up but stretching her arms up to be hugged by Vi, who moved round the edge of the circle, bending over and half-hugging Jimmie and Amit and Anita. Then onto Albert's group – hugs for Tall Tom and Commie Tom and Gregsy and Jamal, a kiss for Clara and a fuss of her absurd little border terrier, Karl Barks. A few eager waves to some of Stewart's book people whom she knew less well. Not that these groups were exactly distinct anymore – Vi and Albert's friends had easily melded.

The grass was covered with scraps of wrapping paper, half full bottles standing precariously erect and empty ones on their sides. Baguettes were split and cigarettes were lit. Brie oozed from its wrapping as if it had a life of its own and from Tall Tom's ghettoblaster came the voice of Björk promising that something important was about to happen.

Vi stood for a minute, opening a still-cool Sol with a hiss, wanting to savour the moment. Stewart had found an ideal spot near the top of Brockwell Park, and beyond it London stretched away, grey yet also glistening somehow in the heat. But in the park, the air was the perfect warmth, gentle and wrapping. A gift. It was like being on holiday.

Conversation simmered, occasionally boiling over into laughter or generous shouting. They were all just slightly too loud, but in the forgivable way of people who are just so pleased to see each other, their voices can't stop overlapping, volume rising. Her friends. Watching them, it felt as if all the cells of her body were very full, thought Vi, as if she was literally swelling with gratitude.

You could choose your own family. You could just make a new one. One that'd accept you for who you really were.

And there, in the middle of it all, Albert. Animated in conversation with Clara, playing with Karl Barks' ears with one hand and grabbing crisps with another, his whole body bobbing along to the music. Smiling. Laughing. The lean of the side of the mouth. The memory of his touch, just earlier – their own secret thing – whizzed between her legs. And he looked up, and smiled, as if he'd felt it too.

Remember this moment, thought Vi. This might just be it.

Chapter 7

October 1994

Vi spotted Clara first, outside the tube station. Waving a roughly hand-stitched 'Fight 4 Your Right 2 Party!' banner in eye-popping acid green on pink, she was hard to miss.

Albert had made Clara, Tall Tom and Commie Tom meet them early, knowing Vi would have to dash about for work; in her parka, she might look like she was there to protest draconian policing powers like everyone else, but actually she was reporting on the march against the Criminal Justice Act for *The Times*. And Albert didn't want to get stuck by himself, unable to find anyone, once crowds built up.

They were expecting a good turnout, after the successes of the previous two demos in May and July. The loathed Tory bill to curb mass gatherings was so clearly intended to crush the very activities and groups that had first brought Vi and Albert together – from raves to road protests, from travellers to squatters – that it was hard not to take it almost personally.

As they began to march, Albert realised he needn't have worried about being left on his own: almost every person he had ever met seemed to be there in the up-for-it crowd. There were mates from environmental protests, old faces from early free parties, and from squatters' rights campaign groups. He passed pals from publishing, that he'd got to know since working for

Rise! Books, and a few stressed-looking organisers from the Advance Party coalition, whom Albert and Stewart helped in the run up, allowing them to use the bookshop as a base from which to distribute flyers and newsletters.

But there was no time to stop to chat: Commie Tom, sporting a 'Chill the Bill' banner, led their own little group in an onward march towards a sound system. The bass rumble emanated from a slow-progressing lorry, while crowds provided their own treble with a ceaseless cacophony of blown whistles. A man in shades bent over the decks as a girl with her hair in six buns on top of her head yelled into a megaphone — 'it's about protecting our freedoms, protecting our civil liberties, protecting our right to have a fucking good time!' — before each drop.

Everyone was loose, everyone was easy. Everyone in their little group dipped into Tall Tom's bag. Everyone except Vi.

'I can't, I'm working,' she'd hissed.

'Oh, go on, darling, have a cheeky half,' said Clara, her eyes already heavy from a joint, the tattooed flesh on her arms wobbling as she waved them out to the side like an exploring octopus.

But Vi remained tight-lipped, and Albert could feel the tension in her shoulders as she walked next to him. The uneasy clash between attending such an event as a protester, and as a reporter — of needing to be seen as impartial, this time. When Clara asked if she wanted to carry the other end of her banner for a bit, Vi shook her head, said she needed her hands free to make notes.

'Right, I better try to see a bit more of what's going on,' Vi said after a while, not looking properly at Albert. 'I'll meet you back at home later.'

She walked off, clutching her notebook like it was armour, her brow furrowed in her focused look.

She had work to do, thought Vi as she wove away through the crowd. She couldn't just dance. She needed to be wherever the action was.

Vi had been head-hunted for her new job at *The Times*. After two and a half years at the *Observer*, her reporting had been good enough that someone had actually noticed it, and phoned her up, and taken her to a slap-up lunch at a bistro with a French name she didn't know how to pronounce. And offered her a proper salary.

'One you deserve,' Paul King, the political editor, had said to her across the table, with an off-handedness that she was sure was studied. To make it clear that, if she went to work for him, she could expect to receive plenty of appreciation. And a proper job title. *Political Correspondent.*

Vi had felt anointed, and elated, after the lunch with Paul. But Albert's reaction had brought her crashing back down. *The Times*! But it was so right-wing, and owned by a union-crushing despot to boot. Surely it was better to stay put, and slowly crawl her way up at a paper she was more closely ideologically aligned to. Where no one would mind, either, if she was a Labour activist on the side.

But Vi didn't call Paul back and turn the job down. Instead, she found herself confessing the job offer to other people. And every time she shared the news, in a low confiding tone, she felt her edges shimmer, luxuriating momentarily in being sought out. *Validated.*

'Of course you should go for it,' everyone said, uniformly, as if following a script. 'For God's sake, Vi, it's not like you're going to chase ambulances for the *News of the World*!' Margot, the *Observer*'s arts editor, scolded her over a sandwich one lunchtime.

But it was Rose who really gave her the permission she needed.

Since Vi and Albert had moved to Islington the previous year, Vi had struck up an independent friendship with Albert's sister. Despite being fantastically busy all the time, Rose regularly took Vi out for nice lunches at trendy restaurants along Upper Street and to air-kissy gallery openings in Mayfair, and Vi would reciprocate by wangling press tickets to political talks at the Southbank Centre or state-of-the-nation plays at the National. Vi found Rose to be ridiculously good company: she made the most rewardingly agog audience for media gossip and insider Westminster knowledge – stuff Albert only rolled his eyes at – and was full of her own juicy titbits about the celebrities and art world stars and fashion people she rubbed shoulders with. But she was sharp too; Rose could just as easily drop into conversation some thoughtful insight about a new Peter Brook production as she could deftly analyse the grunge references in the latest Marc Jacobs collection. An hour with Rose was always delicious, and just a little dizzying.

Vi had thought having a baby might slow Rose down, but it didn't seem to have. Oh sure, she had all the help any woman could hope for – cleaners and nannies and personal assistants – but nonetheless, it still seemed incredible to Vi that Rose managed to be back directing her floral displays and fronting events and posing for magazine features, all within weeks of giving birth. Albert said he thought it was madness, and that if Rose had bothered having a child she should spend some time with her. Vi lost her temper.

'What are you on about? I've never met anyone more naturally bloody maternal in my life than your sister. Rose *adores* Suzie. She's a *fantastic* mother. But she's just also a fantastic florist, and businesswoman, and there's really no need for her to have to choose—'

Albert started muttering something about feminism getting too caught up in capitalism, until Vi glared him into submission.

Even so, Albert was wonderful with Suzie, and spent lots more time round at Rose and Benjamin's airy Holland Park flat than he had done previously. Watching him holding and playing with Suzie made Vi's heart sing.

Why shouldn't it be the *man* who looked after a baby, she thought one evening, as Albert eagerly took on bath-time duties. Wouldn't that be a solution to the vexed question – a question every newspaper and magazine and passing pundit seemed recently completely obsessed with – of how a woman could juggle both kids and a career?

Not that it was a question she herself thought too much about yet. Career first, children later. Probably. Maybe.

Rose had literally groaned when Vi said, over lunch out one day, that she was going to turn down *The Times* job. She stabbed her fork around a mound of goat's cheese and rocket salad furiously with one hand while balancing Suzie with the other.

'This is because of some ... *principle* of Albert's, isn't it? I love my brother, but, Vi – he doesn't live in the real world! This is a *fantastic* opportunity and you have simply got to grab it with both hands.'

Vi hid beneath her choppy fringe as she chased her own salad around a plate. Rose had never sounded more like Amelia, she thought.

'*We* get *The Times*, darling! It's not *that* bad!' laughed Rose incredulously, before continuing, more seriously. 'You know, you would actually probably have a bigger impact, working there. If you want your writing to nudge people to think about things differently. I mean, you're just preaching to the converted at the *Observer* ... aren't you?'

Which was what Vi had tried to tell Albert, a few days later,

after she finally accepted the post. That it was both an opportunity, and a responsibility.

'Christ's sake, Vi!' The scorching disbelief in Albert's eyes, his
bleaching knuckles, as she watched him struggle to keep his
temper. 'I can't believe you'd work for that dirty fucking Rupert
Murdoch rag – after Wapping, after what he did to the unions.'

She'd felt so attacked, and so muzzy-headed from an afternoon being bought celebratory Champagne by Mel, that her
defence came out all wrong.

'OK, but don't you think it's better, right, to take this chance
to be on the inside, and *actually making change*, rather than just …
you know … mucking about on the far-left fringes, and real-*is*-
tically doing … fuck all?'

Deep hurt crumpled Albert's features. Vi had turned away
then, trying to cling to the correctness of the choice. But she
regretted her words, instantly – she didn't really think that
way about his activism, had always admired how Albert would
dedicate his whole self to a cause. Willing to live up a tree in
winter, or get arrested, for what he believed in.

But there was more than one way to make change. And
when it came to it, she did also enjoy working at the paper.
She could – and did – tussle with Paul about how stories were
framed, and he clearly admired such spirit. And really only very
occasionally patronised her for being young and female. ('Our
little star reportress.')

As Vi disappeared into the crowd with her notebook, Albert
experienced a sudden rise of relief – and an equally quick surge
of guilt. Clara danced over to steal his spliff, and he distracted
himself by twirling it around so they spun together as she
reached. They broke into giggles, and Albert felt his shoulders
loosening.

The vibe was good, energy radiating from almost everyone,

every smile and silly sign and mounted speaker. It felt joyfully daft to dance to jungle outside a shut-up Marks & Spencer's or watch someone juggle fire in front of Fortnum & Mason.

'Really, how can anyone look at this and not want to join in?' Albert said out of nowhere. 'Isn't this just clearly a better way to live?' Clara crinkled her plump face into fine smile lines and hugged him and she was soft and warm in his arms, smelling faintly of her Vicks inhaler.

At some point, they lost both the Toms, but Albert didn't care. He and Clara spent the whole day laughing together. She was just so easy to be around, he thought, knowing in some dark corner of his mind that that was partly, if not mostly, due to the pills and the spliffs and the tins they were drinking. But it felt like they moved in sync, seamless and comfortable. Whereas life with Vi was becoming all angles and hard edges.

Later, as they swerved swiftly through scattered groups of balaclava-ed men on Park Lane, it seemed like the peaceful protest was beginning to fray a little. 'Let's just get into Hyde Park, yeah?' said Clara, pulling on his arm. Word was going round that several of the sound systems were setting up there. A celebratory note to end on.

But at the gates to the park there were police everywhere. In riot gear, in lines, advancing. And the mood had definitely turned. A can whistled past Clara's head; there was the smell of burning. The aggression seemed discordant, out of tune with the dopey joyfulness of the rest of the day. Mounted police, their Day-Glo presence on top of horses looking fully surreal, reared up like something out of a nightmare. Albert's pulse started racing. He wondered where Vi was, his head whipping round. And he found he was holding Clara's hand, tightly, as instructions to 'Chill out!' and 'Keep it fluffy!' from one of DJs on a rig competed with more virulent chants of 'Fuck off! Fuck

off!' directed incessantly at the police. More improvised missiles
– smashed-up park benches, even handfuls of dirt – whistled
past and struck the glossy riot shields, advancing towards them
now with intent.

Albert's head flicked round, and he realised the police were
behind them too. Crushing the protest. A girl with dreadlocks
was holding broken spectacles in her hands, bewildered, blood
running all down the front of her dress. A policeman had her
very young-looking friend pressed to the floor. Another was
striking a protester with a truncheon, yelling 'get back' while
giving them no opportunity to do so.

'*Fuck. This,*' said Clara, with feeling. Then they, too, began to
run.

Stopping to catch their breath once out of the park, Albert
and Clara turned to look back, and now protesters and police
were entirely tangled up. Police wouldn't even let people who
wanted to leave out. There was screaming, and kicking and
struggling.

'*Fuck*ing pigs,' said Albert, fury rising at the way their sweet
day had turned so bitter. 'That's just the wrong way – just the
very *worst* approach—'

'Look. I ought to get back to let Karl Barks out for his
evening wee before too long anyway,' interrupted Clara, sooth-
ingly. 'Do you want to just come back to mine for a bit?'

Albert paused, then felt bad for even imagining that there
might be anything in the invitation beyond a natural continua-
tion of the day. Just two friends, keen to end things on a better
note.

He ought to go home. But Vi probably wouldn't be back
yet, and if she was, she'd be busily writing her report. In work
mode; definitely not in chill-out mode. Albert's blood was still
pumping, his mind still jittery. He wasn't *ready* to go home yet.

'Sure. Yeah, why not.'

'Nice one.' Clara led him (by the hand) towards the tube.

When Vi got back to her and Albert's basement flat on Matilda Street, the lights were all out. Fear jumped inside her, knowing how the demo had ended. Then it was quickly overtaken by annoyance. Probably Albert was just at some after-party, as usual.

He still wasn't home by the time she hit her deadline for the morning's edition, delivering her copy over the telephone, before crawling into bed, exhausted. And he wasn't next to her when she woke up at 7.20 a.m., and got ready to go into the office, or when she got back that evening. She rang Stewart; yes, Albert had been in work that day, he was heading home now.

Vi made a cup of tea, and took it out into the garden, allowing her worry to shade to irritation. Wrapping a giant cardigan around her, she lit a fag, and picked up her half-read copy of *Pride and Prejudice* to distract herself. She had recently decided it was silly that her uni course had put her off reading old books for so long, and was working her way back through all the classics she'd only skim-read, with a hangover, as an undergrad. Vi was so absorbed, she didn't hear the patio door slide open.

'Really?' Albert slapped down the newspaper on the little garden table. The wind grabbed at its front pages, whipping them over.

Vi looked up.

'What?' she said, a question that was more like a defence, already. She wrapped her arms across her chest. It wasn't really warm enough for sitting outside.

'Really, Vi? That's what it really felt like, being there, yesterday?' Albert loomed over her, hand thwacking in a frustrated gesture at the copy of *The Times*.

'I'm a reporter, not a columnist. I reported on it. It's not my place to evangelise about repetitive beats.'

'Come on, Vi! You know the police under-report numbers for these things, yet you use their numbers as if they're fact. And the emphasis, on the violence, it makes it sound— that isn't what it was actually—' Albert blew out his cheeks in frustration and raised his hands to his head, shaved these days to a close fur that Vi liked to stroke.

Vi had had exactly this argument over the phone the previous night with Paul King, mounting her own staunch defence of the line 'although exact numbers are likely to be considerably higher than police estimates', that was nonetheless removed from her copy. But being attacked for it by Albert made exasperation rise in the back of her throat. He was clearly in one of his righteous moods – moods that had been increasingly frequent since she'd taken the new job.

There'd been a trail of arguments between them in recent months. Each new fight making them more prickly about perceived slights the next time. Occasionally these spats were explicitly about the paper, or things her colleagues wrote that Albert despised (that Vi despised too, and hated herself for pretending not to). But most were seemingly about more mundane matters: the laundry he hadn't done, the dishes he hadn't done, his come-down when they were meant to be going to see her parents. Her 'wasting' money on fancy clothes, or being too tired to go to a peace camp at a weekend. Coming home late, again, because she was on deadline.

'We have to use police numbers. Don't be *naïve.*' Vi took a sip of tea, and pretended to go back to Austen. The words swam across the page, meaningless.

The wind blew the paper right off the table, and Albert caught it, fumbling it angrily in his hands, and began to read.

'"Military police were also present at the march against the Criminal Justice Bill, to prevent protesters gaining access to

Hyde Park. As they approached police lines at around five p.m., portions of the crowds began to turn nasty. As tensions rose, protest turned swiftly into a riot, dubbed 'The Battle of Park Lane"'.'

Were Albert's hands shaking, or was it just the wind? Looking up, Vi realised clouds had barrelled over, and it was surely about to rain – or storm even. But the last of the evening light still hit the end of their garden, and the contrast of the illuminated plum tree, its purpled, curling leaves lit up against an ominously saturated, slate-grey sky, felt strangely charged. Electric.

'The *crowd* turned nasty, did they?' The scorn in his voice felt like it was peeling a layer of her skin off.

'*Portions*. It says "portions". Even the quote from the chief of police acknowledges it was only certain *parts* of the crowd—'

'Oh yes! So he does! And what's this' – Albert hit the paper for emphasis – 'oh yes, "the despicable behaviour of anarchists—"'

'A minority! Come on, Albert, you were there – *I presume*. A minority did behave badly!'

Albert turned away from her then, his whole body heaving down the garden, tension visibly sweeping his shoulders upwards as his fists clenched. Vi felt, just for a split second, a shiver, that she tried to ascribe to the chilly air blowing in.

Did you throw things? Did you fight?
Is that why you didn't come home last night?
The leaves on the tree trembled.
He turned around.

'You have a … *responsibility*, Vi, to tell the truth! To say what it was really like! You saw how they policed it – fucking chaos, unprovoked attacks. It was textbook police brutality – *textbook*.'

'Have you properly read it, or are you just enjoying shouting at me?' Vi asked, jutting her chin up at him.

There were actually several paragraphs about police brutality,

341

including the moment Vi had seen a policeman repeatedly bring his baton down on the head of a pet dog, being held in a traveller's arms as she tried to move out of the park ('fantastic detail,' Paul said). And there was a particularly vivid description of the mounted police riding right at the crowds. Vi hoped that something of the terror — the actual rising animal terror — of seeing a horse charge towards you when you knew you had iron railings at your back had still come through in her description, even if Paul had stripped out some of her 'bloody poetry'. He'd even let her include the sympathetic quote from Jeremy Corbyn, her local MP in Islington, and about the only one willing to speak out in support of the protesters.

But it was also true that her piece reflected the mob violence Vi had witnessed. The men (for it was almost all men) who had been hurling glass bottles and flaming wooden stakes onto Park Lane with a vicious force of their own, something feral in their eyes, which was absolutely nothing to do with protecting civil liberties or the right to dance in a field. And reporting that was her job too. Her responsibility, now.

'I have read the whole report, Vi, yes.' Albert looked at her, sternly.

'Well, that makes a change.'

'What …?' He sighed with frustration. 'Don't try to turn this round on me, Vi. This isn't about me not being supportive — it's about you betraying a movement you're part of, betraying *yourself*, by reporting what the fucking establishment want to hear rather than how you know it is.'

'Wow. Big words, love. Thanks very much.' Vi shut her book with a snap. 'And where exactly were you last night then?'

The rain began, fat heavy droplets, plopping messily onto the concrete patio, polka-dotting it rapidly.

And Vi's organs seemed to fill with fear as Albert didn't say anything at all.

'Please tell me you didn't get caught up in all that – please tell me you didn't spend a night in the cells...?'

Albert flinched as if she'd slapped him, disgust running across his face.

'No! Fuck's sake, Vi, of course not. I didn't get involved in that violence. That's not... *me.*'

'Well... where were you then? Why didn't you come home?'

'I... I stayed at Clara's.' Albert swallowed.

'Right.'

Around them the tree and bushes and the thin fence blew and bashed moodily, and the rain came down with an increasing insistence.

'We lost everyone else, and she had to get back to let Karl Barks out.' Fuck's sake, stupid name. 'Um. So I just went back to hers to chill out for a bit. And then it got really late. So I just... stayed over.'

'*Right.*'

When they had got back to Clara's, they'd collapsed on the sofa, chatting rubbish and listening to Orbital and letting parts of their bodies touch each other as if it was no big deal, as if they just happened to fall there. A knee resting on a foot. Leg flopping over a lap.

There was a long, uncertain moment before the kiss. And once it was happening it felt altogether wrong to Albert, too sloppy, too tonguey, simply not Vi. And when they pulled away, both of them seemed to contemplate the other while holding their breath for another long, uncertain moment.

Then all the air rushed out of both of them, as they agreed with laughter, *Yeah no – this is a bad idea – what are we thinking? – aaargh, no worries!* But after that the conversation lost its easiness.

Or rather, strained towards easiness, trying to prove the aborted kiss hadn't meant anything, hadn't changed anything, that the evening was completely innocent. They hurriedly opened another bottle of wine, and talked and drank a bit too fast.

Albert passed out on the sofa, and was woken by Karl Barks licking his feet.

'Vi – it wasn't ... it didn't actually—'

'What the *fuck*, Albert.'

He shut his eyes, and tried to force the words to come. To be honest.

'There was ... there was a kiss—'

Before he could finish, before he could explain, Vi turned, and went in through the open patio door, leaving her mug behind to fill with rain.

'Vi! Wait—' he shouted, but he could dimly see her grab a raincoat and run up the stairs of the flat. Heard the slam of the front door.

He stayed, the rain steadily soaking him, unable to move.

Then, as suddenly as it came on, all his adrenaline subsided, and guilt coursed through his veins. Albert felt like an untied balloon farting out all its air. Just as wrinkled and deflated. He went inside.

Albert scrunched the paper in both hands, its wetness making the action wholly unsatisfying. He tossed it in the bin, which needed emptying, and took a Budvar out of the fridge. Taking a slug of beer, he watched the rain run down the patio windows. It turned the garden beyond into a smearing mess of teal and green, the wild, overgrown beds they swore they'd turn into a veg patch hunched at the back of the garden in glowering reprimand.

There was a stack of dishes that needed doing on the side, and it was certainly his turn.

Albert started running the tap. Then he turned it off. *Fuck it.* He made himself a Pot Noodle and sat down on his favourite battered red-leather armchair, in front of the telly, enjoying Gillian Anderson's handsome, concerned face even if fully failing to follow the plot. He rolled and lit a cigarette, something they weren't supposed to do inside.

After all the arguments, Vi's latest tactic when it came to housework was never to remind him about a chore, but also never to do it if it wasn't her turn. For some reason, this made Albert feel as oddly resistant as the previous nagging had. He genuinely didn't care about this stuff – towels overdue a wash, dust bunnies scooching across the floors – because compared to living in a van or up a tree or even in Chaucer Road, the flat was just *fine.*

If she wanted it to be sparklingly, show-home clean – if she wanted a fancy flat like Rose's, or like Mel's – she could clean it. And if she didn't have time to clean because of her 'demanding' job, then that was her own fault.

Albert opened another bottle of Budvar and felt himself slowly soften.

He could call Mel – Vi would certainly be with Mel. Or maybe he should just go round: she only lived fifteen minutes away.

Vi had insisted the reason she wanted them to move into the basement flat on Matilda Street was because she wanted the two of them to live alone. 'I can't stand the bloody chaos of the shared house anymore. And anyway, isn't it time we just lived with each other, a proper couple?'

Albert had been more wary – although the sub-let from a friend of Rose's was an astonishingly bargainous price for Islington, it seemed daft to move north when he worked so far south. But he had been excited not to have to share Vi, and touched that she was willing to give up living with her mates for him. It was only once they'd moved in that he realised how close they were to the sleek top-floor flat Mel had bought herself by Caledonian Road tube.

Albert decided he definitely wasn't going out in the rain after her.

Besides, they'd have probably gone to drink and shout at each other about how shit he was in one of Mel's stupid private members clubs by now. 'How can you call yourself a socialist and pay to be part of an exclusive club?' was one of the more pointless repeated quarrels he and Vi had had in recent months.

Vi would no doubt stay at Mel's, as she had taken to doing whenever she flounced out on him, which had been happening with depressing regularity recently. Or when she just wanted to go out with someone female. It was a mystery to Albert how Mel managed to present a breakfast show when she went out almost every night.

'Don't you have to get up at, like, five a.m.?' shouted Vi as Mel winked at the barman, who'd insisted the tequila shots were on the house.

'Don't worry, babe, I'm used to it: cheese pickle sandwich, rehydration salts, pint of water before bed and I'm right as rain, no matter what happened the night before.'

Holding eye contact, they clonked the stubby neon orange shot glasses, tipped them back and shuddered in unison.

'Anyway, shambolic is the vibe, isn't it?' said Mel, struggling to be heard over the Balearic beats and the hubbub of conversation, the bar busy even on a Monday. 'I think they actually like it if we look like we've been on one.'

This was true, and it annoyed Vi whenever she tuned in to watch Mel over her morning tea and toast.

It had been a feature of Mel's career that she constantly

looked like she was making it up on the spot. In interviews, she'd appear to lose her thread, shifting about on the show's sofa (shaped like a bacon rasher, next to an eggcup armchair) and crossing her long, bare legs distractedly. Distractingly. And the guests — especially older, whiter, maler guests — would jump in, thinking they were saving her. Really, they'd just grabbed the rope with which to hang themselves: giving away something more revealing than they'd intended to, or embarrassing themselves with their obvious eagerness to impress her.

Vi remembered Derek's words: being underestimated is your advantage.

Pretty little young woman.

'Doesn't it piss you off that everyone thinks you're a hot mess? You're not. I see your... your' — Vi couldn't remember the word for *tactics* — 'your scheming!' She wagged her finger sloppily at Mel as they sat back down in the hot pink booth, yet another pair of sea breezes sloshing as they put them on the table.

'I don't care. I honestly don't care! I'm just glad you think I'm hot, babe ...' Mel, also sloppy with drink, jokingly wriggled herself into Vi. Her houndstooth mini skirt was riding up and the edges of her white ribbed cropped top were crimped round the smooth brown skin of her midriff. Vi had felt extraordinarily frumpy when she'd arrived in her cardigan and soggy mac.

'Honestly, darling, you should've said something before now!' Mel continued, rummaging her nose into Vi's hair, and laughing.

I did, thought Vi, something about the close, careless touch rushing her back, way back.

That party in third year. A heady one, everyone already well-soaked after handing in their final dissertations and a day in the sun, almost the entire English course decamping to the beer garden of The Charles. There were people Vi had never spoken to before whom she chatted to with such fervency, over pints and pints of cheap cider, that she experienced a sweet wistfulness for friendships that might-have-been.

A select crew were invited back to Nina Cha's house. Jimmie took charge of the music, and the sentimental mood that had been creeping up on them for weeks intensified as he played the cheesy classics of bad student nights and indie favourites, as well as his beloved Trax records. Ian Curtis mumbled between Tiffany and Cyndi, before Frankie Knuckles took them high. They sang and sang and sang, murdering song after song.

Nina had been in the drama society, and came downstairs at midnight triumphantly carrying armfuls of old costumes she'd been about to take to the charity shop. A whirl of trying on, catwalking, and vogueing very badly. Vi's bare legs stuck out of a pair of Elizabethan-style bottle-green pantaloons. Mel fought Amit over furry zebra-print pedal pushers, and won. She hiked her breasts up obscenely in a cream corset with a self-satisfied grin. *Tighter,* she yelled at Vi as she pulled the corset laces. *Tighter.* Vi pulled and cinched. And something tightened, too, somewhere inside Vi.

Then Jimmie put on 'There is a Light That Never Goes Out', and Amit immediately turned the lights out, amused with himself. As the melody swam up through her torso, Vi felt a strange nostalgia for the moment she was actually living in. And a sudden, sharp urge to cry: for love for her friends, for the ending of this phase. Mel danced over, and took Vi's hands tenderly. They waved them, enmeshed, over their heads in wide loops. Mel bent down so their faces knocked together, their breath hot and conjoining, as they sang about how heavenly it would be to die by each other's side.

Then the eye contact seemed to get heavier, swollen with some new intent. Vi realised she was pressing her pelvic bone in towards Mel's thigh, firm between her legs. Then her lips were warm, and full. Their tongues slow, testing something new.

Vi felt all the bittersweetness burn away in a new flame. She pulled her head back and smiled, enticingly.

'Let's go upstairs,' she whispered, trying to move even closer. But Mel went stiff. Looked away.

It was maybe the only time Vi had seen Mel look conflicted, abashed. But had she really seen it? There'd only been a dim glow of streetlight coming through the thin curtains. Because what had actually happened next was that Mel smiled, the too-big brash toothy grin she still pulled on telly when interviewing people she had to pretend to like.

'Upstairs? All right, calm down, you massive lezza!' And she span away, arms loose, as if the kiss had meant nothing at all.

A mistake. A misunderstanding. *A joke.* And shame smothered Vi in its thick, immoveable blanket.

The memory still made Vi's face feel hot, and she tried to suppress it with a gulp of her cranberry concoction. Shut it down. Pull the blinds on all that. On that whole possibility. As she always did. It was something she tried not to think about. Actually, it was something she no longer even had to try not to think of – she *didn't* ever think about it. Mel was her mate, nothing more. Obviously.

'I mean, I'm sorry, I know we already talked about how shitty Albert is being, but really, he is being *very* shitty? I do actually think that?' Mel's features swam in and out of focus as she spoke, the hazel-brown of her eyes all melted.

Christ, thought Vi, as the room careered around her like a carousel, they were completely trashed.

'Actually – actually – I do think he's just not good enough for you, if he's going to behave like that? Have you considered, you know, just ... not being with him?'

Mel's thick perfume and her breath mingled together, both of them sweet, making a scent almost like cough syrup; cherries and menthol cigarettes.

Vi tried not to picture Albert kissing Clara.

All of a sudden, Vi thought she might be sick.

She wanted to go home.

But then came the image of Albert's cold, silent shoulder in bed, how recently he kept turning away from her under the sheets. Sheets that needed changing. Which led on to a vision of the takeaway cartons he was bound to have left lying about. The cigarettes he'd no doubt rebelliously smoke indoors, leaving a film of filthy fag ash over the sofa, tendrils of tobacco on the coffee table.

She hated being the person who had to care about such pointless shit. Hated clearing up after him, and *really* hated that he then had the gall to even be *superior* about it. As if she was shallow for caring. As if he were always too busy volunteering at the homeless shelter to be able to hang the washing out.

Vi wondered how *home* had become such an unappealing place.

'Can I stay at yours again tonight?'

'Course, babes. My house is your house.'

Vi wondered if she might stay there longer than a night.

Chapter 8

June 1995

As Albert reached forward to pick up a punnet of strawberries, he thought he saw her coming into the grocers. He flinched upright, and realised the brunette looked nothing, really, like Vi. She just had similar hair.

It kept happening, all throughout their six-week, no contact, 'trial separation'. He saw Vi's face everywhere – and it destroyed him every time.

On the number 59, the girl with her head bent over a book.

Several times during an impulsive solo trip to Rome. Her slim limbs round pillars in the Coliseum. Her face at breakfast, a hint of it in the bobble-nose of a Canadian backpacker eating cereal.

Once, most painfully, Albert thought that it was Vi, opening the door to Rise! Books, the bell an overture to 'we can make it work'. Deluded, wishful.

Vi saw Albert too. Several backs-of-heads at Glastonbury. One specific back-of-head at the big, splashy Labour meeting for people interested in becoming prospective MPs. Then the head moved, and it was obviously not Albert.

But she wished, with a painful stab, that he *was* there with her, as she took her tentative first steps towards a new chapter in her career. It might be a time-honoured shift, from journalism to politics, but there were still times when Vi couldn't quite believe she was even *considering* putting herself forward as a potential parliamentary candidate. She had let herself get caught up in the rising excitement in the party – and all the encouragement for new faces to stand had ignited something inside her that had been smouldering for years: a desire to make real change, lasting change.

Albert might've sneered if he was there, however. He didn't share her excitement over New Labour. It had been one of the many subjects they'd bickered over relentlessly.

It was, however, Albert's face that flashed clearly before Vi when, five weeks and two days into their six weeks apart, she thought she might finally kiss someone else. Like he had done. *Bloody Clara.*

The utopian shag-fest Mel had led her to believe was hers for the taking, lightly agitating for *freedom* and *singledom*, hadn't exactly materialised for Vi. And the 'period of exploration' that Vi had silently, internally promised herself had also absolutely not got into gear. She didn't know where to start.

Clearly that was just not her 'thing', after all.

Vi cringed inwardly, remembering the vague fantasy that circled in her head whenever she got drunk for a while, that maybe it would even be Mel... The straightest girl inside the M25. Bizarre thought.

But she hadn't found anyone else, either. Time for experimentation was running out, and Jake Lacewing started to look like her only real option. He was *The Times'* economics reporter, handsome in a thick-haired, rowing-team kind of way, with a habit of scoffing cynically at everything. Including her. But there was something in the way he wound her up that she had long known was sexual, too. When she imagined punching his smug face, it usually turned into a fantasy where his large, muscled arms held her down forcefully.

The reality was less dramatic. There was someone's leaving do, a lot of bad white wine in a pub function room. Jake kept stealing cigarettes off her ('Menthols? You dirty girl'). It was obvious to both of them that one of the times they went to the loo to have a line they would also bang. But when he put a hand around her waist, as arrogantly as if collecting winnings, all Vi could see was Albert. The image of his long, lovely, gentle face.

She pulled away, muttering, 'I can't do this' and hating herself for the cliché. Rushed out of the pub and back to Mel's house. There, on the doormat, was a letter.

It was nudging towards dark as Albert turned onto Matilda Street, the brief moment of dimness just before the streetlights flicked on. The bag of shopping bit into his palm. The air was still, and fumey, as if all of London's choking exhaust had nowhere to escape to. Albert felt like he hadn't been able to take a full breath of fresh air for weeks. Maybe he needed to get out of the city.

He dismissed the phantom almost before he'd registered it. *Isn't. Can't be. Never is.* Then he realised that the figure was sitting on the steps of their house. *Surely next door.* He forced himself to look upwards, as if interested in the bushy leaves of the plane trees. But the person was still there when he looked again. Was, in fact, looking intently in his direction.

Was, in fact, definitely Vi.

And she had, in her hand, a letter.

Oh God. Had he manged to explain—

The letter had been written and posted in a rush the day before, and afterwards Albert half-regretted it. He knew he'd flouted the terms of their agreement – not to get in touch, to have a proper break – and he knew Vi, in all her stubbornness, might be pissed off about that. But Albert had just felt so heavy and sodden with missing her, he was seized with the need to do *something*.

Suddenly, it had seemed like the easiest thing in the world to write *'I'm sorry'*.

In the weeks they'd been apart, all the irritation and resistance that had built up between them had softened and melted away, for him at least. Their arguments – over politics, over her job, over money, over the sodding flipping *washing up* – seemed so petty, so unimportant, compared to the hugeness of their love. And in absence, everything Albert had always admired in Vi became newly, sparkling clear to him. He wanted to tell her how impressed he was by her, how brave he thought her desire to stand as an MP was, how he would do whatever it took to support her in making that happen. (Even if he did think Tony Blair was an arse.)

And he wanted the chance to explain. About Clara. Properly. Vi had obstinately refused to talk about it, saying she 'didn't want to know'. But Albert needed to get through to her, to convey that it really was nothing more than a kiss, and that it wasn't even really a proper kiss – just the start of one, before the realisation, *I do not want this.* That it absolutely could not have meant less.

Their weeks apart had made something else very clear to him: he didn't want freedom, he didn't want other people. He just wanted Vi. And he didn't want to fight with her anymore; he wanted to fight *for* her.

But what if she didn't feel the same?

Vi rose as he approached, one foot held at a child-like angle, unsure, half-keen. Hopeful? Then she smiled, somewhat shyly, and waved the letter. And he started to walk faster towards her. And she seemed to fly into him, and he dropped the shopping.

Oranges rolled all over the pavement. A few strawberries bounced into the gutter.

'I don't want anyone else either,' she said, muffled, into his chest.

Then she drew back from Albert, to look up into his eyes. 'Can I come home now?'

Chapter 9

December 1996

Harold looked smaller than Vi remembered, dwarfed by the large doorway of Farley Hall, forbidding in its heavy timber. Hector, his ageing brown Labrador, leapt in pathetic circles around their legs as they walked from the car.

'Come in, come in. Drive OK? What route did you take?'

Some things were the same no matter who your father was, Vi thought.

'Yes, fine. Sorry we're a bit later than we expected – we got up to Todmorden later than we'd hoped too really.'

It had been Vi's leaving do the night before, and the morning had not been easy.

The Times' editor Peter, as well as Paul, had made farewell speeches in the office that were so full of praise and heartfelt well-wishes for her change in direction – 'you're exactly what this country needs: new hope' – that Vi felt a burning in the back of her throat. They banged her out with aplomb, the entire staff drumming on their desks as she left clutching a box of old notebooks, files and biros. But over pints in The Crown, Paul treated them to all the ruder bits he'd hastily excised from his speech when he realised the editor would be listening: the time Vi fell down the stairs after attempting to match Don Dennis drink-for-drink, the time she'd had to see off the wandering hands of a Tory MP she was interviewing actually on sleaze allegations, and gleefully revisiting the 'storm in a B-cup': when she lost her temper after her expense claim for a white shirt and a bra from M&S got distributed round the whole office ('It was the bloody rain I got caught in, trying to doorstep that bent copper on the way to a trial! I absolutely needed to change!').

Albert had driven them up the M1, with repeated breaks for coffee, and groaning. By the time they parked up behind their little rented cottage, the hills that scooped around Todmorden were darkening to umber, and the town's grey-yellow stone looked grubby in the falling light.

'Come on then,' Albert sighed, lifting Vi's jumper over her head as she grumbled at the thought of spending what was left of the afternoon talking about a planning dispute. Once inside the pub, he marvelled at how she flicked a switch, turning from a hungover lump into Violet Lewis, Your Next MP.

Four middle-aged, deeply concerned residents were huddled around a table in the corner of The Queen's Head. A developer wanted to throw up some houses on open fields on the edge of town, the sort that would likely only attract commuters. The residents were worried about the character of the place. Vi was more worried about affordability, but she promised she'd help them set up a public meeting where objections could be aired – she'd even speak herself.

'Well I think you've got their votes,' Albert said as they walked back to the cottage – an adorably minuscule place that they'd have to move out of if they lived in Todmorden permanently, but that they'd both fallen in love with when searching for a temporary base.

'Do you reckon? They're just the sort of Tories we'll need to sway if we're going to manage it.'

'I think so. You came across as very competent. Able to get things done. That's all those nimbys really want anyway, isn't it?'

'Competent! Imagine if they'd seen me this morning,' she laughed.

Albert kissed her as he unzipped her smart navy jacket, and reached for her big cosy jumper again.

'Yes, very feeble. Cup of tea, or reckon you can cope with getting straight back in the car? We're going to be late as it is. That lot really knew how to stretch out a yarn about central government bureaucracy, eh?'

As they pulled out onto the main road, the rain started. Vi didn't say anything for a while, but just closed her eyes and listened to it hiss against the windscreen and the wheels.

'Do you think there's any chance Calder Valley will really accept me?' Her voice was very small under the sound of the spray.

'Of course, my love,' said Albert. 'Well, most of them. We know you've got a fight on your hands against Sir Donald and his ceaseless Tory reign. And, yes, some of these peanut-minded voters are never going to warm to someone who happened to be born anywhere other than West Yorkshire—'

'You can't say things like that, Albert! Not even in jest – if someone overheard— You need to start *practising*.'

'I know, I know.'

She patted his leg. He did know – Albert had already put in hours and hours supporting her bid to become MP for Calder Valley, willingly following her north. He still co-ran Rise! Books, and he and Stewart talked about maybe – sometime in the future – Albert opening a new branch in Todmorden or Hebden Bridge. But if she won the seat, he'd have to step away from running the Herne Hill bookshop, at least.

Not that they'd count on it just yet: they faced an uphill battle to get Vi elected.

It'd been a long selection process, eleven rounds of interviews before she got to a whole day of hustings in first Halifax and then Hebden Bridge. She was not surprised to be defeated, finally, by a redoubtable local woman in her sixties: already on the council, Old Labour in her bones but willing to talk the talk. Vi warmly told her the best woman had won, and got the train back to London, feeling almost exactly equal parts exhausted, disappointed, and relieved.

And then, less than a month later, the best woman for the job was diagnosed with aggressive breast cancer. Vi had been swiftly chosen to take her place.

'Parachuted in from London,' said the Conservative team, at any available opportunity, gleefully. 'A charismatic, committed, highly electable breath-of-fresh-air,' declared the *Courier*, in an almost fawning interview. Vi had had no problem wrapping their lead reporter round her finger over an 'old-fashioned journalist lunch', winking at him that 'we both know what that means, don't we' while topping up his glass fulsomely.

'But you know what,' Albert continued, 'I reckon the winds of change are blowing through the Calder Valley as much as anywhere else. Even if locals do see you as the height of metro-politan New Labour – which I'm sure they don't, not least because you don't remotely sound like that lot – I honestly think many of them would prefer that to the bloody Tories anyway, the way things are going.'

'Hm.' Vi stared out the window at the passing murky hedge-rows. 'But do you think – do you think that they might feel they just got fobbed off, with the nearest available woman, rather than a proper experienced candidate?'

Albert flicked a glance at her. Publicly, Vi was a passionate, rational advocate for all-female shortlists. And she repeatedly roasted Sir Donald after he dismissed such shortlists in an interview as 'a hen pen – a load of girls picked by the old cocks'. But in private, Albert was surprised how often Vi quietly confessed these fears: that she was chosen for the wrong reasons. That she had not got the nomination on merit, but on gender.

'No. Absolutely not. No one who hears you talking for five minutes could think that, Vi. Of course you're new to the job, but everyone has to be at some point, don't they? And you got this because you're brilliant, not because you've got ovaries.'

Albert smiled at her. But he couldn't help thinking of the time when they'd come up for a meet-and-greet with local councillors and the first to arrive – a greying man with jowls resting on further jowls – had mistaken Vi for a secretary, sent ahead to prepare the room. And asked her to fetch him a glass of water. Or the time she'd been speechifying about New Labour, a new life for Britain, and the phrase 'brave new world' had popped out. Some middle-aged businessman had scoffed loudly. 'Are you really sure you want to be referencing Huxley's sci-fi dystopia, *young lady*?'

But Vi's reply *had* been brilliant: 'I think you'll find it's a quote from Shakespeare, originally. *The Tempest*. Act five. Scene one. Look it up.' The toss of her hair, the tilt of her chin. So self-satisfied!

The memory of it warmed Albert. Vi would do it. She'd show them all.

The country roads were dark and winding, but Albert didn't mind this sort of driving. It was what he'd grown up with, learnt to drive on. As he tried to say to Vi often – but not so often it would sound false – he really did love the Yorkshire countryside. London parks were fine, but he hadn't realised how much he missed woods and moors, the stretch and space of the landscape. There was something nourishing in slipping away into the green, during his few hours off from canvassing duties or playing the perfect partner at openings and functions. Whatever happened at the election, it already felt like a kind of homecoming.

And this part of the world would be an amazing place to bring up kids ... Albert had never been able to picture himself having children in London. It seemed an impossibility, a category error. But now the move might really become permanent, his dread at the thought of completely scotching his work, his activism, and his social life was offset by dim but appealing images of children. Bike rides and river swims. Swinging a little girl over a stile or making dens with his son. He could even be a stay-at-home dad, take the lead on the day-to-day work of raising a family. Whatever happened in the election, Vi clearly wasn't going to give up her career anytime soon – but *he* could. Stewart would let him take a back seat at Rise! Books for a few years without endangering his position there. And after all, what could be a more important job than raising good citizens of the world?

Vi always deflected any comments he made about kids – 'one thing at a time, *please*. I've got to get elected and sort the country out first'. Since they'd determined to stay together, to make it work, Vi also thought that having a family was somewhere in their future. Probably. But this was a critical moment not only for her career, but for the life of the whole bloody United Kingdom – her focus, now, was entirely on Labour's electability. There would be time to consider having babies later. Once she'd got her foot in the door at the Houses of Parliament.

Or maybe much further in the future. Because if she *did* get elected, she wouldn't have time for babies for, well, probably years. She'd seen what the pressure of having baby Suzie, followed quickly by the twins, had done to Rose and her career. Where she'd once sailed effortlessly through the most picture-perfect life, Rose now seemed raggedy with stress, and snarled up with resentment. Her husband Benjamin's routine had barely changed, while she had recently, reluctantly, given over the day-to-day running of Rose Red Blooms to a (younger, single) woman, after finally breaking down and admitting she couldn't do it by herself anymore.

Rose refused to talk to Vi about it, getting teary and then tight-lipped, as if there were shame in failing to spin all those plates fast enough. Or – if she'd had a few glasses of wine, which she now often did – Rose would turn spittingly critical of her husband, and the long hours he worked, leaving her to manage every aspect of caring for the three kids and the household.

'And are you seeing them all before Christmas?' Harold asked over supper (a nut roast for Albert, while Vi and Harold had beef).

'Yes, of course.' Albert's reply was unhelpfully terse.

'We're going over to Rose and Benjamin's, to give the kiddies their presents, the day before Christmas Eve. And then out for dinner somewhere, with Amelia too,' Vi added.

'Le Caprice, no less,' said Albert with a brow raise. Vi kicked him under the table.

Harold gave a grunt that made clear he was about as keen on restaurants patronised by celebrities as Albert was.

'And you'll be back in—' Vi watched him reach for the name, and fail. 'Back with your family for Christmas Day as usual?'

'That's right. Albert will have to endure being woken up by my nephews at five a.m. again I daresay!'

'Well, Christmas is a time for children.'

'You must be looking forward to seeing Suzie and the twins?'

Harold grunted again, and muttered something about how noisy children were, but there was an obvious pride and pleasure below it all.

The one year they'd all had Christmas at Farley Hall, Vi had been quite touched to watch Harold melt like a snowman in the sunshine of his grandchild. He'd indulged Suzie's every whim with a chuckle and, as Albert pointed out to Vi on numerous occasions, gave Suzie more cuddles in those five days than he and Rose had had from him their entire lives.

They hadn't seen Harold in some time, not since Vi's selection had been confirmed, but he didn't mention politics or the campaign during the meal. Vi had a catch in her throat the whole evening, waiting for it.

But as they retired to the drawing room, where a huge fire roared in the grate, Vi felt increasingly sleepy and comfortable, her hangover finally smothered by the rich meat and pudding and red wine. The oppressively grand, panelled room seemed shrunk somewhat by the flickering firelight and boughs of greenery.

'I admire you, actually,' Harold said, out of nowhere, swilling a cognac and looking at the fire, so that Vi wasn't wholly sure he was speaking to her rather than Albert. Or at least, wouldn't have been if it weren't for the fact that Albert had never done anything that Harold would so much as faintly praise, let alone admit to admiring.

'Oh?' asked Albert archly.

'Going into politics. Swinging your weight behind this Tony Blair.'

'Surely not, Father? You do know he's ... *Labour?*'

Vi tried to shoot Albert a look.

'You a fan then, Harold?' Vi sipped her own cognac,

anticipating the usual long broadside about how only the Conservatives knew how to run the economy.

But Harold deflected. 'What made you decide to get stuck in and *do*, rather than just report on it, then?'

'I was getting frustrated, to be honest with you. I wanted to actually ... make some change? Get a bit more hands-on. Do my bit, if I can.'

'Mm,' said Harold, approvingly. 'A sense of calling.'

'Yeah, something like that! And, you know, it seemed like the right moment. I think the country is frustrated too. Ready for change. And, whatever you think of the man himself' – Vi patted Albert's foot, which he'd stretched out across the long red sofa, resting in her lap – 'I do genuinely think he can get us elected.'

'I suspect you may be right.'

'"Electability at any cost!"' Albert almost shouted, in a provocative, mocking tone. He was quite drunk, she realised, watching him sit up so he could slosh more wine into a glass clouded and smudged with fingerprints.

Albert didn't often say things like that anymore. Or not in front of her, anyway; she was sure he did when hanging out with his mates. Commie Tom, certainly, loved to sneer at New Labour.

But presumably the temptation was just too strong in front of his father. Especially when fuelled by the contents of his father's excellent cellar.

'Well, yes, Albert.' Harold spoke as if addressing a silly child. 'There's not much point having principles if you never have the power to enact them.'

Vi winced inwardly: it was strange hearing her own arguments come out of a mouth like Harold's.

'Yes, no, I am *familiar* with the reasoning,' said Albert. 'I just happen to think that socialism without the socialism is somewhat pointless. If you're creating a workers' party that's not actually for the workers, you risk winning a very hollow victory.'

'Ah, yes, and how is it toiling away at the coalface of selling out-of-print books to Stalinists?'

'For fuck's—' Albert shot a contemptuous look at Harold and then leapt to his feet, storming, somewhat unsteadily, out of the room.

Vi looked awkwardly at her own lap. She knew she ought to follow him. But she did not feel inclined to follow him.

She appreciated that Albert had tried very hard since they decided to stay together – the great, loving commitment they made, full of promises that they would support each other's dreams. They were both more careful, now, more generous to each other. That was what being a grown-up was, she supposed: learning not just to compromise, but to actively anticipate what might upset your partner, and not do it.

But – so unfair of her! – Vi actually found Albert's crawling apologies after the occasional slip-ups almost worse than the old obstinate shouting matches or silent stand-offs.

'Sorry about that, Violet.' Harold sighed in a way that suggested he found his son tiresome rather than actually was sorry. *They really are as bad as each other,* Vi thought.

'He's ... he's more supportive than this, usually.'

'Mm. Glad to hear it.'

There was a pause, filled only by the crackle of the fire and the sound of Hector rearranging himself round Harold's feet. Vi thought she should probably get up.

'No, you really should be proud of yourself. It's not an easy choice. It's not an easy *career* – I'm sure you don't need me to tell you how I found that out the hard way – but despite all that, I do believe it is a noble one. You are serving your country. You are doing your ... duty.'

She found herself nodding. 'Yes. Yes, I do actually think I am, you know. It may not be your particular idea of progress – but we're all in this game because we think things could be better for this country, and its people?'

How you could be a Tory and genuinely think you were making things better was – had always been – completely impossible for Vi to wrap her head around. As a thought experiment it produced a fuzzy blankness, like a kind of static, in her head. But even in the depths of despair, from the poll tax to the '92 exit polls, she had tried to hold on to the belief that even Tories thought they were doing the right thing.

'Well, our lot are certainly doing a good job of stuffing things up anyway.'

It took Vi a moment to register what he'd said.

'Oh, do you think so?'

Harold scoffed, and put a hand out to scratch Hector's head, the dog closing his eyes in bliss. Seeming to address the dog, he continued in a tone of pragmatic resignation: 'Oh yes. Of course. I'm not blind. Major's barely got control of them anymore – waste of time, this dratted European question. It'll tear us all apart eventually, if you ask me. And then the sleaze – well, it's shoddy, and it's shabby.'

'And we're brand spanking new ...'

'Yes. You rather are. Modernised, finally. No more of that renationalisation rubbish. And Tony ... well, he's a very fine speaker. Very fine. Bit slick. But *convincing*. And ruthless, in his own way.'

'My God' – Vi enjoyed taking up a teasing tone – 'don't tell me you're tempted?'

Harold looked up. There was a slight smile somewhere in his face even as he frowned, and sat back in his seat.

'Harold – will you cross the floor for me?' Vi leaned forward on her knees, barely able to conceal her glee at the surely ridiculous idea that he might defect to Labour on her account.

'Oh, I'm too old for any of that dramatic nonsense!' Harold waved her away with a chuckle, then sipped his drink slowly. 'But I've always been very impressed with your writing, my dear. Very impressed. And your ambition. Probably don't say these things enough, really, but it's always good to see someone bothering to pull themselves up by their bootstraps.'

I didn't grow up in a slum, thought Vi. And then she remembered how the little terraced cottage her mam had been brought up in really had been called *a slum*, and demolished, something her older relatives still shook their heads over.

'Now, we'll have to be careful about things, of course, but you can count on my support. Obviously can't publicly endorse you, but I will do everything I can to help your campaign in ways that won't get anyone on our backs.' He paused and looked at her with a mixture of real and mock disapproval, the lines blurred in affection, and possibly in cognac. 'We can get you some new clothes for a start!'

'Well, I wasn't planning on campaigning in this old jumper, to be fair...'

Could she take his money? Lord knows, her campaign needed all the help it could get. And it would be for the greater good – for Labour. For change. Wasn't there a pleasing circularity, a brutishly crude form of wealth redistribution, in Conservative peer Lord Harold Brinkhurst helping to fund Violet Lewis's bid to become a Labour MP?

'Anyway, the election could be a way off yet. May, I'd wager. But I shall be watching with interest.' He looked at her, and for a second Vi could see Albert in the lightly enigmatic mischief of his eyes. 'And after all... no one knows which box you put your x in, do they?'

Vi sat back, smiling, stunned.

'Thank you, Harold. That's ... I really don't know what to say.'

'More cognac?'

'Well! I would love to toast you and your nascent communism ...' (Had she gone too far?) 'Joking! I know pale purple is as much as I could dare hope for in a dyed-in-the-wool Tory like you—'

'Oh, a nice rich violet, surely?'

'Ha, very good.' Vi smiled. 'But, honestly, your support means a lot. Now, however, I think I better go and see how that son of yours is doing.'

'Well, good luck there.'

Albert's shoes were no longer in the hallway. Outside chain-smoking, then. Vi wrapped herself in her long black coat and went out the back door. A glowing cigarette tip led the way.

'Heya.'

'Hello.' He sounded glum – moody, or contrite? 'Sorry.'

'Come here, you,' said Vi, putting her arms around him.

Albert sighed, a quick exasperated stream. 'No, I really am sorry. He just winds me up, so reliably. But you know that I support you, and your—'

'Enough of that. Course I know. The big news is ...' Vi took his cigarette and had a drag.

'Thought you were giving up?'

'Really not the moment, Albert!' she said in a high voice, holding the lungful of smoke in.

'Sorry. What's the big news?'

A long, slow, satisfied exhale.

'The big news is ... I think your dad might vote Labour?'

'What?'

'I know!'

'No, seriously: *what?*'

'Maybe he won't actually be able to bring himself to do it, but he definitely teased the idea. He likes Tony Blair. And he likes me!'

'Well of course he likes you.'

'Well I didn't really know that.'

'He thinks you are the only good choice I've ever made.'

'Sweet, that you think you had a choice.'

Albert laughed his soft, low laugh, the one that had the promise of sex curled up in it. He took back his fag, and kissed her gently on the mouth. Then he pulled away, as if remembering.

'Seriously though? He likes Blair?'

'Yeah, seems so.'

'Fuck me. Wonders, and all that.'

Then Vi felt an excitement begin to tingle in her body. She shivered. It was partly the cold, but mostly the great whooshing sense of possibility.

'I mean, this is good news. Really, really good news. Your dad, Albert, a literal actual fucking Tory grandee! Won over!'

Her hands clasped together, and she gave almost a little skip.

'Is that really — I mean, is it really something to celebrate?' Albert's voice was hesitant.

'Um, *yes*!' Vi bumped him with her hip. 'Of course it bloody is! For starters, and on a completely selfish level, your dad just heavily implied he'd be willing to help us out financially, which could be very handy. On "personal", rather than party-political, terms of course.'

Albert felt slightly sick.

'But much more importantly — if we can win over people like him, winning the rest of the country is surely going to be a piece of *piss*. And if we can get a stonking majority, then we can go about fundamentally changing things. Making society kinder, fairer, brighter, better! For everyone!'

She'd slipped into stump mode.

'Yes, but why would someone like him vote for a party who wanted to do that? He must see something else in it!' Albert's voice was rising. 'This is a massive red flag, Vi!'

'A red flag?' She couldn't help the laughter bubbling out, too loud.

'Oh, you know what I mean – it's a warning sign, or it ought to be, that New Labour is just a load of bankrupt bullshit!'

He regretted the explosion as soon as it was out of his mouth. 'Really? Wow, thanks.'

There was a long pause, velvety and close in the cold night.

'Give us a cig.' Her voice sounded small and hard.

Albert rolled, quickly, and handed it to her with the lighter. She was absolutely hopeless at quitting, had come home reeking of menthols the previous evening.

He found his legs taking him quickly down the garden, only dimly lit by the light from a faint half-moon and one upstairs window. But he knew the winding paths well enough to navigate with his eyes shut.

Albert's whole life had been spent running away from his father's politics. Seeking not only alternative principles, but alternative ways of living. Yet the ruling classes wouldn't even allow them that, he thought bitterly. Albert had watched over the previous decade as community after community – the travellers, the eco-activists, the squatters, even the ravers – had been crushed for daring to try to do things differently. For all their free market economics, the Tories didn't recognise true freedom: the freedom to step outside the system. In Britain, you were free to make any lifestyle choice you wanted – as long as someone, somewhere, was getting rich from it.

Perhaps that was why Harold's offer to give Vi money – and

her immediate cheerful acceptance of it – stung so fucking much.

But *Vi*.

Albert stopped walking, tipped his head back, up towards the sky. Stars stretched away, infinitely. The eternal.

What really mattered? She did. It was her, always.

He turned around, and looked at her dim, small shape, still by the back door. He reached a hand out, and she began to walk – with surely deliberate slowness – down the path.

'I'm sorry. *Again*,' he said as she let him wrap her into his chest, and he breathed down into her dark hair.

'It's OK. Albert, I know we have a difference of opinion – a difference of conviction – on this. But I really do think that's … OK? Like, maybe it's better to disagree than for you to spend weeks *not* talking about it and then get a bit sloshed and it all comes out?'

'Yeah. I know.' The cold air had slapped any sense of being drunk out of him, but he knew things had got a little heady after dinner. 'I just … I do support you. One hundred per cent, completely and utterly. And I will do whatever it takes to help you win that seat. And I know that it's a lot of work, and you'll need me to be there for you. But I really am trying.'

'I do know that. It just maybe doesn't need to be at the expense of saying what you actually feel, love! You can disagree on principle, and still support me in practice. I mean, maybe when we get profiled in the *Sunday Times Magazine* you can toe the line …' He could feel her smiling into his jumper. 'But between the two of us, let's keep it honest, eh?'

Albert pulled away, and held her face in his hands, and kissed her all over.

'You, Violet Lewis, are a very wise woman, and I don't know what I've done to deserve you.'

It had been a long day. They could talk about how his father might or might not finance them in the morning. Calmly, generously. Over coffee, and fresh air.

Albert looked, suddenly, towards the oak tree. Even bare in the winter, it seemed to stand proudly at the end of the gardens, spreading its branches like an invitation. A reminder.

It was as if it had spoken, called out to Albert, from deep down within its roots.

'Come with me.' Albert pulled Vi's hand after him as his legs set off at a great pace down the garden.

'What? Albert, it's freezing, let's go back inside now.'

But he powered on, then pulled her down next to him, on the old curved iron bench that bit into the tree's crumpled bark. He held her hand tight.

There was no view to see, of course. *What was he doing?*

'I just – I don't know, I just felt like I had to come and sit here. With you. And this old tree. Like something – someone – told me we should be here together.'

'It's a lovely old tree,' smiled Vi. 'And you're a lovely old thing.'

She kissed him, and it was so soft, so tender, almost tentative, that for a funny second, Vi felt like they were kissing for the first time.

Whatever it takes, thought Albert, as they gently pulled apart. And also: *I love you.*

'Vi, will you marry me?'

Her breath was snatched away.

'What?'

'Violet Lewis, will you marry me?'

Oh God, was it because he thought that would help her get elected? Neither she nor Albert had ever previously been interested in getting married. Was his proposal really just a big gesture of support for her career plans?

It had, after all, been mentioned to them, several times, that married candidates did better – appearing more solid and reliable. Especially new young ones moving out from London. And they'd laughed about it in the same way they'd both always laughed at the idea of marriage itself – an old-fashioned dumb tradition, a bit dusty and faintly sexist.

Vi was sure her being in a relationship with the son of a renowned Conservative peer had been taken into account when she was selected. It was a juicy tit-bit, but one that had, so far, been held in reserve, lest the press also began digging up stories about Albert's own politics and activism. The plan was to insist that was all in the past now, something Albert had been given media training in, greasing up his gritted his teeth. He'd even abstained from protesting the Newbury Bypass earlier that year, watching it on the evening news instead.

'Albert... is this... are you asking me to marry you because you think it would help me *get elected?* I know you want to prove you're here for my career but really...' She laughed, a little uneasily. *Please God, don't let that just be it.*

'Of *course* that's not why, you big silly. I just...'

He looked up at the tree branches, spreading, and then at the roots below, digging into the land, and Albert realised that that was what it was. He wanted to grow with Vi.

'I just love you. I love you so fucking much. And I want to be with you forever, and I want to have a home and children and to watch you get old and to die holding your hand. And whatever happens, however you change, or whatever life – whatever this new millennium! – throws at us, I want to weather it *all* with *you*. I think that would be the very best thing. Don't you?'

Tears sprang into Vi's eyes then, at hearing him say it. The words, so sure and certain and unafraid. And the tears ran into her mouth and Albert's mouth as they kissed. *(Babies though, how would there be time for babies ...)* And such springing, surprising joy at him asking. A pleasure so vast, so sherbetty, that it fizzed and frothed over and overwhelmed any theoretical opposition to the idea of marriage Vi had ever had in a great big fountain of splashy, foamy love.

And at the root of it all, the realisation that she felt the same. The words he'd said could have come from her own heart, too: she wanted to live her life with Albert at her side. To grow, and to grow old, with him.

'Yes, Albert. Yes yes yes.'

Chapter 10

May 1997

When the exit polls were announced at ten p.m., the rush was as great as any Albert had ever known. He realised he was gripping Vi's hand (with its delicate sapphire heirloom engagement ring) so hard he might crush it.

Vi felt her jaw fall open like a cartoon character. *A Labour landslide.* And it took all her restraint not to jump up and down and start snogging Albert like a teenager. She looked round, and Evan had actually picked her mam up in the air. Amelia and Rose were both making exactly the same gesture, clapping their hands together in delight.

Then the hours passed in a blur, time becoming elongated and squashed in unexpected ways. Vi got changed, Rose tenderly pinning an artful arrangement of tiny red rosebuds onto her new dress, tears springing to her eyes. 'Look at you,' she murmured, and then gave Vi a squeeze that threatened to crush the flowers.

They all drove over to the school hall in Elland, arriving just before midnight. It looked like it was hosting several competing sixtieth birthday parties that had yet to get going. People stood aimlessly around in wilted suits, eating curling-up ham sandwiches and drinking instant coffee. In their separate corners, balloons of red, blue and orange bobbed listlessly. But along the back walls, it was a factory of industry, the count in full swing. Boxes kept arriving; the bundles of counted votes kept stacking.

Vi tried not to look at them too much. It looked good. Didn't it? People kept squeezing her arm as they passed, but she didn't dare believe it.

After Sunderland declared and the results started coming in, Vi began to sneak off with Mel behind the back of the temporary classroom; she still didn't want her parents to see her stealing the odd puff.

She wondered about telling Mel. *I'm late.* Only a few days. Probably just the stress. She'd only realised that morning, and had barely had time to consider what it might mean. Because there had been too much in the day already – too much adrenaline, too much potential for anti-climax or joy, too much sheer, soaring, soaking *hope*. There was no space in the air around them, no opening or possibility, for talking about something else so bloody huge.

So badly timed.

(It would be very early days, she wouldn't *have* to keep it—)

But in the loo, after pulling up the sort of disgusting tan tights it occurred to her she'd spent far too much of her life wearing, Vi lightly rested her hand on her lower belly. Maybe it *wasn't* so badly timed. Maybe she would have that, instead of a new job, if the count didn't go in her favour.

Or maybe, if she won, could she maybe even... have *both?*

Albert would be delighted, of course; Albert would help.

Then she remembered how tired and strained Rose had looked, arriving that afternoon, trailing stained muslin cloths and angry messages from clients. Vi took a last naughty drag from Mel's Marlborough, as if it might burn out even the thought of *pregnancy*, and hurried back into the hall.

Albert watched Vi doing an interview down the wire with

the BBC, the second or third she'd already done about the expected new wave of female MPs, the long overdue feminisation of British politics. He loved watching her face when she did these, because she didn't quite look like Vi: it was like someone doing a very good impression of her, but getting her just slightly wrong. He thought how much he'd admire her (and fancy her) if they weren't together. As Mel had said when she'd arrived and seen Vi's red dress: 'Fucking hell, babe, your outfit alone makes a *strong* case for having more women in parliament!' And Vi had hit her, and then remembered she was meant to be being professional.

Albert got another coffee – still undrinkable – and thought that, nice as the sentiment might be, if he had to hear 'Things Can Only Get Better' one more time, he'd have to smash the CD player with a passing clipboard. 'This bloody song,' muttered Evan in his ear, as if he'd heard Albert's thoughts, and winked.

Since he'd proposed to Vi, Evan and Angharad had finally seemed to accept him as part of the family. And thanks to spending more time together during the campaign, a mutual respect had grown up between Evan and Albert, blossoming into – dare he say it – a *fondness,* even. Vi's father shared Albert's antipathy towards Tony Blair ('smarmy, so he is'), and was equally suspicious of the party's dropping of Clause 4, ditching the commitment to the common ownership of the means of production. But he also shared Albert's enormous pride in Vi.

Evan had been canvassing in Wales for months, and spoke loudly to everyone they met about how much he was looking forward to his daughter *finally ousting those Tory bastards* as if it were all a one-woman job, while Vi tried to signal at him to stop swearing. He appeared re-inflated by the campaign, barrel-chested and beaming in a suit Vi had bought him specially. With Harold's money.

The whispers of *recount* came hard on the heels of the murmurs that it was *close, maybe a bit close*. It'd been close the whole campaign – a slog, every vote fought for. And Albert suddenly felt a bit nauseous, although he wasn't sure if it was with hope she'd get it or fear that she'd get it or dread that she wouldn't.

'Well, whatever happens now I think we've done what we need to do as a party, and I feel very proud to have been part of it,' said Vi, with such earnestness that Albert didn't like to say, you don't need to pretend with me. It was a little after three a.m., and the near-hysterical jubilation over Portillo losing his seat had begun to subside. The reality of the situation was starting to feel solid around them. After eighteen years – *eighteen years!* – the Conservatives were finally gone.

Yet the idea of a Labour landslide for the country, but not her constituency, was too much for Albert to get his head around.

Mel had to re-do Vi's face every half-hour or so; she wasn't used to wearing foundation or lipstick and kept smudging it. Her heart rate was as fluttered and feathered as if she'd dropped a whole one, her teeth as firmly clenched.

'Why don't I have any fucking chewing gum?'

And then suddenly it was happening. Officials marching around looking extremely official, microphones squawking into life, people gathering in clumps to be near the people they needed to hug. There were Amelia and Angharad, talking apparently urgently to each other; Rose and Mel, clutching handbags and each other's arms.

'Off you go now. *I love you*,' said Albert, knocking his forehead into hers, interlacing his fingers with hers for a brief pulse of final support. Locking into her eyes.

'I love you too. *Thank you.*' They squeezed fingers.

Then Vi pulled away, took a deep breath and climbed up the green-carpeted steps to the little stage. The eyes of the cameras, and a large crowd of buoyant, almost lairy Labour members and pinched, drained Conservatives, faced her.

Her blood sounded very loud in her ears.

'And the results are ...'

Vi wasn't sure for a second if it was more, or less. Then her side of the room exploded, and she was sure she could hear Evan's voice at the very top of it.

And a smile broke across her face, and her eyes sought Albert's. He caught her gaze, and his heart wanted to pop with the pressure, the ecstatic pride. *She did it. They had done it.* He punched the air for her with a great big daft grin.

I've done it, thought Vi. *It's my turn now.*

And for one moment, they thought that they really could have it all.

21 January

The clock reads 4.04 p.m. He looks around the busy drawing room at Farley Hall, stuffed with friends and family, gathering together in celebration of their birthday. And there she is – watching him, from the other side of the room. Smiling that knowing, intimate smile. For it is their day; their time.

'Oh!' Rose's voice is raised, and stagey, somehow. 'What a beautiful sunset! Do let's go catch the last of it in the garden.'

The rest of their guests seem remarkably willing to put back on their thick winter coats, putting down and then picking up the wrong glasses of Champagne, bundling out the back doors into the cold air.

The two of them share an indulgent glance as Rose strides off, towards the oak tree at the bottom of the garden. Although it's true about the sunset – there is a blood-orange streak just above the line of the horizon, and it shoots almost dark red rays of light across the hills and fields, catching the oak's bare branches. They look like they've been dipped in copper, or licked with fire – a great, crackling canopy.

It must've seen some things, this tree, she thinks, as they approach.

He grabs her hand, warming her already chilling fingers in his own grip. They have their own private camaraderie in the face of such birthday cahoots: all the rustling and whispering, the silly anticipation of childhood, everyone half holding their breath.

And there, squatting on a little table behind the tree, is the most enormous birthday cake she has ever seen. Ridiculously large, really, too large to hide in the drawing room even, with its stacked layers and pillowy folds of icing and cascades of edible flowers delicately arranged around each layer. The hazy glow of scores of candles, struggling a little in the chilly after-noon breeze. Above the cake, a banner – clumsily handmade and reading 'Happy Birthday to you both!' – hangs from the branches; a shuffling semi-circle of cheeky, smiling faces below. Rose beaming, the biggest smile of all.

'Happy birthday to you...'

The squiggly feeling of being the centre of attention. A feeling that, of course, they have shared, together, ever since meeting. He sneaks a look down, at her little smile, and the dimples that reveal the pleasure as well as the slight embarrass-ment. She knocks into his shoulder.

Thank God he found her. Thank God for the all the chances that brought her into his path. The briefest shiver of panic takes him, imagining how easily they might never have met, or might have failed to make it work.

'Happy birthday to you...'

And the other years flicker then through her mind: first shy exchanging of gifts, the snuggling, mutually indulgent breakfasts in bed, the careful mixing of friends or family for fizz and other cakes.

And the quick icicle memory of times that hadn't been so easy. When there was distance between them. When the jollity seemed forced, and being a unit felt chafing, constraining. *Not even allowed her own birthday.*

'Happy birthday, dear...' The usual clatter, as people bump their names into each other, laughing at their own portman-teaus – Vibert, Alberlet – or attempting to go double speed and squeeze them both in.

A great swell of feeling, at being able to surround yourself with people who make life easier. Who help hold you together, like glue. Down the years, and over the bumps.

'Happy birthday *to you!*'

They step forward to the cake, the stupid number of shimmering candles. And they look at each other for a moment, into each other's faces, softly lit in the flicker of celebration. Eyes locking. And here it comes, here it is, the flash of recognition – still as startling as it was, the very first time they met.

'Make a wish!'

They bend over the cake, together, and take a deep breath.

Acknowledgements

I am grateful for support from Arts Council England, whose Project Grants funding enabled me to complete this novel. Special thanks to Elizabeth Briggs for all her help.

Thank you to everyone at RCW, including the best foreign rights team you could dream of, and to all at Orion Fiction. My particular gratitude goes to Lucy Cameron, Alainna Hadjigeorgiou and of course Charlotte Mursell, for her gorgeous enthusiasm for Violet and Albert and for her brilliant, brilliant editing of their story.

Many people helped in the research of this book, and especial thanks are due to Sarah Daniels, Helen Frankel, Stephen Pittam, Jane Tod, Richard Taylor, and Paul Upex for so generously giving up their time to talk with me. I am indebted to many books, but in particular *Altered State* by Matthew Collin, and *This England* by Pete Davies.

To Tom Bromley at the Faber Academy, and all the writers on the work-in-progress course – you were welcome fellow travellers at the start of this long journey, and givers of the very best advice and encouragement.

Thank you to Elaine Feeney, for her generous early support for this novel, which made me grin like mad.

To my South London Lovers: I have so much love and also,

frankly, awe for every single one of you. Thank you for all the faith, feedback, and friendship. I bestow extra special squeezes on my early readers – Heloise Wood, Lizzie Webster, and Gayle Lazda; Ana Fletcher, for being so willing to share her expertise and insight; Daisy Buchanan for her continual encouragement, understanding, and support, and Jude Collins for coming to the rescue with the perfect title.

I owe much gratitude to many people. To Sam Thomas, whose belief in me has usually outstripped my own; thank you for helping me to start, and to keep going. To George Timms, who scooped me up and saved my ass, giving me not one but two rooms of my own at a time when I had none. I will never forget that kindness. To Kate Smith and Helen Newsome, whose room-related generosity also helped this book get finished. You're the best. To Ruth and Graham Fowler, whose hospitality and welcome gave me space to write when the whole world shut down. To Paul Hague, and Ralph Lyle: two of the finest people in the world to talk to about writing – then, now, always. To Alex Ascherson, for all the votes of confidence. To Roxanne Green, Carys Hobbs, and Lara Pedelty, I wish I could tell our teenage selves I'd be writing your names in the back of a book! Thank you, for it all.

To Tristan Kendrick, the most wonderful agent and friend. Who, of all people, knows that I usually use far too many words for whatever I'm trying to say – but I'm not sure there actually are enough to express how important you've been in this process, and how much I have valued all your reassurance and your determined championing of this book.

To Tommo Fowler, my love (how odd to include your surname, but everyone else got one, so here we are). Thank you: for your listening and your loving, your endless patience and your great capacity for celebration. For walking by my side during all of this, and always, always holding my hand.

Finally, enormous love and boundless gratitude to my family: to Lyall, for your quiet unwavering support, and to my mum and dad, Lynda and Martin Williams, who have inspired me, and this book, in more ways than they can possibly know. Thank you for encouraging me to write, to dream, to persist.

Credits

Holly Williams and Orion Fiction would like to thank everyone at Orion who worked on the publication of *What Time is Love?* in the UK.

Editorial
Charlotte Mursell
Sanah Ahmed

Copyeditor
Joanne Gledhill

Proofreader
Sally Partington

Audio
Paul Stark
Jake Alderson

Contracts
Anne Goddard
Humayra Ahmed
Ellie Bowker

Design
Tomás Almeida
Joanna Ridley
Nick May

Editorial Management
Charlie Panayiotou
Jane Hughes
Bartley Shaw
Tamara Morriss

Finance
Jasdip Nandra
Afeera Ahmed
Elizabeth Beaumont
Sue Baker

Marketing
Lucy Cameron

Production
Ruth Sharvell

Publicity
Alainna Hadjigeorgiou

Operations
Jo Jacobs
Sharon Willis

Sales
Jen Wilson
Esther Waters
Victoria Laws
Rachael Hum
Anna Egelstaff
Frances Doyle
Georgina Cutler